AWE AND WONDER

Whether in Brocéliande or Prydain or the cottage of the Fates, whether a slumbering kingdom or the whole cosmos, the geographical province of high fantasy is without limit—and its literary province is only prescribed by the number of wizards, unicorns, demons, and demigods best suited to the elevated nature of the quest or ritual at hand.

Against a phantom tapestry of myth and magic, seemingly simple tales unfold to reveal themes of universal appeal—death and rebirth, the secrets of the netherworld, the soul of a hero, or the mystery of a sin far older than Christendom.

In the hands of such masters of the craft as Lord Dunsany, C. S. Lewis, Peter S. Beagle, Ursula Le Guin, and others represented in this collection, high fantasy has the power to captivate and amaze—to evoke that very special response described by J. R. R. Tolkien as *awe and wonder*.

The Fantastic Imagination:
An Anthology of High Fantasy

Edited by
ROBERT H. BOYER
and
KENNETH J. ZAHORSKI

AVON
PUBLISHERS OF BARD, CAMELOT, DISCUS, EQUINOX AND FLARE BOOKS

TO

Barb and Marijean

For· their patience,

encouragement, and

sense of humor.

THE FANTASTIC IMAGINATION is an original publication of Avon Books. This work has never before appeared in book form.

AVON BOOKS
A division of
The Hearst Corporation
959 Eighth Avenue
New York, New York 10019

Copyright © 1977 by Robert H. Boyer and Kenneth J. Zahorski.
Published by arrangement with the editors.
Library of Congress Catalog Card Number: 76-55545
ISBN: 0-380-00956-0

First Avon Printing, February, 1977

AVON TRADEMARK REG. U.S. PAT. OFF. AND IN
OTHER COUNTRIES, MARCA REGISTRADA,
HECHO EN U.S.A.

Printed in the U.S.A.

ACKNOWLEDGEMENTS

Ludwig Tieck, "The Elves" (translated by Thomas Carlyle), in *Great German Short Stories* (ed. by Lewis Melville and Reginald Hargreaves), Ernest Benn Ltd., London, 1929.

Lord Dunsany, "The Sword of Welleran," from *The Sword of Welleran and Other Stories* by Lord Dunsany. The Devin-Adair Co., Old Greenwich, Conn. 06870. Copyright 1954, The Devin-Adair Company.

George Mac Donald, "The Light Princess." Reprinted from Glenn Edward Sadler, ed. *The Gifts of the Child Christ: Fairy Tales and Stories for the Childlike*. Vol. II. Grand Rapids, Michigan: William Eerdmans Publishing Co., 1973. (Eerdman's copy reprinted from *Adela Cathcart*, 1864).

John Buchan, "The Grove of Ashtaroth," in *The Moon Endureth: Tales and Fancies*. London: Hodder & Stoughton, Ltd., 1935. Permission given by A. P. Watt & Son and The Estate of Lord Tweedsmuir.

James Branch Cabell, "The Music From Behind the Moon." Reprinted with the permission of Farrar, Straus & Giroux, Inc. from *The Witch-Woman* by James Branch Cabell, Copyright 1948 by James Branch Cabell, copyright renewed 1976 by Margaret Cabell.

"The Accommodating Circumstance" by Frank R. Stockton is reprinted by permission of Charles Scribner's Sons from *The Storyteller's Pack: A Frank R. Stockton Reader*.

CONTENTS

Preface

We wish to gratefully acknowledge generous assistance from many sources in the preparation of this anthology. It is appropriate to begin with sincere thanks to our two student assistants, Mr. Mark Allen and Ms. Marla Mellinger. Mark, an enthusiastic sf-fantasy fan and an excellent researcher, helped get the project started. Marla contributed many hours beyond her normal work schedule to carry it through. Further thanks are extended to Ms. Peggy Schlapman, upon whom we always depend to correct our oversights when she proofreads and types any manuscripts; the library staff, in particular Ms. Fran Richter, who speedily, efficiently, and always with a smile, obtained the hundreds of interlibrary loan texts we requested; and Dr. Donald B. King, Dean of St. Norbert College, who provided encouragement and support throughout our project.

ROBERT H. BOYER
KENNETH J. ZAHORSKI
ST. NORBERT COLLEGE

Introduction

This anthology is unique in consisting exclusively of high fantasy. Although novels of high fantasy can readily be found in most bookstores, short fiction of the same type is, we discovered, difficult to locate. Indeed, we rarely found selections of high fantasy in the dozens of anthologies we examined while searching for materials suitable to this volume. In following up leads from *The Short Story Index* or *The Checklist of Fantasy Literature* we unearthed anthologies of ghost stories, folk tales, beast fables, satirical farces, or admixtures of several of these types, but few examples of high fantasy.

Where, and how, did we find most of our selections? At the outset, we knew of four authors we definitely wanted to include: Mac Donald, Dunsany, Lewis, and Tolkien. Beyond these, however, we were tilling new ground. The next step, then, was to compile a comprehensive list of authors and stories. This list led to an examination of more than 140 anthologies and collections of short stories as well as a number of novels and short stories in periodicals. We had the greatest success locating the type of high fantasy we sought in collections of works by a single author. The majority of our selections (nine) are from such volumes.

All told, we read well over a thousand short stories, novels, and novelettes from which we compiled a list of fifteen key selections: thirteen short stories and two self-contained excerpts from novels. All are quality works of high fantasy.

But what, then, is high fantasy? Perhaps this question can best be answered by indicating the sorts of stories which are not, and those which are, high fantasy. High fantasy does not include ghost stories like those of Edgar Allan Poe, or animal fables such as Aesop compiled, or folk tales of the Johnny Appleseed variety, or satirical farces like those written by James Thurber or G. K. Chesterton. High fantasy consists of fairy tales and myth-based tales: fairy tales, those ancient and new stories which take place in the mysterious other world of faërie, such as *Beowulf* or J. R. R. Tolkien's *The Hobbit;* myth tales, stories whose setting is the realm in which gods and men have commerce, as in the Welsh *Mabinogion* or in Lloyd Alexander's *The Foundling and Other Tales of Prydain.*

This is not to say that ghost stories, fables, folk tales, or satirical farces are not fantasy. To the extent that they take place in an unreal world or conjure up people or happenings which, according to realistic norms, are impossible, they are indeed fantasy. But they are not high fantasy.

A number of traits combine to produce a work of high fantasy. High fantasy has an other-world setting, whether this be Middle Earth or Brocéliande, or whether it be the sacred grove of Ashtaroth or the cottage of the Fates. The characters in high fantasy include a generous number of imposing figures who, with their magical or supernatural powers, inspire wonder or fear or often both: Elfin kings, wizards, unicorns, and demigods. High fantasy deals with recognizably archetypal themes and motifs such as the initiation into manhood, death and rebirth, and most frequently with the courage an individual needs to undertake the fateful quest. And, finally, as befits the settings, characters, and themes of high fantasy, the style is elevated, often figurative as it must be to evoke the imaginary worlds it deals with.

The singular effect of the other-worldly setting, the imposing characters, and the memorable themes, along with the high style in which these are portrayed is the creation of an atmosphere which has been best described by Tolkien as one of "awe and wonder."

The stories included in this volume all fit into the category of high fantasy. Most are fairy tales. Two, John Buchan's "The Grove of Ashtaroth" and Lloyd Alexander's "The Foundling," are clear examples of myth fantasy with their conscious indebtedness to Semitic and northern myths respectively. Two of the tales illustrate a not infrequent convergence of fairy tale and myth. In Cabell's "The Music From Behind the Moon," Ettarre, while she is described as "the witch-woman," is clearly related to the Muse of Poetry from classical mythology. And in Mark Van Doren's "The Tall One," the Tall One appears both as a fairy of the trees and as a goddess to whom the woodcutter prays. One story, Peter Beagle's "Come Lady Death," eludes strict classification as either fairy tale or myth fantasy. The setting is an eighteenth-century English ballroom, and most of the characters are conventional. However, the style and the unique appearance of Death as a Cinderella-like fairy princess create the high-fantasy atmosphere found in the other stories.

While the designation as high fantasy has been the primary criterion for including stories in this anthology, it has not been the sole one. In addition to their all being high fantasy—as described above—the stories selected here are good literature. While it may be possible for a story to be of poor quality as literature and yet to be successful as fantasy, we have avoided choosing such. There are a few stories which create a sense of "awe and wonder" while employing cardboard characters, extravagant "sword and sorcery" plots, and artificially ornate styles. Such stories as these have a place in the history of fantasy; they continue to be written and enjoyed. It is tempting to include some here, but we have chosen rather to include only examples of stories which are effective both as literature and as fantasy.

Attention has also been given to including a range of representative authors, covering a considerable period of time, who provide us with a variety of settings, characters, motifs, and themes. Represented here are English, American, and two Continental authors. The earliest piece was composed by the German Ludwig Tieck in 1811 and translated in 1827 by Thomas Carlyle for the English reader. The latest story, "Beliard," appearing in 1974, comes from the pen of the contemporary English writer, Sylvia Townsend Warner. The now classic English writers of fantasy—Mac Donald, Dunsany, Lewis, and Tolkien—appear here under one cover for the first time. Interestingly, most of the American fantasy writers included—Cabell and Stockton are the exceptions—are relatively recent. It seems that American audiences—and consequently American writers—have been slow to appreciate high fantasy. This has changed, however, in recent years, and the U. S. now boasts of a number of young writers of high fantasy such as Alexander, Beagle, and Le Guin.

The fifteen authors represented here illustrate some of the varied contents of, and approaches to, the many-sided world of high fantasy. Frequently, a particular excellence of theme or style, or a unique approach, aided us in our selection.

Several of the stories dramatize traits unique to high fantasy. For instance, John Buchan's "The Grove of Ashtaroth" points out that the other-world of fantasy is at times an ambiguous one for man in terms of being either beneficial or harmful. On the other hand, creatures from the other world do not always understand the emotions and actions of man, as demonstrated by the Loquacious Goblin's question in Alexander Grin's story "The Loquacious Goblin." Ludwig Tieck in "The Elves" provides one of the more interesting examples of how one enters faërie from our world. Shape shifting and the nature of magical powers, two of the most distinctive marks of high fantasy, are dominant concerns of Ursula Le Guin in "The Rule of Names."

The style of high fantasy is, in general, a highly figurative, evocative style, at once lofty and vivid. Still, specific stories offer enchanting variations. Dunsany, perhaps the finest stylist of the group, employs a heroic or epic style in evoking the spirits of the ancient warrior-leaders of an endangered people. In Beagle's "Come Lady Death" the reader is charmed by the elegant style of courtly romance. And in Mark Van Doren's "The Tall One" the reader is moved by the woodcutter's simple, vigorous prayer, spoken in a language which is unadorned yet out of the ordinary.

While humor is not often the primary effect of high fantasy, it is present in abundance in a number of the stories contained here, prominently in Mac Donald's pun-filled "The Light Princess," in Lewis's delightfully witty portrayal of the dimwitted Dufflepuds, and in Stockton's mocking satire on grown-ups in "The Accommodating Circumstance."

Memorable characters emerge in many of the stories. Gollum, Tolkien's creation, shows evil to be a thing of shades rather than of dark versus light. Beagle's story presents Lady Death both as an abstraction and as a humanly appealing young woman, dramatizing that death and beauty are not inseparable.

The stories in this collection reflect the themes common to high fantasy. Cabell's "The Music From Behind the Moon" deals with the familiar quest for fulfillment, but in a most unique fashion. Van Doren's "The Tall One" examines the need for faith in a power beyond our own. And two of the stories concern the ritual initiation of youth into manhood: Bates's "The Peach Tree: A Fantasy" and Alexander's "The Foundling."

These few comments are set down here to give the reader a further idea of the nature of high fantasy and of the contents of this anthology, not to instruct him in what he ought to see in the stories. What is important is that the reader enjoy the magical atmosphere created by these high fantasy tales, and that through enjoying these works he might reflect upon and see afresh his own world.

Perhaps the reason for the increase in production and consumption of fantasy literature since the extraordinary success of Tolkien's works is precisely the fact that having escaped for the moment to an other-world, the reader can meditate on values, unhampered by either the pressures or the rationalizations which so frequently interfere.

R.H.B.
K.J.Z.

JOHANN LUDWIG TIECK

(1773–1853)

Tieck was born in Berlin into a working-class family. His father, a rope maker, was a realistic and sometimes cynical man, while his mother was a mild, imaginative person. Some critics have thus attributed Tieck's blending of realism and the supernatural to parental influence.

Tieck rose to a position of considerable esteem and influence in the world of letters during the first half of the nineteenth century, a period which has been dubbed "The Golden Age of German Literature." As a schoolboy he fell under the influence of two of his masters who encouraged him to write horror stories, which were a popular form at the time. He became so captivated by reading and composing such tales that he reportedly spent a night alone in a church, sitting before a lighted candle, invoking the spirits of the dead.

After completing his studies in European literature, Tieck launched his career as a professional writer. During his career he produced an enormous quantity of work, including plays, poetry, fairy tales (*Märchen*), and short novels (*Novellen*). In addition, he wrote a series of essays on Shakespeare; supervised Dorothea, his daughter, in translating nineteen of Shakespeare's plays; and himself translated *Don Quixote* (1799–1801).

When Goethe died in 1832, Tieck was regarded by many in the literary world as the successor to this greatest of German authors. Posterity has not honored that view; Tieck is regarded primarily as one who influenced great writers but who never became one himself. If Tieck is to regain some of the fame he once had, it will probably be because of two plays and his fairy tales. His two best-known plays, dramatic adaptations of *Puss in Boots* and *Tom Thumb*, are comic attacks on the sentimentalism in the German theater of his time. His finest fairy tales are "The Fair-Haired Eckbert," "The Runenberg," and "The Elves." English audiences in the 1820s had an appetite for German fairy tales, and Thomas Carlyle translated five of Tieck's, including the three here mentioned, in his *German Romances* (1827).

It is for several reasons that Tieck's "The Elves" appears as the first story in this anthology. It is, of course, the oldest selection, and age has some privileges. More important, however, it is an excellent story and pure fairy tale. It recalls to the reader the stories of Tieck's famous contemporaries, the Grimms and Hans Christian Andersen, although Tieck is more elaborate in style. Here is a fairy tale that doesn't end with the "happily ever after" formula, which is not the way good fairy tales should have to end anyway. Yet the ending, while it is perhaps sad, is not permanently so. And the beginning is equally interesting in its description of the passage from our world to faërie. From beginning to end it is an engaging romance, but it is also a thought-provoking one without being too moralizing. Tieck explores the relationship between man and nature, as well as the presence of the supernatural in nature. Another reason for including "The Elves" first is that George Mac Donald almost certainly read it, since he was a great fan of German fairy tales. And, of course, C. S. Lewis and J. R. R. Tolkein have acknowledged their indebtedness to Mac Donald. It is tempting, then to see if some sort of evolution links "The Elves" to some of the later fantasies in this anthology.

R.H.B.
K.J.Z.

❧ The Elves ❧

Johann Ludwig Tieck

(TRANSLATED BY THOMAS CARLYLE)

"Where is our little Mary?" said the father.

"She is playing out upon the green there with our neighbour's boy," replied the mother.

"I wish they may not run away and lose themselves," said he; "they are so thoughtless."

The mother looked for the little ones, and brought them their evening luncheon. "It is warm," said the boy; "and Mary had a longing for the red cherries."

"Have a care, children," said the mother, "and do not run too far from home, and not into the wood; Father and I are going to the fields."

Little Andres answered: "Never fear, the wood frightens us; we shall sit here by the house, where there are people near us."

The mother went in, and soon came out again with her husband. They locked the door, and turned towards the fields to look after their labourers, and see their hay harvest in the meadow. Their house lay upon a little green height, encircled by a pretty ring of paling, which likewise enclosed their fruit and flower garden. The hamlet stretched somewhat deeper down, and on the other side lay the castle of the Count. Martin rented the large farm from this nobleman; and was living in contentment with his wife and only child; for he yearly saved some money, and had the prospect of becoming a man of substance by his industry, for the ground was productive, and the Count not illiberal.

As he walked with his wife to the fields, he gazed

cheerfully round and said: "What a different look this quarter has, Brigitta, from the place we lived in formerly! Here it is all so green; the whole village is bedecked with thick-spreading fruit-trees; the ground is full of beautiful herbs and flowers; all the houses are cheerful and cleanly, the inhabitants are at their ease: nay, I could almost fancy that the woods are greener here than elsewhere, and the sky bluer; and, so far as the eye can reach, you have pleasure and delight in beholding the bountiful Earth."

"And whenever you cross the stream," said Brigitta, "you are, as it were, in another world, all is so dreary and withered; but every traveller declares that our village is the fairest in the country far and near."

"All but that fir-ground," said her husband; "do but look back to it, how dark and dismal that solitary spot is lying in the gay scene: the dingy fir-trees with the smoky huts behind them, the ruined stalls, the brook flowing past with a sluggish melancholy."

"It is true," replied Brigitta; "if you but approach that spot, you grow disconsolate and sad, you know not why. What sort of people can they be that live there, and keep themselves so separate from the rest of us, as if they had an evil conscience?"

"A miserable crew," replied the young Farmer: "gipsies, seemingly, that steal and cheat in other quarters, and have their hoard and hiding place here. I wonder only that his Lordship suffers them."

"Who knows," said the wife, with an accent of pity, "but perhaps they may be poor people, wishing, out of shame, to conceal their poverty; for, after all, no one can say aught ill of them; the only thing is, that they do not go to church, and none knows how they live; for the little garden, which indeed seems altogether waste, cannot possibly support them; and fields they have none."

"God knows," said Martin, as they went along, "what trade they follow; no mortal comes to them; for the place they live in is as if bewitched and excommunicated, so that even our wildest fellows will not venture into it."

Such conversation they pursued, while walking to the fields. That gloomy spot they spoke of lay aside from the hamlet. In a dell, begirt with firs, you might behold a hut, and various ruined office-houses; rarely was smoke seen to mount from it, still more rarely did men appear there; though at times curious people, venturing somewhat nearer, had perceived upon the bench before the hut, some hideous women, in ragged clothes, dandling in their arms some children equally dirty and ill-favoured; black dogs were running up and down upon the boundary; and, of an evening, a man of monstrous size was seen to cross the footbridge of the brook, and disappear in the hut; and, in the darkness, various shapes were observed, moving like shadows round a fire in the open air. This piece of ground, the firs and the ruined huts, formed in truth a strange contrast with the bright green landscape, the white houses of the hamlet, and the stately new-built castle.

The two little ones had now eaten their fruit; it came into their heads to run races; and the little nimble Mary always got the start of the less active Andres. "It is not fair," cried Andres at last: "let us try it for some length, then we shall see who wins."

"As thou wilt," said Mary; "only to the brook we must not run."

"No," said Andres; "but there, on the hill, stands the large pear-tree, a quarter of a mile from this. I shall run by the left, round past the fir-ground; thou canst try it by the right over the fields; so we do not meet till we get up, and then we shall see which of us is swifter."

"Done," cried Mary, and began to run; "for we shall not mar one another by the way, and my father says it is as far to the hill by that side of the Gipsies' house as by this."

Andres had already started, and Mary, turning to the right, could no longer see him. "It is very silly," said she to herself: "I have only to take heart, and run along the bridge, past the hut, and through the yard, and I shall certainly be first." She was already standing by the brook and the clump of firs. "Shall I? No; it is too frightful," said she. A little white dog was standing on the farther side, and barking with might and main. In her terror, Mary thought the dog some monster, and sprang back. "Fy! Fy!" said she: "the dolt is gone half way by this time, while I stand here considering." The little dog kept barking, and, as she looked at it more narrowly, it seemed no longer frightful, but, on the contrary, quite pretty; it had a red collar round its neck, with a glittering bell; and as it raised its head, and shook itself in barking, the little bell sounded with the finest tinkle. "Well, I must risk it!" cried she, "I will run for life; quick, quick, I am through; certainly to Heaven, they cannot eat me up alive in half a minute!" And with this, the gay, courageous little Mary sprang along the footbridge; passed the dog, which ceased its barking and began to fawn on her; and in a moment she was standing on the other bank, and the black firs all round concealed from view her father's house, and the rest of the landscape.

But what was her astonishment when here! The loveliest, most variegated flower-garden, lay round her; tulips, roses, and lilies were glittering in the fairest colours; blue and gold-red butterflies were wavering in the blossoms; cages of shining wire were hung on the espaliers, with many-coloured birds in them, singing beautiful songs; and children, in short white frocks with flowing yellow hair and brilliant eyes, were frolicking about; some playing with lambkins, some feeding the birds, or gathering flowers, and giving them to one another; some, again, were eating cherries, grapes, and ruddy apricots. No hut was to be seen; but instead of it, a large fair house, with a brazen door and lofty statues, stood glancing in the middle of the space. Mary was confounded with surprise, and knew not what to think; but, not being bashful, she went right up to the first of the children, held out her hand, and wished the little creature good-even.

"Art thou come to visit us, then?" said the glittering

child; "I saw thee running, playing on the other side, but thou wert frightened at our little dog."

"So you are not gipsies and rogues," said Mary, "as Andres always told me? He is a stupid thing, and talks of much he does not understand."

"Stay with us," said the strange little girl; "thou wilt like it well."

"But we are running a race."

"Thou wilt find thy comrade soon enough. There, take and eat."

Mary ate, and found the fruit more sweet than any she had ever tasted in her life before; and Andres, and the race, and the prohibition of her parents, were entirely forgotten.

A stately woman, in a shining robe, came towards them, and asked about the stranger child. "Fairest lady," said Mary, "I came running hither by chance, and now they wish to keep me."

"Thou art aware, Zerina," said the lady, "that she can be here but for a little while; besides, thou shouldst have asked my leave."

"I thought," said Zerina, "when I saw her admitted across the bridge, that I might do it; we have often seen her running in the fields, and thou thyself hast taken pleasure in her lively temper. She will have to leave us soon enough."

"No, I will stay here," said the little stranger; "for here it is so beautiful, and here I shall find the prettiest playthings, and store of berries and cherries to boot. On the other side it is not half so grand."

The gold-robed lady went away with a smile; and many of the children now came bounding round the happy Mary in their mirth, and twitched her, and incited her to dance; others brought her lambs, or curious playthings; others made music on instruments, and sang to it.

She kept, however, by the playmate who had first met her; for Zerina was the kindest and loveliest of them all. Little Mary cried and cried again: "I will stay with you forever; I will stay with you, and you shall

be my sisters"; at which the children all laughed, and
embraced her. "Now we shall have a royal sport," said
Zerina. She ran into the palace, and returned with a
little golden box, in which lay a quantity of seeds, like
glittering dust. She lifted of it with her little hand, and
scattered some grains on the green earth. Instantly the
grass began to move, as in waves; and, after a few moments, bright rosebushes started from the ground, shot
rapidly up, and budded all at once, while the sweetest
perfume filled the place. Mary also took a little of the
dust, and, having scattered it, she saw white lilies, and
the most variegated pinks, pushing up. At a signal
from Zerina, the flowers disappeared, and others rose
in their room. "Now," said Zerina, "look for something
greater." She laid two pine seeds in the ground, and
stamped them in sharply with her foot. Two green
bushes stood before them. "Grasp me fast," said she;
and Mary threw her arms about the slender form. She
felt herself borne upwards; for the trees were springing
under them with the greatest speed; the tall pines
waved to and fro, and the two children held each other
fast embraced, swinging this way and that in the red
clouds of the twilight, and kissed each other; while the
rest were climbing up and down the trunks with quick
dexterity, pushing and teasing one another with loud
laughter when they met; if any one fell down in the
press, it flew through the air, and sank slowly and
surely to the ground. At length Mary was beginning to
be frightened; and the other little child sang a few loud
tones, and the trees again sank down, and set them on
the ground as gradually as they had lifted them before
to the clouds.

They next went through the brazen door of the
palace. Here many fair women, elderly and young, were
sitting in the round hall, partaking of the fairest fruits,
and listening to glorious invisible music. In the vaulting
of the ceiling, palms, flowers, and groves stood painted,
among which little figures of children were sporting
and winding in every graceful posture; and with the
tones of the music, the images altered and glowed with

the most burning colours; now the blue and green were
sparkling like radiant light, now these tints faded back
in paleness, the purple flamed up, and the gold took
fire; and then the naked children seemed to be alive
among the flower-garlands and to draw breath, and
emit it through their ruby-coloured lips; so that by fits
you could see the glance of their little white teeth, and
the lighting up of their azure eyes.

From the hall, a stair of brass led down to a subterranean chamber. Here lay much gold and silver, and
precious stones of every hue shone out between them.
Strange vessels stood along the walls, and all seemed
filled with costly things. The gold was worked into
many forms, and glittered with the friendliest red.
Many little dwarfs were busied sorting the pieces from
the heap, and putting them in the vessels; others,
hunch-backed and bandy-legged, with long red noses,
were tottering slowly along, half-bent to the ground,
under full sacks, which they bore as millers do their
grain; and, with much panting, shaking out the gold-
dust on the ground. Then they darted awkwardly to the
right and left, and caught the rolling balls that were
like to run away; and it happened now and then that
one in his eagerness overset the other, so that both fell
heavily and clumsily to the ground. They made angry
faces, and looked askance, as Mary laughed at their
gestures and their ugliness. Behind them sat an old
crumpled little man, whom Zerina reverently greeted;
he thanked her with a grave inclination of his head. He
held a sceptre in his hand, and wore a crown upon his
brow, and all the other dwarfs appeared to regard him
as their master, and obey his nod.

"What more wanted?" asked he, with a surly voice,
as the children came a little nearer. Mary was afraid,
and did not speak; but her companion answered, they
were only come to look about them in the chambers.
"Still your old child's tricks!" replied the dwarf: "Will
there never be an end to idleness?" With this, he
turned again to his employment, kept his people weigh-

ing and sorting the ingots; some he sent away on errands, some he chid with angry tones.

"Who is the gentleman?" said Mary.

"Our Metal-Prince," replied Zerina, as they walked along.

They seemed once more to reach the open air, for they were standing by a lake, yet no sun appeared, and they saw no sky above their heads. A little boat received them, and Zerina steered it diligently forwards. It shot rapidly along. On gaining the middle of the lake, the stranger saw that multitudes of pipes, channels, and brooks, were spreading from the little sea in every direction. "These waters to the right," said Zerina, "flow beneath your garden, and this is why it blooms so freshly; by the other side we get down into the great stream." On a sudden, out of all the channels, and from every quarter of the lake, came a crowd of little children swimming up; some wore garlands of sedge and water-lily; some had red stems of coral, others were blowing on crooked shells; a tumultuous noise echoed merrily from the dark shores; among the children might be seen the fairest women sporting in the waters, and often several of the children sprang about some one of them, and with kisses hung upon her neck and shoulders. All saluted the strangers; and these steered onwards through the revelry out of the lake, into a little river, which grew narrower and narrower. At last the boat came aground. The strangers took their leave, and Zerina knocked against the cliff. This opened like a door, and a female form, all red, assisted them to mount. "Are you all brisk here?" inquired Zerina. "They are just at work," replied the other, "and happy as they could wish; indeed, the heat is very pleasant."

They went up a winding stair, and on a sudden Mary found herself in a most resplendent hall, so that as she entered, her eyes were dazzled by the radiance. Flame-coloured tapestry covered the walls with a purple glow; and when her eye had grown a little used to it, the stranger saw, to her astonishment, that, in the tapestry, there were figures moving up and down in dancing joyfulness; in form so beautiful, and of so fair proportions, that nothing could be seen more graceful; their bodies were as of red crystal, so that it appeared as if the blood were visible within them, flowing and playing in its courses. They smiled on the stranger, and saluted her with various bows; but as Mary was about approaching nearer them, Zerina plucked her sharply back, crying: "Thou wilt burn thyself, my little Mary, for the whole of it is fire."

Mary felt the heat. "Why do the pretty creatures not come out," said she, "and play with us?"

"As thou livest in the Air," replied the other, "so are they obliged to stay continually in Fire, and would faint and languish if they left it. Look now, how glad they are, how they laugh and shout; those down below spread out the fire-floods everywhere beneath the earth, and thereby the flowers, and fruits, and wine, are made to flourish; these red streams again, are to run beside the brooks of water; and thus the fiery creatures are kept ever busy and glad. But for thee it is too hot here; let us return to the garden."

In the garden, the scene had changed since they left it. The moonshine was lying on every flower; the birds were silent, and the children were asleep in complicated groups, among the green groves. Mary and her friend, however, did not feel fatigue, but walked about in the warm summer night, in abundant talk, till morning.

When the day dawned, they refreshed themselves on fruit and milk, and Mary said: "Suppose we go, by way of change, to the firs, and see how things look there?"

"With all my heart," replied Zerina; "thou wilt see our watchmen too, and they will surely please thee; they are standing up among the trees on the mound." The two proceeded through the flower-garden by pleasant groves, full of nightingales; then they ascended a vine-hill; and at last, after long following the windings of a clear brook, arrived at the firs, and the height which bounded the domain. "How does it come," said Mary, "that we have to walk so far here, when without, the circuit is so narrow?"

"I know not," said her friend; "but so it is."

They mounted to the dark firs, and a chill wind blew from without in their faces; a haze seemed lying far and wide over the landscape. On the top were many strange forms standing: with mealy, dusty faces; their misshapen heads not unlike those of white owls; they were clad in folded cloaks of shaggy wool; they held umbrellas of curious skins stretched out above them; and they waved and fanned themselves incessantly with large bat's wings, which flared out curiously beside the woollen roquelaures. "I could laugh, yet I am frightened," cried Mary.

"These are our good trusty watchmen," said her playmate; "they stand here and wave their fans, that cold anxiety and inexplicable fear may fall on every one that attempts to approach us. They are covered so, because without it is now cold and rainy, which they cannot bear. But snow, or wind, or cold air, never reaches down to us; here is an everlasting spring and summer: yet if these poor people on the top were not frequently relieved, they would certainly perish."

"But who are you, then?" said Mary, while again descending to the flowery fragrance; "or have you no name at all?"

"We are called the Elves," replied the friendly child; "people talk about us in the Earth, as I have heard."

They now perceived a mighty bustle on the green. "The fair Bird is come!" cried the children to them: all hastened to the hall. Here, as they approached, young and old were crowding over the threshold, all shouting for joy; and from within resounded a triumphant peal of music. Having entered, they perceived the vast circuit filled with the most varied forms, and all were looking upwards to a large Bird with glancing plumage, that was sweeping slowly round in the dome, and in its stately flight describing many a circle. The music sounded more gaily than before; the colours and lights alternated more rapidly. At last the music ceased; and the Bird, with a rustling noise, floated down upon a glittering crown that hung hovering in air under the high window, by which the hall was lighted from above. His plumage was purple and green, and shining golden streaks played through it; on his head there waved a diadem of feathers, so resplendent that they glanced like jewels. His bill was red, and his legs of a glancing blue. As he moved, the tints gleamed through each other, and the eye was charmed with their radiance. His size was as that of an eagle. But now he opened his glittering beak; and sweetest melodies came pouring from his moved breast, in finer tones than the lovesick nightingale gives forth; still stronger rose the song, and streamed like floods of Light, so that all, the very children themselves, were moved by it to tears of joy and rapture. When he ceased, all bowed before him; he again flew round the dome in circles, then darted through the door, and soared into the light heaven, where he shone far up like a red point, and then soon vanished from their eyes.

"Why are ye all so glad?" inquired Mary, bending to her fair playmate, who seemed smaller than yesterday.

"The King is coming!" said the little one; "many of us have never seen him, and whithersoever he turns his face, there is happiness and mirth; we have long looked for him, more anxiously than you look for spring when winter lingers with you; and now he has announced, by his fair herald, that he is at hand. This wise and glorious Bird, that has been sent to us by the King, is called Phoenix; he dwells far off in Arabia, on a tree, which there is no other that resembles it on Earth, as in like manner there is no second Phoenix. When he feels himself grown old, he builds a pile of balm and incense, kindles it, and dies singing; and then from the fragrant ashes, soars up the renewed Phoenix with unlessened beauty. It is seldom he so wings his course that men behold him; and when once in centuries this does occur, they note it in their annals, and expect remarkable events. But now, my friend, thou and I must part; for the sight of the King is not permitted thee."

Then the lady with the golden robe came through the throng, and beckoning Mary to her, led her into a sequestered walk. "Thou must leave us, my dear child," said she; "the King is to hold his court here for twenty years, perhaps longer; and fruitfulness and blessings will spread far over the land, but chiefly here beside us; all the brooks and rivulets will become more bountiful, all the fields and gardens richer, the wine more generous, the meadows more fertile, and the woods more fresh and green; a milder air will blow, no hail shall hurt, no flood shall threaten. Take this ring, and think of us: but beware of telling anyone of our existence; or we must fly this land, and thou and all around will lose the happiness and blessing of our neighbourhood. Once more, kiss thy playmate, and farewell." They issued from the walk; Zerina wept, Mary stooped to embrace her, and they parted. Already she was on the narrow bridge; the cold air was blowing on her back from the firs; the little dog barked with all its might, and rang its little bell; she looked around, then hastened over, for the darkness of the firs, the bleakness of the ruined huts, the shadows of the twilight, were filling her with terror.

"What a night my parents must have had on my account!" said she within herself, as she stept on the green; "and I dare not tell them where I have been, or what wonders I have witnessed, nor indeed would they believe me." Two men passing by saluted her; and as they went along, she heard them say: "What a pretty girl! Where can she come from?" With quickened steps she approached the house: but the trees which were hanging last night loaded with fruit were now standing dry and leafless; the house was differently painted, and a new barn had been built beside it. Mary was amazed, and thought she must be dreaming. In this perplexity she opened the door; and behind the table sat her father, between an unknown woman and a stranger youth. "Good God! Father," cried she, "where is my mother?"

"Thy mother!" said the woman, with a forecasting tone, and sprang towards her: "Ha, thou surely canst not—Yes, indeed, indeed thou art my lost, long-lost dear, only Mary!" She had recognised her by a little brown mole beneath the chin, as well as by her eyes and shape. All embraced her, all were moved with joy, and the parents wept. Mary was astonished that she almost reached to her father's stature; and she could not understand how her mother had become so changed and faded; she asked the name of the stranger youth. "It is our neighbour's Andres," said Martin. "How comest thou to us again, so unexpectedly, after seven long years? Where hast thou been? Why didst thou never send us tidings of thee?"

"Seven years!" said Mary, and could not order her ideas and recollections. "Seven whole years?"

"Yes, yes," said Andres, laughing, and shaking her trustfully by the hand; "I have won the race, good Mary; I was at the pear-tree and back again seven years ago, and thou, sluggish creature, art but just returned!"

They again asked, they pressed her; but remembering her instruction, she could answer nothing. It was they themselves chiefly that, by degrees, shaped a story for her: How, having lost her way, she had been taken up by a coach, and carried to a strange remote part, where she could not give the people any notion of her parents' residence; how she was conducted to a distant town, where certain worthy persons brought her up and loved her; how they had lately died, and at length she had recollected her birthplace, and so returned. "No matter how it is!" exclaimed her mother; "enough, that we have thee again, my little daughter, my own, my all!"

Andres waited supper, and Mary could not be at home in anything she saw. The house seemed small and dark; she felt astonished at her dress, which was clean and simple, but appeared quite foreign; she looked at the ring on her finger, and the gold of it glittered strangely, enclosing a stone of burning red. To her father's question, she replied that the ring also was a present from her benefactors.

She was glad when the hour of sleep arrived, and she hastened to her bed. Next morning she felt much more collected; she had now arranged her thoughts a little, and could better stand the questions of the people in the village, all of whom came in to bid her welcome. Andres was there too with the earliest, active, glad, and serviceable beyond all others. The blooming maiden of fifteen had made a deep impression on him; he had passed a sleepless night. The people of the castle likewise sent for Mary, and she had once more to tell her story to them, which was now grown quite familiar to her. The old Count and his Lady were surprised at her good-breeding; she was modest, but not embarrassed; she made answer courteously in good phrases to all their questions; all fear of noble persons and their equipage had passed away from her; for when she measured these halls and forms by the wonders and the high beauty she had seen with the Elves in their hidden abode, this earthly splendour seemed but dim to her, the presence of men was almost mean. The young lords were charmed with her beauty.

It was now February. The trees were budding earlier than usual; the nightingale had never come so soon; the spring rose fairer in the land than the oldest men could recollect it. In every quarter, little brooks gushed out to irrigate the pastures and meadows; the hills seemed heaving, the vines rose higher and higher, the fruit-trees blossomed as they had never done; and a swelling fragrant blessedness hung suspended heavily in rosy clouds over the scene. All prospered beyond expectation; no rude day, no tempest injured the fruits; the wine flowed blushing in immense grapes; and the inhabitants of the place felt astonished, and were captivated as in a sweet dream. The next year was like its forerunner; but men had now become accustomed to the marvellous. In autumn Mary yielded to the pressing entreaties of Andres and her parents; she was betrothed to him, and in winter they were married.

She often thought with inward longing of her residence behind the fir-trees; she continued serious and still. Beautiful as all that lay around her was, she knew of something yet more beautiful; and from the remembrance of this, a faint regret attuned her nature to soft melancholy. It smote her painfully when her father and mother talked about the gipsies and vagabonds, that dwelt in the dark spot of ground. Often she was on the point of speaking out in defence of those good beings, whom she knew to be the benefactors of the land; especially to Andres, who appeared to take delight in zealously abusing them. Yet still she repressed the word that was struggling to escape her bosom. So passed this year; in the next, she was solaced by a little daughter, whom she named Elfrida, thinking of the designation of her friendly Elves.

The young people lived with Martin and Brigitta, the house being large enough for all; and helped their parents in conducting their now extended husbandry. The little Elfrida soon displayed peculiar faculties and gifts; for she could walk at a very early age, and could speak perfectly before she was a twelvemonth old; and after some few years, she had become so wise and clever, and of such wondrous beauty, that all people regarded her with astonishment; and her mother could not keep away the thought that her child resembled one of those shining little ones in the space behind the Firs. Elfrida cared not to be with other children; but seemed to avoid, with a sort of horror, their tumultuous amusements; and liked best to be alone. She would then retire into a corner of the garden, and read, or work diligently with her needle; often also you might see her sitting, as if deep sunk in thought; or violently walking up and down the alleys, speaking to herself. Her parents readily allowed her to have her will in these things, for she was healthy, and waxed apace; only her strange sagacious answers and observations often made them anxious. "Such wise children do not grow to age," her grandmother, Brigitta, many times observed; "they are too good for this world; the child, besides, is beautiful beyond nature, and will never find its proper place on Earth."

The little girl had this peculiarity, that she was very loath to let herself be served by any one, but endeavoured to do everything herself. She was almost the earliest riser in the house; she washed herself carefully, and dressed without assistance: at night she was equally careful; she took special heed to pack up her clothes and washed them with her own hands, allowing no one, not even her mother, to meddle with her articles. The mother humoured her in this caprice, not thinking it of any consequence. But what was her astonishment, when, happening one holiday to insist, regardless of Elfrida's tears and screams, on dressing her out for a visit to the castle, she found upon her breast, suspended by a string, a piece of gold of a strange form, which she directly recognised as one of that sort she had seen in such abundance in the subterranean vault! The little thing was greatly frightened; and at last confessed that she had found it in the garden, and as she liked it much, had kept it carefully: she at the same time prayed so earnestly and pressingly to have it back, that Mary fastened it again on its former place, and, full of thoughts, went out with her in silence to the castle.

Sidewards from the farmhouse lay some offices for the storing of produce and implements; and behind these there was a little green, with an old grove, now visited by no one as, from the new arrangement of the buildings, it lay too far from the garden. In this solitude Elfrida delighted most; and it occurred to nobody to interrupt her here, so that frequently her parents did not see her for half a day. One afternoon her mother chanced to be in these buildings, seeking for some lost article among the lumber; and she noticed that a beam of light was coming in, through a chink in the wall. She took a thought of looking through this aperture, and seeing what her child was busied with; and it happened that a stone was lying loose, and could be pushed aside, so that she obtained a view right into the grove. Elfrida was sitting there on a little bench, and beside her the well-known Zerina; and the children were playing, and amusing one another, in the kindliest unity. The Elf embraced her beautiful companion, and said mournfully: "Ah! dear little creature, as I sport with thee, so have I sported with thy mother, when she was a child; but you mortals so soon grow tall and thoughtful! It is very hard: wert thou but to be a child as long as I!"

"Willingly would I do it," said Elfrida; "but they all say, I shall come to sense, and give over playing altogether; for I have great gifts, as they think, for growing wise. Ah! and then I shall see thee no more, thou dear Zerina! Yet it is with us as with the fruit-tree flowers: how glorious the blossoming apple-tree, with its red bursting buds! It looks so stately and broad; and every one, that passes under it, thinks surely something great will come of it; then the sun grows hot, and the buds come joyfully forth; but the wicked kernel is already there, which pushes off and casts away the fair flower's dress; and now, in pain and waxing, it can do nothing 'more, but must grow to fruit in harvest. An apple, to be sure, is pretty and refreshing; yet nothing to the blossom of spring. So it is also with us mortals: I am not glad in the least at growing to be a tall girl. Ah! Could I but once visit you!"

"Since the King is with us," said Zerina, "it is quite impossible; but I will come to thee, my darling, often, often; and none shall see me either here or there. I will pass invisible through the air, or fly over to thee like a bird. O! we will be much, much together, while thou art still little. What can I do to please thee?"

"Thou must like me very dearly," said Elfrida, "as I like thee in my heart. But come, let us make another rose."

Zerina took the well-known box from her bosom, threw two grains from it on the ground; and instantly a green bush stood before them, with two deep-red roses, bending their heads, as if to kiss each other. The children plucked them smiling, and the bush disappeared. "O that it would not die so soon!" said Elfrida; "this red child, this wonder of the Earth!"

"Give it me here," said the little Elf; then breathed thrice upon the budding rose, and kissed it thrice. "Now," said she, giving back the rose, "it will continue fresh and blooming till winter."

"I will keep it," said Elfrida, "as an image of thee; I will guard it in my little room, and kiss it night and morning, as if it were thyself."

"The sun is setting," said the other; "I must go home." They embraced again, and Zerina vanished.

In the evening, Mary clasped her child to her breast, with a feeling of alarm and veneration. She henceforth allowed the good little girl more liberty than formerly; and often calmed her husband when he came to search for the child; which for some time he was wont to do, as her retiredness did not please him; and he feared that, in the end, it might make her silly, or even pervert her understanding. The mother often glided to the chink; and almost always found the bright Elf beside her child, employed in sport, or in earnest conversation.

"Wouldst thou like to fly?" inquired Zerina once.

"O well! How well!" replied Elfrida; and the fairy clasped her mortal playmate in her arms, and mounted with her from the ground, till they hovered above the grove. The mother, in alarm, forgot herself, and pushed out her head in terror to look after them; when Zerina, from the air, held up her finger, and threatened yet smiled; then descended with the child, embraced her, and disappeared. After this, it happened more than once that Mary was observed by her; and every time, the shining little creature shook her head, or threatened, yet with friendly looks.

Often, in disputing with her husband, Mary had said in her zeal: "Thou dost injustice to the poor people in the hut!" But when Andres pressed her to explain why she differed in opinion from the whole village, nay, from his Lordship himself; and how she could understand it better than the whole of them, she still broke off embarrassed, and became silent. One day, after dinner, Andres grew more violent than ever; and maintained that, by one means or another, the crew must be packed away, as a nuisance to the country; when his wife, in anger, said to him: "Hush! for they are benefactors to thee and to every one of us."

"Benefactors!" cried the other, in astonishment: "These rogues and vagabonds?"

In her indignation, she was now at last tempted to relate to him, under promise of the strictest secrecy, the history of her youth: and as Andres at every word grew more incredulous, and shook his head in mockery, she took him by the hand, and led him to the chink; where, to his amazement, he beheld the glittering Elf sporting with his child, and caressing her in the grove. He knew not what to say; an exclamation of astonishment escaped him, and Zerina raised her eyes. On the instant she grew pale, and trembled violently; not with friendly, but with indignant looks, she made the sign of threatening, and then said to Elfrida: "Thou canst not help it, dearest heart; but they will never learn sense, wise as they believe themselves." She embraced the little one with stormy haste; and then, in the shape of a raven, flew with hoarse cries over the garden, toward the Firs.

In the evening, the little one was very still; she kissed her rose with tears; Mary felt depressed and frightened, Andres scarcely spoke. It grew dark. Suddenly there went a rustling through the trees; birds flew to and fro with wild screaming, thunder was heard to roll, the Earth shook, and tones of lamentation moaned in the air. Andres and his wife had not courage to rise; they shrouded themselves within the curtains, and with fear and trembling awaited the day. Towards morning, it grew calmer; and all was silent when the Sun, with his cheerful light, rose over the wood.

Andres dressed himself; and Mary now observed

that the stone of the ring upon her finger had become quite pale. On opening the door, the sun shone clear on their faces, but the scene around them they could scarcely recognise. The freshness of the wood was gone; the hills were shrunk, the brooks were flowing languidly with scanty streams, the sky seemed grey; and when you turned to the Firs, they were standing there no darker or more dreary than the other trees. The huts behind them were no longer frightful; and several inhabitants of the village came and told about the fearful night, and how they had been across the spot where the gipsies had lived; how these people must have left the place at last, for their huts were standing empty, and within had quite a common look, just like the dwellings of other poor people: some of their household gear was left behind.

Elfrida in secret said to her mother: "I could not sleep last night; and in my fright at the noise, I was praying from the bottom of my heart, when the door suddenly opened, and my playmate entered to take leave of me. She had a travelling pouch slung round her, a hat on her head, and a large staff in her hand. She was very angry at thee; since on thy account she had now to suffer the severest and most painful punishments, as she had always been so fond of thee; for all of them, she said, were very loath to leave this quarter."

Mary forbade her to speak of this; and now the ferryman came across the river, and told them new wonders. As it was growing dark, a stranger man of large size had come to him, and hired his boat till sunrise; and with this condition, that the boatman should remain quiet in his house, at least should not cross the threshold of his door. "I was frightened," continued the old man, "and the strange bargain would not let me sleep. I slipped softly to the window, and looked towards the river. Great clouds were driving restlessly through the sky, and the distant woods were rustling fearfully; it was as if my cottage shook, and moans and lamentations glided round it. On a sudden, I perceived a white streaming light, that grew broader and broader, like many thousands of falling stars; sparkling and waving, it proceeded forward from the dark Fir-ground, moved over the fields, and spread itself along towards the river. Then I heart a trampling, a jingling, a bustling, and rushing, nearer and nearer; it went forwards to my boat, and all stept into it, men and women, as it seemed, and children; and the tall stranger ferried them over. In the river were by the boat swimming many thousands of glittering forms; in the air white clouds and lights were wavering; and all lamented and bewailed that they must travel forth so far, far away, and leave their beloved dwelling. The noise of the rudder and the water creaked and gurgled between-whiles, and then suddenly there would be silence. Many a time the boat landed, and went back, and was again laden; many heavy casks, too, they took along with them, which multitudes of horrid-looking little fellows carried and rolled; whether they were devils or goblins, Heaven only knows. Then came, in waving brightness, a stately freight; it seemed an old man, mounted on a small white horse, and all were crowding round him. I saw nothing of the horse but its head; for the rest of it was covered with costly glittering cloths and trappings: on his brow the old man had a crown, so bright that, as he came across, I thought the sun was rising there, and the redness of the dawn glimmering in my eyes. Thus it went on all night; I at last fell asleep in the tumult, half in joy, half in terror. In the morning all was still; but the river is, as it were, run off, and I know not how I am to steer my boat in it now."

The same year there came a blight; the woods died away, the springs ran dry; and the scene, which had once been the joy of every traveller, was in autumn standing waste, naked and bald; scarcely showing here and there, in the sea of sand, a spot or two where grass, with a dingy greenness, still grew up. The fruit-trees all withered, the vines faded away, and the aspect of the place became so melancholy, that the Count, with his people, next year left the castle, which in time decayed and fell to ruins.

Elfrida gazed on her rose day and night with deep longing, and thought of her kind playmate; and as it drooped and withered, so did she also hang her head; and before the spring the little maiden had herself faded away. Mary often stood upon the spot before the hut, and wept for the happiness that had departed. She wasted herself away like her child, and in a few years she too was gone. Old Martin, with his son-in-law, returned to the quarter where he had lived before.

LORD DUNSANY

(1878–1957)

Lord Dunsany, novelist, poet, and playwright, was born in London, the son of an Irish nobleman. He was educated at Eton and Sandhurst and served in both the Boer War and World War I. During World War II, he held the chair of Byron Professor of English Literature in Athens, and was there when Nazi troops invaded and captured the city. He subsequently disappeared for some time, finally arriving in Dublin in 1942 but refusing to explain what had ensued during his disappearance. Dunsany was a dynamic and athletic individual who loved to play sports and travel. He crisscrossed America on reading tours, and spent a great deal of time hunting lions on safari in Africa. It is difficult to believe that he could do all these things and still find time to write over sixty books.

His literary career began in 1905 with the publication of his novel *The Gods of Pegana*. Other novels include *Time and the Gods* (1906), *The King of Elfland's Daughter* (1924), *The Charwoman's Shadow* (1926), and *The Wise Woman* (1933). In 1909, at the request of W. B. Yeats, Dunsany wrote a drama, *The Glittering Gate,* for production at the Abbey Theatre. Evidently both Yeats and Dunsany were pleased with the results, since the play was followed by a number of others, including *The Gods of the Mountain* (1911), *The Laughter of the Gods* (1919), *If* (1921), *Alexander* (1925), and *Plays for Earth and Air* (1937). Besides his novels and plays, Dunsany published two volumes of verse, a series of autobiographies, numerous essays, short-story collections, and even a translation of Horace. He is generally recognized as one of the finest, and most influential, fantasy writers of the past century and a half. Many have tried to imitate his lyrical prose style, but few have succeeded.

"The Sword of Welleran" is a striking example of Dunsany's inimitable brand of heroic fantasy. He handles his subject with such authority that the reader immediately feels a part of the imaginary kingdom in which Merimna is located. The songs of the sentries, the grandeur of the landscapes, the soul-wrenching anguish of the warrior spirits, the valiant defense of Merimna against the invading tribes—all seem genuine and believable. Lord Dunsany uses many effective literary techniques to create the exotic and pensive atmosphere which permeates the work, but especially noteworthy is his use of evocative names: Cyresian, Welleran, Soorenard, Mommolek, Rollory, Akanax, Iraine, Rold, Sajar-Ho, Seejar. Dunsany seemed to possess an instinctive sense of the magical and arresting, and thus he was able to create high fantasy in its purest form.

❧ The Sword of Welleran ❧

Lord Dunsany

Where the great plain of Tarphet runs up, as the sea in estuaries, among the Cyresian mountains, there stood long since the city of Merimna well-nigh among the shadows of the crags. I have never seen a city in the world so beautiful as Merimna seemed to me when first I dreamed of it. It was a marvel of spires and figures of bronze, and marble fountains, and trophies of fabulous wars, and broad streets given over wholly to the Beautiful. Right through the centre of the city there went an avenue fifty strides in width, and along each side of it stood likenesses in bronze of the Kings of all the countries that the people of Merimna had ever known. At the end of that avenue was a colossal chariot with three bronze horses driven by the winged figure of Fame, and behind her in the chariot the huge form of Welleran, Merimna's ancient hero, standing with extended sword. So urgent was the mien and attitude of Fame, and so swift the pose of the horses, that you had sworn that the chariot was instantly upon you, and that its dust already veiled the faces of the Kings. And in the city was a mighty hall wherein were stored the trophies of Merimna's heroes. Sculptured it was and domed, the glory of the art of masons a long while dead, and on the summit of the dome the image of Rollory sat gazing across the Cyresian mountains toward the wide lands beyond, the lands that knew his sword. And beside Rollory, like an old nurse, the fig-

33

ure of Victory sat, hammering into a golden wreath of laurels for his head the crowns of fallen Kings.

Such was Merimna, a city of sculptured Victories and warriors of bronze. Yet in the time of which I write the art of war had been forgotten in Merimna, and the people almost slept. To and fro and up and down they would walk through the marble streets, gazing at memorials of the things achieved by their country's swords in the hands of those that long ago had loved Merimna well. Almost they slept, and dreamed of Welleran, Soorenard, Mommolek, Rollory, Akanax, and young Iraine. Of the lands beyond the mountains that lay all round about them they knew nothing, save that they were the theatre of the terrible deeds of Welleran, that he had done with his sword. Long since these lands had fallen back into the possession of the nations that had been scourged by Merimna's armies. Nothing now remained to Merimna's men save their inviolate city and the glory of the remembrance of their ancient fame. At night they would place sentinels far out in the desert, but these always slept at their posts dreaming of Rollory, and three times every night a guard would march around the city clad in purple, bearing lights and singing songs of Welleran. Always the guard went unarmed, but as the sound of their song went echoing across the plain towards the looming mountains, the desert robbers would hear the name of Welleran and steal away to their haunts. Often dawn would come across the plain, shimmering marvellously upon Merimna's spires, abashing all the stars, and find the guard still singing songs of Welleran, and would change the colour of their purple robes and pale the lights they bore. But the guard would go back leaving the ramparts safe, and one by one the sentinels in the plain would awake from dreaming of Rollory and shuffle back into the city quite cold. Then something of the menace would pass away from the faces of the Cyresian mountains, that from the north and the west and the south lowered upon Merimna, and clear in the morning the statues and the pillars would arise in the old inviolate city. You would wonder that an unarmed guard and sentinels that slept could defend a city that was stored with all the glories of art, that was rich in gold and bronze, a haughty city that had erst oppressed its neighbours, whose people had forgotten the art of war. Now this is the reason that, though all her other lands had long been taken from her, Merimna's city was safe. A strange thing was believed or feared by the fierce tribes beyond the mountains, and it was credited among them that at certain stations round Merimna's ramparts there still rode Welleran, Soorenard, Mommolek, Rollory, Akanax, and young Iraine. Yet it was close on a hundred years since Iraine, the youngest of Merimna's heroes, fought his last battle with the tribes.

Sometimes indeed there arose among the tribes young men who doubted and said: "How may a man for ever escape death?"

But graver men answered them: "Hear us, ye whose wisdom has discerned so much, and discern for us how a man may escape death when two score horsemen assail him with their swords, all of them sworn to kill him, and all of them sworn upon their country's gods; as often Welleran hath. Or discern for us how two men alone may enter a walled city by night, and bring away from it that city's king, as did Soorenard and Mommolek. Surely men that have escaped so many swords and so many sleety arrows shall escape the years and Time."

And the young men were humbled and became silent. Still, the suspicion grew. And often when the sun set on the Cyresian mountains, men in Merimna discerned the forms of savage tribesmen black against the light, peering towards the city.

All knew in Merimna that the figures round the ramparts were only statues of stone, yet even there a hope lingered among a few that some day their old heroes would come again, for certainly none had ever seen them die. Now it had been the wont of these six warriors of old, as each received his last wound and knew it to be mortal, to ride away to a certain deep ravine

and cast his body in, as somewhere I have read great
elephants do, hiding their bones away from lesser
beasts. It was a ravine steep and narrow even at the
ends, a great cleft into which no man could come by
any path. There rode Welleran alone, panting hard;
and there later rode Soorenard and Mommolek, Mommolek with a mortal wound upon him not to return,
but Soorenard was unwounded and rode back alone
from leaving his dear friend resting among the mighty
bones of Welleran. And there rode Soorenard, when
his day was come, with Rollory and Akanax, and Rollory rode in the middle and Soorenard and Akanax on
either side. And the long ride was a hard and weary
thing for Soorenard and Akanax, for they both had
mortal wounds; but the long ride was easy for Rollory,
for he was dead. So the bones of these five heroes
whitened in an enemy's land, and very still they were,
though they had troubled cities, and none knew where
they lay saving only Iraine, the young captain, who was
but twenty-five when Mommolek, Rollory and Akanax
rode away. And among them were strewn their saddles
and their bridles, and all the accoutrements of their
horses, lest any man should ever find them afterwards
and say in some foreign city: "Lo! the bridles or the
saddles of Merimna's captains, taken in war," but their
beloved trusty horses they turned free.

Forty years afterwards, in the hour of a great victory, his last wound came upon Iraine, and the wound
was terrible and would not close. And Iraine was the
last of the captains, and rode away alone. It was a long
way to the dark ravine, and Iraine feared that he
would never come to the resting-place of the old
heroes, and he urged his horse on swiftly, and clung to
the saddle with his hands. And often as he rode he fell
asleep, and dreamed of earlier days, and of the times
when he first rode forth to the great wars of Welleran,
and of the time when Welleran first spake to him, and
of the faces of Welleran's comrades when they led
charges in the battle. And ever as he awoke a great
longing arose in his soul as it hovered on his body's

brink, a longing to lie among the bones of the old heroes. At last when he saw the dark ravine making a scar across the plain, the soul of Iraine slipped out through his great wound and spread its wings, the pain departed from the poor hacked body and, still urging his horse forward, Iraine died. But the old true horse cantered on till suddenly he saw before him the dark ravine and put his forefeet out on the very edge of it and stopped. Then the body of Iraine came toppling forward over the right shoulder of the horse, and his bones mingle and rest as the years go by with the bones of Merimna's heroes.

Now there was a little boy in Merimna named Rold. I saw him first, I, the dreamer, that sit before my fire asleep, I saw him first as his mother led him through the great hall where stand the trophies of Merimna's heroes. He was five years old, and they stood before the great glass casket wherein lay the sword of Welleran, and his mother said: "The sword of Welleran." And Rold said: "What should a man do with the sword of Welleran?" And his mother answered: "Men look at the sword and remember Welleran." And they went on and stood before the great red cloak of Welleran, and the child said: "Why did Welleran wear this great red cloak?" And his mother answered: "It was the way of Welleran."

When Rold was a little older he stole out of his mother's house quite in the middle of the night when all the world was still, and Merimna asleep dreaming of Welleran, Soorenard, Mommolek, Rollory, Akanax, and young Iraine. And he went down to the ramparts to hear the purple guard go by singing of Welleran. And the purple guard came by with lights, all singing in the stillness, and dark shapes out in the desert turned and fled. And Rold went back again to his mother's house with a great yearning towards the name of Welleran, such as men feel for very holy things.

And in time Rold grew to know the pathway all round the ramparts, and the six equestrian statues that were there guarding Merimna still. These statues were not like other statues, they were so cunningly wrought of many-coloured marbles that none might be quite sure until very close that they were not living men. There was a horse of dappled marble, the horse of Akanax. The horse of Rollory was of alabaster, pure white, his armour was wrought out of a stone that shone, and his horseman's cloak was made of a blue stone, very precious. He looked northward.

But the marble horse of Welleran was pure black, and there sat Welleran upon him looking solemnly westwards. His horse it was whose cold neck Rold most loved to stroke, and it was Welleran whom the watchers at sunset on the mountains the most clearly saw as they peered towards the city. And Rold loved the red nostrils of the great black horse and his rider's jasper cloak.

Now beyond the Cyresians the suspicion grew that Merimna's heroes were dead, and a plan was devised that a man should go by night and come close to the figures upon the ramparts and see whether they were Welleran, Soorenard, Mommolek, Rollory, Akanax, and young Iraine. And all were agreed upon the plan, and many names were mentioned of those who should go, and the plan matured for many years. It was during these years that watchers clustered often at sunset upon the mountains but came no nearer. Finally, a better plan was made, and it was decided that two men who had been by chance condemned to death should be given a pardon if they went down into the plain by night and discovered whether or not Merimna's heroes lived. At first the two prisoners dared not go, but after a while one of them, Seejar, said to his companion, Sajar-Ho: "See now, when the King's axeman smites a man upon the neck that man dies."

And the other said that this was so. Then said Seejar: "And even though Welleran smite a man with his sword no more befalleth him than death."

Then Sajar-Ho thought for a while. Presently he said: "Yet the eye of the King's axeman might err at the moment of his stroke or his arm fail him, and the eye of Welleran hath never erred nor his arm failed. It were better to bide here."

Then said Seejar: "Maybe that Welleran is dead and that some other holds his place upon the ramparts, or even a statue of stone."

But Sajar-Ho made answer: "How can Welleran be dead when he even escaped from two score horsemen with swords that were sworn to slay him, and all sworn upon our country's gods?"

And Seejar said: "This story his father told my grandfather concerning Welleran. On the day that the fight was lost on the plains of Kurlistan he saw a dying horse near to the river, and the horse looked piteously toward the water but could not reach it. And the father of my grandfather saw Welleran go down to the river's brink and bring water from it with his own hand and give it to the horse. Now we are in as sore a plight as was that horse, and as near to death; it may be that Welleran will pity us, while the King's axeman cannot because of the commands of the King."

Then said Sajar-Ho: "Thou wast ever a cunning arguer. Thou broughtest us into this trouble with thy cunning and thy devices, we will see if thou canst bring us out of it. We will go."

So news was brought to the King that the two prisoners would go down to Merimna.

That evening the watchers led them to the mountain's edge, and Seejar and Sajar-Ho went down towards the plain by the way of a deep ravine, and the watchers watched them go. Presently their figures were wholly hid in the dusk. Then night came up, huge and holy, out of waste marshes to the eastwards and low lands and the sea; and the angels that watched over all men through the day closed their great eyes and slept, and the angels that watched over all men through the night awoke and ruffled their deep blue feathers and stood up and watched. But the plain became a thing of mystery filled with fears. So the two spies went down the deep ravine, and coming to the plain sped stealthily across it. Soon they came to the line of sentinels asleep

upon the sand, and one stirred in his sleep calling on
Rollory, and a great dread seized upon the spies and
they whispered "Rollory lives," but they remembered
the King's axeman and went on. And next they came
to the great bronze statue of Fear, carved by some
sculptor of the old glorious years in the attitude of
flight towards the mountains, calling to her children as
she fled. And the children of Fear were carved in the
likeness of the armies of all the trans-Cyresian tribes
with their backs towards Merimna, flocking after Fear.
And from where he sat on his horse behind the ramparts the sword of Welleran was stretched out over
their heads as ever it was wont. And the two spies
kneeled down in the sand and kissed the huge bronze
foot of the statue of Fear, saying: "O Fear, Fear." And
as they knelt they saw lights far off along the ramparts
coming nearer and nearer, and heard men singing of
Welleran. And the purple guard came nearer and went
by with their lights, and passed on into the distance
round the ramparts still singing of Welleran. And all
the while the two spies clung to the foot of the statue,
muttering: "O Fear, Fear." But when they could hear
the name of Welleran no more they arose and came to
the ramparts and climbed over them and came at once
upon the figure of Welleran, and they bowed low to the
ground, and Seejar said: "O Welleran, we came to see
whether thou didst yet live." And for a long while they
waited with their faces to the earth. At last Seejar
looked up towards Welleran's terrible sword, and it
was still stretched out pointing to the carved armies
that followed after Fear. And Seejar bowed to the
ground again and touched the horse's hoof, and it
seemed cold to him. And he moved his hand higher
and touched the leg of the horse, and it seemed quite
cold. At last he touched Welleran's foot, and the armour on it seemed hard and stiff. Then as Welleran
moved not and spake not, Seejar climbed up at last and
touched his hand, the terrible hand of Welleran, and it
was marble. Then Seejar laughed aloud, and he and
Sajar-Ho sped down the empty pathway and found

Rollory, and he was marble too. Then they climbed down over the ramparts and went back across the plain, walking contemptuously past the figure of Fear, and heard the guard returning round the ramparts for the third time, singing of Welleran; and Seejar said: "Ay, you may sing of Welleran, but Welleran is dead and a doom is on your city."

And they passed on and found the sentinel still restless in the night and calling on Rollory. And Sajar-Ho muttered: "Ay, you may call on Rollory, but Rollory is dead and naught can save your city."

And the two spies went back alive to their mountains again, and as they reached them the first ray of the sun came up red over the desert behind Merimna and lit Merimna's spires. It was the hour when the purple guard were wont to go back into the city with their tapers pale and their robes a brighter colour, when the cold sentinels came shuffling in from dreaming in the desert; it was the hour when the desert robbers hid themselves away, going back to their mountain caves; it was the hour when gauze-winged insects are born that only live for a day; it was the hour when men die that are condemned to death; and in this hour a great peril, new and terrible, arose for Merimna and Merimna knew it not.

Then Seejar turning said: "See how red the dawn is and how red the spires of Merimna. They are angry with Merimna in Paradise and they bode its doom."

So the two spies went back and brought the news to their King, and for a few days the Kings of those countries were gathering their armies together; and one evening the armies of four Kings were massed together at the top of the deep ravine, all crouching below the summit waiting for the sun to set. All wore resolute and fearless faces, yet inwardly every man was praying to his gods, unto each one in turn.

Then the sun set, and it was the hour when the bats and the dark creatures are abroad and the lions come down from their lairs, and the desert robbers go into the plains again, and fevers rise up winged and hot out of chill marshes, and it was the hour when safety leaves the thrones of Kings, the hour when dynasties change. But in the desert the purple guard came swinging out of Merimna with their lights to sing of Welleran, and the sentinels lay down to sleep.

Now into Paradise no sorrow may ever come, but may only beat like rain against its crystal walls, yet the souls of Merimna's heroes were half aware of some sorrow far away as some sleeper feels that some one is chilled and cold yet knows not in his sleep that it is he. And they fretted a little in their starry home. Then unseen there drifted earthward across the setting sun the souls of Welleran, Soorenard, Mommolek, Rollory, Akanax, and young Iraine. Already when they reached Merimna's ramparts it was just dark, already the armies of the four Kings had begun to move, jingling, down the deep ravine. But when the six warriors saw their city again, so little changed after so many years, they looked towards her with a longing that was nearer to tears than any that their souls had known before, crying to her:

"O Merimna, our city: Merimna, our walled city.

"How beautiful thou art with all thy spires, Merimna. For thee we left the earth, its kingdoms and little flowers, for thee we have come away for awhile from Paradise.

"It is very difficult to draw away from the face of God—it is like a warm fire, it is like dear sleep, it is like a great anthem, yet there is a stillness all about it, a stillness full of lights.

"We have left Paradise for awhile for thee, Merimna.

"Many women have we loved, Merimna, but only one city.

"Behold now all the people dream, all our loved people. How beautiful are dreams! In dreams the dead may live, even the long dead and the very silent. Thy lights are all sunk low, they have all gone out, no sound is in thy streets. Hush! Thou art like a maiden that shutteth up her eyes and is asleep, that draweth her breath softly and is quite still, being at ease and untroubled.

"Behold now the battlements, the old battlements. Do men defend them still as we defended them? They are worn a little, the battlements," and drifting nearer they peered anxiously. "It is not by the hand of man that they are worn, our battlements. Only the years have done it and indomitable Time. Thy battlements are like the girdle of a maiden, a girdle that is round about her. See now the dew upon them, they are like a jewelled girdle.

"Thou art in great danger, Merimna, because thou art so beautiful. Must thou perish to-night because we no more defend thee, because we cry out and none hear us, as the bruised lilies cry out and none have known their voices?"

Thus spake those strong-voiced, battle-ordering captains, calling to their dear city, and their voices came no louder than the whispers of little bats that drift across the twilight in the evening. Then the purple guard came near, going round the ramparts for the first time in the night, and the old warriors called to them, "Merimna is in danger! Already her enemies gather in the darkness." But their voices were never heard because they were only wandering ghosts. And the guard went by and passed unheeding away, still singing of Welleran.

Then said Welleran to his comrades: "Our hands can hold swords no more, our voices cannot be heard, we are stalwart men no longer. We are but dreams, let us go among dreams. Go all of you, and thou too, young Iraine, and trouble the dreams of all the men that sleep, and urge them to take the old swords of their grandsires that hang upon the walls, and to gather at the mouth of the ravine; and I will find a leader and make him take my sword."

Then they passed up over the ramparts and into their dear city. And the wind blew about, this way and that, as he went, the soul of Welleran who had upon his day withstood the charges of tempestuous armies.

And the souls of his comrades, and with them young Iraine, passed up into the city and troubled the dreams of every man who slept, and to every man the souls said in their dreams: "It is hot and still in the city. Go out now into the desert, into the cool under the mountains, but take with thee the old sword that hangs upon the wall for fear of the desert robbers."

And the god of that city sent up a fever over it, and the fever brooded over it and the streets were hot; and all that slept awoke from dreaming that it would be cool and pleasant where the breezes came down the ravine out of the mountains; and they took the old swords that their grandsires had, according to their dreams, for fear of the desert robbers. And in and out of dreams passed the souls of Welleran's comrades, and with them young Iraine, in great haste as the night wore on; and one by one they troubled the dreams of all Merimna's men and caused them to arise and go out armed, all save the purple guard who, heedless of danger, sang of Welleran still, for waking men cannot hear the souls of the dead.

But Welleran drifted over the roofs of the city till he came to the form of Rold lying fast asleep. Now Rold was grown strong and was eighteen years of age, and he was fair of hair and tall like Welleran, and the soul of Welleran hovered over him and went into his dreams as a butterfly flits through trellis-work into a garden of flowers, and the soul of Welleran said to Rold in his dreams: "Thou wouldst go and see again the sword of Welleran, the great curved sword of Welleran. Thou wouldst go and look at it in the night with the moonlight shining upon it."

And the longing of Rold in his dreams to see the sword caused him to walk still sleeping from his mother's house to the hall wherein were the trophies of the heroes. And the soul of Welleran urging the dreams of Rold caused him to pause before the great red cloak, and there the soul said among his dreams: "Thou art cold in the night; fling now a cloak around thee."

And Rold drew round about him the huge red cloak of Welleran. Then Rold's dreams took him to the sword, and the soul said to the dreams: "Thou hast a longing to hold the sword of Welleran: take up the sword in thy hand."

But Rold said: "What should a man do with the sword of Welleran?"

And the soul of the old captain said to the dreamer: "It is a good sword to hold: take up the sword of Welleran."

And Rold, still sleeping and speaking aloud, said: "It is not lawful; none may touch the sword."

And Rold turned to go. Then a great and terrible cry arose in the soul of Welleran, all the more bitter for that he could not utter it, and it went round and round his soul finding no utterance, like a cry evoked long since by some murderous deed in some old haunted chamber that whispers through the ages heard by none.

And the soul of Welleran cried out to the dreams of Rold: "Thy knees are tied! Thou art fallen in a marsh! Thou canst not move."

And the dreams of Rold said to him: "Thy knees are tied, thou art fallen in a marsh," and Rold stood still before the sword. Then the soul of the warrior wailed among Rold's dreams, as Rold stood before the sword.

"Welleran is crying for his sword, his wonderful curved sword. Poor Welleran, that once fought for Merimna, is crying for his sword in the night. Thou wouldst not keep Welleran without his beautiful sword when he is dead and cannot come for it, poor Welleran who fought for Merimna."

And Rold broke the glass casket with his hand and took the sword, the great curved sword of Welleran; and the soul of the warrior said among Rold's dreams: "Welleran is waiting in the deep ravine that runs into the mountains, crying for his sword."

And Rold went down through the city and climbed

over the ramparts, and walked with his eyes wide open but still sleeping over the desert to the mountains.

Already a great multitude of Merimna's citizens were gathered in the desert before the deep ravine with old swords in their hands, and Rold passed through them as he slept holding the sword of Welleran, and the people cried in amaze to one another as he passed: "Rold hath the sword of Welleran!"

And Rold came to the mouth of the ravine, and there the voices of the people woke him. And Rold knew nothing that he had done in his sleep, and looked in amazement at the sword in his hand and said: "What art thou, thou beautiful thing? Lights shimmer in thee, thou art restless. It is the sword of Welleran, the curved sword of Welleran!"

And Rold kissed the hilt of it, and it was salt upon his lips with the battle-sweat of Welleran. And Rold said: "What should a man do with the sword of Welleran?"

And all the people wondered at Rold as he sat there with the sword in his hand muttering, "What should a man do with the sword of Welleran?"

Presently there came to the ears of Rold the noise of a jingling up in the ravine, and all the people, the people that knew naught of war, heard the jingling coming nearer in the night; for the four armies were moving on Merimna and not yet expecting an enemy. And Rold gripped upon the hilt of the great curved sword, and the sword seemed to lift a little. And a new thought came into the hearts of Merimna's people as they gripped their grandsires' swords. Nearer and nearer came the heedless armies of the four Kings, and old ancestral memories began to arise in the minds of Merimna's people in the desert with their swords in their hands sitting behind Rold. And all the sentinels were awake holding their spears, for Rollory had put their dreams to flight, Rollory that once could put to flight armies and now was but a dream struggling with other dreams.

And now the armies had come very near. Suddenly

Rold leaped up, crying: "Welleran! And the sword of Welleran!" And the savage, lusting sword that had thirsted for a hundred years went up with the hand of Rold and swept through a tribesman's ribs. And with the warm blood all about it there came a joy into the curved soul of that mighty sword, like to the joy of a swimmer coming up dripping out of warm seas after living for long in a dry land. When they saw the red cloak and that terrible sword a cry ran through the tribal armies, "Welleran lives!" And there arose the sounds of the exulting of victorious men, and the panting of those that fled, and the sword singing softly to itself as it whirled dripping through the air. And the last that I saw of the battle as it poured into the depth and darkness of the ravine was the sword of Welleran sweeping up and falling, gleaming blue in the moonlight whenever it arose and afterwards gleaming red, and so disappearing into the darkness.

But in the dawn Merimna's men came back, and the sun arising to give new life to the world, shone instead upon the hideous things that the sword of Welleran had done. And Rold said: "O sword, sword! How horrible thou art! Thou art a terrible thing to have come among men. How many eyes shall look upon gardens no more because of thee? How many fields must go empty that might have been fair with cottages, white cottages with children all about them? How many valleys must go desolate that might have nursed warm hamlets, because thou hast slain long since the men that might have built them? I hear the wind crying against thee, thou sword! It comes from the empty valleys. It comes over the bare fields. There are children's voices in it. They were never born. Death brings an end to crying for those that had life once, but these must cry for ever. O sword! sword! why did the gods send thee among men?" And the tears of Rold fell down upon the proud sword but could not wash it clean.

And now that the ardour of battle had passed away, the spirits of Merimna's people began to gloom a little, like their leader's, with their fatigue and with the cold of the morning; and they looked at the sword of Welleran in Rold's hand and said: "Not any more, not any more for ever will Welleran now return, for his sword is in the hand of another. Now we know indeed that he is dead. O Welleran, thou wast our sun and moon and all our stars. Now is the sun fallen down and the moon broken, and all the stars are scattered as the diamonds of a necklace that is snapped off one who is slain by violence."

Thus wept the people of Merimna in the hour of their great victory, for men have strange moods, while beside them their old inviolate city slumbered safe. But back from the ramparts and beyond the mountains and over the lands that they had conquered of old, beyond the world and back again to Paradise, went the souls of Welleran, Soorenard, Mommolek, Rollory, Akanax, and young Iraine.

GEORGE MAC DONALD

(1824–1905)

George Mac Donald, Scottish novelist, poet, and writer of children's stories, was born at Huntley, Aberdeenshire, the son of a farmer. He was educated at Aberdeen University and Highbury Theological College. In 1850, Mac Donald became a Congregationalist minister at Arundel, but after a few years he retired, partly because of health problems, and partly because of theological considerations. Devoting the rest of his long life to the writing of literature, he published scores of books, including popular novels of Scottish peasant life and volumes of collected sermons and theological treatises. The latter attracted the attention of C. S. Lewis, who was greatly impressed by the deep religious feeling which permeates all Mac Donald's works.

In the past decade or so, Mac Donald's fantasy writings have gained great popularity. *Phantastes: A Faerie Romance* (1858) and *Lilith* (1895) are generally considered to be two of the best adult fantasy novels ever written. Of equally fine quality are his collections of children's stories, including *At the Back of the North Wind* (1871), *Ranald Bannerman's Boyhood* (1871), and *The Princess and the Goblin* (1872). Although troubled by ill health, Mac Donald seems to have lived a happy, eventful, and rewarding life. He became a famous and popular writer, and established a number of close friendships with some of the leading literary figures of the day. He seemed happiest, however, when reading one of his stories to his huge, and adoring, family of eleven children.

"The Light Princess" is one of Mac Donald's most

charming and inventive fairy tales. It is full of surprising events and clever contrivances. Perhaps the most ingenious device is the central one, the Princess's weightlessness. Once her sour aunt's evil spell has deprived the Princess of her "gravity" she gets into one embarrassing predicament after another, much to the chagrin of her royal parents. It is not princess-like, after all, to be used as a ball by the servants of the castle. Another memorable device is the mysterious "White Snake of Darkness" which is used by the evil aunt later in the narrative. The story is also distinctive because of its subtle, but devastating, satire. Especially poignant are the epsiodes involving the two court Metaphysicals—Hum-Drum the Materialist and Kopy-Keck the Spiritualist. But perhaps the most amazing thing about this story is that it remains a fairy tale in the finest and purest sense of the term, even while mercilessly parodying many of the stock ingredients of the genre.

❦ The Light Princess ❦

George Mac Donald

I

WHAT! NO CHILDREN?

Once upon a time, so long ago that I have quite forgotten the date, there lived a king and queen who had no children.

And the king said to himself, "All the queens of my acquaintance have children, some three, some seven, and some as many as twelve; and my queen has not one. I feel ill-used." So he made up his mind to be cross with his wife about it. But she bore it all like a good patient queen as she was. Then the king grew very cross indeed. But the queen pretended to take it all as a joke, and a very good one too.

"Why don't you have any daughters, at least?" said he. "I don't say *sons;* that might be too much to expect." "I am sure, dear king, I am very sorry," said the queen.

"So you ought to be," retorted the king; "you are not going to make a virtue of *that,* surely."

But he was not an ill-tempered king, and in any matter of less moment would have let the queen have her own way with all his heart. This, however, was an affair of state.

The queen smiled.

"You must have patience with a lady, you know, dear king," said she.

She was, indeed, a very nice queen, and heartily sorry that she could not oblige the king immediately.

The king tried to have patience, but he succeeded very badly. It was more than he deserved, therefore, when, at last, the queen gave him a daughter—as lovely a little princess as ever cried.

II

WON'T I, JUST?

The day grew near when the infant must be christened. The king wrote all the invitations with his own hand. Of course somebody was forgotten.

Now it does not generally matter if somebody *is* forgotten, only you must mind who. Unfortunately, the king forgot without intending to forget; and so the chance fell upon the Princess Makemnoit, which was awkward. For the princess was the king's own sister; and he ought not to have forgotten her. But she had made herself so disagreeable to the old king, their father, that he had forgotten her in making his will; and so it was no wonder that her brother forgot her in writing his invitations. But poor relations don't do anything to keep you in mind of them. Why don't they? The king could not see into the garret she lived in, could he?

She was a sour, spiteful creature. The wrinkles of contempt crossed the wrinkles of peevishness, and made her face as full of wrinkles as a pat of butter. If ever a king could be justified in forgetting anybody, this king was justified in forgetting his sister, even at a christening. She looked very odd, too. Her forehead was as large as all the rest of her face, and projected over it like a precipice. When she was angry, her little eyes flashed blue. When she hated anybody, they shone yellow and green. What they looked like when she loved anybody, I do not know; for I never heard of her loving anybody but herself, and I do not think she could have managed that if she had not somehow got used to herself. But what made it highly imprudent in the king to forget her was—that she was awfully clever. In fact, she was a witch; and when she bewitched anybody, he very soon had enough of it; for she beat all the wicked fairies in wickedness, and all the clever ones in cleverness. She despised all the modes we read of in history, in which offended fairies and witches have taken their revenges; and therefore, after waiting and waiting in vain for an invitation, she made up her mind at last to go without one, and make the whole family miserable, like a princess as she was.

So she put on her best gown, went to the palace, was kindly received by the happy monarch, who forgot that he had forgotten her, and took her place in the procession to the royal chapel. When they were all gathered about the font, she contrived to get next to it, and throw something into the water; after which she maintained a very respectful demeanour till the water was applied to the child's face. But at that moment she turned round in her place three times, and muttered the following words, loud enough for those beside her to hear:—

> "Light of spirit, by my charms,
> Light of body every part,
> Never weary human arms—
> Only crush thy parents' heart!"

They all thought she had lost her wits, and was repeating some foolish nursery rhyme; but a shudder went through the whole of them notwithstanding. The baby, on the contrary, began to laugh and crow; while the nurse gave a start and a smothered cry, for she thought she was struck with paralysis: she could not feel the baby in her arms. But she clasped it tight and said nothing.

The mischief was done.

III

SHE CAN'T BE OURS

Her atrocious aunt had deprived the child of all her gravity. If you ask me how this was effected, I answer, "In the easiest way in the world. She had only to destroy gravitation." For the princess was a philosopher, and knew all the *ins* and *outs* of the laws of gravitation as well as the *ins* and *outs* of her boot-lace. And being a witch as well, she could abrogate those laws in a moment; or at least so clog their wheels and rust their bearings, that they would not work at all. But we have more to do with what followed than with how it was done.

The first awkwardness that resulted from this unhappy privation was, that the moment the nurse began to float the baby up and down, she flew from her arms towards the ceiling. Happily, the resistance of the air brought her ascending career to a close within a foot of it. There she remained, horizontal as when she left her nurse's arms, kicking and laughing amazingly. The nurse in terror flew to the bell, and begged the footman, who answered it, to bring up the house-steps directly. Trembling in every limb, she climbed upon the steps, and had to stand upon the very top, and reach up, before she could reach the floating tail of the baby's long clothes.

When the strange fact came to be known, there was a terrible commotion in the palace. The occasion of its discovery by the king was naturally a repetition of the nurse's experience. Astonished that he felt no weight when the child was laid in his arms, he began to wave her up and—not down; for she slowly ascended to the ceiling as before, and there remained floating in perfect comfort and satisfaction, as was testified by her peals of tiny laughter. The king stood staring up in speechless amazement, and trembled so that his beard shook like grass in the wind. At last, turning to the queen, who was just as horror-struck as himself, he said, gasping, staring, and stammering,—

"She *can't* be ours, queen!"

Now the queen was much cleverer than the king, and had begun already to suspect that "this effect defective came by cause."

"I am sure she is ours," answered she. "But we ought to have taken better care of her at the christening. People who were never invited ought not to have been present."

"Oh, ho!" said the king, tapping his forehead with his forefinger, "I have it all. I've found her out. Don't you see it, queen? Princess Makemnoit has bewitched her."

"That's just what I say," answered the queen.

"I beg your pardon, my love; I did not hear you.— John! bring the steps I get on my throne with."

For he was a little king with a great throne, like many other kings.

The throne-steps were brought, and set upon the dining-table, and John got upon the top of them. But he could not reach the little princess, who lay like a baby-laughter-cloud in the air, exploding continuously.

"Take the tongs, John," said his Majesty; and getting up on the table, he handed them to him.

John could reach the baby now, and the little princess was handed down by the tongs.

IV

WHERE IS SHE?

One fine summer day, a month after these her first adventures, during which time she had been very carefully watched, the princess was lying on the bed in the queen's own chamber, fast asleep. One of the windows was open, for it was noon, and the day was so sultry that the little girl was wrapped in nothing less ethereal than slumber itself. The queen came into the room, and not observing that the baby was on the bed, opened another window. A frolicsome fairy wind, which had been watching for a chance of mischief, rushed in at the one window, and taking its way over the bed where the child was lying, caught her up, and rolling and floating her along like a piece of flue, or a dandelion seed, carried her with it through the opposite window, and away. The queen went down-stairs, quite ignorant of the loss she had herself occasioned.

When the nurse returned, she supposed that her Majesty had carried her off, and, dreading a scolding, delayed making inquiry about her. But hearing nothing, she grew uneasy, and went at length to the queen's boudoir, where she found her Majesty.

"Please, your Majesty, shall I take the baby?" said she.

"Where is she?" asked the queen.

"Please forgive me. I know it was wrong."

"What do you mean?" said the queen, looking grave.

"Oh! don't frighten me, your Majesty!" exclaimed the nurse, clasping her hands.

The queen saw that something was amiss, and fell down in a faint. The nurse rushed about the palace, screaming, "My baby! my baby!"

Every one ran to the queen's room. But the queen

could give no orders. They soon found out, however, that the princess was missing, and in a moment the palace was like a beehive in a garden; and in one minute more the queen was brought to herself by a great shout and a clapping of hands. They had found the princess fast asleep under a rose-bush, to which the elvish little wind-puff had carried her, finishing its mischief by shaking a shower of red rose-leaves all over the little white sleeper. Startled by the noise the servants made, she woke, and, furious with glee, scattered the rose-leaves in all directions, like a shower of spray in the sunset.

She was watched more carefully after this, no doubt; yet it would be endless to relate all the odd incidents resulting from this peculiarity of the young princess. But there never was a baby in a house, not to say a palace, that kept the household in such constant good humour, at least below-stairs. If it was not easy for her nurses to hold her, at least she made neither their arms nor their hearts ache. And she was so nice to play at ball with! There was positively no danger of letting her fall. They might throw her down, or knock her down, or push her down, but couldn't *let* her down. It is true, they might let her fly into the fire or the coal-hole, or through the window; but none of these accidents had happened as yet. If you heard peals of laughter resounding from some unknown region, you might be sure enough of the cause. Going down into the kitchen, or *the room,* you would find Jane and Thomas, and Robert and Susan, all and sum, playing at ball with the little princess. She was the ball herself, and did not enjoy it the less for that. Away she went, flying from one to another, screeching with laughter. And the servants loved the ball itself better even than the game. But they had to take some care how they threw her, for if she received an upward direction, she would never come down again without being fetched.

V

WHAT IS TO BE DONE?

But above-stairs it was different. One day, for instance, after breakfast, the king went into his counting-house, and counted out his money.

The operation gave him no pleasure.

"To think," said he to himself, "that every one of these gold sovereigns weighs a quarter of an ounce, and my real, live, flesh-and-blood princess weighs nothing at all!"

And he hated his gold sovereigns, as they lay with a broad smile of self-satisfaction all over their yellow faces.

The queen was in the parlour, eating bread and honey. But at the second mouthful she burst out crying, and could not swallow it. The king heard her sobbing. Glad of anybody, but especially of his queen, to quarrel with, he clashed his gold sovereigns into his money-box, clapped his crown on his head, and rushed into the parlour.

"What is all this about?" exclaimed he. "What are you crying for, queen?"

"I can't eat it," said the queen, looking ruefully at the honey-pot.

"No wonder!" retorted the king. "You've just eaten your breakfast—two turkey eggs, and three anchovies."

"Oh, that's not it!" sobbed her Majesty. "It's my child, my child!"

"Well, what's the matter with your child? She's neither up the chimney nor down the draw-well. Just hear her laughing."

Yet the king could not help a sigh, which he tried to turn into a cough, saying,—

"It is a good thing to be light-hearted, I am sure, whether she be ours or not."

"It is a bad thing to be light-headed," answered the queen, looking with prophetic soul far into the future.

" 'Tis a good thing to be light-handed," said the king.

" 'Tis a bad thing to be light-fingered," answered the queen.

" 'Tis a good thing to be light-footed," said the king.

" 'Tis a bad thing—" began the queen; but the king interrupted her.

"In fact," said he, with the tone of one who concludes an argument in which he has had only imaginary opponents, and in which, therefore, he has come off triumphant—"in fact, it is a good thing altogether to be light-bodied."

"But it is a bad thing altogether to be light-minded," retorted the queen, who was beginning to lose her temper.

This last answer quite discomfited his Majesty, who turned on his heel, and betook himself to his counting-house again. But he was not half-way towards it, when the voice of his queen overtook him.

"And it's a bad thing to be light-haired," screamed she, determined to have more last words, now that her spirit was roused.

The queen's hair was black as night; and the king's had been, and his daughter's was, golden as morning. But it was not this reflection on his hair that arrested him; it was the double use of the word *light*. For the king hated all witticisms, and punning especially. And besides, he could not tell whether the queen meant light-*haired* or light-*heired*; for why might she not aspirate her vowels when she was ex-asperated herself?

He turned upon his other heel, and rejoined her. She looked angry still, because she knew that she was guilty, or, what was much the same, knew that he thought so.

"My dear queen," said he, "duplicity of any sort is exceedingly objectionable between married people of any rank, not to say kings and queens; and the most objectionable form duplicity can assume is that of punning."

"There!" said the queen, "I never made a jest, but I broke it in the making. I am the most unfortunate woman in the world!"

She looked so rueful, that the king took her in his arms; and they sat down to consult.

"Can you bear this?" said the king.

"No, I can't," said the queen.

"Well, what's to be done?" said the king.

"I'm sure I don't know," said the queen. "But might you not try an apology?"

"To my older sister, I suppose you mean?" said the king.

"Yes," said the queen.

"Well, I don't mind," said the king.

So he went the next morning to the house of the princess, and, making a very humble apology, begged her to undo the spell. But the princess declared, with a grave face, that she knew nothing at all about it. Her eyes, however, shone pink, which was a sign that she was happy. She advised the king and queen to have patience, and to mend their ways. The king returned disconsolate. The queen tried to comfort him.

"We will wait till she is older. She may then be able to suggest something herself. She will know at least how she feels, and explain things to us."

"But what if she should marry?" exclaimed the king, in sudden consternation at the idea.

"Well, what of that?" rejoined the queen.

"Just think! If she were to have children! In the course of a hundred years the air might be as full of floating children as of gossamers in autumn."

"That is no business of ours," replied the queen. "Besides, by that time they will have learned to take care of themselves."

A sigh was the king's only answer.

He would have consulted the court physicians; but he was afraid they would try experiments upon her.

VI

SHE LAUGHS TOO MUCH

Meantime, notwithstanding awkward occurrences, and griefs that she brought upon her parents, the little princess laughed and grew—not fat, but plump and tall. She reached the age of seventeen, without having fallen into any worse scrape than a chimney; by rescuing her from which, a little bird-nesting urchin got fame and a black face. Nor thoughtless as she was, had she committed anything worse than laughter at everybody and everything that came in her way. When she was told, for the sake of experiment, that General Clanrunfort was cut to pieces with all his troops, she laughed; when she heard that the enemy was on his way to besiege her papa's capital, she laughed hugely; but when she was told that the city would certainly be abandoned to the mercy of the enemy's soldiery—why, then she laughed immoderately. She never could be brought to see the serious side of anything. When her mother cried, she said,—

"What queer faces mamma makes! And she squeezes water out of her cheeks! Funny mamma!"

And when her papa stormed at her, she laughed, and danced round and round him, clapping her hands, and crying—

"Do it again, papa. Do it again! It's such fun! Dear, funny papa!"

And if he tried to catch her, she glided from him in an instant, not in the least afraid of him, but thinking it part of the game not to be caught. With one push of her foot, she would be floating in the air above his head; or she would go dancing backwards and forwards and sideways, like a great butterfly. It happened several times, when her father and mother were holding a consultation about her in private, that they were interrupted by vainly repressed outbursts of laughter over their heads; and looking up with indignation, saw her floating at full length in the air above them, whence she regarded them with the most comical appreciation of the position.

One day an awkward accident happened. The princess had come out upon the lawn with one of her attendants, who held her by the hand. Spying her father at the other side of the lawn, she snatched her hand from the maid's, and sped across to him. Now when she wanted to run alone, her custom was to catch up a stone in each hand, so that she might come down again after a bound. Whatever she wore as part of her attire had no effect in this way: even gold, when it thus became as it were a part of herself, lost all its weight for the time. But whatever she only held in her hands retained its downward tendency. On this occasion she could see nothing to catch up but a huge toad, that was walking across the lawn as if he had a hundred years to do it in. Not knowing what disgust meant, for this was one of her peculiarities, she snatched up the toad and bounded away. She had almost reached her father, and he was holding out his arms to receive her, and take from her lips the kiss which hovered on them like a butterfly on a rosebud, when a puff of wind blew her aside into the arms of a young page, who had just been receiving a message from his Majesty. Now it was no great peculiarity in the princess that, once she was set agoing, it always cost her time and trouble to check herself. On this occasion there was no time. She *must* kiss—and she kissed the page. She did not mind it much; for she had no shyness in her composition; and she knew, besides, that she could not help it. So she only laughed, like a musical box. The poor page fared the worst. For the princess, trying to correct the unfortunate tendency of the kiss, put out her hands to keep her off the page; so that along with the kiss, he received, on the other cheek, a slap with a huge black toad, which she poked right into his eye. He tried to laugh, too, but the attempt resulted in such an odd contortion of countenance, as showed that there was no danger of his pluming himself on the kiss. As for the king, his dignity was greatly hurt, and he did not speak to the page for a whole month.

I may here remark that it was very amusing to see her run, if her mode of progression would properly be called running. For first she would make a bound, then, having alighted, she would run a few steps and make another bound. Sometimes she would fancy she had reached the ground before she actually had, and her feet would go backwards and forwards, running upon nothing at all, like those of a chicken on its back. Then she would laugh like the very spirit of fun; only in her laugh there was something missing. What it was, I find myself unable to describe. I think it was a certain tone, depending upon the possibility of sorrow—*morbidezza,* perhaps. She never smiled.

VII

TRY METAPHYSICS

After a long avoidance of the painful subject, the king and queen resolved to hold a council of three upon it; and so they sent for the princess. In she came, sliding and flitting and gliding from one piece of furniture to another, and put herself at last in an arm-chair, in a sitting posture. Whether she could be said *to sit,* seeing she received no support from the seat of the chair, I do not pretend to determine.

"My dear child," said the king, "you must be aware by this time that you are not exactly like other people."

"Oh, you dear funny papa! I have got a nose, and two eyes, and all the rest. So have you. So has mamma."

"Now be serious, my dear, for once," said the queen.

"No, thank you, mamma; I had rather not."

"Would you not like to be able to walk like other people?" said the king.

"No indeed, I should think not. You only crawl. You are such slow coaches!"

"How do you feel, my child?" he resumed, after a pause of discomfiture.

"Quite well, thank you."

"I mean, what do you feel like?"

"Like nothing at all, that I know of."

"You must feel like something."

"I feel like a princess with such a funny papa, and such a dear pet of a queen-mamma!"

"Now really!" began the queen; but the princess interrupted her.

"Oh, yes," she added, "I remember. I have a curious feeling sometimes, as if I were the only person that had any sense in the whole world."

She had been trying to behave herself with dignity; but now she burst into a violent fit of laughter, threw herself backwards over the chair, and went rolling about the floor in an ecstasy of enjoyment. The king picked her up easier than one does a down quilt, and replaced her in her former relation to the chair. The exact preposition expressing this relation I do not happen to know.

"Is there nothing you wish for?" resumed the king, who had learned by this time that it was useless to be angry with her.

"Oh, you dear papa!—yes," answered she.

"What is it, my darling?"

"I have been longing for it—oh, such a time!—ever since last night."

"Tell me what it is."

"Will you promise to let me have it?"

The king was on the point of saying *Yes*, but the wiser queen checked him with a single motion of her head.

"Tell me what it is first," said he.

"No no. Promise first."

"I dare not. What is it?"

"Mind, I hold you to your promise.—It is—to be tied to the end of a string—a very long string indeed, and be flown like a kite. Oh such fun! I would rain rose-water, and hail sugar-plums, and snow whipped-cream, and—and—and—"

A fit of laughing checked her; and she would have been off again over the floor, had not the king started up and caught her just in time. Seeing that nothing but talk could be got out of her, he rang the bell, and sent her away with two of her ladies-in-waiting.

"Now, queen," he said, turning to her Majesty, "what *is* to be done?"

"There is but one thing left," answered she. "Let us consult the college of Metaphysicians."

"Bravo!" cried the king; "we will."

Now at the head of this college were two very wise Chinese philosophers—by name Hum-Drum, and Kopy-Keck. For them the king sent; and straightway they came. In a long speech he communciated to them what they knew very well already—as who did not?—namely, the peculiar condition of his daughter in relation to the globe on which she dwelt; and requested them to consult together as to what might be the cause and probable cure of her *infirmity*. The king laid stress upon the word, but failed to discover his own pun. The queen laughed; but Hum-Drum and Kopy-Keck heard with humility and retired in silence.

Their consultation consisted chiefly in propounding and supporting, for the thousandth time, each his favourite theories. For the condition of the princess afforded delightful scope for the discussion of every question arising from the division of thought—in fact, of all the Metaphysics of the Chinese Empire. But it is only justice to say that they did not altogether neglect the discussion of the practical question, *what was to be done*.

Hum-Drum was a Materialist, and Kopy-Keck was a

Spiritualist. The former was slow and sententious; the latter was quick and flighty: the latter had generally the first word; the former the last.

"I reassert my former assertion," began Kopy-Keck, with a plunge. "There is not a fault in the princess, body or soul; only they are wrong put together. Listen to me now, Hum-Drum, and I will tell you in brief what I think. Don't speak. Don't answer me. I *won't* hear you till I have done.—At that decisive moment, when souls seek their appointed habitations, two eager souls met, struck, rebounded, lost their way, and arrived each at the wrong place. The soul of the princess was one of those, and she went far astray. She does not belong by rights to this world at all, but to some other planet, probably Mercury. Her proclivity to her true sphere destroys all the natural influence which this orb would otherwise possess over her corporeal frame. She cares for nothing here. There is no relation between her and this world.

"She must therefore be taught, by the sternest compulsion, to take an interest in the earth as the earth. She must study every department of its history—its animal history; its vegetable history; its mineral history; its social history; its moral history; its political history; its scientific history; its literary history; its musical history; its artistical history; above all, its metaphysical history. She must begin with the Chinese dynasty and end with Japan. But first of all she must study geology, and especially the history of the extinct races of animals—their natures, their habits, their loves, their hates, their revenges. She must—"

"Hold, h-o-o-old!" roared Hum-Drum. "It is certainly my turn now. My rooted and insubvertible conviction is that the causes of the anomalies evident in the princess's condition are strictly and solely physical. But that is only tantamount to acknowledging that they exist. Hear my opinion.—From some cause or other, of no importance to our inquiry, the motion of her heart has been reversed. The remarkable combination of the suction and the force-pump works the wrong way—I mean in the case of the unfortunate princess: it draws in where it should force out, and forces out where it should draw in. The offices of the auricles and the ventricles are subverted. The blood is sent forth by the veins, and returns by the arteries. Consequently it is running the wrong way through all her corporeal organism—lungs and all. Is it then at all mysterious, seeing that such is the case, that on the other particular of gravitation as well, she should differ from normal humanity? My proposal for the cure is this:—

"Phlebotomize until she is reduced to the last point of safety. Let it be effected, if necessary, in a warm bath. When she is reduced to a state of perfect asphyxy, apply a ligature to the left ankle, drawing it as tight as the bone will bear. Apply, at the same moment, another of equal tension around the right wrist. By means of plates constructed for the purpose, place the other foot and hand under the receivers of two airpumps. Exhaust the receivers. Exhibit a pint of French brandy, and await the result."

"Which would presently arrive in the form of grim Death," said Kopy-Keck.

"If it should, she would yet die in doing our duty," retorted Hum-Drum.

But their Majesties had too much tenderness for their volatile offspring to subject her to either of the schemes of the equally unscrupulous philosophers. Indeed, the most complete knowledge of the laws of nature would have been unserviceable in her case; for it was impossible to classify her. She was a fifth imponderable body, sharing all the other properties of the ponderable.

VIII

TRY A DROP OF WATER

Perhaps the best thing for the princess would have been to fall in love. But how a princess who had no gravity could fall into anything is a difficulty—perhaps *the* difficulty. As for her own feelings on the subject, she did not even know that there was such a beehive of honey and stings to be fallen into. But now I come to mention another curious fact about her.

The palace was built on the shores of the loveliest lake in the world; and the princess loved this lake more than father or mother. The root of this preference no doubt, although the princess did not recognise it as such, was, that the moment she got into it, she recovered the natural right of which she had been so wickedly deprived—namely, gravity. Whether this was owing to the fact that water had been employed as the means of conveying the injury, I do not know. But it is certain that she could swim and dive like the duck that her old nurse said she was. The manner in which this alleviation of her misfortune was discovered was as follows.

One summer evening, during the carnival of the country, she had been taken upon the lake by the king and queen, in the royal barge. They were accompanied by many of the courtiers in a fleet of little boats. In the middle of the lake she wanted to get into the lord chancellor's barge, for his daughter, who was a great favourite with her, was in it with her father. Now though the old king rarely condescended to make light of his misfortune, yet, happening on this occasion to be in a particularly good humour, as the barges approached each other, he caught up the princess to throw her into the chancellor's barge. He lost his balance, however, and dropping into the bottom of the barge, lost his hold of his daughter; not, however, before imparting to her the downward tendency of his own person, though in a somewhat different direction; for, as the king fell into the boat, she fell into the water. With a burst of delighted laughter she disappeared in the lake. A cry of horror ascended from the boats. They had never seen the princess go down before. Half the men were under water in a moment; but they had all, one after another, come up to the surface again for breath, when—tinkle, tinkle, babble, and gush! came the princess's laugh over the water from far away. There she was, swimming like a swan. Nor would she come out for king or queen, chancellor or daughter. She was perfectly obstinate.

But at the same time she seemed more sedate than usual. Perhaps that was because a great pleasure spoils laughing. At all events, after this, the passion of her life was to get into the water, and she was always the better behaved and the more beautiful the more she had of it. Summer and winter it was quite the same; only she could not stay so long in the water when they had to break the ice to let her in. Any day, from morning till evening in summer, she might be descried—a streak of white in the blue water—lying as still as the shadow of a cloud, or shooting along like a dolphin; disappearing, and coming up again far off just where one did not expect her. She would have been in the lake of a night too, if she could have had her way; for the balcony of her window overhung a deep pool in it; and through the shallow reedy passage she could have swum out into the wide wet water, and no one would have been any the wiser. Indeed, when she happened to wake in the moonlight, she could hardly resist the temptation. But there was the sad difficulty of getting into it. She had as great a dread of the air as some children have of the water. For the slightest gust of wind would blow her away; and a gust might arise in the stillest moment. And if she gave herself a push towards the water and just failed of reaching it, her situation would be dreadfully awkward, irrespective of the wind; for at best there she would have to remain, suspended in her night-gown, till she was seen and angled for by somebody from the window.

"Oh! if I had my gravity," thought she, contemplating the water, "I would flash off this balcony like a long white sea-bird headlong into the darling wetness. Heigh-ho!"

This was the only consideration that made her wish to be like other people.

Another reason for her being fond of the water was that in it alone she enjoyed any freedom. For she could not walk out without a *cortège,* consisting in part of a troop of light-horse, for fear of the liberties which the wind might take with her. And the king grew more apprehensive with increasing years, till at last he would not allow her to walk abroad at all without some twenty silken cords fastened to as many parts of her dress, and held by twenty noblemen. Of course horseback was out of the question. But she bade good-by to all this ceremony when she got into the water.

And so remarkable were its effects upon her, especially in restoring her for the time to the ordinary human gravity, that Hum-Drum and Kopy-Keck agreed in recommending the king to bury her alive for three years; in the hope that, as the water did her so much good, the earth would do her yet more. But the king had some vulgar prejudices against the experiment, and would not give his consent. Foiled in this, they yet agreed in another recommendation; which, seeing that one imported his opinions from China and the other from Thibet, was very remarkable indeed. They argued that, if water of external origin and application could be so efficacious, water from a deeper source might work a perfect cure; in short, that if the poor afflicted princess could by any means be made to cry, she might recover her lost gravity.

But how was this to be brought about? Therein lay all the difficulty—to meet which the philosophers were not wise enough. To make the princess cry was as im-

possible as to make her weigh. They sent for a professional beggar; commanded him to prepare his most
touching oracle of woe; helped him out of the court
charade-box, to whatever he wanted for dressing up,
and promised great rewards in the event of his success.
But it was all in vain. She listened to the mendicant
artist's story, and gazed at his marvellous make-up, till
she could contain herself no longer, and went into the
most undignified contortions for relief, shrieking, positively screeching with laughter.

When she had a little recovered herself, she ordered
her attendants to drive him away, and not give him a
single copper; whereupon his look of mortified discomfiture wrought her punishment and his revenge, for it
sent her into violent hysterics, from which she was with
difficulty recovered.

But so anxious was the king that the suggestion
should have a fair trial, that he put himself in a rage
one day, and, rushing up to her room gave her an awful whipping. Yet not a tear would flow. She looked
grave, and her laughing sounded uncommonly like
screaming—that was all. The good old tyrant, though
he put on his best gold spectacles to look, could not
discover the smallest cloud in the serene blue of her
eyes.

IX

PUT ME IN AGAIN

It must have been about this time that the son of a
king, who lived a thousand miles from Lagobel, set out
to look for the daughter of a queen. He travelled far
and wide, but as sure as he found a princess, he found
some fault in her. Of course he could not marry a mere
woman, however beautiful; and there was no princess
to be found worthy of him. Whether the prince was so

near perfection that he had a right to demand perfection itself, I cannot pretend to say. All I know is, that he was a fine, handsome, brave, generous, well-bred, and well-behaved youth, as all princes are.

In his wanderings he had come across some reports about our princess; but as everybody said she was bewitched, he never dreamed that she could bewitch him. For what indeed could a prince do with a princess that had lost her gravity? Who could tell what she might not lose next? She might lose her visibility, or her tangibility; or, in short, the power of making impressions upon the radical sensorium; so that he should never be able to tell whether she was dead or alive. Of course he made no further inquiries about her.

One day he lost sight of his retinue in a great forest. These forests are very useful in delivering princes from their courtiers, like a sieve that keeps back the bran. Then the princes get away to follow their fortunes. In this they have the advantage of the princesses, who are forced to marry before they have had a bit of fun. I wish our princesses got lost in a forest sometimes.

One lovely evening, after wandering about for many days, he found that he was approaching the outskirts of this forest; for the trees had got so thin that he could see the sunset through them; and he soon came upon a kind of heath. Next he came upon signs of human neighbourhood; but by this time it was getting late, and there was nobody in the fields to direct him.

After travelling for another hour, his horse, quite worn out with long labour and lack of food, fell, and was unable to rise again. So he continued his journey on foot. At length he entered another wood—not a wild forest, but a civilized wood, through which a footpath led him to the side of a lake. Along this path the prince pursued his way through the gathering darkness. Suddenly he paused, and listened. Strange sounds came across the water. It was, in fact, the princess laughing. Now there was something odd in her laugh, as I have already hinted; for the hatching of a real hearty laugh requires the incubation of gravity; and perhaps this was how the prince mistook the laughter for screaming. Looking over the lake, he saw something white in the water; and, in an instant, he had torn off his tunic, kicked off his sandals, and plunged in. He soon reached the white object, and found that it was a woman. There was not light enough to show that she was a princess, but quite enough to show that she was a lady, for it does not want much light to see that.

Now I cannot tell how it came about,—whether she pretended to be drowning, or whether he frightened her, or caught her so as to embarrass her,—but certainly he brought her to shore in a fashion ignominious to a swimmer, and more nearly drowned than she had ever expected to be; for the water had got into her throat as often as she had tried to speak.

At the place to which he bore her, the bank was only a foot or two above the water; so he gave her a strong lift out of the water, to lay her on the bank. But, her gravitation ceasing the moment she left the water, away she went up into the air, scolding and screaming.

"You naughty, *naughty*, NAUGHTY, *NAUGHTY* man!" she cried.

No one had ever succeeded in putting her into a passion before.—When the prince saw her ascend, he thought he must have been bewitched, and have mistaken a great swan for a lady. But the princess caught hold of the topmost cone upon a lofty fir. This came off; but she caught at another; and, in fact, stopped herself by gathering cones, dropping them as the stalks gave way. The prince, meantime, stood in the water, staring, and forgetting to get out. But the princess disappearing, he scrambled on shore, and went in the direction of the tree. There he found her climbing down one of the branches towards the stem. But in the darkness of the wood, the prince continued in some bewilderment as to what the phenomenon could be; until, reaching the ground, and seeing him standing there, she caught hold of him, and said,—

"I'll tell papa."

"Oh no, you won't" returned the prince.

"Yes, I will," she persisted. "What business had you to pull me down out of the water, and throw me to the bottom of the air? I never did you any harm."

"Pardon me. I did not mean to hurt you."

"I don't believe you have any brains; and that is a worse loss than your wretched gravity. I pity you."

The prince now saw that he had come upon the bewitched princess, and had already offended her. But before he could think what to say next, she burst out angrily, giving a stamp with her foot that would have sent her aloft again but for the hold she had of his arm,—

"Put me up directly."

"Put you up where, you beauty?" asked the prince.

He had fallen in love with her almost, already; for her anger made her more charming than any one else had ever beheld her; and, as far as he could see, which certainly was not far, she had not a single fault about her, except, of course, that she had not any gravity. No prince, however, would judge of a princess by weight. The loveliness of her foot he would hardly estimate by the depth of the impression it could make in mud.

"Put you up where, you beauty?" asked the prince.

"In the water, you stupid!" answered the princess.

"Come, then," said the prince.

The condition of her dress, increasing her usual difficulty in walking, compelled her to cling to him; and he could hardly persuade himself that he was not in a delightful dream, notwithstanding the torrent of musical abuse with which she overwhelmed him. The prince being therefore in no hurry, they came upon the lake at quite another part, where the bank was twenty-five feet high at least; and when they had reached the edge, he turned towards the princess, and said,—

"How am I to put you in?"

"That is your business," she answered, quite snappishly. "You took me out—put me in again."

"Very well," said the prince; and, catching her up in his arms, he sprang with her from the rock. The princess had just time to give one delighted shriek of laughter before the water closed over them. When they came to the surface, she found that, for a moment or two, she could not even laugh, for she had gone down with such a rush, that it was with difficulty she recovered her breath. The instant they reached the surface—

"How do you like falling in?" said the prince.

After some effort the princess panted out,—

"Is that what you call *falling in?*"

"Yes," answered the prince, "I should think it a very tolerable specimen."

"It seemed to me like going up," rejoined she.

"My feeling was certainly one of elevation too," the prince conceded.

The princess did not appear to understand him, for she retorted his question:—

"How do *you* like falling in?" said the princess.

"Beyond everything," answered he; "for I have fallen in with the only perfect creature I ever saw."

"No more of that: I am tired of it," said the princess.

Perhaps she shared her father's aversion to punning.

"Don't you like falling in, then?" said the prince.

"It is the most delightful fun I ever had in my life," answered she. "I never fell before. I wish I could learn. To think I am the only person in my father's kingdom that can't fall!"

Here the poor princess looked almost sad.

"I shall be most happy to fall in with you any time you like," said the prince, devotedly.

"Thank you. I don't know. Perhaps it would not be proper. But I don't care. At all events, as we have fallen in, let us have a swim together."

"With all my heart," responded the prince.

And away they went, swimming, and diving, and floating, until at last they heard cries along the shore, and saw lights glancing in all directions. It was now quite late, and there was no moon.

"I must go home," said the princess. "I am very sorry, for this is delightful."

"So am I," returned the prince. "But I am glad I haven't a home to go to—at least, I don't exactly know where it is."

"I wish I hadn't one either," rejoined the princess, "it is so stupid! I have a great mind," she continued, "to play them all a trick. Why couldn't they leave me alone? They won't trust me in the lake for a single night!—You see where that green light is burning? That is the window of my room. Now if you would just swim there with me very quietly, and when we are all but under the balcony, give me such a push—*up* you call it—as you did a little while ago, I should be able to catch hold of the balcony, and get in at the window: and then they may look for me till tomorrow morning!"

"With more obedience than pleasure," said the prince, gallantly; and away they swam, very gently.

"Will you be in the lake to-morrow night?" the prince ventured to ask.

"To be sure I will. I don't think so. Perhaps," was the princess's somewhat strange answer.

But the prince was intelligent enough not to press her further; and merely whispered, as he gave her the parting lift, "Don't tell." The only answer the princess returned was a roguish look. She was already a yard above his head. The look seemed to say, "Never fear. It is too good fun to spoil that way."

So perfectly like other people had she been in the water, that even yet the prince could scarcely believe his eyes when he saw her ascend slowly, grasp the balcony, and disappear through the window. He turned, almost expecting to see her still by his side. But he was alone in the water. So he swam away quietly, and watched the lights roving about the shore for hours after the princess was safe in her chamber. As soon as they disappeared, he landed in search of his tunic and sword, and after some trouble, found them again. Then he made the best of his way round the lake to the other side. There the wood was wilder, and the shore steeper—rising more immediately towards the mountains which surrounded the lake on all sides, and kept sending it messages of silvery streams from morning to night, and all night long. He soon found a spot whence he could see the green light in the princess's room, and where, even in the broad daylight, he would be in no danger of being discovered from the opposite shore. It was a sort of cave in the rock, where he provided himself a bed of withered leaves, and lay down too tired for hunger to keep him awake. All night long he dreamed that he was swimming with the princess.

X

LOOK AT THE MOON

Early the next morning the prince set out to look for something to eat, which he soon found at a forester's hut, where for many following days he was supplied with all that a brave prince could consider necessary. And having plenty to keep him alive for the present, he would not think of wants not yet in existence. Whenever Care intruded, this prince always bowed him out in the most princely manner.

When he returned from his breakfast to his watch-cave, he saw the princess already floating about in the lake, attended by the king and queen—whom he knew by their crowns—and a great company in lovely little boats, with canopies of all the colours of the rainbow, and flags and streamers of a great many more. It was a very bright day, and soon the prince burned up with the heat, began to long for the cold water and the cool princess. But he had to endure till twilight; for the boats had provisions on board, and it was not till the sun went down that the gay party began to vanish. Boat after boat drew away to the shore, following that of the king and queen, till only one, apparently the princess's own boat, remained. But she did not want to go home even yet, and the prince thought he saw her order the boat to the shore without her. At all events, it rowed away; and now, of all the radiant company, only one white speck remained. Then the prince began to sing.

And this is what he sang:—

> "Lady fair,
> Swan-white,
> Lift thine eyes,
> Banish night
> By the might
> Of thine eyes.

> "Snowy arms,
> Oars of snow,
> Oar her hither,
> Plashing low.
> Soft and slow,
> Oar her hither.

> "Stream behind her
> O'er the lake,
> Radiant whiteness!
> In her wake
> Following, following for her sake,
> Radiant whiteness!

> "Cling about her,
> Waters blue;
> Part not from her,
> But renew
> Cold and true
> Kisses round her.

> "Lap me round,
> Waters sad
> That have left her;
> Make me glad,
> For ye had
> Kissed her ere ye left her."

Before he had finished his song, the princess was just under the place where he sat, and looking up to find him. Her ears had led her truly.

"Would you like a fall, princess?" said the prince, looking down.

"Ah! there you are! Yes, if you please, prince," said the princess, looking up.

"How do you know I am a prince, princess?" said the prince.

"Because you are a very nice young man, prince," said the princess.

"Come up then, princess."

"Fetch me, prince."

The prince took off his scarf, then his sword-belt, then his tunic, and tied them all together, and let them down. But the line was far too short. He unwound his turban, and added it to the rest, when it was all but long enough; and his purse completed it. The princess just managed to lay hold of the knot of money, and was beside him in a moment. This rock was much higher than the other, and the splash and the dive were tremendous. The princess was in ecstasies of delight, and their swim was delicious.

Night after night they met, and swam about in the dark clear lake; where such was the prince's gladness, that (whether the princess' way of looking at things infected him, or he was actually getting light-headed) he often fancied that he was swimming in the sky instead of the lake. But when he talked about being in heaven, the princess laughed at him dreadfully.

When the moon came, she brought them fresh pleasure. Everything looked strange and new in her light, with an old, withered, yet unfading newness. When the moon was nearly full, one of their great delights was to dive deep in the water, and then, turning round, look up through it at the great blot of light close above them, shimmering and trembling and wavering, spreading and contracting, seeming to melt away, and again grow solid. Then they would shoot up through the blot; and lo! there was the moon, far off, clear and steady and cold, and very lovely, at the bottom of a deeper and bluer lake than theirs, as the princess said.

The prince soon found out that while in the water the princess was very like other people. And besides this, she was not so forward in her questions or pert in her replies at sea as on shore. Neither did she laugh so much; and when she did laugh, it was more gently. She seemed altogether more modest and maidenly in the water than out of it. But when the prince, who had really fallen in love when he fell in the lake, began to talk to her about love, she always turned her head towards him and laughed. After a while she began to look puzzled, as if she were trying to understand what he meant, but could not—revealing a notion that he meant something. But as soon as ever she left the lake, she was so altered, that the prince said to himself, "If I marry her, I see no help for it: we must turn merman and mermaid, and go out to sea at once."

XI

HISS!

The princess's pleasure in the lake had grown to a passion, and she could scarcely bear to be out of it for an hour. Imagine then her consternation, when diving with the prince one night, a sudden suspicion seized her that the lake was not so deep as it used to be. The prince could not imagine what had happened. She shot to the surface, and, without a word, swam at full speed toward the higher side of the lake. He followed, begging to know if she was ill, or what was the matter. She never turned her head, or took the smallest notice of his question. Arrived at the shore, she coasted the rocks with minute inspection. But she was not able to come to a conclusion, for the moon was very small, and so she could not see well. She turned therefore and swam home, without saying a word to explain her conduct to the prince, of whose presence she seemed no longer conscious. He withdrew to his cave, in great perplexity and distress.

Next day she made many observations, which, alas! strengthened her fears. She saw that the banks were too dry; and that the grass on the shore, and the trailing plants on the rocks, were withering away. She caused marks to be made along the borders, and examined them, day after day, in all directions of the wind; till at last the horrible idea became a certain fact—that the surface of the lake was slowly sinking.

The poor princess nearly went out of the little mind she had. It was awful to her to see the lake, which she loved more than any living thing, lie dying before her eyes. It sank away, slowly vanishing. The tops of rocks that had never been seen till now, began to appear far down in the clear water. Before long they were dry in the sun. It was fearful to think of the mud that would soon lie there baking and festering, full of lovely creatures dying, and ugly creatures coming to life, like the unmaking of a world. And how hot the sun would be without any lake! She could not bear to swim in it any more, and began to pine away. Her life seemed bound up with it; and ever as the lake sank, she pined. People said she would not live an hour after the lake was gone.

But she never cried.

Proclamation was made to all the kingdom, that whosoever should discover the cause of the lake's decrease, would be rewarded after a princely fashion. Hum-Drum and Kopy-Keck applied themselves to their physics and metaphysics; but in vain. Not even they could suggest a cause.

Now the fact was that the old princess was at the root of the mischief. When she heard that her niece found more pleasure in the water than anyone else had out of it, she went into a rage, and cursed herself for her want of foresight.

"But," said she, "I will soon set all right. The king and the people shall die of thirst; their brains shall boil and frizzle in their skulls before I will lose my revenge."

And she laughed a ferocious laugh, that made the hairs on the back of her black cat stand erect with terror.

Then she went to an old chest in the room, and opening it, took out what looked like a piece of dried seaweed. This she threw into a tub of water. Then she threw some powder into the water, and stirred it with her bare arm, muttering over it words of hideous sound, and yet more hideous import. Then she set the tub aside, and took from the chest a huge bunch of a hundred rusty keys, that clattered in her shaking hands. Then she sat down and proceeded to oil them all. Before she had finished, out from the tub, the water of which had kept on a slow motion ever since she had ceased stirring it, came the head and half the body of a huge gray snake. But the witch did not look round. It grew out of the tub, waving itself backwards and forwards with a slow horizontal motion, till it reached the princess, when it laid its head upon her shoulder, and gave a low hiss in her ear. She started—but with joy; and seeing the head resting on her shoulder, drew it toward her and kissed it. Then she drew it all out of the tub, and wound it round her body. It was one of those dreadful creatures which few have ever beheld—the White Snakes of Darkness.

Then she took the keys and went down to her cellar; and as she unlocked the door she said to herself—

"This is worth living for!"

Locking the door behind her, she descended a few steps into the cellar, and crossing it, unlocked another door into a dark, narrow passage. She locked this also behind her, and descended a few more steps. If any one had followed the witch-princess, he would have heard her unlock exactly one hundred doors, and descend a few steps after unlocking each. When she had unlocked the last, she entered a vast cave, the roof of which was supported by huge natural pillars of rock. Now this room was the underside of the bottom of the lake.

She then untwined the snake from her body, and held it by the tail high above her. The hideous creature stretched up its head towards the roof of the cavern, which it was just able to reach. It then began to move its head backwards and forwards, with a slow oscillating motion, as if looking for something. At the same moment the witch began to walk round and round the cavern, coming nearer to the centre every circuit; while the head of the snake described the same path over the floor, for she kept holding it up. And still it kept slowly oscillating. Round and round the cavern they went, ever lessening the circuit, till at last the snake made a sudden dart, and clung to the roof with its mouth.

"That's right, my beauty!" cried the princess, "drain it dry."

She let it go, left it hanging, and sat down on a great stone, with her black cat, which had followed her all round the cave, by her side. Then she began to knit and mutter awful words. The snake hung like a huge leech, sucking at the stone; the cat stood with his back arched, and his tail like a piece of cable, looking up at the snake; and the old woman sat and knitted and muttered. Seven days and seven nights they remained thus; when suddenly the serpent dropped from the roof as if exhausted, and shrivelled up till it was again like a piece of dried seaweed. The witch started to her feet, picked it up, put it in her pocket, and looked up at the roof. One drop of water was trembling on the spot where the snake had been sucking. As soon as she saw that, she turned and fled, followed by her cat. Shutting the door in a terrible hurry, she locked it, and having muttered some frightful words, sped to the next, which also she locked and muttered over; and so with all the hundred doors, till she arrived in her own cellar. There she sat down on the floor ready to faint, but listening with malicious delight to the rushing of the water, which she could hear distinctly through all the hundred doors.

But this was not enough. Now that she had tasted revenge, she lost her patience. Without further measures, the lake would be too long in disappearing. So the next night, with the last shred of the dying old moon rising, she took some of the water in which she had revived the snake, put it in a bottle, and set out, accompanied by her cat. Before morning she had made the entire circuit of the lake, muttering fearful words as she crossed every stream, and casting into it some of the water out of her bottle. When she had finished the circuit she muttered yet again, and flung a handful of water towards the moon. Thereupon every spring in the country ceased to throb and bubble, dying away like the pulse of a dying man. The next day there was no sound of falling water to be heard along the borders of the lake. The very courses were dry; and the mountains showed no silvery streaks down their dark sides. And not alone had the fountains of mother Earth ceased to flow; for all the babies throughout the country were crying dreadfully—only without tears.

XII

WHERE IS THE PRINCE?

Never since the night when the princess left him so abruptly had the prince had a single interview with her. He had seen her once or twice in the lake; but as far as he could discover, she had not been in it any more at night. He had sat and sung, and looked in vain for his Nereid; while she, like a true Nereid, was wasting away with her lake, sinking as it sank, withering as it dried. When at length he discovered the change that was taking place in the level of the water, he was in great alarm and perplexity. He could not tell whether the lake was dying because the lady had forsaken it; or whether the lady would not come because the lake had begun to sink. But he resolved to know so much at least.

He disguised himself, and, going to the palace, requested to see the lord chamberlain. His appearance at once gained his request; and the lord chamberlain, being a man of some insight, perceived that there was more in the prince's solicitation than met the ear. He felt likewise that no one could tell whence a solution of the present difficulties might arise. So he granted the prince's prayer to be made shoeblack to the princess. It was rather cunning in the prince to request such an easy post, for the princess could not possibly soil as many shoes as other princesses.

He soon learned all that could be told about the princess. He went nearly distracted; but after roaming about the lake for days, and diving in every depth that remained, all that he could do was to put an extra polish on the dainty pair of boots that was never called for.

For the princess kept her room, with the curtains drawn to shut out the dying lake. But could not shut it out of her mind for a moment. It haunted her imagination so that she felt as if the lake were her soul, drying up within her, first to mud, then to madness and death. She thus brooded over the change, with all its dreadful accompaniments, till she was nearly distracted. As for the prince, she had forgotten him. However much she had enjoyed his company in the water, she did not care for him without it. But she seemed to have forgotten her father and mother too.

The lake went on sinking. Small slimy spots began to appear, which glittered steadily amidst the changeful shine of the water. These grew to broad patches of mud, which widened and spread, with rocks here and there, and foundering fishes and crawling eels swarming. The people went everywhere catching these, and looking for anything that might have dropped from the royal boats.

At length the lake was all but gone, only a few of the deepest pools remaining unexhausted.

It happened one day that a party of youngsters found themselves on the brink of one of these pools in the very centre of the lake. It was a rocky basin of considerable depth. Looking in, they saw at the bottom something that shone yellow in the sun. A little boy jumped in and dived for it. It was a plate of gold covered with writing. They carried it to the king.

On one side of it stood these words:

> "Death alone from death can save.
> Love is death, and so is brave.
> Love can fill the deepest grave.
> Love loves on beneath the wave."

Now this was enigmatical enough to the king and courtiers. But the reverse of the plate explained it a little. Its writing amounted to this:

"If the lake should disappear, they must find the hole through which the water ran. But it would be useless to try to stop it by any ordinary means. There was but one effectual mode—The body of a living man should alone stanch the flow. The man must give himself of his own will; and the lake must take his life as it filled. Otherwise the offering would be of no avail. If the nation could not provide one hero, it was time it should perish."

XIII

HERE I AM

This was a very disheartening revelation to the king—not that he was unwilling to sacrifice a subject, but that he was hopeless of finding a man willing to sacrifice himself. No time was to be lost, however, for the princess was lying motionless on her bed, and taking no nourishment but lake-water, which was now none of the best. Therefore the king caused the contents of the wonderful plate of gold to be published throughout the country.

No one, however, came forward.

The prince, having gone several days' journey into the forest, to consult a hermit whom he had met there on his way to Lagobel, knew nothing of the oracle till his return.

When he had acquainted himself with all the particulars, he sat down and thought—

"She will die if I don't do it, and life would be nothing to me without her; so I shall lose nothing by doing it. And life will be as pleasant to her as ever, for she will soon forget me. And there will be so much more beauty and happiness in the world!—To be sure, I shall not see it." (Here the poor prince gave a sigh.) "How lovely the lake will be in the moonlight, with that glorious creature sporting in it like a wild goddess!—It is rather hard to be drowned by inches, though. Let me see—that will be seventy inches of me to drown." (Here he tried to laugh, but could not.) "The longer the better, however," he resumed: "For can I not bargain that the princess shall be beside me all the time? So I shall see her once more, kiss her perhaps,—who knows? and die looking in her eyes. It will be no death. At least, I shall not feel it. And to see the lake filling for the beauty again!—All right! I am ready."

He kissed the princess's boot, laid it down, and hurried to the king's apartment. But feeling, as he went, that anything sentimental would be disagreeable, he resolved to carry off the whole affair with nonchalance. So he knocked at the door of the king's counting-house, where it was all but a capital crime to disturb him.

When the king heard the knock he started up, and opened the door in a rage. Seeing only the shoeblack, he drew his sword. This, I am sorry to say, was his usual mode of asserting his regality when he thought his dignity was in danger. But the prince was not in the least alarmed.

"Please your majesty, I'm your butler," said he.

"My butler! you lying rascal! What do you mean?"

"I mean, I will cork your big bottle."

"Is the fellow mad?" bawled the king, raising the point of his sword.

"I will put a stopper—plug—what you call it, in your leaky lake, grand monarch," said the prince.

The king was in such a rage that before he could speak he had time to cool, and to reflect that it would be great waste to kill the only man who was willing to be useful in the present emergency, seeing that in the end the insolent fellow would be as dead as if he had died by his majesty's own hand.

"Oh!" said he at last, putting up his sword with difficulty, it was so long; "I am obliged to you, you young fool! Take a glass of wine?"

"No, thank you," replied the prince.

"Very well," said the king. "Would you like to run and see your parents before you make your experiment?"

"No, thank you," said the prince.

"Then we will go and look for the hole at once," said his majesty, and proceeded to call some attendants.

"Stop, please your majesty; I have a condition to make," interposed the prince.

"What!" exclaimed the king, "a condition! and with me! How dare you?"

"As you please," returned the prince, coolly. "I wish your majesty a good morning."

"You wretch! I will have you put in a sack, and stuck in the hole."

"Very well, your majesty," replied the prince, becoming a little more respectful, lest the wrath of the king should deprive him of the pleasure of dying for the princess. "But what good will that do your majesty? Please to remember that the oracle says the victim must offer himself."

"Well, you *have* offered yourself," retorted the king.

"Yes, upon one condition."

"Condition again!" roared the king, once more drawing his sword. "Begone! Somebody else will be glad enough to take the honor off your shoulders."

"Your majesty knows it will not be easy to get another to take my place."

"Well, what is your condition?" growled the king, feeling that the prince was right.

"Only this," replied the prince: "that, as I must on no account die before I am fairly drowned, and the waiting will be rather wearisome, the princess, your daughter, shall go with me, feed me with her own hands, and look at me now and then to comfort me; for you must confess it *is* rather hard. As soon as the water is up to my eyes, she may go and be happy, and forget her poor shoeblack."

Here the prince's voice faltered, and he very nearly grew sentimental, in spite of his resolution.

"Why didn't you tell me before what your condition was? Such a fuss about nothing!" exclaimed the king.

"Do you grant it?" persisted the prince.

"Of course I do," replied the king.

"Very well. I am ready."

"Go and have some dinner, then, while I set my people to find the place."

The king ordered out his guards, and gave directions to the officers to find the hole in the lake at once. So the bed of the lake was marked out in divisions and thoroughly examined, and in an hour or so the hole was discovered. It was in the middle of a stone, near the centre of the lake, in the very pool where the golden plate had been found. It was a three-cornered hole of no great size. There was water all round the stone, but very little was flowing through the hole.

XIV

THIS IS VERY KIND OF YOU

The prince went to dress for the occasion, for he was resolved to die like a prince.

When the princess heard that a man had offered to die for her, she was so transported that she jumped off the bed, feeble as she was, and danced about the room for joy. She did not care who the man was; that was nothing to her. The hole wanted stopping; and if only a man would do, why, take one. In an hour or two more everything was ready. Her maid dressed her in haste, and they carried her to the side of the lake. When she saw it she shrieked, and covered her face with her hands. They bore her across to the stone, where they had already placed a little boat for her. The water was not deep enough to float it, but they hoped it would be, before long. They laid her on cushions, placed in the boat wines and fruits and other nice things, and stretched a canopy over all.

In a few minutes the prince appeared. The princess recognized him at once, but did not think it worthwhile to acknowledge him.

"Here I am," said the prince. "Put me in."

"They told me it was a shoeblack," said the princess.

"So I am," said the prince. "I blacked your little boots three times a day, because they were all I could get of you. Put me in."

The courtiers did not resent his bluntness, except by saying to each other that he was taking it out in impudence.

But how was he to be put in? The golden plate contained no instructions on this point. The prince looked at the hole, and saw but one way. He put both his legs into it, sitting on the stone, and stooping forward, covered the corner that remained open with his two hands. In this uncomfortable position he resolved to abide his fate, and turning to the people, said,—

"Now you can go."

The king had already gone home to dinner.

"Now you can go," repeated the princess after him, like a parrot.

The people obeyed her and went.

Presently a little wave flowed over the stone, and wetted one of the prince's knees. But he did not mind it much. He began to sing, and the song he sang was this:

"As a world that has no well,
Darkly bright in forest dell;
As a world without the gleam
Of the downward-going stream;
As a world without the glance
Of the ocean's fair expanse;
As a world where never rain
Glittered on the sunny plain:—
Such, my heart, thy world would be,
If no love did flow in thee.

"As a world without the sound
Of the rivulets underground;
Or the bubbling of the spring
Out of darkness wandering;
Or the mighty rush and flowing
Of the river's downward going;
Or the music-showers that drop
On the outspread beech's top;
Or the ocean's mighty voice,
When his lifted waves rejoice;—
Such, my soul, thy world would be,
If no love did sing in thee.

"Lady, keep thy world's delight;
Keep the waters in thy sight.
Love hath made me strong to go,

> For thy sake, to realms below,
> Where the water's shine and hum
> Through the darkness never come:
> Let, I pray, one thought of me
> Spring, a little well, in thee;
> Lest thy loveless soul be found
> Like a dry and thirsty ground."

"Sing again, prince. It makes it less tedious," said the princess.

But the prince was too much overcome to sing any more, and a long pause followed.

"This is very kind of you, prince," said the princess at last, quite coolly, as she lay in the boat with her eyes shut.

"I am sorry I can't return the compliment," though the prince; "but you are worth dying for, after all."

Again a wavelet, and another, and another flowed over the stone, and wetted both the prince's knees; but he did not speak or move. Two—three—four hours passed in this way, the princess apparently asleep, and the prince very patient. But he was much disappointed in his position, for he had none of the consolation he had hoped for.

At last he could bear it no longer.

"Princess!" said he.

But at the moment up started the princess, crying,—

"I'm afloat! I'm afloat!"

And the little boat bumped against the stone.

"Princess!" repeated the prince, encouraged by seeing her wide awake and looking eagerly at the water.

"Well?" said she, without looking round.

"Your papa promised that you should look at me, and you haven't looked at me once."

"Did he? Then I suppose I must. But I am so sleepy!"

"Sleep then, darling, and don't mind me," said the poor prince.

"Really, you are very good," replied the princess. "I think I will go to sleep again."

"Just give me a glass of wine and a biscuit first," said the prince, very humbly.

"With all my heart," said the princess, and gaped as she said it.

She got the wine and the biscuit, however, and leaning over the side of the boat toward him, was compelled to look at him.

"Why, prince," she said, "you don't look well! Are you sure you don't mind it?"

"Not a bit," answered he, feeling very faint indeed. "Only I shall die before it is of any use to you, unless I have something to eat."

"There, then," said she, holding out the wine to him.

"Ah! you must feed me. I dare not move my hands. The water would run away directly."

"Good gracious!" said the princess; and she began at once to feed him with bits of biscuit and sips of wine.

As she fed him, he contrived to kiss the tips of her fingers now and then. She did not seem to mind it, one way or the other. But the prince felt better.

"Now, for your own sake, princess," said he, "I cannot let you go to sleep. You must sit and look at me, else I shall not be able to keep up."

"Well, I will do anything I can to oblige you," answered she, with condescension; and, sitting down, she did look at him, and kept looking at him with wonderful steadiness, considering all things.

The sun went down, and the moon rose, and, gush after gush, the waters were rising up the prince's body. They were up to his waist now.

"Why can't we go and have a swim?" said the princess. "There seems to be water enough just about here."

"I shall never swim more," said the prince.

"Oh, I forgot," said the princess, and was silent.

So the water grew and grew, and rose up and up on the prince. And the princess sat and looked at him. She fed him now and then. The night wore on. The waters rose and rose. The moon rose likewise higher and higher, and shone full on the face of the dying prince. The water was up to his neck.

"Will you kiss me, princess?" said he, feebly. The nonchalance was all gone now.

"Yes, I will," answered the princess, and kissed him with a long, sweet, cold kiss.

"Now," said he, with a sigh of content, "I die happy."

He did not speak again. The princess gave him some wine for the last time: he was past eating. Then she sat down again, and looked at him. The water rose and rose. It touched his chin. It touched his lower lip. It touched between his lips. He shut them hard to keep it out. The princess began to feel strange. It touched his upper lip. He breathed through his nostrils. The princess looked wild. It covered his nostrils. Her eyes looked scared, and shone strange in the moonlight. His head fell back; the water closed over it, and the bubbles of his last breath bubbled up through the water. The princess gave a shriek, and sprang into the lake.

She laid hold first of one leg, and then of the other, and pulled and tugged, but she could not move either. She stopped to take breath, and that made her think that he could not get any breath. She was frantic. She got hold of him, and held his head above the water, which was possible now his hands were no longer on the hole. But it was of no use, for he was past breathing.

Love and water brought back all her strength. She got under the water, and pulled and pulled with her whole might, till at last she got one leg out. The other easily followed. How she got him into the boat she never could tell; but when she did, she fainted away. Coming to herself, she seized the oars, kept herself steady as best she could, and rowed and rowed, though she had never rowed before. Round rocks, and over shallows, and through mud she rowed, till she got to the landing-stairs of the palace. By this time her people were on the shore, for they had heard her shriek. She made them carry the prince to her own room, and lay him in her bed, and light a fire, and send for the doctors.

"But the lake, your highness!" said the chamberlain, who, roused by the noise, came in, in his nightcap.

"Go and drown yourself in it!" she said.

This was the last rudeness of which the princess was ever guilty; and one must allow that she had good cause to feel provoked with the lord chamberlain.

Had it been the king himself, he would have fared no better. But both he and the queen were fast asleep. And the chamberlain went back to his bed. Somehow, the doctors never came. So the princess and her old nurse were left with the prince. But the old nurse was a wise woman, and knew what to do.

They tried everything for a long time without success. The princess was nearly distracted between hope and fear, but she tried on and on, one thing after another, and everything over and over again.

At last, when they had all but given it up, just as the sun rose, the prince opened his eyes.

XV

LOOK AT THE RAIN!

The princess burst into a passion of tears, and *fell* on the floor. There she lay for an hour, and her tears never ceased. All the pent-up crying of her life was spent now. And a rain came on, such as had never been seen in that country. The sun shone all the time, and the great drops, which fell straight to the earth, shone likewise. The palace was in the heart of a rainbow. It was a rain of rubies, and sapphires, and emeralds, and topazes. The torrents poured from the mountains like molten gold; and if it had not been for its subterraneous outlet, the lake would have overflowed and inundated the country. It was full from shore to shore.

But the princess did not heed the lake. She lay on the floor and wept. And this rain within doors was far more wonderful than the rain out of doors. For when it abated a little, and she proceeded to rise, she found, to her astonishment, that she could not. At length, after many efforts, she succeeded in getting upon her feet. But she tumbled down again directly. Hearing her fall, her old nurse uttered a yell of delight, and ran to her, screaming,—

"My darling child! she's found her gravity!"

"Oh, that's it! is it?" said the princess, rubbing her shoulder and her knee alternately. "I consider it very unpleasant. I feel as if I should be crushed to pieces."

"Hurrah!" cried the prince from the bed. "If you've come round, princess, so have I. How's the lake?"

"Brimful," answered the nurse.

"Then we're all happy."

"That we are indeed!" answered the princess, sobbing.

And there was rejoicing all over the country that rainy day. Even the babies forgot their past troubles, and danced and crowed amazingly. And the king told stories, and the queen listened to them. And he divided the money in his box, and she the honey in her pot, among all the children. And there was such jubilation as was never heard of before.

Of course the prince and princess were betrothed at once. But the princess had to learn to walk, before they could be married with any propriety. And this was not so easy at her time of life, for she could walk no more than a baby. She was always falling down and hurting herself.

"Is this the gravity you used to make so much of?" said she one day to the prince, as he raised her from the floor. "For my part, I was a great deal more comfortable without it."

"No, no, that's not it. This is it," replied the prince,

as he took her up, and carried her about like a baby, kissing her all the time. "This is gravity."

"That's better," said she. "I don't mind that so much."

And she smiled the sweetest, loveliest smile in the prince's face. And she gave him one little kiss in return for all his; and he thought them overpaid, for he was beside himself with delight. I fear she complained of her gravity more than once after this, notwithstanding.

It was a long time before she got reconciled to walking. But the pain of learning it was quite counterbalanced by two things, either of which would have been sufficient consolation. The first was, that the prince himself was her teacher; and the second, that she could tumble into the lake as often as she pleased. Still, she preferred to have the prince jump in with her; and the splash they made before was nothing to the splash they made now.

The lake never sank again. In process of time, it wore the roof of the cavern quite through, and was twice as deep as before.

The only revenge the princess took upon her aunt was to tread pretty hard on her gouty toe the next time she saw her. But she was sorry for it the very next day, when she heard that the water had undermined her house, and that it had fallen in the night, burying her in its ruins; whence no one ever ventured to dig up her body. There she lies to this day.

So the prince and princess lived and were happy; and had crowns of gold, and clothes of cloth, and shoes of leather, and children of boys and girls, not one of whom was ever known, on the most critical occasion, to lose the smallest atom of his or her due proportion of gravity.

JOHN BUCHAN
(1875–1940)

John Buchan, distinguished statesman and writer, was born in Perth, Scotland, the son of a minister. He was educated at Glasgow University and Oxford, where he established a reputation as an outstanding scholar. In 1901, he was called to the Bar at the Middle Temple, and in the same year he became private secretary to Lord Milner, High Commissioner for South Africa. After a two-year term in Africa, he returned to England and joined a publishing firm. During World War I, he became Director of Information and wrote a twenty-four-volume history of the War. In 1935, he was appointed Governor-General of Canada and raised to the peerage. The newly titled first Baron Tweedsmuir became chancellor of Edinburgh University in 1938. The life of this extraordinarily gifted man came to a tragic end in 1940 as a result of a brain concussion brought on by an accidental fall.

Although Buchan had a busy professional life in government, he somehow found time for writing. During a literary career as a journalist, novelist, biographer, and historian he wrote over sixty works. He is probably best known for his adventure stories, of which the most popular are *The Watcher by the Threshold* (1902), *Prester John* (1910), *The Thirty-Nine Steps* (1915), *Greenmantle* (1916), *Mr. Standfast* (1919), and *The Three Hostages* (1924). Those familiar with C. S. Lewis's *That Hideous Strength* might recall Lewis saying that Mark Studdock had missed reading Buchan—along with Mac Donald—and that, as a consequence, he lacked an appreciation for mystery.

At first glance, Africa might seem a highly unlikely setting for a work of high fantasy, but one must remember that a century ago this vast and mysterious continent seemed as other-worldly to the Englishman as any fictional creation. The writings of Joseph Conrad, H. Rider Haggard, and John Buchan will attest to the enchanting spell this land exercised upon its visitors. In "The Grove of Ashtaroth," the reader will find Buchan's enchantment manifested in the rich and memorable descriptions of Welgevonden, Lawson's lush and exotic estate. This verdant expanse is an almost perfect example of the archetypal Eden where irresistible evil lurks in the paradisaical garden. The pagan presence of the goddess Ashtaroth seems as natural here as a supernatural agent in an Edgar Allen Poe thriller. "Ashtaroth" is not only an exceptionally fine example of myth fantasy, but one of the rare instances of high fantasy built upon a foundation of scriptural myth.

❧ The Grove of Ashtaroth ❧

John Buchan

"C'est enfin que dans leurs prunelles
Rit et pleure—fastidieux—
L'amour des choses éternelles,
Des vieux morts et des anciens dieux!"
                    —PAUL VERLAINE

I

We were sitting around the camp fire, some thirty miles north of a place called Taqui, when Lawson announced his intention of finding a home. He had spoken little the last day or two, and I had guessed that he had struck a vein of private reflection. I thought it might be a new mine or irrigation scheme, and I was surprised to find that it was a country house.

"I don't think I shall go back to England," he said, kicking a sputtering log into place. "I don't see why I should. For business purposes I am far more useful to the firm in South Africa than in Throgmorton Street. I have no relation left except a third cousin, and I have never cared a rush for living in town. That beastly house of mine in Hill Street will fetch what I gave for it—Isaacson cabled about it the other day, offering for furniture and all. I don't want to go into Parliament, and I hate shooting little birds and tame deer. I am one of those fellows who are born Colonial at heart, and I don't see why I shouldn't arrange my life as I please.

101

Besides, for ten years I have been falling in love with this country, and now I am up to the neck."

He flung himself back in the camp chair till the canvas creaked, and looked at me below his eyelids. I remember glancing at the lines of him, and thinking what a fine make of a man he was. In his untanned field-boots, breeches and grey shirt, he looked the born wilderness hunter, though less than two months before he had been driving down to the City every morning in the sombre regimentals of his class. Being a fair man, he was gloriously tanned, and there was a clear line at his shirt-collar to mark the limits of his sunburn. I had first known him years ago, when he was a broker's clerk working on half-commission. Then he had gone to South Africa, and soon I heard he was a partner in a mining house which was doing wonders with some gold areas in the North. The next step was his return to London as the new millionaire—young, good-looking, wholesome in mind and body, and much sought after by the mothers of marriageable girls. We played polo together, and hunted a little in the season, but there were signs that he did not propose to become the conventional English gentleman. He refused to buy a place in the country, though half the Homes of England were at his disposal. He was a very busy man, he declared, and had not time to be a squire. Besides, every few months he used to rush out to South Africa. I saw that he was restless, for he was always badgering me to go big-game hunting with him in some remote part of the earth. There was that in his eyes, too, which marked him out from the ordinary blond type of our countrymen. They were large and brown and mysterious, and the light of another race was in their odd depths.

To hint such a thing would have meant a breach of friendship, for Lawson was very proud of his birth. When he first made his fortune he had gone to the Heralds to discover his family, and these obliging gentlemen had provided a pedigree. It appeared that he was a scion of the house of Lowson or Lowieson, an ancient and rather disreputable clan on the Scottish side of the Border. He took a shooting in Teviotdale on the strength of it, and used to commit lengthy Border ballads to memory. But I had known his father, a financial journalist who never quite succeeded, and I had heard of a grandfather who sold antiques in a back street at Brighton. The latter, I think, had not changed his name, and still frequented the synagogue. The father was a progressive Christian, and the mother had been a blonde Saxon from the Midlands. In my mind there was no doubt, as I caught Lawson's heavy-lidded eyes fixed on me. My friend was of a more ancient race than the Lowsons of the Border.

"Where are you thinking of looking for your house?" I asked. "In Natal or in the Cape Peninsula? You might get the Fishers' place if you paid a price."

"The Fishers' place be hanged!" he said crossly. "I don't want any stuccoed, overgrown Dutch farm. I might as well be at Roehampton as in the Cape."

He got up and walked to the far side of the fire, where a lane ran down through the thornscrub to a gully of the hills. The moon was silvering the bush of the plains, forty miles off and three thousand feet below us.

"I am going to live somewhere hereabouts," he answered at last.

I whistled. "Then you've got to put your hand in your pocket, old man. You'll have to make everything, including a map of the countryside."

"I know," he said, "that's where the fun comes in. Hang it all, why shouldn't I indulge my fancy? I'm uncommonly well off, and I haven't chick or child to leave it to. Supposing I'm a hundred miles from railhead, what about it? I'll make a motor-road and fix up a telephone. I'll grow most of my supplies, and start a colony to provide labour. When you come and stay with me, you'll get the best food and drink on earth, and sport that will make your mouth water. I'll put Lochleven trout in these streams,—at six thousand feet you can do anything. We'll have a pack of hounds, too, and we can drive pig in the woods, and if we want big game there are the Mangwe flats at our feet. I tell you I'll make such a country-house as nobody ever dreamed of. A man will come plumb out of stark savagery into lawns and rose-gardens." Lawson flung himself into his chair again and smiled dreamily at the fire.

"But why here, of all places?" I persisted. I was not feeling very well and did not care for the country.

"I can't quite explain. I think it's the sort of land I have always been looking for. I always fancied a house on a green plateau in a decent climate looking down on the tropics. I like heat and colour, you know, but I like hills too, and greenery, and the things that bring back Scotland. Give me a cross between Teviotdale and the Orinoco, and by Gad! I think I've got it here."

I watched my friend curiously, as with bright eyes and eager voice he talked of his new fad. The two races were very clear in him—the one desiring gorgeousness, the other athirst for the soothing spaces of the North. He began to plan out the house. He would get Adamson to design it, and it was to grow out of the landscape like a stone on the hillside. There would be wide verandahs and cool halls, but great fireplaces against winter time. It would all be very simple and fresh—"clean as morning" was his odd phrase; but then another idea supervened, and he talked of bringing the Tintorets from Hill Street. "I want it to be a civilised house, you know. No silly luxury, but the best pictures and china and books. . . . I'll have all the furniture made after the old plain English models out of native woods. I don't want second-hand sticks in a new country. Yes, by Jove, the Tintorets are a great idea, and all those Ming pots I bought. I had meant to sell them, but I'll have them out here."

He talked for a good hour of what he would do, and his dream grew richer as he talked, till by the time we went to bed he had sketched something more like a palace than a country-house. Lawson was by no means a luxurious man. At present he was well content with a Wolseley valise, and shaved cheerfully out of a tin mug. It struck me as odd that a man so simple in his habits should have so sumptuous a taste in bric-a-brac. I told myself, as I turned in, that the Saxon mother from the Midlands had done little to dilute the strong wine of the East.

It drizzled next morning when we inspanned, and I mounted my horse in a bad temper. I had some fever on me, I think, and I hated this lush yet frigid tableland, where all the winds on earth lay in wait for one's marrow. Lawson was, as usual, in great spirits. We were not hunting, but shifting our hunting-ground, so all morning we travelled fast to the north along the rim of the uplands.

At midday it cleared, and the afternoon was a pageant of pure colour. The wind sank to a low breeze; the sun lit the infinite green spaces, and kindled the wet forest to a jewelled coronal. Lawson gaspingly admired it all, as he cantered bareheaded up a bracken-clad slope. "God's country," he said twenty times. "I've found it." Take a piece of Sussex downland; put a stream in every hollow and a patch of wood; and at the edge, where the cliffs at home would fall to the sea, put a cloak of forest muffling the scarp and dropping thousands of feet to the blue plains. Take the diamond air of the Gornergrat, and the riot of colour which you get by a West Highland lochside in late September. Put flowers everywhere, the things we grow in hothouses, geraniums like sun-shades and arums like trumpets. That will give you a notion of the countryside we were in. I began to see that after all it was out of the common.

And just before sunset we came over a ridge and found something better. It was a shallow glen, half a mile wide, down which ran a blue-grey stream in linns like the Spean, till at the edge of the plateau it leaped into the dim forest in a snowy cascade. The opposite side ran up in gentle slopes to a rocky knoll, from which the eye had a noble prospect of the plains. All down the glen were little copses, half moons of green edging some silvery shore of the burn, or delicate clusters of tall trees nodding on the hill brow. The place so satsified the eye that for the sheer wonder of its perfection we stopped and stared in silence for many minutes.

Then "The House," I said, and Lawson replied softly, "The House!"

We rode slowly into the glen in the mulberry gloaming. Our transport wagons were half an hour behind, so we had time to explore. Lawson dismounted and plucked handfuls of flowers from the water meadows. He was singing to himself all the time—an old French catch about *Cadet Rousselle* and his *trois maisons*.

"Who owns it?" I asked.

"My firm, as like as not. We have miles of land about here. But whoever the man is, he has got to sell. Here I build my tabernacle, old man. Here, and nowhere else!"

In the very centre of the glen, in a loop of the stream, was one copse which even in that half light struck me as different from the others. It was of tall, slim, fairy-like trees, the kind of wood the monks painted in old missals. No, I rejected the thought. It was no Christian wood. It was not a copse, but a "grove,"—one such as Artemis may have flitted through in the moonlight. It was small, forty or fifty yards in diameter, and there was a dark something at the heart of it which for a second I thought was a house.

We turned between the slender trees, and—was it fancy?—an odd tremor went through me. I felt as if I were penetrating the *temenos* of some strange and lovely divinity, the goddess of this pleasant vale. There was a spell in the air, it seemed, and an odd dead silence.

Suddenly my horse started at a flutter of light wings. A flock of doves rose from the branches, and I saw the burnished green of their plumes against the opal sky. Lawson did not seem to notice them. I saw his keen eyes staring at the centre of the grove and what stood there.

It was a little conical tower, ancient and lichened, but, so far as I could judge, quite flawless. You know the famous Conical Temple at Zimbabwe, of which prints are in every guidebook. This was of the same type, but a thousandfold more perfect. It stood about thirty feet high, of solid masonry, without door or window or cranny, as shapely as when it first came from the hands of the old builders. Again I had the sense of breaking in on a sanctuary. What right had I, a common vulgar modern, to be looking at this fair thing, among these delicate trees, which some white goddess had once taken for her shrine?

Lawson broke in on my absorption. "Let's get out of this," he said hoarsely, and he took my horse's bridle (he had left his own beast at the edge) and led him back to the open. But I noticed that his eyes were always turning back and that his hand trembled.

"That settles it," I said after supper. "What do you want with your medieval Venetians and your Chinese pots now? You will have the finest antique in the world in your garden—a temple as old as time, and in a land which they say has no history. You had the right inspiration this time."

I think I have said that Lawson had hungry eyes. In his enthusiasm they used to glow and brighten; but now, as he sat looking down at the olive shades of the glen, they seemed ravenous in their fire. He had hardly spoken a word since we left the wood.

"Where can I read about these things?" he asked, and I gave him the names of books.

Then, an hour later, he asked me who were the builders. I told him the little I knew about Phoenician and Sabaean wanderings, and the ritual of Sidon and Tyre. He repeated some names to himself and went soon to bed.

As I turned in, I had one last look over the glen, which lay ivory and black in the moon. I seemed to hear a faint echo of wings, and to see over the little

grove a cloud of light visitants. "The Doves of Ashtaroth have come back," I said to myself. "It is a good
omen. They accept the new tenant." But as I fell
asleep I had a sudden thought that I was saying something rather terrible.

II

Three years later, pretty nearly to a day, I came back
to see what Lawson had made of his hobby. He had
bidden me often to Welgevonden, as he chose to call
it—though I do not know why he should have fixed a
Dutch name to a countryside where Boer never trod.
At the last there had been some confusion about dates,
and I wired the time of my arrival, and set off without
an answer. A motor met me at the queer little wayside
station of Taqui, and after many miles on a doubtful
highway I came to the gates of the park, and a road on
which it was a delight to move. Three years had
wrought little difference in the landscape. Lawson had
done some planting,—conifers and flowering shrubs
and such-like,—but wisely he had resolved that Nature
had for the most part forestalled him. All the same, he
must have spent a mint of money. The drive could not
have been beaten in England, and fringes of mown turf
on either hand had been pared out of the lush
meadows. When we came over the edge of the hill and
looked down on the secret glen, I could not repress a
cry of pleasure. The house stood on the farther ridge,
the viewpoint of the whole neighbourhood; and its
brown timbers and white rough-cast walls melted into
the hillside as if it had been there from the beginning
of things. The vale below was ordered in lawns and
gardens. A blue lake received the rapids of the stream,
and its banks were a maze of green shades and glorious
masses of blossom. I noticed, too, that the little grove
we had explored on our first visit stood alone in a big
stretch of lawn, so that its perfection might be clearly

seen. Lawson had excellent taste, or he had had the best advice.

The butler told me that his master was expected home shortly, and took me into the library for tea. Lawson had left his Tintorets and Ming pots at home after all. It was a long, low room, panelled in teak half-way up the walls, and the shelves held a multitude of fine bindings. There were good rugs on the parquet floor, but no ornaments anywhere, save three. On the carved mantelpiece stood two of the old soapstone birds which they used to find at Zimbabwe, and between, on an ebony stand, a half moon of alabaster, curiously carved with zodiacal figures. My host had altered his scheme of furnishing, but I approved the change.

He came in about half-past six, after I had consumed two cigars and all but fallen asleep. Three years make a difference in most men, but I was not prepared for the change in Lawson. For one thing, he had grown fat. In place of the lean young man I had known, I saw a heavy, flaccid being, who shuffled in his gait, and seemed tired and listless. His sunburn had gone, and his face was as pasty as a city clerk's. He had been walking, and wore shapeless flannel clothes, which hung loose even on his enlarged figure. And the worst of it was, that he did not seem over-pleased to see me. He murmured something about my journey, and then flung himself into an armchair and looked out of the window.

I asked him if he had been ill.

"Ill! No!" he said crossly. "Nothing of the kind. I'm perfectly well."

"You don't look as fit as this place should make you. What do you do with yourself? Is the shooting as good as you hoped?"

He did not answer, but I thought I heard him mutter something like "shooting be damned."

Then I tried the subject of the house. I praised it extravagantly, but with conviction. "There can be no place like it in the world," I said.

He turned his eyes on me at last, and I saw that they were as deep and restless as ever. With his pallid face they made him look curiously Semitic. I had been right in my theory about his ancestry.

"Yes," he said slowly, "there is no place like it—in the world."

Then he pulled himself to his feet. "I'm going to change," he said. "Dinner is at eight. Ring for Travers, and he'll show you your room."

I dressed in a noble bedroom, with an outlook over the garden-vale and the escarpment to the far line of the plains, now blue and saffron in the sunset. I dressed in an ill temper, for I was seriously offended with Lawson, and also seriously alarmed. He was either very unwell or going out of his mind, and it was clear, too, that he would resent any anxiety on his account. I ransacked my memory for rumours, but found none. I had heard nothing of him except that he had been extraordinarily successful in his speculations, and that from his hill-top he directed his firm's operations with uncommon skill. If Lawson was sick or mad, nobody knew of it.

Dinner was a trying ceremony. Lawson, who used to be rather particular in his dress, appeared in a kind of smoking suit with a flannel collar. He spoke scarcely a word to me, but cursed the servants with a brutality which left me aghast. A wretched footman in his nervousness spilt some sauce over his sleeve. Lawson dashed the dish from his hand, and volleyed abuse with a sort of epileptic fury. Also he, who had been the most abstemious of men, swallowed disgusting quantities of champagne and old brandy.

He had given up smoking, and half an hour after we left the dining-room, he announced his intention of going to bed. I watched him as he waddled upstairs, with a feeling of angry bewilderment. Then I went to the library and lit a pipe. I would leave first thing in the morning—on that I was determined. But as I sat gazing at the moon of alabaster and the soapstone birds my anger evaporated, and concern took its place. I remembered what a fine fellow Lawson had been, what good times we had had together. I remembered especially that evening when we had found this valley and given rein to our fancies. What horrid alchemy in the place had turned a gentleman into a brute? I thought of drink and drugs and madness and insomnia, but I could fit none of them into my conception of my friend. I did not consciously rescind my resolve to depart, but I had a notion that I would not act on it.

The sleepy butler met me as I went to bed. "Mr. Lawson's room is at the end of your corridor, sir," he said. "He don't sleep over well, so you may hear him stirring in the night. At what hour would you like breakfast, sir? Mr. Lawson mostly has his in bed."

My room opened from the great corridor, which ran the full length of the front of the house. So far as I could make out, Lawson was three rooms off, a vacant bedroom and his servant's room being between us. I felt tired and cross, and tumbled into bed as fast as possible. Usually I sleep well, but now I was soon conscious that my drowsiness was wearing off and that I was in for a restless night. I got up and laved my face, turned the pillows, thought of sheep coming over a hill and clouds crossing the sky; but none of the old devices were of any use. After about an hour of make-believe I surrendered myself to facts, and, lying on my back, stared at the white ceiling and the patches of moonshine on the walls.

It certainly was an amazing night. I got up, put on a dressing-gown, and drew a chair to the window. The moon was almost at its full, and the whole plateau swam in a radiance of ivory and silver. The banks of the stream were black, but the lake had a great belt of light athwart it, which made it seem like a horizon, and the rim of land beyond it like a contorted cloud. Far to the right I saw the delicate outlines of the little wood which I had come to think of as the Grove of Ashtaroth. I listened. There was not a sound in the air. The land seemed to sleep peacefully beneath the moon, and yet I had a sense that the peace was an illusion. The place was feverishly restless.

I could have given no reason for my impression, but there it was. Something was stirring in the wide moon-lit landscape under its deep mask of silence. I felt as I had felt on the evening three years ago when I had ridden into the grove. I did not think that the influence, whatever it was, was maleficent. I only knew that it was very strange, and kept me wakeful.

By-and-by I bethought me of a book. There was no lamp in the corridor save the moon, but the whole house was bright as I slipped down the great staircase and across the hall to the library. I switched on the lights and then switched them off. They seemed a profanation, and I did not need them.

I found a French novel, but the place held me and I stayed. I sat down in an arm-chair before the fireplace and the stone birds. Very odd those gawky things, like prehistoric Great Auks, looked in the moonlight. I remember that the alabaster moon shimmered like translucent pearl, and I fell to wondering about its history. Had the old Sabaeans used such a jewel in their rites in the Grove of Ashtaroth?

Then I heard footsteps pass the window. A great house like this would have a watchman, but these quick shuffling footsteps were surely not the dull plod of a servant. They passed on to the grass and died away. I began to think of getting back to my room.

In the corridor I noticed that Lawson's door was ajar, and that a light had been left burning. I had the unpardonable curiosity to peep in. The room was empty, and the bed had not been slept in. Now I knew whose were the footsteps outside the library window.

I lit a reading-lamp and tried to interest myself in *La Cruelle Enigme*. But my wits were restless, and I could not keep my eyes on the page. I flung the book aside and sat down again by the window. The feeling came over me that I was sitting in a box at some play. The glen was a huge stage, and at any moment the players might appear on it. My attention was strung as high as if I had been waiting for the advent of some world-famous actress. But nothing came. Only the shadows shifted and lengthened as the moon moved across the sky.

Then quite suddenly the restlessness left me and at the same moment the silence was broken by the crow of a cock and the rustling of trees in a light wind. I felt very sleepy, and was turning to bed when again I heard footsteps without. From the window I could see a figure moving across the garden towards the house. It was Lawson, got up in the sort of towel dressing-gown that one wears on board ship. He was walking slowly and painfully, as if very weary. I did not see his face, but the man's whole air was that of extreme fatigue and dejection.

I tumbled into bed and slept profoundly till long after daylight.

III

The man who valeted me was Lawson's own servant. As he was laying out my clothes I asked after the health of his master, and was told that he had slept ill and would not rise till late. Then the man, an anxious-faced Englishman, gave me some information on his own account. Mr. Lawson was having one of his bad turns. It would pass away in a day or two, but till it had gone he was fit for nothing. He advised me to see Mr. Jobson, the factor, who would look to my entertainment in his master's absence.

Jobson arrived before luncheon, and the sight of him was the first satisfactory thing about Welgevonden. He was a big, gruff Scot from Roxburghshire, engaged, no doubt, by Lawson as a duty to his Border ancestry. He had short, grizzled whiskers, a weather-worn face, and a shrewd, calm blue eye. I knew now why the place was in such perfect order.

We began with sport, and Jobson explained what I

could have in the way of fishing and shooting. His exposition was brief and business-like, and all the while I could see his eye searching me. It was clear that he had much to say on other matters than sport.

I told him that I had come here with Lawson three years before, when he chose the site. Jobson continued to regard me curiously. "I've heard tell of ye from Mr. Lawson. Ye're an old friend of his, I understand."

"The oldest," I said. "And I am sorry to find that the place does not agree with him. Why it doesn't I cannot imagine, for you look fit enough. Has he been seedy for long?"

"It comes and it goes," said Mr. Jobson. "Maybe once a month he has a bad turn. But on the whole it agrees with him badly. He's no' the man he was when I first came here."

Jobson was looking at me very seriously and frankly. I risked a question.

"What do you suppose is the matter?"

He did not reply at once, but leaned forward and tapped my knee.

"I think it's something that doctors canna cure. Look at me, sir. I've always been counted a sensible man, but if I told you what was in my head you would think me daft. But I have one word for you. Bide till to-night is past and then speir your question. Maybe you and me will be agreed."

The factor rose to go. As he left the room he flung me back a remark over his shoulder—"Read the eleventh chapter of the First Book of Kings."

After luncheon I went for a walk. First I mounted to the crown of the hill and feasted my eyes on the unequalled loveliness of the view. I saw the far hills in Portuguese territory, a hundred miles away, lifting up thin blue fingers into the sky. The wind blew light and fresh, and the place was fragrant with a thousand delicate scents. Then I descended to the vale, and followed the stream up through the garden. Poinsettias and oleanders were blazing in coverts, and there was a paradise of tinted water-lilies in the slacker reaches. I saw good trout rise at the fly, but I did not think about fishing. I was searching my memory for a recollection which would not come. By-and-by I found myself beyond the garden, where the lawns ran to the fringe of Ashtaroth's Grove.

It was like something I remembered in an old Italian picture. Only, as my memory drew it, it should have been peopled with strange figures—nymphs dancing on the sward, and a prick-eared faun peeping from the covert. In the warm afternoon sunlight it stood, ineffably gracious and beautiful, tantalising with a sense of some deep hidden loveliness. Very reverently I walked between the slim trees, to where the little conical tower stood half in the sun and half in shadow. Then I noticed something new. Round the tower ran a narrow path, worn in the grass by human feet. There had been no such path on my first visit, for I remembered the grass growing tall to the edge of the stone. Had the Kaffirs made a shrine of it, or were there other and strange votaries?

When I returned to the house I found Travers with a message for me. Mr. Lawson was still in bed, but he would like me to go to him. I found my friend sitting up and drinking strong tea—a bad thing, I should have thought, for a man in his condition. I remember that I looked about the room for some sign of the pernicious habit of which I believed him a victim. But the place was fresh and clean, with the windows wide open, and, though I could not have given my reasons, I was convinced that drugs or drink had nothing to do with the sickness.

He received me more civilly, but I was shocked by his looks. There were great bags below his eyes, and his skin had the wrinkled puffy appearance of a man in dropsy. His voice, too, was reedy and thin. Only his great eyes burned with some feverish life.

"I am a shocking bad host," he said, "but I'm going

to be still more inhospitable. I want you to go away. I hate anybody here when I'm off colour."

"Nonsense," I said; "you want looking after. I want to know about this sickness. Have you had a doctor?"

He smiled wearily. "Doctors are no earthly use to me. There's nothing much the matter I tell you. I'll be all right in a day or two, and then you can come back. I want you to go off with Jobson and hunt in the plains till the end of the week. It will be better fun for you, and I'll feel less guilty."

Of course I pooh-poohed the idea, and Lawson got angry. "Damn it, man," he cried, "why do you force yourself on me when I don't want you? I tell you your presence here makes me worse. In a week I'll be as right as the mail, and then I'll be thankful for you. But get away now; get away, I tell you."

I saw that he was fretting himself into a passion. "All right," I said soothingly; "Jobson and I will go off hunting. But I am horribly anxious about you, old man."

He lay back on his pillows. "You needn't trouble. I only want a little rest. Jobson will make all arrangements, and Travers will get you anything you want. Good-bye."

I saw it was useless to stay longer, so I left the room. Outside I found the anxious-faced servant. "Look here," I said, "Mr. Lawson thinks I ought to go, but I mean to stay. Tell him I'm gone if he asks you. And for Heaven's sake keep him in bed."

The man promised, and I thought I saw some relief in his face.

I went to the library, and on the way remembered Jobson's remark about First Kings. With some searching I found a Bible and turned up the passage. It was a long screed about the misdeeds of Solomon, and I read it through without enlightenment. I began to re-read it, and a word suddenly caught my attention—

"For Solomon went after Ashtaroth, the goddess of the Zidonians."

That was all, but it was like a key to a cipher. Instantly there flashed over my mind all that I had heard or read of that strange ritual which seduced Israel to sin. I saw a sunburnt land and a people vowed to the stern service of Jehovah. But I saw, too, eyes turning from the austere sacrifice to lonely hill-top groves and towers and images, where dwelt some subtle and evil mystery. I saw the fierce prophets, scourging the votaries with rods, and a nation penitent before the Lord; but always the backsliding again, and the hankering after forbidden joys. Ashtaroth was the old goddess of the East. Was it not possible that in all Semitic blood there remained transmitted through the dim generations, some craving for her spell? I thought of the grandfather in the back street at Brighton and of those burning eyes upstairs.

As I sat and mused my glance fell on the inscrutable stone birds. They knew all those old secrets of joy and terror. And that moon of alabaster! Some dark priest had worn it on his forehead when he worshipped like Ahab, "all the host of Heaven." And then I honestly began to be afraid. I, a prosaic, modern Christian gentleman, a half-believer in casual faiths, was in the presence of some hoary mystery of sin far older than creeds or Christendom. There was fear in my heart—a kind of uneasy disgust, and above all a nervous eerie disquiet. Now I wanted to go away, and yet I was ashamed of the cowardly thought. I pictured Ashtaroth's Grove with sheer horror. What tragedy was in the air? What secret awaited twilight? For the night was coming, the night of the Full Moon, the season of ecstasy and sacrifice.

I do not know how I got through that evening. I was disinclined for dinner, so I had a cutlet in the library and sat smoking till my tongue ached. But as the hours passed a more manly resolution grew up in my mind. I owed it to old friendship to stand by Lawson in this extremity. I could not interfere—God knows, his reason seemed already rocking,—but I could be at hand in case my chance came. I determined not to undress, but to watch through the night. I had a bath, and changed into light flannels and slippers. Then I took up my position in a corner of the library close to the window, so that I could not fail to hear Lawson's footsteps if he passed.

Fortunately I left the lights unlit, for as I waited I grew drowsy, and fell asleep. When I woke the moon had risen, and I knew from the feel of the air that the hour was late. I sat very still, straining my ears, and as I listened I caught the sound of steps. They were crossing the hall, stealthily, and nearing the library door. I huddled into my corner as Lawson entered.

He wore the same towel dressing-gown, and he moved swiftly and silently as if in a trance. I watched him take the alabaster moon from the mantelpiece and drop it in his pocket. A glimpse of white skin showed that the gown was his only clothing. Then he moved past me to the window, opened it, and went out.

Without any conscious purpose I rose and followed, kicking off my slippers that I might go quietly. He was running, running fast, across the lawns in the direction of the Grove—an odd shapeless antic in the moonlight. I stopped, for there was no cover, and I feared for his reason if he saw me. When I looked again he had disappeared among the trees.

I saw nothing for it but to crawl, so on my belly I wormed my way over the dripping sward. There was a ridiculous suggestion of deer-stalking about the game which tickled me and dispelled my uneasiness. Almost I persuaded myself I was tracking an ordinary sleep-walker. The lawns were broader than I imagined, and it seemed an age before I reached the edge of the Grove. The world was so still that I appeared to be making a most ghastly amount of noise. I remember that once I heard a rustling in the air, and looked up to see the green doves circling about the tree-tops.

There was no sign of Lawson. On the edge of the Grove I think that all my assurance vanished. I could see between the trunks to the little tower, but it was quiet as the grave, save for the wings above. Once more there came over me the unbearable sense of anticipation I had felt the night before. My nerves tingled with mingled expectation and dread. I did not think that any harm would come to me, for the powers of the air seemed not malignant. But I knew them for powers, and felt awed and abased. I was in the presence of the "host of Heaven," and I was no stern Israelitish prophet to prevail against them.

I must have lain for hours waiting in that spectral place, my eyes riveted on the tower and its golden cap of moonshine. I remember that my head felt void and light, as if my spirit were becoming disembodied and leaving its dew-drenched sheath far below. But the most curious sensation was of something drawing me to the tower, something mild and kindly and rather feeble, for there was some other and stronger force keeping me back. I yearned to move nearer, but I could not drag my limbs an inch. There was a spell somewhere which I could not break. I do not think I was in any way frightened now. The starry influence was playing tricks with me, but my mind was half asleep. Only I never took my eyes from the little tower. I think I could not, if I had wanted to.

Then suddenly from the shadows came Lawson. He was stark-naked, and he wore, bound across his brow, the half-moon of alabaster. He had something, too, in his hand,—something which glittered.

He ran round the tower, crooning to himself and flinging wild arms to the skies. Sometimes, the crooning changed to a shrill cry of passion, such as a maenad may have uttered in the train of Bacchus. I could make out no words, but the sound told its own tale. He was absorbed in some infernal ecstasy. And as he ran, he drew his right hand across his breast and arms, and I saw that it held a knife.

I grew sick with disgust,—not terror, but honest physical loathing. Lawson, gashing his fat body, affected me with an overpowering repugnance. I wanted to go forward and stop him and I wanted, too, to be a hundred miles away. And the result was that I stayed still. I believe my own will held me there, but I doubt if in any case I could have moved my legs.

The dance grew swifter and fiercer. I saw the blood dripping from Lawson's body, and his face ghastly white above his scarred breast. And then suddenly the horror left me; my head swam; and for one second—one brief second—I seemed to peer into a new world. A strange passion surged up in my heart. I seemed to see the earth peopled with forms not human, scarcely divine, but more desirable than man or god. The calm face of Nature broke up for me into wrinkles of wild knowledge. I saw the things which brush against the soul in dreams, and found them lovely. There seemed no cruelty in the knife or the blood. It was a delicate mystery of worship, as wholesome as the morning song of birds. I do not know how the Semites fround Ashtaroth's ritual; to them it may well have been more rapt and passionate than it seemed to me. For I saw in it only the sweet simplicity of Nature, and all riddles of lust and terror soothed away as a child's nightmares are calmed by a mother. I found my legs able to move, and I think I took two steps through the dusk towards the tower.

And then it all ended. A cock crew, and the homely noises of earth were renewed. While I stood dazed and shivering, Lawson plunged through the Grove toward me. The impetus carried him to the edge, and he fell fainting just outside the shade.

My wits and common-sense came back to me with my bodily strength. I got my friend on my back, and staggered with him towards the house. I was afraid in real earnest now, and what frightened me most was the thought that I had not been afraid sooner. I had come very near the "abomination of the Zidonians."

At the door I found the scared valet waiting. He had apparently done this sort of thing before.

"Your master has been sleep-walking and has had a fall." I said. "We must get him to bed at once."

We bathed the wounds as he lay in a deep stupor, and I dressed them as well as I could. The only danger

lay in his utter exhaustion, for happily the gashes were
not serious, and no artery had been touched. Sleep and
rest would make him well, for he had the constitution
of a strong man. I was leaving the room when he
opened his eyes and spoke. He did not recognize me,
but I noticed that his face had lost its strangeness, and
was once more that of the friend I had known. Then I
suddenly bethought me of an old hunting remedy
which he and I always carried on our expeditions. It is
a pill made up from an ancient Portuguese prescrip-
tion. One is an excellent specific for fever. Two are in-
valuable if you are lost in the bush, for they send a
man for many hours into a deep sleep, which prevents
suffering and madness, till help comes. Three give a
painless death. I went to my room and found the little
box in my jewel-case. Lawson swallowed two, and
turned wearily on his side. I bade his man let him sleep
till he woke, and went off in search of food.

IV

I had business on hand which would not wait. By
seven, Jobson, who had been sent for, was waiting for
me in the library. I knew by his grim face that here I
had a very good substitute for a prophet of the Lord.

"You were right," I said. "I have read the eleventh
chapter of First Kings, and I have spent such a night as
I pray God I shall never spend again."

"I thought you would," he replied. "I've had the
same experience myself."

"The Grove?" I said.

"Ay, the wud," was the answer in broad Scots.

I wanted to see how much he understood.

"Mr. Lawson's family is from the Scottish Border?"

"Ay. I understand they come off Borthwick Water
side," he replied, but I saw by his eyes that he knew
what I meant.

"Mr. Lawson is my oldest friend," I went on, "and I
am going to take measures to cure him. For what I am

going to do I take the sole responsibility. I will make that plain to your master. But if I am to succeed I want your help. Will you give it me? It sounds like madness, and you are a sensible man and may like to keep out of it. I leave it to your discretion."

Jobson looked me straight in the face. "Have no fear for me," he said: "there is an unholy thing in that place, and if I have the strength in me I will destroy it. He has been a good master to me, and, forbye, I am a believing Christian. So say on, sir."

There was no mistaking the air. I had found my Tishbite.

"I want men," I said,—"as many as we can get."

Jobson mused. "The Kaffirs will no' gang near the place, but there's some thirty white men on the tobacco farm. They'll do your will, if you give them an indemnity in writing."

"Good," said I. "Then we will take our instructions from the only authority which meets the case. We will follow the example of King Josiah." I turned up the twenty-third chapter of Second Kings, and read—

"And the high places that were before Jerusalem, which were on the right hand of the Mount of Corruption, which Solomon the king of Israel had builded for Ashtaroth the abomination of the Zidonians . . . did the king defile.

"And he brake in pieces the images, and cut down the groves, and filled their places with the bones of men.

"Moreover the altar that was at Beth-el, and the high place which Jeroboam the son of Nebat, who made Israel to sin, had made, both the altar and the high place he brake down, and burned the high place, and stamped it small to powder, and burned the grove."

Jobson nodded. "It'll need dinnymite. But I've plenty of yon down at the workshops. I'll be off to collect the lads."

Before nine the men had assembled at Jobson's house. They were a hardy lot of young farmers from home, who took their instructions docilely from the masterful factor. On my orders they had brought their shotguns. We armed them wtih spades and woodmen's axes, and one man wheeled some coils of rope in a handcart.

In the clear, windless air of morning the Grove, set amid its lawns, looked too innocent and exquisite for ill. I had a pang of regret that a thing so fair should suffer; nay, if I had come alone, I think I might have repented. But the men were there, and the grim-faced Jobson was waiting for orders. I placed the guns, and sent beaters to the far side. I told them that every dove must be shot.

It was only a small flock, and we killed fifteen at the first drive. The poor birds flew over the glen to another spinney, but we brought them back over the guns and seven fell. Four more were got in the trees, and the last I killed myself with a long shot. In half an hour there was a pile of little green bodies in the sward.

Then we went to work to cut down the trees. The slim stems were an easy task to a good woodman, and one after another they toppled to the ground. And meantime, as I watched, I became conscious of a strange emotion.

It was as if someone were pleading with me. A gentle voice, not threatening, but pleading—something too fine for the sensual ear, but touching inner chords of the spirit. So tenuous it was and distant that I could think of no personality behind it. Rather it was the viewless, bodiless grace of this delectable vale, some old exquisite divinity of the groves. There was the heart of all sorrow in it, and the soul of all loveliness. It seemed a woman's voice, some lost lady who had brought nothing but goodness unrepaid to the world. And what the voice told me was that I was destroying her last shelter.

That was the pathos of it—the voice was homeless. As the axes flashed in the sunlight and the wood grew

thin, that gentle spirit was pleading with me for mercy
and a brief respite. It seemed to be telling of a world
for centuries grown coarse and pitiless, of long sad
wanderings, of hardly-won shelter, and a peace which
was the little all she sought from men. There was nothing terrible in it. No thought of wrong-doing. The spell,
which to Semitic blood held the mystery of evil, was to
me, of the Northern race, only delicate and rare and
beautiful. Jobson and the rest did not feel it, I with my
finer senses caught nothing but the hopeless sadness of
it. That which had stirred the passion in Lawson was
only wringing my heart. It was almost too pitiful to
bear. As the trees crashed down and the men wiped
the sweat from their brows, I seemed to myself like the
murderer of fair women and innocent children. I
remember that the tears were running over my cheeks.
More than once I opened my mouth to countermand the
work, but the face of Jobson, that grim Tishbite, held
me back.

I knew now what gave the Prophets of the Lord
their mastery, and I knew also why the people sometimes stoned them.

The last tree fell, and the little tower stood like a ra-
vished shrine, stripped of all defense against the world.
I heard Jobson's voice speaking. "We'd better blast
that stane thing now. We'll trench on four sides and lay
the dinnymite. Ye're no' looking weel, sir. Ye'd better
go and sit down on the braeface."

I went up the hillside and lay down. Below me, in
the waste of shorn trunks, men were running about,
and I saw the mining begin. It all seemed like an aim-
less dream in which I had no part. The voice of that
homeless goddess was still pleading. It was the inno-
cence of it that tortured me. Even so must a merciful
Inquisitor have suffered from the plea of some fair girl
with the aureole of death on her hair. I knew I was
killing rare and unrecoverable beauty. As I sat dazed
and heartsick, the whole loveliness of Nature seemed to
plead for its divinity. The sun in the heavens, the mel-
low lines of upland, the blue mystery of the far plains,

were all part of that soft voice. I felt bitter scorn for myself. I was guilty of blood; nay, I was guilty of the sin against light which knows no forgiveness. I was murdering innocent gentleness—and there would be no peace on earth for me. Yet I sat helpless. The power of a sterner will constrained me. And all the while the voice was growing fainter and dying away into unutterable sorrow.

Suddenly a great flame sprang to heaven, and a pall of smoke. I heard men crying out, and fragments of stone fell around the ruins of the grove. When the air cleared, the little tower had gone out of sight.

The voice had ceased and there seemed to me to be a bereaved silence in the world. The shock moved me to my feet, and I ran down the slope to where Jobson stood rubbing his eyes.

"That's done the job. Now we maun get up the tree roots. We've no time to howk. We'll just blast the feck o' them."

The work of destruction went on, but I was coming back to my senses. I forced myself to be practical and reasonable. I thought of the night's experience and Lawson's haggard eyes, and I screwed myself into a determination to see the thing through. I had done the deed; it was my business to make it complete. A text in Jeremiah came into my head: *"Their children remember their altars and their groves by the green trees upon the high hills."* I would see to it that this grove should be utterly forgotten.

We blasted the tree-roots, and, yoking oxen, dragged the debris into a great heap. Then the men set to work with their spades, and roughly levelled the ground. I was getting back to my old self, and Jobson's spirit was becoming mine.

"There is one thing more," I told him. "Get ready a couple of ploughs. We will improve upon King Josiah." My brain was a medley of Scripture precedents, and I was determined that no safeguard should be wanting.

We yoked the oxen again and drove the ploughs

over the site of the grove. It was rough ploughing, for the place was thick with bits of stone from the tower, but the slow Afrikander oxen plodded on, and sometime in the afternoon the work was finished. Then I sent down to the farm for bags of rock-salt, such as they use for cattle. Jobson and I took a sack apiece, and walked up and down the furrows, sowing them with salt.

The last act was to set fire to the pile of tree-trunks. They burned well, and on the top we flung the bodies of the green doves. The birds of Ashtaroth had an honorable pyre.

Then I dismissed the much-perplexed men, and gravely shook hands with Jobson. Black with dust and smoke I went back to the house, where I bade Travers pack my bags and order the motor. I found Lawson's servant, and heard from him that his master was sleeping peacefully. I gave him some directions, and then went to wash and change.

Before I left I wrote a line to Lawson. I began by transcribing the verses from the twenty-third chapter of Second Kings. I told him what I had done, and my reason. "I take the whole responsibility upon myself," I wrote. "No man in the place had anything to do with it but me. I acted as I did for the sake of our old friendship, and you will believe it was no easy task for me. I hope you will understand. Whenever you are able to see me send me word, and I will come back and settle with you. But I think you will realise that I have saved your soul."

The afternoon was merging into twilight as I left the house on the road to Taqui. The great fire, where the Grove had been, was still blazing fiercely, and the smoke made a cloud over the upper glen, and filled all the air with a soft violet haze. I knew that I had done well for my friend, and that he would come to his senses and be grateful. My mind was at ease on that score, and in something like comfort I faced the future. But as the car reached the ridge I looked back to the vale I had outraged. The moon was rising and silvering the smoke, and through the gaps I could see the tongues of fire. Somehow, I know not why, the lake, the stream, the garden-coverts, even the green slopes of hill, wore an air of loneliness and desecration.

And then my heartache returned, and I knew that I had driven something lovely and adorable from its last refuge on earth.

JAMES BRANCH CABELL

(1879–1958)

James Branch Cabell, American novelist, was born in
Richmond, Virginia, and educated at William and
Mary College. Before devoting himself entirely to a
literary career he spent some time in newspaper work
in both Richmond and New York City. Cabell's
success as a writer began with the publication of *Jurgen* in 1919. Like so many of his other works, *Jurgen*
displays an eroticism which quickly prompted charges
of obscenity. It is very probable that these charges,
coupled with the fact that the novel was banned in
several cities, helped the work achieve such a high
degree of popularity. Cabell enjoyed great success as a
writer for the next three decades, especially among college students who appreciated the erudition of his writings and also his preoccupation with the search for an
ideal state.

Most of his works deal with medieval romance and
chivalry, and are often set in the imaginary kingdom of
Poictesme. The impressive Poictesme Cycle consists of
the following works: *The Eagle's Shadow* (1904), *The
Line of Love* (1905), *Gallantry* (1907), *Chivalry*
(1909), *The Cords of Vanity* (1909), *The Rivet in
Grandfather's Neck* (1915), *The Certain Hour*
(1916), *From the Hidden Way* (1916), *The Cream of
the Jest* (1917), *Jurgen* (1919), *Domnei* (1920), *Figures of Earth* (1921), *The Jewel Merchants* (1921),
The High Place (1923), *The Music From Behind the
Moon* (1926), *The Silver Stallion* (1926), and *Something about Eve* (1927).

Cabell's unusually fertile imagination is effectively

displayed in this poignant tale of Madoc's eternal pursuit of the "skirling" music of Ettarre the witchwoman. The reader follows Madoc's career from his youthful position as poet at the "cultured court of Netan, the High King of Marr and Kett," to his old age when he drifts about the countryside "as a vagabond, a trifle crazed, a trifle ragged, but utterly satisfied to follow after that music which none ever heard." The adventures which befall the protagonist as he is irresistibly drawn by Ettarre's siren song are as varied and fabulous as one can hope to find in any work of high fantasy. Perhaps the highlight of all Madoc's journeys, however, is his unforgettable trip to the moon on the back of the spectacular hippogriffin.

❧ The Music From Behind the Moon ❧

EPITOME OF A POET

J. B. Cabell

Judge thou the lips of those that rose up against me all the day. Behold their sitting down, and their rising up: I am their music.

PART ONE

OF MADOC IN HIS YOUTH

—*De grâce, belle dame, si je puis vous demander ce que j'ai à coeur de savoir, dites-moi pourquoi vous êtes assise ici toute seule?*
—*Je vais te le dire, mon pauvre Madoc, avec franchise.*

THE TEXT FROM GENESIS

To such as will listen I plan here to tell the story of Madoc and some little part of the story of Ettarre.

Now this is a regrettably familiar tale. It may possibly have begun with Lamech, in the Book of Genesis,—who was, in any event, the first well-thought-of citizen upon known record to remark, "I have slain a young man to my hurt!" And poets tell us that many poets whose bodies had survived to middle age have repeated this glum observation, although probably not ever since then, when Lamech spoke without tact, to their co-partners alike in the homicide and in married life.

Moreover, this is a regrettably inconclusive tale, without any assured ending. Nor is there any assured prophesying, either, that the next thousand years or so will remedy that defect in this tale, because the story of Ettarre is not lightly to be ended by the death of any woman's body which for a while Ettarre has been wearing.

And, lastly, this is a regrettably true tale such as no correct-thinking person ought to regard seriously.

1

FOUR VIEWS OF A POET

Lean red-haired Madoc was the youngest and the least promising of the poets about the cultured court of Netan, the High King of Marr and Kett. When it was Madoc's turn to take out his bronze harp from its bag of otter-skin, and to play at a banquet, he assisted nobody's digestion. And, as the art-loving King would put it, twisting half-fretfully at his long white beard, what else was the lad there for?

The best-thought-of connoisseurs declared the songs of Madoc to be essentially hollow and deficient in, as they phrased it in their technical way, red blood: to which verdict the wives and the sweethearts of these connoisseurs were only too apt to reply that, anyhow, the boy was quite nice-looking. The unthinking women thus confirmed the connoisseurs in their disapproval.

But the strangest matter of all, in a world where poets warm themselves mainly by self-esteem, was that not even to young Madoc did his songs appear miraculous beyond any description.

To Madoc's hearing his songs ran confusedly; they strained toward a melody which stayed forever uncaptured; and they seemed to him to be thin parodies of an elvish music, not wholly of this earth, some part of which he had heard very long ago and had half forgotten, but the whole of which music remained unheard by any mortal ears.

2

THE WOMAN LIKE A MIST

Now, upon a May evening, when a plump amber-colored moon stayed as yet low behind the willows in the east, this same young Madoc bathed with an old ceremony. Thereafter he sat beside the fountain meditatively disposing of his allotted portion of thin wine and of two cheese sandwiches. A woman came to him, white-limbed and like a living mist in that twilight.

"Hail, friend!" said Madoc.

She replied, with hushed and very lovely laughter, "I am not your friend."

He said, "Well, peace be with you, in any event!"

She answered, "There is for you, poor Madoc, no more peace, now that I have come to you all the long way from behind the moon."

And then that woman did a queer thing, for she laid to her young breasts her hands, and from the flesh of her body she took out her red heart, and upon her heartstrings she made a music.

It was a strange and troubling music she made there in the twilight, and after that slender mistlike woman had ended her music-making, and had vanished as a white wave falters and is gone, then Madoc could not recall the theme or even one cadence of her music-making, nor could he put the skirling of it out of his mind. Moreover, there was upon him a loneliness and a hungering for what he could not name.

3

WHAT WISDOM ADVISED

Therefore Madoc comes to the dark and ivy-covered tower of Jonathas the Wise. And the lean and kindly man put forth his art. He burned, in a tall brazier, camphor and sulphur and white resin and incense and salt: he invoked the masters of the lightning and of volcanoes and of starlight; and he recited the prayer of the Salamanders.

Then Jonathas sighed, and he looked compassionately over his spectacles. "The person that troubles you, my poor Madoc, is Ettarre the witch-woman, whom Dom Manuel the Redeemer begot in Poictesme; and whom the Norns have ordained to live with Sargatanet, Lord of the Waste Beyond the Moon, until the 725 years of her poisonous music-making are ended."

Madoc said, "How may a struggling poet avoid the spells of this witch and of this wizard?"

Jonathas replied: "There is for a poet no defense against their malice, because their weapon is that song which is an all-consuming fire. Still, as one nail drives out the other, and as one fire consumes another fire, so something may be done against the destroying pair with this."

And thereupon, lean kindly Jonathas gave to young Madoc a very large quill pen fashioned out of a feather which had fallen from the black wings of Lucifer, the Father of All Lies.

4

ONE PATRIOT'S REWARD

With this pen Madoc began to write down his songs
before he sang them: and the pen made for him a new
kind of song.

Now the connoisseurs nodded approval. "The senti-
ment is wholesome, and, in these degenerate days, regrettably rare." King Netan clapped his hands, he
laughed aloud, and he gave Madoc a greyhoud, a white
tunic worked with green embroidery, and seven chests
of gold coin.

Thereafter Madoc lacked for no reward, and every
week he had a lovelier lady for his love. At all the
royal banquets he sang his new song, of how enviable
were Netan's people in every heritage and in their
sturdy racial qualities, and of how contemptible the
other nations appeared in comparison: and everybody
applauded his remarkable rightness.

But Madoc one day put aside his harp, he removed
an amorous countess from about his neck, and he went
alone out of Netan's shield-hung hall. All at that banquet were applauding Madoc; but through the shouting
he could hear a skirling music which derided his patriotic perjuries: and Madoc knew that the fatherland he
was praising showed as an unimportant pimple on the
broad face of the world, and that its history, or the history of any other people, was but a very little parenthe-
sis in Earth's history.

5

SOME VERY ANCIENT GAMES

So Madoc fled from the cultured court of Netan, where the superb emotions of patriotism were denied him by that music which a pallid and pestiferous witch was devising in the Waste Beyond the Moon. He fled southward, into the fertile land of Marna.

In a green field, beneath a flowering apple tree, a young woman was playing at chess against a veiled opponent. His face could not be seen, but the gray hand with which he now moved a bishop had four talons like the claw of a vulture. The woman was clothed in blue: about her yellow hair she wore a circlet of silver inset with many turquoises, and about her wrists also were bands of silver, and in her face was the bright pride of youth.

At the sight of Madoc this woman arose, she smiled, and in a clear sweet voice she cried out the magic word of the south, saying, "Berith!"

The veiled man was not any longer there, but beyond the apple tree you saw a thin gray wolf running away very swiftly.

The lovely girl then told young Madoc that she was Ainath, the queen over all this country, and he told her that he was a wandering minstrel. Ainath in reply said she did not know much about music, but she knew what she liked, and among the things that she especially liked was the appearance of Madoc.

6

LEADS TO A COFFIN

Nor did Madoc dislike the appearance of Ainath. Nowhere in her appearance could he find any flaw: she
was, indeed, so confident of her perfection that she hid
from him no portion of her loveliness, and she refused
to cheat him by leaving his knowledge superficial.

Her generosity and her fond loving ways led Madoc
quite to overlook, if not entirely to condone, this
queen's alliance with the Old Believers, when Madoc
by-and-by had found out the nature of Ainath's veiled
opponent and what game it was that Ainath played
within reach of the fiend's talons.

Meanwhile with Madoc she played other games,
night after night, inside the carved and intricately
colored sarcophagus in which, when the time came,
Queen Ainath must be laid away under the dark and
fertile land of Marna; for it was the intent of this far-
seeing queen to make of her coffin a hospitable place,
and to endear it with memories of countless frolics and
of much loving friendship, so that (when the time
came) she might lie down in her last home without any
feeling of strangeness about her being there yet again,
or any unwelcome association of ideas.

Now it was Madoc who, for the while, assisted
Ainath in this poetic wise plan, and with all the vigor
which was in him he set lovingly to work to keep that
coffin dear to her.

7

REWARD OF THE OPTIMIST

Now also, for Queen Ainath, and for the shepherds who served Ainath, young Madoc wrote noble songs. It was not of any local patriotic prevarications that Madoc sang in the green fields of Marna, but of an optimism which was international and all-embracing.

"This is a fair world," sang Madoc, "very lovingly devised for human kind. Let us give praise for the excellence of this world, and—not exactly this morning, but tomorrow afternoon perhaps, or at any rate, next week—let us be doing exceedingly splendid things in this world wherein everything is ordered for the best when you come to consider matters properly."

The kindly shepherd people said, as they cuddled each other in pairs, "This Madoc is the king of poets, sweetheart, for he makes us see that, after all, this world is a pretty good sort of place."

But Madoc looked with dismay upon their smirking faces, which seemed to him, beneath their hawthorn garlands, as witless as were the faces of their sheep: and upon the face of Madoc there was no smirk. For all the while that he made his benevolent music he could hear another music, skirling: and this other music derided the wholesome optimism which was in the singing but not in the parched heart of Madoc, and this other music called him, resistlessly, toward his allotted doom.

PART TWO

OF MADOC IN THIS WORLD

Je t'ai secrètement accompagné partout,
dans les luttes et dans les combats, sur les
routes, dans les rues et partout: ma musique t'a
préservé des atteintes et des agréments et des
illusions du monde.

8

"THE BRAVEST ARE THE TENDEREST"

Madoc fled from the shepherd land and from the hospitable coffin of Queen Ainath, wherein optimism was denied him. Now he goes westerly, into the mountainous country of the Emperor Pandras, the third of that name.

There Madoc encountered a gleaming company of archers and spearmen with red lions blazoned upon their shields. Their Emperor rode before them, in red armor, mounted upon a roan stallion: and they went thus marching to make war against the people of Ethion, as was their annual custom.

"Our old traditions and our national honor must be preserved," declared the Emperor, "but, nevertheless, this year a war is rather inconvenient."

Then Madoc sang the newest song which he had made with his black pen. He sang very movingly of how many young men would be killed in the impending war, and of how this fact would be a source of considerable distress to their mothers.

The spearmen and the archers dropped each a tear from each eye: the Emperor himself was heard to clear his throat. "I have a mother," said one warrior.

His neighbor replied, "I have not; but I formerly had one, and the principle is the same."

The entire army agreed that the principle was excellent; a retreat was sounded; and war was deferred.

9

PHILANTHROPY PROSPERS

Then Madoc made yet other songs for the war-loving people of the Emperor Pandras. He made fine stirring songs about philanthropy, and many simple chanteys such as workmen use at their labors.

The warriors turned from their belligerent raids, to the building of schoolhouses and hospitals and public drinking-fountains and domed temples for their three national deities. Laboring, these warriors sang the songs which Madoc had made, and his songs put a new vigor in them: their philanthropic endeavors went forward the more nimbly because of Madoc's noble and inspiring songs.

"Build," Madoc sang, "for the welfare of those who come hereafter! Create for them a fairer and more enlightened world! Build, as befits the children of the great Builder!"

But in a while he heard another music: he reflected how stupid were these perspiring and large-muscled persons who toiled for the welfare of a problematic and, it well might be, an unmeritorious posterity, for people who had done nothing whatever to place anybody under any least obligations: and his songs, which brought benevolence and vigor into the living of all other persons appeared to Madoc rather silly now that again he had heard the skirling music of Ettarre the witch-woman.

10

SPOILS OF THE VICTOR

But the people of Ethion, after they had waited a reasonable while for their annual war to begin, lost patience before this disrespect for tradition, and bestirred themselves. They invaded the country of the Emperor Pandras. They were driven back and were slaughtered cosily, in their own homes, which were then destroyed.

"Our triumph is gratifying," said Pandras, after he had attended divine worship and had sent for Madoc. "Only, now that we have won this war, it seems right we should pay for it; now that we have laid waste the cities of Ethion, to rebuild them is our manifest duty: and in consequence I shall have to redouble, or perhaps it would be more simple merely to multiply by five, the taxes which are now being paid by my people."

"Yes, Majesty," said Madoc, sighing somewhat.

"It follows, Madoc, that immediately after we have tried and hanged the surviving leaders of Ethion, we shall need a new song from you, as to the brotherhood of all mankind and as to the delight which a proper-minded person gets out of discomfort when it helps his enemies to live at ease, because otherwise my people may not enjoy paying five times as many taxes."

"I withdraw, sir, to complete this song," said Madoc, and after that, he withdrew, not merely from the presence of Pandras, but from out of the country of Pandras.

11

THE COMFORTABLE MUSIC

Just so did it fare with Madoc in many kingdoms. He wandered everywhither, writing noble songs with his black pen. He sang these songs before great notabilities, before the Soldan of Ethiopia under a purple awning worked with silver crescents, and before the Pope of Rome in a white marble room quite empty of all furnishing, and before the Old Man of the Mountains beside a fire in a grove of fir trees at midnight. Everywhere people of every estate delighted in Madoc's songmaking, and they applauded the refining influence of his art.

Wheresoever Madoc sang, though it were in a thieves' kitchen or in the dark cell of a prison, his comforting music became a spur to the magnanimity of his hearers. They overflowed forthwith with altruism and kindliness and every manner of virtue which was not too immediately expensive: they loved their fellows, upon no provocation detectable by Madoc: and they exulted to be the favored children and the masterworks of Whoever happened to be their tribal god, in a universe especially designed for them and their immediate relatives to occupy.

And Madoc envied the amiable notions which he provoked but might not share. For always, when his music soared at its most potent, he heard the skirling of another nature of music, which was all a doubtfulness and a discontent.

12

PUZZLE OF ALL ARTISTS

Yet, as it seemed, no other person heard that skirling music. No other person willed to hear a music which doubtfulness and discontent made unexhilarating. They thronged, instead, to hear the sugared and the grandiose music which Madoc peddled, and which, like a drug, buoyed up its hearers with self-approval as concerned the present and with self-confidence as touched what was to come.

They listened, and they grinned complacently, who were—the kings and the archbishops and the barons and the plowmen alike,—each one of them already a skeleton and a grinning death's-head so very thinly veiled with flesh and hair. They grinned, while at the feet of each lay crouched the inescapable gloom of his shadow, to serve as an ever-present reminder of that darkness which would presently leap and devour him. Meanwhile they listened to the bedrugging music which Madoc peddled: and every heart made of red, moving dust, upon a brief vacation from the lawns and gutters of earth, was exulting.

It troubled Madoc whenever he heard any of his hearers talk exaltedly about the songs which Madoc made with his black quill, and it troubled Madoc that not any of the noble songs which he was making could ever wholly shut out from Madoc's ears the skirling music of Ettarre the witch-woman.

13

LEADS TO A LIZARD

Therefore he went to Maya of the Fair Breasts, who
controlled Wednesday. Before her at that instant stood
an amber basin with green stones set about the rim of
it. Inside this basin was the appearance of a shining lizard with very red, protuberant eyes which moved and
glittered as the panting creature whispered to Dame
Maya about that which was to come.

When Madoc came, the wise woman arose and put
aside her cold, familiar counsellor. She went toward
young Madoc with a light of wooing in her proud and
sullen face. He found her exceedingly handsome, but
he said nothing about this.

Instead, before her kindling gaze, he looked downward. Thus it was that he saw the lizard had put on the
appearance of a tiny silver-colored pig. As Madoc
looked, this pig became a little horse, and then a sheep,
and after that an ox, drifting out of one dwarfed bright
shaping into another shaping just as a cloud changes.
But Madoc said nothing about this, either.

He said only, "Do you, who are all-wise, show me
that way in which I may win to the accursed witch Ettarre, who has made empty my life, who permits no
magnanimities to flourish in my parched heart, and
who turns to mockery the noble songs that I write with
the quill pen made of a feather from the wing of the
Father of All Lies!"

14

HOW POETS MAY REFORM

Dame Maya led him to a peaceful place where every kind of domestic animal was dozing in her fine market-garden upon Mispec Moor. Sheep and asses and pigs and oxen and draught-horses all rested comfortably in this peaceful place. They had not any care in the world, and no desires save those which food and sleeping satisfied.

The wise woman said, "Through a magic well known to me, poor Madoc, you may become as one of these who have been my husbands."

He asked, "Were these once men?"

Maya of the Fair Breasts answered him, reassuringly, "Yes: all these quiet and useful creatures at one time were mere poets, troubled as you are now troubled, and all these have I saved from that music which is made by the witch-woman, as presently I will save you."

Madoc cried out, "I do not ask for salvation, but for vengeance!"

She said, "In vengeance there is neither ease nor wisdom; but upon Mispec Moor are both."

Madoc replied, "Nevertheless, I prefer that you tell me in what way I may come to the accursed witch, and may make an end of her music and of her also."

The sullen wise woman answered, standing now more near to him, "That way I will not ever tell you, because I like too much your appearance."

15

RIGHT-THINKING REMEDIED

Then Madoc sang yet another of the songs which he
had written with the quill from the wing of the Father
of All Lies. He sang of how much good there is in
even the very worst of us, and of that priceless spark of
divinity which glows in every human breast and needs
but properly to be fostered.

The well-nourished beasts that once had been poets
arose forthwith, and each lurched clumsily about upon
his hind legs. "Let us be worthy, yet, even yet, of that
heritage which we have denied! Let us abandon this
wicked market-garden wherein are only ease and glut-
tony, let us discomfort the world's ease everywhere
with right-thinking and with very other high-minded
kind of intrepid morality!"

So they babbled and floundered about Madoc, who
all the while sang on exaltedly and thought what silly
creatures seemed these bemired and madly aspiring
overfed animals.

But Dame Maya winced to see her fair name as a
competent wife thus imperiled, now that all her trans-
figured husbands were in revolt. She hastily told Madoc
the way to the Waste Beyond the Moon: he ended his
singing: and the domestic animals fell back contentedly
into the incurious sloth and the fat ease of the wise
woman's market-garden, out of which Madoc passed
toward his allotted doom.

PART THREE

OF MADOC IN THE MOON

*Le chevalier Madoc lui dit: Vous voir est ce
qui pouvait m'arriver de plus agréable, et je
voudrais être avec vous jusqu'à la mort.
—Cela peut bien être, dit la jeune fille.*

16

LEADS TO THE MOON

All that which Maya of the Fair Breasts had commanded Madoc performed, with his sword and a
forked rod and a cup and a five-pointed talisman. This
magic brought to him a monster shaped like a
feathered lion, but eight-and-one-half times as large,
and having the head and wings of a fighting-cock.
Upon the breast of the hippogriffin grew red plumage;
its back was of a dark blue color; and its wings were
white.

Such was the gaily tinted steed upon which Madoc
rode, along strange and unhealthy highways. The spirits of the air beset him: sylphs beckoned to this fine
young fellow: Lilith, that very dreadful and delicious
Bride of the Serpent, pursued him a great way, because
she liked the appearance of Madoc. Nevertheless, he
won unhurt to the pale mists and the naked desert
space behind the moon.

Ettarre was at her accursed music: the gray place

throbbed with it: it seemed the heartbeat of the universe, and the winds that moved between the stars were attuned to its doubtfulness and discontent.

"Turn, witch, and die!" cried Madoc furiously, as he came toward Ettarre with his sword drawn.

She made an end of her skirling music, she rose, and now for the first time he saw the face of Ettarre. Then Madoc knew it was not hatred which had drawn him to her.

17

MORE LUNAR HAPPENINGS

He put her lips away from his lips. Madoc saw that the desert place was changed. About them now was a quiet-colored paradise: lilies abounded everywhere, and many climbing white roses also were lighted by the clear and tempered radiancy of early dawn. White rabbits were frisking to every side. Instead of that music which was all a doubtfulness and a discontent, you could now hear doves calling to their mates very softly.

"Love has wrought this lovely miracle," Ettarre remarked, without any sign of disapproval.

Madoc replied: "Love has brought beauty into this place. Now also shall my ever-living love bring liberty to you, and loose you from all bonds excepting only my embraces."

Ettarre answered: "I like your appearance: your embrace is strong and comforting: but there can be no liberty for me until the 725 years of my post-lunar music-making are ended. No man may alter any word of the Norns' decree: and they have decreed that for 725 years my master Sargatanet shall retain me here as his scholar and his prisoner."

Madoc said, jealously: "What else has this Sargatanet taught you save music? No, do you not tell me that, but do you tell me instead the way to your music-master, whom I intend to discharge."

18

TRUISMS COME HIGH

Thereafter hand in hand they passed toward Sargatanet where he sat under a vine which bore fruit of five different colors. Kneeling before the porphyry throne of Sargatanet at that instant were the five lords of hunger and fire and cold, of darkness and of madness. To each of these he was assigning the vexations to be completed during that week.

When his servants had departed earthward, to work the will of Sargatanet among mankind, and to stir up in human hearts the doubtfulness and the discontent which endlessly oppressed the heart of Sargatanet, then the gaunt master of the Waste Beyond the Moon bent down toward where Madoc and Ettarre stood at his ankle. He heard the plea of Madoc, and he heard the threats of Madoc, impartially; and Sargatanet shrugged his winged shoulders.

"That which is written by the Norns," said Sargatanet, "cannot be evaded. The Norns have written all Earth's history, they have recorded its Contents and its Colophon also. No man nor any god may alter any word of that which the Gray Three have written. For one, I would not grieve if such an evasion were possible, because Ettarre has now been my scholar and my prisoner for some 592 years. And you know what women are. That is why I do not bother to criticize seriously the writing of the three Norns."

19

THE NATURE OF WOMEN

Then Madoc said: "I am not certain that I do know what women are; but I know their ways are pleasant. Their lips have been dear to me. They have yet other possessions in which I have taken delight. A woman is a riddle without any answer; she is not mere bed-furnishing; she is a rapture very brightly colored; she is a holiness which I am content to adore without understanding: and among all women who keep breath in them Ettarre has not her equal.

"And besides," Madoc continued, "Ettarre is more durable than are other women; for she is more than 592 years old; and never in the moon would you suspect it. Hers and hers only, it has been remarked by the diffident voice of understatement, is that perfect beauty of which all young poets have had their fitful glimpses. Her beauty is ageless. Her beauty has in it no flaw. And so, even if the completeness of the beauty of Ettarre may demolish common-sense, yet a generous-minded person will be ready to condone its excesses. A generous-minded person will concede, without any cowardly beating about the bushes of reticence, that among all women who keep breath in them Ettarre has not her equal."

Sargatanet replied: "Do you please stop talking. For we know what poets are; and all we immortals know what women are. But we cannot do anything whatever about it."

20

LOVE SCORES A POINT

Then Sargatanet lifted the two lovers 592 feet, and through as many dead years, to the stone table beside his throne; and now before them lay open a book of which the pages were as tall as Sargatanet. This was the book in which the Norns had written the history of our world and all that has been upon Earth and all that will ever be.

"As I was saying," Sargatanet continued, "we know what women are. They very certainly do not excel as creative writers. Their imagination needs chastening; their bent is toward the excessively romantic. Thus the gray ladies have written a great deal of nonsense, and they have permitted entirely too much to hinge upon love affairs. Nevertheless, no man nor any god may alter any word of the Norns' out-of-date nonsense, of which all men and gods are a portion. So do these ladies keep the feminine privilege of the last word. And here it is written, plainly enough, that I shall retain Ettarre until the 725 years of her captivity are ended."

Madoc walked far up the page to inspect that entry in the giant book. "There is no need," said Madoc, "to alter any word."

With that, he took out the quill pen which had fallen from the wing of the Father of All Lies, he stooped, and with this pen Madoc inserted after the digit seven a decimal point.

21

THE PEN OF THE CENSOR

And then of course—because whatsoever is written in the Book of the Norns must be fulfilled, and figures in particular cannot lie—then a changing followed of all that which had been since seven years and three months after the beginning of Ettarre's captivity in the Waste Beyond the Moon.

Everything which had existed upon Earth during the last 584 years passed very swiftly and confusedly before the eyes of Madoc, as these things swirled backward into oblivion, now that none of these things had ever happened.

Twenty generations of mankind and all their blusterings upon land and sea went by young Madoc in the appearance of a sandstorm. Each grain of sand was a town or, it might be, an opulent and famous city, just as that city had been builded laboriously and painfully by some twenty generations of a people's cluttered, flustered, humdrum, troubleful, lumped hubbub, ungrudged because of that people's high dreams.

All the toil and glory and folly and faith and irrational happiness of the many millions whom Madoc's pen had put out of living had now not ever existed, because that which is written in the Book of the Norns must be fulfilled. And it was now written in this book that the bondage of Ettarre should endure for only seven and a quarter years.

22

NEAR YGGDRASILL

Not ever before had anybody essayed to cheat the Norns in quite this fashion: and so, from their quiet studio, by Yggdrasill, the Gray Three noticed this quaint expurgating of their work almost at once.

Verdandi, in fact, took off her reading glasses so as to observe just what was happening over yonder. "Oh, yes, I see!" she said comfortably. "It is only a poet altering the history of Earth."

Her sisters glanced up from their writing: and they all smiled. Urdhr remarked, "These poets! They are always trying to escape their allotted doom."

But Skuld looked rather pensively at each of the two other literary ladies before she said, "One almost pities them at times."

Then Urdhr laughed outright. "My darling, you waste sympathy in this sweet fashion because we also were poets when we wrote Earth's Epic. For myself, I grant we made a mistake to put any literary people in the book. Still, it is a mistake to which most beginners are prone: and that story, you must remember, was one of our first efforts. All inexperienced girls must necessarily write balderdash. So we put poets in that book, and death, and love, and common-sense, and I can hardly remember what other incredibilities."

With that, they all laughed again, to think of their art's crude beginnings.

23

THE CALL OF EARTH

"A poet is bold. There is no god in any current mythology who would have made bold to cheat the Norns," said Sargatanet, with odd quietness.

Madoc replied, "My pen is almighty; my pen is equally good at music-making and at arithmetic."

Sargatanet looked, for some while, with very pale blue eyes, at the two midgets down there beside his gold-sandaled feet. "Your pen makes music," Sargatanet then said, "such as all men delight in. Yet it cannot make my music. Your pen cannot write down nor may it cancel any line of the music which I eternally devise to be an eternal vexing to every poet, no matter what may be his boldness."

But, in the while that Sargatanet spoke such nonsense. Madoc had uplifted his Ettarre to the back of his hippogriffin. "I have done with all vexations!" Madoc cried out, as the glittering monster spread its huge white wings, and, flapping upward from behind the moon, plunged mightily toward Earth.

Thereafter the hippogriffin went as a comet goes, because its heart remembered that upon this Earth, among the dear hills of Noenhir, were its warm nest builded out of cedar trees and its loved mate brooding over her agate-colored eggs. And upon the monster's back, exulting Madoc also passed with a high heart, toward his allotted doom.

PART FOUR

OF MADOC IN THE OLD TIME

*Ils vécurent ainsi pendant quelque temps: et
la plume noire lui donna de l'argent, du bien,
tout ce qu'il faut pour vivre heureux dans le
monde. Ensuite le chevalier Madoc partit en-
core pour voyager.*

24

THE OLD TIME REITERATES

Thus it was that Madoc and his Ettarre returned to an
Earth rejuvenated by Madoc's pen, and lived in the old
time which long and long ago had perished before the
time of Madoc.

Now the Northmen ruled as lords of Noenhir, where
the hippogriffin had left its riders. These Northmen
were an unsophisticated and hardy people, exceedingly
brave and chaste, whose favorite recreations were
drunkenness and song-making and piracy.

They welcomed the singer who could make such
comfortable and uplifting songs as Madoc wrote with
the quill which had fallen from the wing of the Father
of All Lies. Madoc sang to them about their own importance, about the excellence of their daily habits, and
about the splendid and luxurious future which was in
store for their noble Nordic race: he made for them
that music which incites mankind toward magnanimity.

Under their winged helmets the ruddy faces of the attendant pirates were aglow with altruism and kindliness and every manner of virtue. In their thorps and homesteads they welcomed Madoc, and paid him well. So Madoc built at Noenhir a fine wooden hall: he and his Ettarre began housekeeping: and Madoc had not anything to trouble him, and his fair wife's embraces were now as dear to him as once had been the embraces of Ainath.

25

CONFECTIONER'S REPOSE

Madoc had not anything to trouble him. For many years he made his songs, and these songs made his hearers better and more happy. The only difference was that Madoc, now, had invested some little faith in his optimistic and uplifting songs; and much of what they said appeared to Madoc to be, quite possibly, almost true, here and there.

Madoc lived statelily, with all manner of comfort, in his broad hall, with dragons handsomely painted upon each end of it, and with a stout palisade of oak logs enclosing everything. The most prominent thieves and cutthroats in the country delighted to hear and to reward the singing of Madoc; Druids had crowned Madoc with the sacred mistletoe, as the king of skalds; the fame of Madoc was spread everywhither about the world: and the renowned poet had not anything to trouble him, and no heavier task confronted Madoc than to make praiseworthy music.

But Ettarre made no more music. "How was it that little air of yours used to run, my darling?" her illustrious husband would ask, very carelessly.

And Ettarre would reply, with the common sense of a married woman: "How can I remember a music I never learned until centuries after this morning? And besides, what time have I for such fiddle-faddle with all these children on my hands?"

26

WHAT WAS NOT TROUBLE

Madoc knew that he had not anything to trouble him. You were not really troubled by your vagrant notion that the face of Ainath or the face of Maya, or the more terrible strange pallor of Queen Lilith's face, seemed now and then to be regarding the well-thought-of poet that was Madoc, with a commingling— for so illogical are all daydreams—of derision and of pity.

Nor could you call it a trouble that, now and then, in such misleading reveries as were apt to visit idle persons when upon the plains and hills of Noenhir the frail tints of spring were resting lightly, and ever so briefly, the women whom tall, red-haired young Madoc had thrust aside, because of the magic laid upon the prime of his manhood, seemed to have been more dear and more desirable than anybody could expect a mere boy to appreciate.

Nor was it a trouble—rather, was it, when properly regarded, a blessing—that the one woman whom you had ever loved was endlessly wrangling nowadays over your meals and the validity of your underclothing, and over the faithlessness of all servants, and over the doings of her somewhat tedious children; and was endowed nowadays, with the chronic and the never wholly smothered dissatisfaction which is the mark of a competent housekeeper. Madoc very well knew that he had not anything to trouble him.

27

TOO MUCH IS NOT ENOUGH

Meanwhile love's graduates lived with large ease and
splendor. About their rheumatic knees were now the
flaxen heads of grandchildren: they had broad farm-
lands, and thralls to do their bidding, and many cattle
lowed in their barns. Life had given them all the good
things which life is able to give. And Madoc had no
desires save those which food and sleeping satisfied,
and lean red-haired Madoc now was lean and gray and
pompous, and unaccountably peevish also.

He rarely wrote new songs. But everywhere his elder
songs had been made familiar, in all quarters of the
world, by the best-thought-of pirates and sea rovers, as
the sort of thing of which the decadent younger generation was incapable. Everybody everywhere was
charmed by their resonant beguilement. Even the most
callow poets admitted that with a little more frankness
about sexual matters and the unfairness of social condi-
tions the old fellow would have been passable.

Madoc, in brief, had not any care or need, nor, it
was plain, any contentment. He fell more and more often to asking Ettarre if she could not recollect, just for
the fun of the thing, a strain or two of the music from
behind the moon with which she used to keep him
without any home and miserable. And the old lady
would tell him more and more pettishly that she had
no patience whatever with his nonsense.

28

THE RESPECTABLE GESTURE

Then his wife died. She died sedately, with the best
medical and churchly aid, and after an appropriate
leave-taking of her numerous family. There was a loneliness upon Madoc when he saw her white and shriv-
eled old body,—so troublingly made strange by the
forlorn aloofness of the dead,—lying upon the neat bed
among four torches of pine wood. His loneliness closed
over him like a cold flood.

He thought confusedly of the fierce loving which had
been between them in their youth; and of their high
adventuring because of a music which was not wholly
of this earth; and of the ensuing so many years through
which a sensible, unmoonstruck married couple had
shared in all and in howsoever trivial matters loyally;
and of how those fallen pale lips would not ever find
fault with him any more. It was then that he fetched
the black pen with which Madoc had written his
world-famous songs; and he laid his pen in the cold
hand of Ettarre.

"I call you all to witness," said Madoc, "that this
day has robbed my living of its purpose and of every
joy. I call you all to witness that I shall make no more
songs now that I have lost my heart's arbiter and my
art's arbitrary and most candid critic. Let my fame end
with my happiness! Let the provokers of each perish in
the one burning!"

29

"THIS TRULY DOES NOT DIE"

Thereafter Madoc stood beside the funeral pyre. About him were his children and his grandchildren. A company of white-robed boys, from the temple of the local goddess of fertility, were singing what many persons held to be the very noblest of Madoc's many superb songs, the poet's great hymn about human immortality and about the glorious heritage of man that is the ever-living and beloved heir of Heaven.

Four bondwomen were killed, and their bodies were arranged gracefully about the pyre, along with the furnishings of Ettarre's toilet table and her cooking utensils and her sewing implements. Then fire was laid to all. Ettarre's frail aged body was burned so, with the black pen that was in her hand.

The white-robed boys sang very movingly; and they enumerated sweetly and comfortably, and exultantly, the joys into which this noble and most virtuous lady had entered yesterday afternoon. But old Madoc heard another music, unheard through all the years in which he had held Ettarre away from her lunar witcheries to be his bedfellow upon Earth: and the bereaved widower shocked everybody by laughing aloud, now that he heard once more the skirling music from behind the moon which, whether it stayed heard or unheard, was decreed to be the vexing of him who had cheated the Norns.

30

LEADS TO CONTENTMENT

Such was the end of his prosperity and honor, and such was the beginning of his happiness. Old Madoc went now as a vagabond, a trifle crazed, a trifle ragged, but utterly satisfied to follow after that music which none other heard.

Its maker fled always a little before him, inaccessibly: she held before her that with which she made her music, upon no cumbersome bronze harp but upon her heartstrings: her averted face he could not see, nor did he any longer wonder if it were Ettarre or some other who guided him. It was enough that Madoc followed after the music woven out of all doubtfulness and discontent which rang more true than any other music.

He followed its sweet skirling down the lanes and streets in which home-keeping persons chanted the famous songs of Madoc. Everywhere the smiling old wanderer could see his fellows living more happily and more worthily because of the contentedness and the exultant faith which was in these songs.

He was glad that he had made these songs, to be a cordial to guiltless men who had not cheated the Norns. Meanwhile—for him who had outwitted the Gray Three,—there stayed always yonder, always just ahead, another music, which was not wholly of this earth, and which a vagabond alone might be following after always, as was his allotted doom.

THE BEST POSSIBLE POSTSCRIPT

Such is the story of Madoc: but of the story of Ettarre this is only a very little part. For her story is not lightly to be ended (so do the learned declare) by the death of any woman's body which for a while Ettarre has been wearing: nor is her music-making ended either (the young say), no matter to what ears time and conformity may have brought deafness.

I think we oldsters hardly need to debate the affair, with so many other matters to be discussed and put in order, now that all evenings draw in. If there be any music coming from behind the moon it echoes faintlier than does the crackling of the hearth fire; it is drowned by the piping voices of our children. We—being human—may pause to listen now and then, half wistfully, it may be, for an unrememberable cadence which only the young hear: yet we whom time has made deaf to this music are not really discontent; and common decency forbids one to disturb the home circle (as that blundering Lamech did, you may remember) by crying out, "I have slain a young man to my hurt!"

EXPLICIT

FRANK RICHARD STOCKTON

(1834–1902)

Frank R. Stockton, noted American humorist, was
born in Philadelphia and received his formal education
from the common schools of that city. After gradua-
tion, he became a successful wood engraver, but writing remained his first love. As a young boy he
voraciously read fairy tales, and while still in school he
began writing his own. Many of these were good
enough to be accepted for publication. He kept at his
writing while practicing the art of engraving, but the
success of *Ting-a-Ling* (1870), a collection of short
stories for children, prompted him to devote all his
time and energy to writing. Thus, in 1872, he turned to
journalism, and spent the next ten years or so working
for newspaper and magazine concerns. During this
period he also continued to write many children's
works, including *Roundabout Rambles in Lands of
Fact and Fancy* (1872), *Tales Out of School* (1875),
A Jolly Fellowship (1880), *The Floating Prince and
Other Fairy Tales* (1881), and *The Story of Viteau*
(1884). In 1879 Stockton published the book that was
to make him famous, *Rudder Grange*. It was so successful that he wrote two sequels: *The Rudder
Grangers Abroad* (1891) and *Pomona's Travels*
(1894). After Stockton retired from the magazine
business he wrote his most popular novel, *The Casting
Away of Mrs. Lecks and Mrs. Aleshine* (1886). Stockton's humorous novels are truly delightful, but he is
probably best remembered for his short stories, the
most widely known of which is "The Lady or the Tiger" (1884). Those who knew him well described him

as a gentle man with an enviable capacity for always looking at the bright and humorous side of life.

In many respects "The Accommodating Circumstance" resembles the traditional fairy tale. Within its pages the reader will find a cruel prince, narrow escapes, chivalrous deeds, an abundance of magic, and the inevitable marriage of beautiful maiden and charming hero. However, the quaint and whimsical humor of Stockton simply will not allow one of his stories to become typical or commonplace, and so the reader can expect to find a number of delightful surprises. Most obvious, is the device of the accommodating circumstance itself. Brought into being through a magical incantation, the sprightly "Green Goblin of the Third Word" literally becomes the accommodating circumstance of this memorable tale. The device is effectively handled by Stockton, and creates much of the narrative's lively and engaging action. Unique, too, is the central episode of the story, which features a curious "School for Men," where the students (full-grown men, of course) are taught the proper treatment of boys—by schoolmasters who are boys. Depend upon Stockton to develop such a delightful and satiric reversal of situation and perspective.

❧ The Accommodating Circumstance ❧

Frank R. Stockton

It was on a bright afternoon, many, many years ago, that a young baron stood on the stone steps that led down from the door of his ancestral home. That great castle was closed and untenanted, and the baron was taking leave of it forever. His father, who was now dead, had been very unfortunate, and had been obliged to sell his castle and his lands. But he had made it a condition that the nobleman who bought the estate should allow the young baron to occupy it until he was twenty-one years of age.

This period had now arrived, and although the purchaser, who did not need the castle, had told the baron that he might remain there as long as he chose, the young man was too high-spirited to depend upon the charity of anyone, and he determined to go forth and seek a fortune for himself. His purpose was to go to the town of the Prince of Zisk, a journey of a few days, and to offer to join an army which the prince intended to lead against a formidable band of robbers who had set up a stronghold in his dominions. If he should distinguish himself in this army, the young baron hoped that he might rise to an honorable position. At any rate, he would earn a livelihood for himself and be dependent upon no one.

But it was a very sad thing for him to leave this home where he was born and where he had spent most of his life. His parents were dead, he had no relatives, and now he was to leave the house which had been so dear to him. He stood with one foot upon the ground and the other upon the bottom step and looked up to the great hall door, which he had shut and locked behind him, as if he were unwilling to make the movement which would finally separate him from the old place.

As he stood thus, he heard someone approaching, and turning, he saw an old woman and a young girl coming toward the castle. Each carried a small bundle, and besides these, the young girl had a little leathern bag, which was fastened securely to her belt.

"Good sir," said the woman, "can you tell me if we can rest for the night in this castle? My granddaughter and I have walked since early morning, and I am very tired. It is a long time since we have passed a house, and I fear we might not come to another one today."

The baron hesitated for a moment. It was true that there was no other house for several miles, and the old woman looked as if she was not able to walk any farther. The castle was shut up and deserted, for he had discharged his few servants that morning and he was just about to leave it himself; but for all that, he could not find it in his heart to say that there was no refuge there for these two weary travelers. His family had always been generous and hospitable, and although there was very little that he could offer now, he felt that he must do what he could and not send away an old woman and a young girl to perish on the road in the cold winter night which was approaching.

"The castle is a bare and empty place," he said, "but you can rest here for the night." And so saying, he went up the steps, opened the door, and invited the travelers to enter.

Of course if they stayed there that night, he must do so also, for he could not leave the castle in the care of strangers, although these appeared to be very inoffensive people. And thus he very unexpectedly re-entered the home he thought he had left forever.

There was some wood by the fireplace in the great hall, and the baron made a fire. He had left no provisions in the house, having given everything of the kind to the servants, but he had packed into his wallet a goodly store of bread, meat, and cheese, and with these he spread a meal for the wayfarers. When they had been strengthened by the food and warmed by the fire, the old woman told her story.

"You must not think, kind sir," she said, "that we are poor outcasts and wanderers. I have a very pleasant little home of my own, where my granddaughter and myself have lived very happily ever since she was a little baby, and now, as you see, she is quite grown up. But Litza—that is her name—has a godmother who is a very peculiar person, whom we are all obliged to obey; and she came to us yesterday and gave Litza a little iron box, which is in that leathern bag she carries, and charged her to start with me the next morning and take it to its destination."

In order to account for the condition of his house, the baron then told his story. Litza and her grandmother were grieved to hear the account of the young nobleman's ill fortune, and the old woman said if they prevented his journey they might yet try to go on.

"Oh, no," said the baron. "I was starting too late anyway, for it had taken me so long to bid good-bye to my old home. It will be just as well for me to go to-morrow. So you and your granddaughter shall have a room here tonight, and all will be well."

The next morning, after a breakfast which quite finished the baron's provisions, the three set out together, as their roads lay in the same direction. About noon the old woman became very tired and hungry. There was no house in sight, and the road seemed quite deserted.

"If I had known it would be so far," she said to herself, "we would not have come. I am too old to walk for two days. If I could only remember the meaning of the words, I would surely try them now. But I cannot remember—I cannot remember."

When this old woman was a little girl, she had lived with Litza's godmother, who was the daughter of a magician and was now over a hundred years old. From this person she had learned five magical words, which, when repeated, would each bring up a different kind of goblin or spirit. In her youth Litza's grandmother had never used these words, for she was a timid girl; and now for years, although she remembered the words, she had entirely forgotten what sort of creature each one would call forth. Some of these beings were good, and some she knew were very bad, and so, for fear of repeating the wrong word, she had never used any one of them. But now she felt that if ever she needed the help of goblin or fairy, she needed it this day.

"I can walk no farther," she said, "and that young man cannot carry me. If I do not use my words, I must perish here. I will try one of them, come what may." And so, with fear and trembling, she repeated aloud the third word.

Instantly there appeared before her a strange being. He was of a pale pea-green color, with great black eyes, and long arms and legs which seemed continually in motion. He jumped into the air, he snapped his fingers over his head, and suddenly taking from his pockets two empty bottles and an earthern jar, he began tossing them in the air, catching them dexterously as they fell.

"Who on earth are you?" said the old woman, much astonished.

"I am the Green Goblin of the Third Word," replied the other, still tossing up his jar and bottles, "but I am generally known as the Accommodating Circumstance."

"I don't know exactly what that may be," said the old woman, "but I wish that instead of a juggler with empty bottles and jars you were a pastrycook with a basket full of something to eat."

Instantly the goblin changed into a pastrycook carrying a large basket filled with hot meat pies and buns. The old woman jumped to her feet with delight and beckoned to the others, who had just turned around to see where she was.

"Come here," she cried. "Here is a pastrycook who has arrived just in the nick of time."

The party now made a good meal, for which the old woman would not allow the baron to pay anything, as it was a repast to which she had invited him. And then they moved on again, the pastrycook following. But although the grandmother was refreshed by the food, she was still very tired. She fell back a little and walked by the side of the pastrycook.

"I wish," she said, "that you were a man with a chair on your back. Then you might carry me."

Instantly the pastrycook changed into a stout man in a blue blouse, with a wooden armchair strapped to his back. He stooped down, and the old woman got into the chair. He then walked on and soon overtook the baron and Litza.

"Ah!" cried the old woman. "See what good fortune has befallen me! The pastrycook has gone, and this man with his chair has just arrived. Now I can travel with ease and comfort."

"What wonderful good fortune!" cried Litza.

"Wonderful good fortune, indeed!" exclaimed the baron, equally pleased.

The four now pursued their way, the old woman comfortably nodding in the chair, to which the baron had secured her with his belt. In about an hour the road branched, and the baron asked the chair man which way led to the town of Zisk. But the man, who was a dull, heavy fellow, did not know, and the baron took the road to the right. After walking two or three miles, they came to a wide river, at the edge of which the road stopped. On a post was a signboard on which was painted "Blow ye horn for ye ferryman." Below this hung a large horn, with a small pair of bellows attached to the mouthpiece.

"That is a good idea," said the baron. "One ought to be able to blow a horn very well with a pair of bellows." And so saying, he seized the handle of the bellows and blew a blast upon the horn that made Litza and her grandmother clap their hands to their ears. "I think that will bring the ferryman," said the baron, as he helped the old woman to get out of her chair.

In a few minutes they heard the sound of oars, and a boat made its appearance from behind a point of land to the right. To their surprise it was rowed by a boy about fourteen years old. When the boat touched the shore, they all got in.

"I am afraid you cannot row so heavy a load," said the baron to the boy; "but perhaps this good man will help you."

The boy, who was well dressed and of a grave demeanor, looked sternly at the baron. "Order must be kept in the boat," he said. "Sit down, all of you, and I will attend to the rowing." And he began to pull slowly but steadily from the shore. But instead of rowing directly across the river, he rounded the high point to the right and then headed toward an island in the stream.

"Where are you taking us?" asked the baron.

"This is the place to land," replied the boy gruffly. And in a few strokes he ran the boat ashore at the island.

A large house stood not far away from the water, and the baron thought he would go there and make some inquiries, for he did not like the manner of the boy in the boat. He accordingly stepped ashore and, followed by the rest of his party, approached the house. When they reached it, they saw over the door, in large black letters, the words "School for Men." Two boys, well dressed and sedate, came out to meet them and ushered them in.

"What is this place?" asked the baron, looking about him.

"It is a school," was the reply, "established by boys for the proper instruction and education of men. We have found that there are no human beings who need to be taught so much as men; and it is to supply this long-felt want that we have set up our school. By diverting the ferry from its original course we have obtained a good many scholars who would not otherwise have entered."

"What do you teach men?" asked the baron.

"The principal thing we try to teach them," said the other, "is the proper treatment of boys. But you will know all about this in good time."

"What I wish most now to know," said the baron, smiling, "is whether or not we can all obtain lodging here tonight. It is already growing dark."

"Did these two ladies come with you?" asked the boy.

"Yes," answered the baron.

"It was very good of them," said the boy. "Of course they can stay here all night. We always try to accommodate friends who come with scholars."

It was past suppertime at the school, but the baron and his party were provided with a good meal, and Litza and her grandmother were shown to a guest chamber on the ground floor. One boy then took charge of the chair-carrier, while another conducted the baron to a small chamber upstairs, where he found everything very comfortable and convenient.

"You can sit up and read for an hour or two," said the boy. "We don't put our scholars all into one great room like a barrack and make them put out their lights and go to bed just at the time when other people begin to enjoy the evening."

When the baron arose the next morning, he was informed that the principal wished to see him, and he was taken downstairs into a room where there was a very solemn-looking boy sitting in an armchair before a fire. This was the principal, and he arose and gravely shook hands with the baron.

"I am glad to welcome you to our school," he said, "and I hope you will do honor to it."

"I have no intention of remaining here," said the baron.

The principal regarded him with a look of great severity. "Silence, sir!" he said. "It pains me to think of the sorrow which will fill the hearts of your children

or your young relatives if they could hear you de-
liberately declare that you did not wish to avail yourself of the extraordinary educational opportunities
which are offered to you here."

The principal then rang a bell, and two of the largest
scholars, who acted as monitors, entered the room.
"Take this new pupil," he said to them, "to the schoolroom and have him entered in the lowest class. He has
much to learn."

The baron saw that it would be useless to resist
these two tall fellows, who conducted him from the
room, and he peacefully followed them to the large
schoolroom where he was put in a class and given a
lesson to learn.

The subject of the lesson was the folly of supposing
that boys ought not to be trusted with horses, bat-
tleaxes, and all the arms used in war and hunting.
There were twelve reasons proving that men were very
wrong in denying these privileges to boys, and the
baron was obliged to learn them all by heart.

At the other end of the room he saw the chair-carrier, who was hard at work over a lesson on the
wickedness of whipping boys. On the wall, at one end
of the room, was the legend, in large letters, "The
Boy: Know Him, and You Are Educated." At the
other end were the words "Respect Your Youngers."

In the afternoon the baron studied sixteen rules
which proved that boys ought to be consulted in regard
to the schools they were sent to, the number of their
holidays, the style of their new clothes, and many other
things which concerned them more than anyone else.
At the end of the afternoon session the principal made
a short address the school, in which he said that in four
days it would be Christmas, at which time the scholars
would have a month's holiday.

"We believe," he said, "that scholars ought to have
at least that much time at Christmas; and besides, your
instructors need relaxation. But," said he, with a severe
look at the baron, "disaffected newcomers must not

suppose that they will be allowed this privilege. Such pupils will remain here during the holidays."

After this speech, school was dismissed, and the scholars were allowed three hours to play.

The baron was disturbed when he found that he would not be permitted to leave. He had heard that the Prince of Zisk intended to start on his expedition immediately after Christmas; and if he did not get to the town very soon, he could not join his army. So he determined to escape.

Walking about, he met Litza and her grandmother. The old woman was much troubled. She had been told that she could leave whenever she chose, but she felt she could not go away without the chair-carrier, and he was detained as a pupil. She would not explain her trouble to her granddaughter, for she did not wish her to know anything about the magical nature of the assistance she had received. In a few moments the chair-carrier also made his appearance, and then the baron, seeing that none of the boys were in sight, proposed that they should go down to the beach and escape in a ferryboat.

The boat was found there, with the oars, and they all jumped in. The baron and the chair-carrier then each seized an oar and pushed off. They were not a dozen yards from the shore when several of the boys, accompanied by some of the larger pupils, came running down to the beach. The baron could not help smiling when he saw them, and resting on his oar, he made a little speech.

"My young friends," he said, "you seem to have forgotten, when you set up your school, that men, when they become scholars, are as likely to play truant as if they were boys."

To these remarks the boy teachers made no answer, but the big scholars on shore looked at each other and grinned. Then they all stooped down and took hold of a long chain that lay coiled in the shallow water. They began to pull, and the baron soon perceived that the other end of the chain was attached to the boat. He and the chair man pulled as hard as they could at the oars, but in spite of their efforts they were steadily drawn to shore. Litza and her grandmother were then sent to their room, while the baron and the chair man were put to bed without their suppers.

The next day the old grandmother walked about by herself, more troubled than ever, for she was very anxious that Litza should fulfill her mission and that they should get back home before Christmas. And yet she would not go away and leave her magical companion. Just then she saw the chair-carrier looking out of a second-story window, with a blanket wrapped around him.

"Come down here," she said.

"I can't," he answered. "They say I am to stay in bed all day, and they have taken away my clothes."

"You might as well be back with your goblin companions," said the old woman, "for all the use you are to me. I wish you were somebody who could set things straight here."

Instantly there stood by her side a school trustee. He was a boy of grave and pompous demeanor, handsomely dressed, and carrying a large gold-headed cane.

"My good woman," he said, in a stately voice, "is there anything I can do to serve you?"

"Yes, sir," she replied. "My granddaughter and I"—she pointed to Litza, who just then came up—"wish to leave this place as soon as possible and to pursue our journey."

"Of course you may do so," said he. "This is not a school for women."

"But, Grandma," said Litza, "it would be a shame to go away without the poor baron, who is as anxious to get on as we are."

"There is a gentleman here, sir," said the old woman, "who does not wish to stay."

"Did you bring him?" asked the trustee.

"Yes, sir; he came with us."

"And you wish to take him away again?" said he.

"Yes, sir; we do," said Litza.

"Very well, then," said the trustee, severely; "he

shall be dismissed. We will have no pupils here whose children or guardians desire their removal. I will give orders in regard to the matter."

In a few moments the baron's clothes were brought to him, and he was told that he might get out of bed and leave the establishment. When he came down and joined Litza and her grandmother, he looked about him and said, "Where is the chair-carrier? I cannot consent to go away and leave him here."

"Do not trouble yourself about that man," said the grandmother. "He has already taken himself away."

The party, accompanied by the trustee, proceeded to the boat, where the boy ferryman was waiting for them. To the surprise of the baron the trustee got in with them, and they were all rowed to the other side of the river, where they found the road that led to Zisk. The school trustee walked with them, delivering his opinions in regard to the education of men. The baron grew very tired of hearing this talk.

"I am much obliged to this person," he thought, "for having enabled me to get away from that queer school; but he certainly is a dreadful bore. I wish he were going on some other road."

Litza and her grandmother agreed with the baron, and the old woman would gladly have changed the trustee into a chair-carrier again, but she had no opportunity of doing so, for the pompous little fellow never fell back behind the rest of the party, where he could be transformed unobserved. So they all walked on together until they reached the middle of a great plain, when suddenly a large body of horsemen appeared from behind a clump of trees at no great distance.

"It is a band of robbers!" said the baron, stopping and drawing his sword. "I know their flag. And they are coming directly toward us."

The grandmother and Litza were terribly frightened, and the baron turned very pale, for what could his one sword do against all those savage horsemen? As for the school trustee, he was glad to fall back now, and he

crouched behind the baron, nearly scared out of his
wits. He even pushed the old woman aside, so as to
better conceal himself.

"You wretched coward!" she exclaimed. "I wish you
were somebody able to defend us against these robbers."

Instantly there was a great clank of steel, and in the
place of the trustee there stood an immense man, fully
eight feet high, clothed in mail, and armed to the teeth.
At his left side he carried a great sword, and on the
other a heavy mace. In his hand he held a strong bow,
higher than himself. His belt was filled with daggers
and arrows, and at his back was an immense shield.

"Hold this in front of your party," he said to the
baron, setting the shield down before him, "and I will
attend to these rascals."

Quickly fitting a long arrow to his bow, he sent it
directly through the foremost horseman and killed a
man behind him. Arrow after arrow flew through the
air, until half the robbers lay dead on the field. The
rest turned to fly, but the armed giant sprang in among
them, his sword in one hand and his mace in the other,
and in less than five minutes he had slain every one of
them.

"Now, then," said he, returning and taking up his
bow and shield, "I think we may proceed without further fear."

The baron and Litza were no less delighted at their
deliverance than surprised at the appearance of this de-
fender, and the old woman was obliged to explain the
whole matter to them. "I did not want you to know
anything about it," she said to Litza, "for a young girl's
head should not be filled with notions of magic; but the
case was very urgent, and I could not hesitate."

"I am very glad you did not hesitate," said the
baron, "for in a few minutes we should all have been
killed. There was certainly never anything so useful as
your Accommodating Circumstance."

The armed giant was a quiet and obliging fellow,

and he offered to carry the old woman on his shoulder, which she found a very comfortable seat.

Toward evening they arrived in sight of the town of Zisk, and the baron said to the grandmother, "I am very much afraid you will lose your giant, for when the prince sees such a splendid soldier he will certainly enlist him into his army."

"Oh, dear!" cried the old woman, slipping down from the giant's shoulder. "I wish this great fellow was somebody who could not possibly be of any use to the prince as a soldier."

Instantly there toddled toward her a little baby about a year old. She had a white cap on her funny little head and was very round and plump. She had scarcely taken three steps when she stumbled and sat down very suddenly, and then she began to try to pull off one of her little shoes. They all burst out laughing at this queer little creature, and Litza rushed toward the baby and snatched her up in her arms.

"You dear little thing!" she said. "The prince will never take you for a soldier."

"No," said the baron, laughing, "and she can never grow up into one."

It was too late for the baron to see the Prince of Zisk that day, and the party stopped for the night at a little inn in the town. The next morning, as the baron was about to go to the palace, he asked Litza what was her business in Zisk and if he could help her.

"All my godmother told me to do," said the young girl, "was to give this box to the noblest man in Zisk, and of course he is the prince."

"Yes," said the baron; "and as I am on my way to the palace, I may help you to see him."

"Go you with the baron," said the grandmother to Litza, "and I will stay here and take care of this baby. And as soon as you come back I will change her into a long-legged man with two chairs on his back, and we will get home to my cottage as fast as we can."

When the baron and the young girl reached the palace they found the prince in his audience chamber, surrounded by officers and courtiers. Litza stood by the door, while the baron approached the prince and respectfully told him why he had come.

"You are the very man we want!" cried the prince. "I have conceived a most admirable plan of conquering my robber foes, and you shall carry it out. The day after tomorrow is Christmas, and these highwaymen always keep this festival as if they were decent people and good Christians. They gather together all their wives and children and their old parents, and they sing carols and make merry all day long. At this time they never think of attacking anybody or of being attacked, and if we fall upon them then, we can easily destroy them all, young and old, and thus be rid of the wretches forever. I have a strong body of soldiers ready to send, but they must be led by a man of rank, and all my officers of high degree wish to remain here with their families to celebrate Christmas. Now, you are a stranger and have nothing to keep you here, and you are the very man to lead my soldiers. Destroy that colony of robbers, and you shall have a good share of the booty that you find there."

"Oh, Prince!" exclaimed the baron. "Would you have me, on holy Christmas Day, when these families are assembled together to celebrate the blessed festival, rush upon them with an armed band and slay them, old and young, women and children, at the very foot of the Christmas tree? No man needs occupation more than I, but this is a thing I cannot do."

"Impudent upstart!" cried the prince in a rage. "If you cannot do this, there is nothing for you here. Begone!"

Without an answer the baron turned and left the hall. Litza, who still stood by the door, did not now approach the prince but ran after the baron, who was walking rapidly away. "This is yours," she said, taking the iron box from her little bag. "You are the noblest man."

The baron, surprised, objected to receiving the box,

but Litza was firm. "I was told," she said, "to give it to the noblest man in Zisk, and I have done so."

When the baron found that he must keep the box, he asked Litza what was in it.

"I do not know," said Litza; "but the key is fastened to the handle."

They sat down under a tree in a quiet corner of the palace grounds and opened the box. Something inside was covered with a piece of velvet, on top of which lay a golden locket. The baron opened it and beheld a portrait of the beautiful Litza. "Why, you have given me yourself!" he cried, delighted.

"So it appears," said Litza, looking down upon the ground.

"And will you marry me?" he cried.

"If you wish it," said Litza. So that matter was settled.

The two then went to the inn and told the grandmother what had occurred. She looked quite pleased when she heard this story, and then she asked what else was in the box.

"I found so much," said the baron, "that I did not think of looking for anything more." He then opened the box, and lifting the piece of velvet, found it filled with sparkling diamonds.

"That is Litza's dowry," cried the old woman. "It was a wise thing in her godmother to send her out to look for a noble husband, for one would never have come to my little cottage to look for her. But it seems to me that the box might as well have been given to you at your castle. It would have saved us a weary journey."

"But if we had not taken that journey," said Litza, "we should not have become so well acquainted, and I would not have known he was the noblest man."

"It is all right," said the grandmother, "and your dowry will enable the baron to buy his castle again and to live there as his ancestors did before him."

The grandmother desired to leave Zisk immediately, but the baron objected. "There is something I wish to do today," he said; "and if we start early tomorrow morning on horseback, we can reach my castle before dark."

The old woman agreed to this, and the baron continued: "I would like you to lend me the baby for the rest of the day; and when the sundial in the courtyard shall mark three hours after noon, you will please open this piece of paper and wish what I have written upon it."

The grandmother took the folded piece of paper and let him have the baby. She and Litza wondered much what he was going to do, but they asked no questions.

The baron had learned that it was a three hours' walk from the town to the stronghold of the robbers, and just at noon he set out for that place, carrying the baby in his arms. Before he had gone a mile he wished that the baby had been changed into somebody who could walk, but it was too late now.

At three hours after noon the grandmother was about to open the paper when Litza exclaimed, "Before you wish anything, dear Grandmother, let me read what the baron has written."

Litza then took the paper and read it. "It is just what I expected," she cried. "He has gone out to fight the robbers, and he wants you to change the baby into that great armed giant to help him. But don't you do it, for the baron will certainly be killed, there are so many robbers in that place. Please change the baby into a very strong, fleet man who knows the country and who will take the baron in his arms and bring him back here just as fast as he can."

"I will wish that," said the grandmother. And she did so.

The baron had just arrived in sight of the robbers' stronghold when he was very much surprised to find that, instead of carrying a baby in his arms, he himself was in the grasp of a tall, powerful man who was carrying him at the top of his speed toward the town. The baron kicked and struggled much worse than the baby had, but the man paid no attention to his violent remonstrances and soon set him down in the courtyard of the inn.

"This is your doing," he said to Litza. "I wished to show the prince that it was not fear that kept me from fighting the robbers, and you have prevented me."

"You have proved that you are brave," said Litza, "and that is enough. The prince is a bad man; let him fight his own robbers."

The baron could not be angry at this proof of Litza's prudent affection. And the next morning the party left the town on three horses, which the baron bought with one of his diamonds. The tall, fleet man who knew the country acted as guide and led them by a byroad which did not pass near the School for Men. They arrived at the castle early on Christmas Eve, and the baron sent for his servants, his friends, and a priest, and he and Litza were married amid great rejoicing, for everybody was glad to see him come to his own again.

The next day Litza and the baron asked the grandmother to show them her magical servant in his original form. The old woman called the tall, fleet guide and transformed him into the Green Goblin of the Third Word. This strange creature wildly danced and skipped before them, and taking a watermelon and three pumpkins from his pocket, he tossed them up, keeping two of them always in the air.

The baron and his wife were very much amused by the antics of the goblin, and Litza exclaimed, "Oh, Grandmother, if I were you I would keep him this way always. He would be wonderfully amusing, and I am sure he could carry you about and scare away robbers, and do ever so many things."

"A merry green goblin might suit you," said the old woman, shaking her head, "but it would not suit me. I want to return to my own little home, and what I now wish is a suitable companion."

Instantly the goblin changed into a healthy middle-aged woman of agreeable manners and willing to make herself useful. With this "suitable companion" the old grandmother returned after the holidays to her much-loved cottage, where she was often visited by the young baron and his wife; but although they sometimes asked it, she never let them see the green goblin again.

"When a circumstance is just as accommodating as you want it to be," she said, "the less you meddle with it the better."

HERBERT ERNEST BATES

(1905-1974)

H. E. Bates, novelist, essayist, and short-story writer, was born at Rushden, Northamptonshire. After completing his formal education at the Kettering Grammar School, he worked first on a local newspaper, and then as a clerk in a leather warehouse. During this latter employment he wrote and published his first novel, *The Two Sisters* (1926). In the same year, he published a drama, *The Days of Glory*. Bates served as a squadron leader in the RAF during World War II, and several of his stories recounting his wartime experiences were first published under the pseudonym "Flying-Officer X." A prolific and widely read writer who tried his hand at practically every form of literature, Bates was most successful as a writer of short stories. Included among his many collections are *Day's End* (1928), *Seven Tales and Alexander* (1929), *The Woman Who Had Imagination* (1934), *The Flying Goat* (1939), and *The Bride Comes to Evensford* (1949). Critics have consistently praised Bates for his sensitive and knowledgeable portrayals of common folk, and for his concise and polished prose style. He died January 29, 1974, in Canterbury, England.

"The Peach Tree" is not as memorable for its plot as for the soft, exotic, and loving descriptions of the mysterious garden at the end of the wall. Although perhaps not quite as rich as C. S. Lewis's sensuous descriptions of the floating islands of Perelandra, sections of this tale certainly compare favorably with Lewis's writings. Like the rare perfumes of the wondrous garden, an atmosphere of tender melancholy hangs over the story. But there is thematic substance as well. Like many other thoughtful writers, Bates deals with the intriguing concept of appearance versus reality. The final effect of "The Peach Tree" is not unlike that of Shakespeare's *A Midsummer Night's Dream*; the reader is left wondering where illusion ends and reality begins, and whether our entire concept of reality is somehow deficient. Is the garden real? Only the children will ever really know.

❧ The Peach-Tree ❧

A FANTASY

H. E. Bates

I

Every afternoon, after their grandfather had covered his face with his bandana handkerchief, the children went down the long, sloping path to play under the peach-tree at the bottom of the garden. Their three little heads bobbed up and down and lost themselves in the bright spring grass as they ran. Their feet sounded like tiny drums, and over everything echoed their voices, like the calling of birds across water.

Because it grew in a hollow the children never saw the peach-tree until they were almost near enough to touch its boughs. Sometimes, as they ran through the grass, they would pause, and look at themselves and ask: 'Is it gone?' And then gaze at each other with round eyes, as if to say: 'What if it's there no longer?' But day after day they ran suddenly into the hollow where, sheltered by the high stone wall running behind, it waited for them with its slender arms outstretched, but never weary, as if ready to bless them.

At sight of it the children would not speak, but to themselves they thought, 'It's here, it's here! How silly we were!'

And the hollow over which the peach-tree reigned like a young green king would take them into its bosom.

Here was the beginning of a change for them. In the garden and the house, even after their grandfather had

185

covered his face with his great handkerchief, their
sweet voices were never still. They would call to each
other as if from one star to another, and laugh and
clap their hands. But the moment their feet touched
the grass under the peach-tree they changed, their
voices grew very soft, as if not to disturb the blossoms
sleeping so lightly above, and laughter crept into their
eyes.

It was so sudden a change that for a long time they
were silent, kneeling and sitting in the grass without
moving. When at last they got to their feet it was softly
and with care, as if the peach-tree had cast a spell
over them. It seemed to them they must think, and
speak, and act and dream, just as the tree did.

They grew to love the tree more and more. Sometimes it seemed to them full of dreams, sometimes of
awakenings, and day after day its light, slender arms
were outstretched for them.

Then one day they found that the peach-tree had
changed too. They stood on the edge of the hollow
with breathless delight and gazed at it. 'It's turned, it's
changed!' they cried. They tried to touch it with their
hands.

The peach-tree had blossomed. All its little awakenings and dreams, all its whispers seemed to have come
into this single awakening. It was one pale cloud of
blossoms; a mass of delicate pink snow against the
grass; a crowd of the palest fingers against the blue
sky. To the children it had for the first time the gift of
laughter. They had heard its whispers and sighs before.
But these new sounds, these airy, silvery notes which it
seemed came from the throats of the blossoms themselves, they caught as one catches at a new and more
lovely voice.

Day after day it had its blossoming arms outstretched for them. At the height of its flowering it
seemed to sing to them. Early bees sang, too. For days
its blossoms rose up in the bright air, delicate but
strong, pale but unfading, airy and yet never floating
away.

Then one afternoon the blossoms began to fall on the grass at the children's feet. All that day the children laughed and tried to catch them as they fell—and all the next day and the next. On the grass the blossoms were like pink snow. The children built castles and towers with them and blew them away.

But soon there came a day when the peach-tree changed again. It seemed to the children that the hollow where it grew was full of tears, things that to them were faded and ugly, bringing them thoughts which made their lips and eyes lose their brightness. As they sat down on the grass and looked up into the arms of the peach-tree, no longer like a cloud of pinkish snow, no more like a crowd of quivering fingers against the sky, they were quiet and sad.

Not only the children, but the tree itself seemed sad at this loss. It bent over them heavily and silently, as if trying to tell them this or as if reproaching its weary self for having let all its loveliness slip away.

But the children understood nothing of this. They only knew that the fragrant and delicate beauty of the tree had fallen to the ground, that it was dying there, and would never rise again; they only knew that the blossoms were no longer things which sang to them.

Nevertheless, every afternoon after their grandfather had put his bandana handkerchief over his face, they still came and played under the peach-tree. They were not so happy, but still their voices were softer and their eyes more joyful than elsewhere. Only their long silences seemed to reproach the tree.

At last, when it seemed that one of their silences must last for ever, the two older children got to their feet and said:

'We are tired of sitting here always.'

'Where are you going?' asked the other. He was very small.

The boy did not hear; the girl answered for him: 'Along by the wall—as far as we can see, until we can go no further.'

The little boy put chin in his hands and spoke softly:

'I'm not coming. You can go.'

They made no answer. Without moving his head the boy watched the other children go from beneath the peach-tree into the sunshine. He listened for the sound of their feet in the grass. Soon he guessed they had gone far along by the wall, where in summer-time nettles and thistles and mallow grew thickly about the feet of the hollyhocks and half the wall was hidden. He saw it all very clearly. His little blue eyes shone with thought. Now and then he listened. But only silence came from that part of the garden where they had gone.

II

That afternoon, as on all other afternoons, the boy sat and let his fancy play under the beautiful slender arms of the peach-tree. He sat deep in thought, while above him the tree seemed to hang with especial care, as though not wanting to lose him. All the time it seemed to be straining itself to put forward some new wonder.

The boy did not notice this. He was content with the memory of the tree as a cloud of snow, as a host of quivering fingers. He liked to linger over its gentle perfume as it had reached him day after day.

Suddenly, in the heart of these dreams, he heard the voices of the other children returning. They bounded wildly towards him through the long grasses, stumbling, panting with excitement and laughter.

They fell breathlessly in the grass at his side. Their words ran over each other.

'Such wonderful things—trees with flowers on, ever so wonderful—red and purple and orange. And in the grass—in the grass, stones, red and green, sparkling—you'd never believe! Trees so high you can't see their tops—and birds with long blue tails and scarlet eyes and green wings. They're like butterflies—only the butterflies settle on your head and tickle your eyes with their wings. And then—oh! then there's a pool, a long way inside, right under the darkest trees—and in it you can see the shadows of things that aren't there. Really, really—it's true! They move and change—all colors—and the fruits on the trees don't taste like themselves, but like one another. Oh! it's strange—it's lovely—it goes on and on—we never got to the end!'

To the boy their voices were strange. He gazed at them through all this with large eyes, not understanding. At last he murmured:

'Where have you been?—what have you found?'

They buried their faces in the grass again.

'The garden! the garden—it's sweet, it's wonderful. You must come! We never got to the end, but we shall, we shall!'

He had only one cry. 'Where? Where?'

The children glanced at each other—their voices fell to a whisper. They waved their hands carelessly. 'We couldn't tell you, it's so strange. We can only take you.'

The boy did not move. The other children tried to lift him to his feet.

He protested a little. 'No, no!' and they let him fall again.

Their voices were still excited and wondrous. 'Oh! the trees—there were such blossoms—such fruit!' they cried.

Without saying anything the boy thought solemnly: 'Not more wonderful than the peach-tree.'

He dared not say this. In silence he listened to the other children talking wildly of the scented, blossoming garden which had given them such new and marvellous thoughts, and of which the secret was to them more precious than the peach-tree even at the time when it was like a cloud of snow.

As he listened he kept looking upwards. It seemed to him that whatever the other children had seen he could not leave the peach-tree.

'You must come!—to-morrow we will take you,' the children cried to him.

But he put his chin in his hands and shook his head.

To-morrow came—and other to-morrows. And every day, as before, when their grandfather had covered his face with his bandana handkerchief, the children went to play at the bottom of the garden. But now only the smallest of them remained under the peach-tree. The eyes and voices of the others no longer grew bright and soft beneath it, and they loved its plain, slender arms no more.

Every day the boy watched them vanish where the nettles and thistles twined about the feet of the hollyhocks. And day after day he heard them return excitedly through the grass and listened as they flung themselves on the ground under the peach-tree and whispered of the things they had seen again. 'Trees with blossoms, bright stones, birds with crimson wings, strange fruit and scents, and the pool with the shadows of the things you cannot see!'

Again and again, as he heard all this, the boy thought: 'Not so lovely as the peach-tree when it blossomed.'

It was this thought always which each day kept him silent when the other children cried 'We will take you—to-morrow, to-morrow!'

He saw the tree straining and growing, heard its sighs, and seemed to feel its spirit imploring to have patience only a little longer. The whisper of its leaves was no longer as if they kissed each other, but as if they whispered to him: 'Soon! Soon!'

III

One day the boy found in the grass beneath the peach-tree little green fruits which shone delicately in his hand. He looked up into the branches: against the sky shone others like them, hanging shyly among the leaves, like birds' eggs of a soft, gleaming green.

The boy pondered. Here was another change. He did not understand. It had come so quietly, so mysteriously, with not half the beauty of the tree in blossom. With grave stares he looked up at the boughs: an instinct came and possessed him. He bit his teeth hard into one of the delicate green fruits that had fallen.

He jumped to his feet with a cry of dismay. His lips felt drawn and rough, his tongue curled itself up in his mouth, his teeth were like stones against each other. There were tears in his round, bewildered eyes.

'Sour! Sour!'

He flung the little green fruit away and buried his face in the grass.

On that day, as on all others, the children went to fetch him as they came running from the secret garden. Their faces were beaming, they were full of laughter, they had the stain of strange fruits on their lips. They flung themselves on the grass and cried to him.

'Such wonderful things! Why do you stay here?—why don't you come? Things you never saw before—you never dreamed. Pomegranates that taste like plums—quinces and custard-fruit, melons and cocoanuts, figs like gourds, and peaches that have all the flavours of all the strangest fruits in the East in them growing on trees higher than churches.'

The boy turned his eyes from the grass. He did not understand. He pondered on the greatness of the new trees.

'Do you climb them?' he asked.

'Climb? They have scarlet teeth on their trunks. Only the apes with ivory feet and ebony fingers climb them.'

'Apes!' There were stars of fear in his eyes. 'Don't they bleed?'

'Sometimes the teeth cut their breasts—then they bleed two drops of bright blue. And where they fall on the ground a peacock springs up.'

'And they?—the peacocks.'

'They have voices like nightingales.'

The boy remained in an awed wonder, asking himself if these things were true.

'What other things?' he asked presently.

'Everything.'

All that day and all the next and the next the boy thought on this. But he would not be dragged away from the peach-tree. He lay there with visions which very slowly he began to see that the tree had never given him. Voices spoke to him, he saw strange-footed apes in trees, he heard echoes of sounds he never made, he lived in a state of silver wonder.

Sometimes the taste of the sour fruit of the peach-tree came into his mouth again. Then he would say: 'It has cheated me!'

Gradually he began to hate this sourness more and more. The peach-tree had cheated him, the peach-tree had cheated him!

IV

There came a day when the boy crept from beneath the shadow of the peach-tree and walked timidly along by the high stone wall. The other children had already disappeared. He had waited for them to go with fear in his heart: he was half ashamed that they should see him.

He made his way very carefully, seeking protection from the tall hollyhocks, making no sound. But his heart throbbed fast and he trembled.

The wall seemed as if it would never end. Ahead of him the boy could see no change, no sign of the secret garden. He listened, but he could not hear the shrieks of the apes, nor the peacocks which sang like nightingales. There were no new scents, the air smelled as it had always done—heavy with pinks and clover, with stocks and jasmine, with grass and roses.

But the boy never once looked back at the peach-tree. At last he wandered so far off that he could not have seen it had he turned. And it still seemed to him that the wall would never end.

Then suddenly, as if the wind had blown him there, he was in the garden—the secret garden, among the magic of new airs, new sounds, swaying under the breath of new perfumes! His coming there was a mystery—there was no wall, not one familiar stone, not a single scent he knew.

He went forward warily in the grass: from beneath his feet shot up a bird with a precious stone in its mouth. It flew to the top of a tree with purple leaves and dropped the jewel. The boy watched it: it fell into his arms. They became heavy with pink birds with scarlet feet. The boy let them fall, and they flew away.

When he walked on the echo of his feet was like music.

He looked at his feet: they gleamed in the grass like silver. They bore him suddenly into a forest of crimson trees, where the birds were as the other children had led him to believe, only to his eyes even more wonderful, where the trees bore blossoms that were not their own, so that the quince had a flower like lilac, the mulberry like a tiger-lily, and the peach like a peony.

Some trees were in flower, some had fruit on them. The boy's feet gleamed.

He ate the fruit of the trees, eating pomegranates with the taste of mangoes. From the highest branches the apes with ivory feet and ebony fingers shrieked at him and brought him the things he dreamed of. The things he asked for they never brought—only sometimes they shed their bright blue blood, as if to reproach him, and peacocks sprang up where the drops fell.

For a long time he wandered in the forest. He was not frightened. His head was full of dreams. The apes brought him whatever he dreamed of, the peacocks sang, there was always something more wonderful.

He came to a pool. He whispered across it: the echo was like the chatter of parrots. When he shouted it murmured, as if heavy with dreams, as if sleepily asking for something. He felt a desire to pick up a stone and disturb its dark surface. When the stone touched the pool a crimson swan sprang up; its eyes were black; it talked to him.

'Your mouth is stained,' it said first.

'That's through eating pomegranates,' said the boy.

'How far have you been?' it asked.

'Not far. Where is the peach-tree with flowers like peonies? I have lost it.'

'You think it is over there, behind the black grasses,' answered the swan.

It disappeared. And the boy found that the swan's words were true, and that the peach-tree was where he thought it must be.

He went there. Its scent came to him strongly. And then, after a moment, behind the wall of black grasses, the peach-tree with peony flowers made a red stain in the forest. And it seemed to the boy to give out the heaviest, most wondrous perfume he had ever known.

Petals fell warmly on his face as he stretched himself under its branches. He felt the touch of a new spirit. Underneath its arms he thought only of the colour of its flowers, their scent, the blessing they seemed to give him. Of the other peach-tree, the quiet, green, straining one, he thought nothing. He could not even imagine what it looked like: the great mass of burning crimson above him dazzled his eyes.

V

The boy returned at last, as he had seen the other children return, suddenly, mysteriously, from the new garden to the old. Of the apes and peacocks, the jewels and fruit, of the pool and the peach-tree with peony blooms, he never ceased thinking. But he said nothing of them, nothing of the garden. It was as if he were half ashamed, half afraid of what had come.

When the children urged him to go with them he only smiled. But when they had disappeared, he sprang

up from beneath the peach-tree, green and silent and
watchful as ever, and followed the wall until the secret
garden was all about him again. And every day he saw
things there which filled him with wonder. Every day
he ate the wondrous fruit, dreamed in the forest, and
watched the apes run up and down the scarlet trees.
Every day he lay under the peach-tree with peony blossoms that dazzled his eyes.

The days went on and on.

One day, under the peach-tree in the old garden, he
sat waiting for the other children to go. The air was
warm and drowsy. He thought of the other garden,
even more lovely. But the children beside him never
moved themselves. 'Are they never going?' thought the
boy. A long time went past, but the children did not
stir.

'Aren't you going to the garden to-day?' he asked
aloud.

They shook their heads. 'No more!' they said. 'It's
winter in the garden now; there's snow, the pool is
frozen, the apes and swans have gone and hidden
themselves, the trees are bare, the peacocks never
sing—it's dreary and silent.'

The boy's heart grew cold. He could not believe
these things. Only yesterday it had been so warm, so
wonderful in the garden. Some of the peonies, he
knew, were only just opening themselves.

Feverishly he escaped from the old peach-tree and
ran along by the wall, trembling, afraid. He could not
bear to think of winter in the garden. He saw the pool
frozen and dark, the flowers dead, the trees bare, the
peacocks shivering—and, last of all, the peach-tree
stripped of its peony-blooms.

Then suddenly he was in the garden. There was a
rush of warm air, warm scents, of the most beautiful of
sounds—the peacocks singing. The boy glanced about
him—there was no winter! no snow! no darkness! He
was able to smell even the farthest blossoms. He saw
jewels and birds. The apes brought him the things of
his dreams, he stained his lips with fruits, he talked to

the swan. And all that afternoon he lay under the peach-tree in a great gladness that there was no winter—but only summer, summer, summer, summer!

As he returned it seemed to him that never before had the peach-tree shed such a dazzling light on him. It made him tremble. In the old garden he could not see clearly what things were. But he heard the voices of the other children, calling from the old peach-tree:

'Come quickly! Where have you been? Such wonderful things—you'd never believe!'

Very dimly he could see them rolling in the grass, their eyes shining.

'The peaches are ripe! The peaches are ripe!' they shouted.

The boy glanced at them, at the grass, and at the peach-tree itself. He could see nothing.

'The peaches are ripe! They're red and gold—oh! look!—do look!'

The boy did not pause, did not speak. As if in a dream he went slowly up the path until their voices were like no more than echoes:

'The peaches are ripe! The peaches are ripe!' he heard them say.

But he thought only of the day when the peach-tree had cheated him and he had cried 'Sour! Sour!' and then of the new peach-tree with the blossoms that were like peonies, with its everlasting wonder in a summer that would never end. He passed out of the reach of the children's voices. His eyes were alight, his lips were stained with purple, his head sang with the sound of peacocks singing like nightingales, and in the air he caught the echoes of those things that never were, never are, and never will be.

ALEXANDER GRIN

(1880–1932)

Alexander Grin, whose real name was Alexander Stepenovich Grinevsky, was born in Vyatka (now Kirov), a small Russian town west of the Urals. Though his father had hoped he would become a doctor, Alexander dreamed from childhood of sailing away to visit distant lands such as India and America. And while he never got further from Russia than Alexandria, Egypt—and that for just a few hours—Grin successfully created his own secondary world which he called Greenlandia, and which he peopled out of his own imagination.

Grin's preparation for his eventual career as a writer was obtained in the school of experience. He left school at the age of sixteen and became an apprentice sailor. After this attempt failed, Grin spent the next fifteen years at a variety of unusual jobs such as putting out fires in the oil fields of Baku, prospecting for gold in the Urals, and the rather unromantic one of serving as bath attendant for the railway. None of these provided him with more than a bare subsistence-level existence.

He finally was afforded the opportunity to begin his writing career when he was imprisoned by the Czarist police for treason. He had earlier joined the Socialist Revolutionary Party and had become an agitator. He spent a year and a half in prison (1903–1905) before he was released and then promptly arrested and sent to Siberia. This time he escaped, however, and fled to Petersburg, where he sold his first story in 1906. He assumed a pen name but was found out anyway and sent again to Siberia (1908) where he continued to write.

By 1912 he was back in Russia and able to support himself with his writings, which had gained some popularity.

After serving in the Red Army and fighting off malaria, Grin completed his best-known novel, *Scarlet Sails* (1923). During the Second World War, this novel was adapted as a ballet and performed in Moscow by the Bolshoi. In 1961 the film version of *Scarlet Sails* appeared.

Grin, after having been a socialist revolutionary fifteen years before the revolution, withdrew from politics and pretty much from society in 1923. From then until his death he lived in the Crimea in poverty and obscurity. But it was his most productive period, in which he wrote most of his longer works: *The Golden Chain; She Who Runs on the Waves; The Road to Nowhere.* His works were so different from the usual type that the censors paid them little heed, until 1945 when they were banned because they were too Western. At one time, in fact, they were thought to have been translations from an English or American writer. However, the ban was lifted in 1955, and since then Grin has become one of the most popular and widely read writers in Russian literary history. In 1966 nearly a half million copies of his six-volume collected works were put out in hardback. Unfortunately, he is still little known in the West because few of his works have been translated.

Grin writes about what he called "The Beautiful Unknown," a world which is unreachable in reality but not in fantasy. He has been accused of being unable to deal with reality, but the story which follows belies this claim. One can sometimes deal with reality more effectively in fantasy, as Grin shows in "The Loquacious Goblin." Reversal of perspective, a technique used effectively in many fantasy works, is the key device in this brief narrative. Instead of hearing of the world of goblins from human lips, we hear of the world of humans from the mouth of a loquacious goblin. It is an ingenious device, and it creates an unusual effect in this tale.

❧ The Loquacious Goblin ❧

Alexander Grin

"I stood by the window, humming a song about Anna. . .

—H. HORNUNG

I

A house goblin suffering from toothache: isn't that slander against a creature who has so many witches and sorcerers at his command that he can safely gobble sugar by the barrel? But that's how it was, a fact. There he was, a small, sad-looking goblin sitting by the cold range, which had long forgotten what a fire was like. Rhythmically shaking his disheveled head, he held his bandaged cheek, moaning piteously like a child, and his red, turbid eyes reflected suffering.

Rain was pouring. I had entered this deserted house to shelter from the downpour and had suddenly caught sight of him who had forgotten that he should vanish. . . .

"It doesn't matter now," he said in the voice of an agitated parrot. "It doesn't matter now, for no one will believe that you have seen me anyhow."

Making a pair of horns with my fingers to ward off the evil eye just in case, I replied:

"Don't be afraid. I won't shoot you with a silver bullet, nor will I pronounce an incantation. But why are you here? The house is empty."

"Oi-oi. And yet I find it hard to quit this spot," the little goblin explained. "Now listen. I'll tell you everything. So be it. As it is, my teeth are aching. It's a relief to talk. It eases the pain . . . oi! My dear fellow, it was all a question of a single hour, and that is why I got stuck here. My people . . ."—here he sighed plaintively—"my people, well, in a word, our people, after they departed, have been grooming their horses' tails for quite a while on the other side of the hills, but I just can't get away because I must understand what happened.

"Just look at the holes in the ceiling and the cracked walls, and then imagine to yourself this place all neat with shining copper vessels, white transparent curtains, and the house as full of flowers as the forest; a brightly polished floor; and the range, on which you are sitting as on a cold gravestone, all red-hot with the dinner simmering in pots and exuding an appetizing aroma.

"There were quarries, granite quarries in the vicinity. A married couple, a rare pair, inhabited the house. The husband's name was Philip, and his wife was called Annie. She was twenty, and he was twenty-five. Now, if this pleases you, she was just like this." Here the goblin plucked a tiny wildflower, which had sprung up out of the earth accumulated through the years in a crack on the windowsill, and demonstratively presented it to me. "I liked the husband too, but I was fonder of her, for she was more than just a good housekeeper; we goblins find great relish in what links people closer to us. Well, she used to try and catch fish in the stream with her bare hands, and she also used to tap on the big stone that stands at the crossroads and listen for long moments to the ever fainter ringing sound it made, and she used to laugh on seeing a yellow patch of sunlight on a wall. Don't be so surprised: there is a magic in all this, the fine knowledge of a beautiful soul; but only we, the cloven-footed, are able to detect its signs. Ordinary folk are so unperceptive.

" 'Annie,' the husband would cry out joyfully whenever he returned at dinnertime from the quarry, where he held a job in the office, 'I am not alone! I have Ralph with me.' But the joke was repeated so often that Annie, smiling and unperturbed, would only lay the table for two. Annie and Philip always met as if they were discovering each other for the first time. She would run towards him and he would carry her back in his arms.

"In the evening he would pull out a batch of letters from his old friend Ralph, in whose company he had spent part of his life before marriage, and he would read the letters aloud to Annie, who, propping her head with her hands, listened to the familiar words about the sea and the glittering, wonderful sunbeams on the far side of our vast country, about volcanoes and pearl-fishing, tempests and conflicts in the shadow of huge forests. And each word rang out to her like the stone that sang so long and ringingly at the crossroads when she tapped it.

" 'He will arrive soon,' Philip would say. 'He will come to visit us as soon as his three-masted schooner, the *Sinbad*, berths in the harbor at Gress. To reach our place takes only an hour by train and then an hour more from the station.'

"Sometimes Annie would show interest in some aspect of Ralph's life; and Philip would begin to tell her enthusiastically about Ralph's daring, his peculiarities, his magnanimity and his strange destiny, reminiscent of a fairy tale: his early poverty, his gold strike, his purchase of a schooner, and all the lacework of legendary exploit woven of a ship's tackle, sea foam, gambling and trade, peril and discovery. Eternal gambling. Eternal excitement. Eternal music of sea shore and sea wave.

"I never heard them quarrel, and I hear everything. I never saw them exchange a cold glance, and I see everything. 'I feel sleepy,' Annie would say at night, and he would carry her to the bed, laying her down and wrapping her up like a child. Falling asleep, she would say: 'Phil, who is that whispering in the tops of the trees? Who is that walking on the roof? Whose face is it I see in the stream beside mine?' And he would answer in a troubled way, peering into her half-closed eyes: 'It's a raven walking on the roof; the wind in the trees; pebbles glittering in the stream. Sleep now and don't walk about barefoot.'

"Then he would sit down at the table to finish his routine report; afterwards, he would wash, arrange the logs and go to bed, falling asleep at once and always forgetting everything he dreamt. He never tapped on the singing stone that stood at the crossroads, where the fairies wove astonishing carpets from grains of dust and moonbeams.

II

"Well, listen . . . There isn't much more for me to tell about the three people who put me, the goblin, into such a quandary. One sunny, fully flowering day, Philip, with a notebook in his hand, was marking off piles of granite; and Annie, in the meantime, was returning with purchases from the station. As usual, she stopped by her stone and, as always, made it sing out by tapping it with a key. The stone was a fragment of ancient rock, about half as tall as herself. When one tapped it, the stone would sing out, ringing fainter, and fainter; but, when one thought that it had stopped ringing, it was enough to apply one's ear to it to be able still to detect a barely audible voice inside the mass.

"Our forest paths are veritable gardens. Their beauty grips the heart. The flowers and the branches above one's head peer through their fingers at the sun, which changes in color, for the eyes quickly tire of it and begin to wander aimlessly. The white sand reflected the yellow, chalky and somber green hues. On a day such as that cold water was the best thing.

"Annie halted, listening to the forest singing in her breast. Then she began to tap on the stone, breaking into a smile whenever a new wave of ringing sound imposed itself upon the fading sound. Thus she amused herself, imagining that no one could see her; but then, suddenly, a man came striding round the corner of the path and approached her. His steps sounded softer and softer, and finally he stopped. Annie, continuing to smile, glanced at him without being startled or without stepping back. It was as if he had always stood there.

"He was swarthy, very swarthy, and the sea had left upon his face the imprint of a scurrying wave. But it was a beautiful face, reflecting a soul at once desperate and tender. His dark eyes gazed at Annie, darkening and gleaming more intensely; and Annie's luminous eyes shone gently back.

"As you have rightly concluded, I always followed her about, for there were snakes in that forest.

"The stone had long grown silent, but this man and this woman still gazed at each other without uttering a word. Then he held out his hand, and slowly she offered her own, and their hands joined them together. Then he took her head carefully, so carefully that I was afraid to breathe, and kissed her on the lips. Her eyes closed.

"They moved apart then, and the stone stood between them as before. Suddenly Philip appeared, striding towards them. Annie, catching sight of him, hastened to meet him:

" 'Here's Ralph. He has arrived.' "

" 'Yes, he has,' Philip said, unable even to shout for joy. Finally he tossed his hat in the air and embraced the new arrival. 'Ralph, you have already met Annie. It is she.' His rugged, generous face glowed from the excitement of the meeting. 'You will stay with us, Ralph; we shall show you everything. And we'll talk to our heart's content. Ralph, dear friend, my wife also has been awaiting your arrival.'

"Annie placed her hand on her husband's shoulder and directed her frankest, warmest and purest glance at him and then, without changing her expression, gazed at Ralph as if he were as close to her as her husband.

" 'I'll be back soon,' Ralph said. 'Phil, I wasn't sure of your address. I thought I was on the wrong track and therefore I left my luggage at the station. I'll go back and fetch it now.'

"They agreed on the details and separated," the goblin said. "That is all I know. But I can't understand it. Perhaps you will explain to me."

"Did Ralph return?" I asked.

"They waited for him, but he only wrote them a note from the station to say he had met an acquaintance who had offered him a profitable deal."

"And what happened to them?"

"They died . . . died long ago . . . some thirty years back. She drank some cold water on a hot day. She caught a chill to begin with. His hair was half-gray when he followed the coffin. Then he disappeared. It was rumored that he had locked himself up in a room with a brazier. But that's not the point. . . . My teeth are still aching, and still I don't understand . . ."

"And that's how it will remain," I replied politely, shaking his shaggy, unwashed paw in farewell. "Only we, five-fingered folk, can read the signs of the human heart. Goblins are so unperceptive."

JOHN RONALD REUEL TOLKIEN

(1892–1973)

Tolkien, the single most prominent figure in reclaiming both popular and scholarly attention for fantasy literature, became a legend while still living, due to a combination of enormous popularity and shyness. As with many authors, he cherished his privacy and guarded against undue publicity. He gave interviews infrequently and wrote little about himself. The outline of his public life is well known, and an official biography, presently being compiled by Humphrey Carpenter with the help and approval of the Tolkien family, should afford a more intimate portrait of the man. The best we can do here is to briefly rehearse a few of the high points of this extraordinary man's career.

Tolkien was born in South Africa of British parents and returned to England with his mother and brother in 1896 after the death of his father. He was educated at King Edward VI School in Birmingham and at Exeter College, Oxford. During World War I, he served with the Lancashire Fusiliers.

For a good many years, Tolkien enjoyed the quiet life of an Oxford don. To judge from a comment by the poet W. H. Auden, Tolkien was an effective lecturer. Auden, years after his student days at Oxford, vividly recalled being so taken by Tolkien's reading of a long passage of *Beowulf* that Old English became a lasting influence on his own poetry. Tolkien lectured on both Old and Middle English language and literature and also wrote numerous scholarly articles. "Beowulf: The Monsters and The Critics" is his classic attack on the many doubtful interpretations of the Old English epic. Tolkien regarded the work as an heroic tragedy of Northern myth rather than as a Christian allegory. Another scholarly work which is still the best in its field is the Tolkien and Gordon edition of *Gawain and The Green Knight,* for which Tolkien compiled an extensive glossary to facilitate the reading in the original.

The quiet years continued even after the appearance of *The Hobbit* in 1937. During World War II Tolkien met almost weekly with a group called "The Inklings." The most faithful—and most famous—members of the group were Tolkien, C. S. Lewis, and Charles Williams. They met to read and discuss their works in progress. During these years Tolkien was working on a sequel to *The Hobbit,* which turned out to be the *Lord of the Rings Trilogy* (LOTR): *The Fellowship of the Rings* (1954), *The Two Towers* (1954), and *The Return of the King* (1955).

With the appearance of the trilogy the quiet years were over, and Tolkien, quite unwillingly, became a celebrity. Yet he somehow, over the next eighteen years, maintained a good deal of privacy. Relatively little is known, for example, about his still unpublished *The Silmarillion,* another epic fantasy which also takes place in Middle Earth, but in an earlier time than in LOTR.* Tolkien left Oxford in 1969 (he had retired from teaching in 1959) to insure the privacy of his last years.

One of Tolkien's objections to his fans was their hunting for hidden meanings in his works. He maintained that he wrote to tell a story, not an allegory. Whether allegory is present or not is arguable, but the success of his stories as stories is incontestable. The selection which follows is chapter five of *The Hobbit* in which the reader—and Bilbo—first meet Gollum. The chapter is important to the whole trilogy because it discusses Gollum's "precious," the ring of power. Of itself, however, this chapter is memorable It is an exciting story with an admixture of humor and high seri-

---

*At this time, *The Silmarillion* is being prepared for publication by Tolkien's eldest son Christopher.

ousness which only the best storyteller can achieve successfully. And the setting, described in simple but unforgettable imagery, evokes as palpable a shudder from the reader as it did from Bilbo.

❧ Riddles in the Dark ❧

J. R. R. Tolkien

When Bilbo opened his eyes, he wondered if he had; for it was just as dark as with them shut. No one was anywhere near him. Just imagine his fright! He could hear nothing, see nothing, and he could feel nothing except the stone of the floor.

Very slowly he got up and groped about on all fours, till he touched the wall of the tunnel; but neither up nor down it could he find anything: nothing at all, no sign of goblins, no sign of dwarves. His head was swimming, and he was far from certain even of the direction they had been going in when he had his fall. He guessed as well as he could, and crawled along for a good way, till suddenly his hand met what felt like a tiny ring of cold metal lying on the floor of the tunnel. It was a turning point in his career, but he did not know it. He put the ring in his pocket almost without thinking; certainly it did not seem of any particular use at the moment. He did not go much further, but sat down on the cold floor and gave himself up to complete miserableness, for a long while. He thought of himself frying bacon and eggs in his own kitchen at home—for he could feel inside that it was high time for some meal or other; but that only made him miserabler.

He could not think what to do; nor could he think what had happened; or why he had been left behind; or why, if he had been left behind, the goblins had not caught him; or even why his head was so sore. The truth was he had been lying quiet, out of sight and out of mind, in a very dark corner for a long while.

After some time he felt for his pipe. It was not broken, and that was something. Then he felt for his pouch, and there was some tobacco in it, and that was something more. Then he felt for matches and he could not find any at all, and that shattered his hopes completely. Just as well for him, as he agreed when he came to his senses. Goodness knows what the striking of matches and the smell of tobacco would have brought on him out of dark holes in that horrible place. Still at the moment he felt very crushed. But in slapping all his pockets and feeling all round himself for matches his hand came on the hilt of his little sword—the little dagger that he got from the trolls, and that he had quite forgotten; nor do the goblins seem to have noticed it, as he wore it inside his breeches.

Now he drew it out. It shone pale and dim before his eyes. "So it is an elvish blade, too," he thought; "and goblins are not very near, and yet not far enough."

But somehow he was comforted. It was rather splendid to be wearing a blade made in Gondolin for the goblin wars of which so many songs had been sung; and also he had noticed that such weapons made a great impression on goblins that came upon them suddenly.

"Go back?" he thought. "No good at all! Go sideways? Impossible! Go forward? Only thing to do! On we go!" So up he got, and trotted along with his little sword held in front of him and one hand feeling the wall, and his heart all of a patter and a pitter.

Now certainly Bilbo was in what is called a tight place. But you must remember it was not quite so tight for him as it would have been for me or for you. Hobbits are not quite like ordinary people; and after all if their holes are nice cheery places and properly aired, quite different from the tunnels of the goblins, still they are more used to tunnelling than we are, and they do not easily lose their sense of direction underground— not when their heads have recovered from being bumped. Also they can move very quietly, and hide easily, and recover wonderfully from falls and bruises, and they have a fund of wisdom and wise sayings that men have mostly never heard or have forgotten long ago.

I should not have liked to have been in Mr. Baggins' place, all the same. The tunnel seemed to have no end. All he knew was that it was still going down pretty steadily and keeping in the same direction in spite of a twist and a turn or two. There were passages leading off to the side every now and then, as he knew by the glimmer of his sword, or could feel with his hand on the wall. Of these he took no notice, except to hurry past for fear of goblins or half-imagined dark things coming out of them. On and on he went, and down and down; and still he heard no sound of anything except the occasional whirr of a bat by his ears, which startled him at first, till it became too frequent to bother about. I do not know how long he kept on like this, hating to go on, not daring to stop, on, on, until he was tireder than tired. It seemed like all the way to tomorrow and over it to the days beyond.

Suddenly without any warning he trotted splash into water! Ugh! it was icy cold. That pulled him up sharp and short. He did not know whether it was just a pool in the path, or the edge of an underground stream that crossed the passage, or the brink of a deep dark sub-terranean lake. The sword was hardly shining at all. He stopped, and he could hear, when he listened hard, drops drip-drip-dripping from an unseen roof into the water below; but there seemed no other sort of sound.

"So it is a pool or a lake, and not an underground river," he thought. Still he did not dare to wade out into the darkness. He could not swim; and he thought, too, of nasty slimy things, with big bulging blind eyes, wriggling in the water. There are strange things living in the pools and lakes in the hearts of mountains: fish whose fathers swam in, goodness only knows how many years ago, and never swam out again, while their eyes grew bigger and bigger and bigger from trying to see in the blackness; also there are other things more slimy than fish. Even in the tunnels and caves the goblins have made for themselves there are other things living unbeknown to them that have sneaked in from outside to lie up in the dark. Some of these caves, too, go back in their beginnings to ages before the goblins, who only widened them and joined them up with passages, and the original owners are still there in odd corners, slinking and nosing about.

Deep down here by the dark water lived old Gollum. I don't know where he came from, nor who or what he was. He was Gollum—as dark as darkness, except for two big round pale eyes. He had a boat, and he rowed about quite quietly on the lake; for lake it was, wide and deep and deadly cold. He paddled it with large feet dangling over the side, but never a ripple did he make. Not he. He was looking out of his pale lamp-like eyes for blind fish, which he grabbed with his long fingers as quick as thinking. He liked meat too. Goblin he thought good, when he could get it; but he took care they never found him out. He just throttled them from behind, if they ever came down alone anywhere near the edge of the water, while he was prowling about. They very seldom did, for they had a feeling that something unpleasant was lurking down there, down at the very roots of the mountain. They had come on the lake, when they were tunnelling down long ago, and they found they could go no further; so there their road ended in that direction, and there was no reason to go that way—unless the Great Goblin sent them. Sometimes he took a fancy for fish from the lake, and sometimes neither goblin nor fish came back.

Actually Gollum lived on a slimy island of rock in the middle of the lake. He was watching Bilbo now from the distance with his pale eyes like telescopes. Bilbo could not see him, but he was wondering a lot about Bilbo, for he could see that he was no goblin at all.

Gollum got into his boat and shot off from the island, while Bilbo was sitting on the brink altogether flummoxed and at the end of his way and his wits. Suddenly up came Gollum and whispered and hissed:

"Bless us and splash us, my preciousss! I guess it's a choice feast; at least a tasty morsel it'd make us, gollum!" And when he said *gollum* he made a horrible swallowing noise in his throat. That is how he got his name, though he always called himself 'my precious.'

The hobbit jumped nearly out of his skin when the hiss came in his ears, and he suddenly saw the pale eyes sticking out at him.

"Who are you?" he said, thrusting his dagger in front of him.

"What iss he, my preciouss?" whispered Gollum (who always spoke to himself through never having anyone else to speak to). This is what he had come to find out, for he was not really very hungry at the moment, only curious; otherwise he would have grabbed first and whispered afterwards.

"I am Mr. Bilbo Baggins. I have lost the dwarves and I have lost the wizard, and I don't know where I am; and I don't want to know, if only I can get away."

"What's he got in his handses?" said Gollum, looking at the sword, which he did not quite like.

"A sword, a blade which came out of Gondolin!"

"Sssss" said Gollum, and became quite polite. "Praps ye sits here and chats with it a bitsy, my preciousss. It like riddles, praps it does, does it?" He was anxious to appear friendly, at any rate for the moment, and until he found out more about the sword and the hobbit, whether he was quite alone really, whether he was good to eat, and whether Gollum was really hungry. Riddles were all he could think of. Asking them, and sometimes guessing them, had been the only game he had ever played with other funny creatures sitting in their holes in the long, long ago, before he lost all his friends and was driven away, alone, and crept down, down, into the dark under the mountains.

"Very well," said Bilbo, who was anxious to agree, until he found out more about the creature, whether he was quite alone, whether he was fierce or hungry, and whether he was a friend of the goblins.

"You ask first," he said, because he had not had time to think of a riddle.

So Gollum hissed:

> *What has roots as nobody sees,*
> *Is taller than trees,*
> *Up, up it goes,*
> *And yet never grows?*

"Easy!" said Bilbo. "Mountain, I suppose."

"Does it guess easy? It must have a competition with us, my preciouss! If precious asks, and it doesn't answer, we eats it, my preciousss. If it asks us, and we doesn't asnwer, then we does what it wants, eh? We shows it the way out, yes!"

"All right!" said Bilbo, not daring to disagree, and nearly bursting his brain to think of riddles that could save him from being eaten.

> *Thirty white horses on a red hill,*
> *First they champ,*
> *Then they stamp,*
> *Then they stand still.*

That was all he could think of to ask—the idea of eating was rather on his mind. It was rather an old one, too, and Gollum knew the answer as well as you do.

"Chestnuts, chestnuts," he hissed. "Teeth! teeth! my preciousss; but we has only six!" Then he asked his second:

> *Voiceless it cries,*
> *Wingless flutters,*

> *Toothless bites,*
> *Mouthless mutters.*

"Half a moment!" cried Bilbo, who was still thinking uncomfortably about eating. Fortunately he had once heard something rather like this before, and getting his wits back he thought of the answer. "Wind, wind of course," he said, and he was so pleased that he made up one on the spot. "This'll puzzle the nasty little underground creature," he thought:

> *An eye in a blue face*
> *Saw an eye in a green face.*
> *"That eye is like to this eye"*
> *Said the first eye,*
> *"But in low place,*
> *Not in high place."*

"Ss, ss, ss," said Gollum. He had been underground a long long time, and was forgetting this sort of thing. But just as Bilbo was beginning to wonder what Gollum's present would be like, Gollum brought up memories of ages and ages and ages before, when he lived with his grandmother in a hole in a bank by a river. "Sss, sss, my preciouss," he said. "Sun on the daisies it means, it does."

But these ordinary aboveground everyday sort of riddles were tiring for him. Also they reminded him of days when he had been less lonely and sneaky and nasty, and that put him out of temper. What is more they made him hungry; so this time he tried something a bit more difficult and more unpleasant:

> *It cannot be seen, cannot be felt,*
> *Cannot be heard, cannot be smelt.*
> *It lies behind stars and under hills,*
> *   And empty holes it fills.*
> *It comes first and follows after,*
> *   Ends life, kills laughter.*

Unfortunately for Gollum Bilbo had heard that sort of thing before; and the answer was all round him any way. "Dark!" he said without even scratching his head or putting on his thinking cap.

> *A box without hinges, key, or lid,*
> *Yet golden treasure inside is hid.*

he asked to gain time, until he could think of a really hard one. This he thought a dreadfully easy chestnut, though he had not asked it in the usual words. But it proved a nasty poser for Gollum. He hissed to himself, and still he did not answer; he whispered and spluttered.

After some while Bilbo became impatient. "Well, what is it?" he said. "The answer's not a kettle boiling over, as you seem to think from the noise you are making."

"Give us a chance; let it give us a chance, my preciouss—ss—ss."

"Well," said Bilbo, after giving him a long chance, "what about your guess?"

But suddenly Gollum remembered thieving from nests long ago, and sitting under the river bank teaching his grandmother, teaching his grandmother to suck—"Eggses!" he hissed. "Eggses it is!" Then he asked:

> *Alive without breath,*
> *As cold as death;*
> *Never thirsty, ever drinking,*
> *All in mail never clinking.*

He also in his turn thought this was a dreadfully easy one, because he was always thinking of the answer. But he could not remember anything better at the moment, he was so flustered by the egg-question. All the same it was a poser for poor Bilbo, who never had anything to do with the water if he could help it. I imagine you know the answer, of course, or can guess it as easy as winking, since you are sitting comfortably at home and have not the danger of being eaten to disturb your thinking. Bilbo sat and cleared his throat once or twice, but no answer came.

After a while Gollum began to hiss with pleasure to himself: "Is it nice, my preciousss? Is it juicy? Is it scrumptiously crunchable?" He began to peer at Bilbo out of the darkness.

"Half a moment," said the hobbit shivering. "I gave you a good long chance just now."

"It must make haste, haste!" said Gollum, beginning to climb out of his boat on to the shore to get at Bilbo. But when he put his long webby foot in the water, a fish jumped out in a fright and fell on Bilbo's toes.

"Ugh!" he said, "it is cold and clammy!"—and so he guessed. "Fish! fish!" he cried. "It is fish!"

Gollum was dreadfully disappointed; but Bilbo asked another riddle as quick as ever he could, so that Gollum had to get back into his boat and think.

> *No-legs lay on one-leg, two-legs sat near on three-legs, four-legs got some.*

It was not really the right time for this riddle, but Bilbo was in a hurry. Gollum might have had some trouble guessing it, if he had asked it at another time. As it was, talking of fish, "no-legs" was not so very difficult, and after that the rest was easy. "Fish on a little table, man at the table sitting on a stool, the cat has the bones" that of course is the answer, and Gollum soon gave it. Then he thought the time had come to ask something hard and horrible. This is what he said:

> *This thing all things devours:*
> *Birds, beasts, trees, flowers;*
> *Gnaws iron, bites steel;*
> *Grinds hard stones to meal;*
> *Slays king, ruins town,*
> *And beats high mountain down.*

Poor Bilbo sat in the dark thinking of all the horrible names of all the giants and ogres he had ever heard told of in tales, but not one of them had done all these things. He had a feeling that the answer was quite different and that he ought to know it, but he could not think of it. He began to get frightened, and that is bad for thinking. Gollum began to get out of his boat. He flapped into the water and paddled to the bank; Bilbo could see his eyes coming toward him. His tongue seemed to stick in his mouth; he wanted to shout out: "Give me more time! Give me time!" But all that came out with a sudden squeal was:

"Time! Time!"

Bilbo was saved by pure luck. For that of course was the answer.

Gollum was disappointed once more; and now he was getting angry, and also tired of the game. It had made him very hungry indeed. This time he did not go back to the boat. He sat down in the dark by Bilbo. That made the hobbit most dreadfully uncomfortable and scattered his wits.

"It's got to ask uss a quesstion, my preciouss, yes, yess, yesss. Jusst one more question to guess, yes, yess," said Gollum.

But Bilbo simply could not think of any question with that nasty wet cold thing sitting next to him, and pawing and poking him. He scratched himself, he pinched himself; still he could not think of anything.

"Ask us! ask us!" said Gollum.

Bilbo pinched himself and slapped himself; he gripped on his little sword; he even felt in his pocket with his other hand. There he found the ring he had picked up in the passage and forgotten about.

"What have I got in my pocket?" he said aloud. He was talking to himself, but Gollum thought it was a riddle, and he was frightfully upset.

"Not fair! Not fair!" he hissed. "It isn't fair, my precious, is it, to ask us what it's got in its nassty little pocketses?"

Bilbo seeing what had happened and having nothing better to ask stuck to his question, "What have I got in my pocket?" he said louder.

"S-s-s-s-s," hissed Gollum. "It must give us three guesseses, my preciouss, three guesseses."

"Very well! Gues away!" said Bilbo.

"Handses!" said Gollum.

"Wrong," said Bilbo, who had luckily just taken his hand out again. "Guess again!"

"S-s-s-s-s," said Gollum more upset than ever. He thought of all the things he kept in his own pockets: fish-bones, goblins' teeth, wet shells, a bit of bat-wing, a sharp stone to sharpen his fangs on, and other nasty things. He tried to think what other people kept in their pockets.

"Knife!" he said at last.

"Wrong!" said Bilbo, who had lost his some time ago. "Last guess!"

Now Gollum was in a much worse state than when Bilbo had asked him the egg-question. He hissed and spluttered and rocked himself backwards and forwards, and slapped his feet on the floor, and wriggled and squirmed; but still he did not dare to waste his last guess.

"Come on!" said Bilbo. "I am waiting!" He tried to sound bold and cheerful, but he did not feel at all sure how the game was going to end, whether Gollum guessed right or not.

"Time's up!" he said.

"String, or nothing!" shrieked Gollum, which was not quite fair—working in two guesses at once.

"Both wrong," cried Bilbo very much relieved; and he jumped at once to his feet, put his back to the nearest wall, and held out his little sword. He knew, of course, that the riddle-game was sacred and of immense antiquity, and even wicked creatures were afraid to cheat when they played at it. But he felt he could not trust this slimy thing to keep any promise at a pinch. Any excuse would do for him to slide out of it. And after all that last question had not been a genuine riddle according to the ancient laws.

But at any rate Gollum did not at once attack him. He could see the sword in Bilbo's hand. He sat still, shivering and whispering. At last Bilbo could wait no longer.

"Well?" he said. "What about your promise? I want to go. You must show me the way."

"Did we say so, precious? Show the nassty little Baggins the way out, yes, yes. But what has it got in its pocketses, eh? Not string, precious, but not nothing. Oh no! gollum!"

"Never you mind," said Bilbo. "A promise is a promise."

"Cross it is, impatient, precious," hissed Gollum. "But it must wait, yes it must. We can't go up the tunnels so hasty. We must go and get some things first, yes, things to help us."

"Well, hurry up!" said Bilbo, relieved to think of Gollum going away. He thought he was just making an excuse and did not mean to come back. What was Gollum talking about? What useful thing could he keep out on the dark lake? But he was wrong. Gollum did mean to come back. He was angry now and hungry. And he was a miserable wicked creature, and already he had a plan.

Not far away was his island, of which Bilbo knew nothing, and there in his hiding-place he kept a few wretched oddments, and one very beautiful thing, very beautiful, very wonderful. He had a ring, a golden ring, a precious ring.

"My birthday-present!" he whispered to himself, as he had often done in the endless dark days. "That's what we wants now, yes; we wants it!"

He wanted it because it was a ring of power, and if you slipped that ring on your finger, you were invisible; only in the full sunlight could you be seen, and then only by your shadow, and that would be shaky and faint.

"My birthday-present! It came to me on my birthday, my precious." So he had always said to himself. But who knows how Gollum came by that present, ages ago in the old days when such rings were still at large in the world? Perhaps even the Master who ruled them could not have said. Gollum used to wear it at first, till it tired him; and then he kept it in a pouch next his skin, till it galled him; and now usually he hid it in a hole in the rock on his island, and was always going back to look at it. And still sometimes he put it on, when he could not bear to be parted from it any longer, or when he was very, very, hungry, and tired of fish. Then he would creep along dark passages looking for stray goblins. He might even venture into places where the torches were lit and made his eyes blink and smart; for he would be safe. Oh yes, quite safe. No one would see him, no one would notice him, till he had his fingers on their throat. Only a few hours ago he had worn it, and caught a small goblin-imp. How it squeaked! He still had a bone or two left to gnaw, but he wanted something softer.

"Quite safe, yes," he whispered to himself. "It won't see us, will it, my precious? No. It won't see us, and its nassty little sword will be useless, yes quite."

That is what was in his wicked little mind, as he slipped suddenly from Bilbo's side, and flapped back to his boat, and went off into the dark. Bilbo thought he had heard the last of him. Still he waited a while; for he had no idea how to find his way out alone.

Suddenly he heard a screech. It sent a shiver down his back. Gollum was cursing and wailing away in the gloom, not very far off by the sound of it. He was on his island, scrabbling here and there, searching and seeking in vain.

"Where is it? Where iss it?" Bilbo heard him crying. "Losst it is, my precious, lost, lost! Curse us and crush us, my precious is lost!"

"What's the matter?" Bilbo called. "What have you lost?"

"It mustn't ask us," shrieked Gollum. "Not its

business, no, gollum! It's losst, gollum, gollum, gollum."

"Well, so am I," cried Bilbo, "and I want to get unlost. And I won the game, and you promised. So come along! Come and let me out, and then go on with your looking!" Utterly miserable as Gollum sounded, Bilbo could not find much pity in his heart, and he had a feeling that anything Gollum wanted so much could hardly be something good. "Come along!" he shouted.

"No, not yet, precious!" Gollum answered. "We must search for it, it's lost, gollum."

"But you never guessed my last question, and you promised," said Bilbo.

"Never guessed!" said Gollum. Then suddenly out of the gloom came a sharp hiss. "What has it got in its pocketses? Tell us that. It must tell first."

As far as Bilbo knew, there was no particular reason why he should not tell. Gollum's mind had jumped to a guess quicker than his; naturally, for Gollum had brooded for ages on this one thing, and he was always afraid of its being stolen. But Bilbo was annoyed at the delay. After all, he had won the game, pretty fairly, at a horrible risk. "Answers were to be guessed not given," he said.

"But it wasn't a fair question," said Gollum. "Not a riddle, precious, no."

"Oh well, if it's a matter of ordinary questions," Bilbo replied, "then I asked one first. What have you lost? Tell me that!"

"What has it got in its pocketses?" The sound came hissing louder and sharper, and as he looked towards it, to his alarm Bilbo now saw two small points of light peering at him. As suspicion grew in Gollum's mind, the light of his eyes burned with a pale flame.

"What have you lost?" Bilbo persisted.

But now the light in Gollum's eyes had become a green fire, and it was coming swiftly nearer. Gollum was in his boat again, paddling wildly back to the dark shore; and such a rage of loss and suspicion was in his heart that no sword had any more terror for him.

Bilbo could not guess what had maddened the wretched creature, but he saw that all was up, and that Gollum meant to murder him at any rate. Just in time he turned and ran blindly back up the dark passage down which he had come, keeping close to the wall and feeling it with his left hand.

"What has it got in its pocketses?" he heard the hiss loud behind him, and the splash as Gollum leapt from his boat. "What have I, I wonder?" he said to himself, as he panted and stumbled along. He put his left hand in his pocket. The ring felt very cold as it quietly slipped on to his groping forefinger.

The hiss was close behind him. He turned now and saw Gollum's eyes like small green lamps coming up the slope. Terrified he tried to run faster, but suddenly he struck his toes on a snag in the floor, and fell flat with his little sword under him.

In a moment Gollum was on him. But before Bilbo could do anything, recover his breath, pick himself up, or wave his sword, Gollum passed by, taking no notice of him, cursing and whispering as he ran.

What could it mean? Gollum could see in the dark. Bilbo could see the light of his eyes palely shining even from behind. Painfully he got up, and sheathed his sword, which was now glowing faintly again, then very cautiously he followed. There seemed nothing else to do. It was no good crawling back down to Gollum's water. Perhaps if he followed him, Gollum might lead him to some way of escape without meaning to.

"Curse it! curse it! curse it!" hissed Gollum. "Curse the Baggins! It's gone! What has it got in its pocketses? Oh we guess, we guess, my precious. He's found it, yes he must have. My birthday-present."

Bilbo pricked up his ears. He was at last beginning to guess himself. He hurried a little, getting as close as he dared behind Gollum, who was still going quickly, not looking back, but turning his head from side to side, as Bilbo could see from the faint glimmer on the walls.

"My birthday-present! Curse it! How did we lose it,

my precious? Yes, that's it. When we came this way last, when we twisted that nassty young squeaker. That's it. Curse it! It slipped from us, after all these ages and ages! It's gone, gollum."

Suddenly Gollum sat down and began to weep, a whistling and gurgling sound horrible to listen to. Bilbo halted and flattened himself against the tunnel wall. After a while Gollum stopped weeping and began to talk. He seemed to be having an argument with himself.

"It's no good going back there to search, no. We doesn't remember all the places we've visited. And it's no use. The Baggins has got it in its pocketses; the nassty noser has found it, we says."

"We guesses, precious, only guesses. We can't know till we find the nassty creature and squeezes it. But it doesn't know what the present can do, does it? It'll just keep it in its pocketses. It doesn't know, and it can't go far. It's lost itself, the nassty nosey thing. It doesn't know the way out. It said so."

"It said so, yes; but it's tricksy. It doesn't say what it means. It won't say what it's got in its pocketses. It knows. It knows a way in, it must know a way out, yes. It's off to the back-door. To the back-door, that's it."

"The goblinses will catch it then. It can't get out that way, precious."

"Ssss, sss, gollum! Goblinses! Yes, but if it's got the present, our precious present, then goblinses will get it, gollum! They'll find it, they'll find out what it does. We shan't ever be safe again, never, gollum! One of the goblinses will put it on, and then no one will see him. He'll be there but not seen. Not even our clever eyeses will notice him; and he'll come creepsy and tricksy and catch us, gollum, gollum!"

"Then let's stop talking, precious, and make haste. If the Baggins has gone that way, we must go quick and see. Go! Not far now. Make haste!"

With a spring Gollum got up and started shambling off at a great pace. Bilbo hurried after him, still cautiously, though his chief fear now was of tripping on another snag and falling with a noise. His head was in a whirl of hope and wonder. It seemed that the ring he had was a magic ring: it made you invisible! He had heard of such things, of course, in old old tales; but it was hard to believe that he really had found one, by accident. Still there it was: Gollum with his bright eyes had passed him by, only a yard to one side.

On they went, Gollum flip-flapping ahead, hissing and cursing; Bilbo behind going as softly as a hobbit can. Soon they came to places where, as Bilbo had noticed on the way down, side-passages opened, this way and that. Gollum began at once to count them.

"One left, yes. One right, yes. Two right, yes, yes. Two left, yes, yes." And so on and on.

As the count grew he slowed down, and he began to get shaky and weepy; for he was leaving the water further and further behind, and he was getting afraid. Goblins might be about, and he had lost his ring. At last he stopped by a low opening, on their left as they went up.

"Seven right, yes. Six left, yes!" he whispered. "This is it. This is the way to the back-door, yes. Here's the passage!"

He peered in, and shrank back. "But we durstn't go in, precious, no we durstn't. Goblinses down there. Lots of goblinses. We smells them. Ssss!"

"What shall we do? Curse them and crush them! We must wait here, precious, wait a bit and see."

So they came to a dead stop. Gollum had brought Bilbo to the way out after all, but Bilbo could not get in! There was Gollum sitting humped up right in the opening, and his eyes gleamed cold in his head, as he swayed it from side to side between his knees.

Bilbo crept away from the wall more quietly than a mouse; but Gollum stiffened at once, and sniffed, and his eyes went green. He hissed softly but menacingly. He could not see the hobbit, but now he was on the alert, and he had other senses that the darkness had sharpened: hearing and smell. He seemed to be crouched right down with his flat hands splayed on the floor, and his head thrust out, nose almost to the stone. Though he was only a black shadow in the gleam of his own eyes, Bilbo could see or feel that he was tense as a bowstring, gathered for a spring.

Bilbo almost stopped breathing, and went stiff himself. He was desperate. He must get away, out of this horrible darkness, while he had any strength left. He must fight. He must stab the foul thing, put its eyes out, kill it. It meant to kill him. No, not a fair fight. He was invisible now. Gollum had no sword. Gollum had not actually threatened to kill him, or tried to yet. And he was miserable, alone, lost. A sudden understanding, a pity mixed with horror, welled up in Bilbo's heart: a glimpse of endless unmarked days without light or hope of betterment, hard stone, cold fish, sneaking and whispering. All these thoughts passed in a flash of a second. He trembled. And then quite suddenly in another flash, as if lifted by a new strength and resolve, he leaped.

No great leap for a man, but a leap in the dark. Straight over Gollum's head he jumped, seven feet forward and three in the air; indeed, had he known it, he only just missed cracking his skull on the low arch of the passage.

Gollum threw himself backwards, and grabbed as the hobbit flew over him, but too late: his hands snapped on thin air, and Bilbo, falling fair on his sturdy feet, sped off down the new tunnel. He did not turn to see what Gollum was doing. There was a hissing and cursing almost at his heels at first, then it stopped. All at once there came a bloodcurdling shriek, filled with hatred and despair. Gollum was defeated. He dared go no further. He had lost: lost his prey, and lost, too, the only thing he had ever cared for, his precious. The cry brought Bilbo's heart to his mouth, but still he held on. Now faint as an echo, but menacing, the voice came behind:

"Thief, thief, thief! Baggins! We hates it, we hates it, we hates it for ever!"

Then there was a silence. But that too seemed menacing to Bilbo. "If goblins are so near that he smelt them," he thought, "then they'll have heard his shrieking and cursing. Careful now, or this way will lead you to worse things."

The passage was low and roughly made. It was not too difficult for the hobbit, except when, in spite of all care, he stubbed his poor toes again, several times, on nasty jagged stones on the floor. "A bit low for goblins, at least for the big ones," thought Bilbo, not knowing that even the big ones, the orcs of the mountains, go along at a great speed stooping low with their hands almost on the ground.

Soon the passage that had been sloping down began to go up again, and after a while it climbed steeply. That slowed Bilbo down. But at last the slope stopped, the passage turned a corner, and dipped down again, and there, at the bottom of a short incline, he saw, filtering round another corner—a glimpse of light. Not red light, as of fire or lantern, but a pale out-of-doors sort of light. Then Bilbo began to run.

Scuttling as fast as his legs would carry him he turned the last corner and came suddenly right into an open space where the light, after all that time in the dark, seemed dazzlingly bright. Really it was only a leak of sunshine in through a doorway, where a great door, a stone door, was left standing open.

Bilbo blinked, and then suddenly he saw the goblins: goblins in full armour with drawn swords sitting just inside the door, and watching it with wide eyes, and watching the passage that led to it. They were aroused, alert, ready for anything.

They saw him sooner than he saw them. Yes, they saw him. Whether it was an accident, or a last trick of the ring before it took a new master, it was not on his finger. With yells of delight the goblins rushed upon him.

A pang of fear and loss, like an echo of Gollum's misery, smote Bilbo, and forgetting even to draw his sword he struck his hands into his pockets. And there was the ring still, in his left pocket, and it slipped on his finger. The goblins stopped short. They could not see a sign of him. He had vanished. They yelled twice as loud as before, but not so delightedly.

"Where is it?" they cried.

"Go back up the passage!" some shouted.

"This way!" some yelled. "That way!" others yelled.

"Look out for the door," bellowed the captain.

Whistles blew, armour clashed, swords rattled, goblins cursed and swore and ran hither and thither, falling over one another and getting very angry. There was a terrible outcry, to-do, and disturbance.

Bilbo was dreadfully frightened, but he had the sense to understand what had happened and to sneak behind a big barrel which held drink for the goblin-guards, and so get out of the way and avoid being bumped into, trampled to death, or caught by feel.

"I must get to the door, I must get to the door!" he kept on saying to himself, but it was a long time before he ventured to try. Then it was like a horrible game of blindman's-buff. The place was full of goblins running about, and the poor little hobbit dodged this way and that, was knocked over by a goblin who could not make out what he had bumped into, scrambled away on all fours, slipped between the legs of the captain just in time, got up, and ran for the door.

It was still ajar, but a goblin had pushed it nearly to. Bilbo struggled but he could not move it. He tried to squeeze through the crack. He squeezed and squeezed, and he stuck! It was awful. His buttons had got wedged on the edge of the door and the door-post. He could see outside into the open air: there were a few steps running down into a narrow valley between tall mountains; the sun came out from behind a cloud and shone bright on the outside of the door—but he could not get through.

Suddenly one of the goblins inside shouted: "There is a shadow by the door. Something is outside!"

Bilbo's heart jumped into his mouth. He gave a terrific squirm. Buttons burst off in all directions. He was through, with a torn coat and waistcoat, leaping down the steps like a goat, while bewildered goblins were still picking up his nice brass buttons on the doorstep.

Of course they soon came down after him, hooting and hallooing, and hunting among the trees. But they don't like the sun: it makes their legs wobble and their heads giddy. They could not find Bilbo with the ring on, slipping in and out of the shadow of the trees, running quick and quiet, and keeping out of the sun; so soon they went back grumbling and cursing to guard the door. Bilbo had escaped.

CLIVE STAPLES LEWIS

(1898–1963)

C. S. Lewis was an extraordinary man of diverse talents. He was a respected scholar and teacher, a reputable literary critic, a knowledgeable social commentator, a persuasive essayist, a critically acclaimed poet and novelist, a fervent Christian Apologist, and a popular author of children's literature. Born in Belfast, Ireland, the son of a solicitor, Lewis was educated at Malvern and University College, Oxford. Before taking his M.A. he received numerous honors, and established a reputation as an outstanding scholar. When World War I broke out Lewis joined the armed forces and served with the Somerset Light Infantry. Once out of the service, he re-entered the world of Academe and spent the remainder of his life there. He was a Fellow of Magdalen College, Oxford, from 1925 to 1954, and then was appointed Professor of Medieval and Renaissance English at Cambridge in 1956. He held this chair until his death in 1963.

Lewis's writing career covers a long span of approximately forty years. As early as 1926, he published a long poem, *Dymer,* under the pseudonym Clive Hamilton, and in the ensuing years he wrote and published a number of scholarly texts and theological treatises. Perhaps the best known of his critical works is *The Allegory of Love* (1936), which still remains the definitive study of the courtly-love tradition in literature. Lewis freely admitted that much of his writing was devoted to bringing theology to the masses, and this he did with works such as *The Pilgrim's Regress* (1933), *The Screwtape Letters* (1942), *Christian Behavior* (1943), and *Mere Christianity* (1952). *Surprised by Joy* (1955) is his spiritual autobiography. Lewis's sterling reputation as writer could safely rest with the aforementioned works, but perhaps his most popular writings are those which comprise the *Outer Space Trilogy* and *The Chronicles of Narnia*. He began writing the trilogy in 1938 with *Out of the Silent Planet; Perelandra* followed in 1943; and, finally, *That Hideous Strength* in 1945. The seven volumes which make up the Narnia series were written in rapid succession during the early and mid-fifties: *The Lion, The Witch and The Wardrobe* (1950), *Prince Caspian* (1951), *The Voyage of the "Dawn Treader"* (1952). *The Silver Chair* (1953), *The Horse and His Boy* (1954), *The Magician's Nephew* (1955), and *The Last Battle* (1956).

An anthology of high fantasy simply would not be complete without a selection from *The Chronicles of Narnia*, which have delighted readers of all ages for the past two decades. Especially memorable are some of the episodes in *The Voyage of the "Dawn Treader,"* and it is from this book that our selection is drawn. Lewis was a superb literary craftsman who did many things well, but he was especially successful in juxtaposing the serious and the comic. In this episode we first witness Lucy's poignant and joyful reunion with Aslan, with all its serious spiritual overtones, and then are treated to the hilarious antics of the unforgettable dufflepuds—those bouncy little monopods who are constantly doing silly things like "planting boiled potatoes to save cooking them when . . . dug up." Magic is, of course, the primary ingredient in all of the *Chronicles,* and there is an abundance of it here.

❧ The Magician's Book ❧

C. S. Lewis

The invisible people feasted their guests royally. It was very funny to see the plates and dishes coming to the table and not to see anyone carrying them. It would have been funny even if they had moved along level with the floor, as you would expect things to do in invisible hands. But they didn't. They progressed up the long dining-hall in a series of bounds or jumps. At the highest point of each jump a dish would be about fifteen feet up in the air; then it would come down and stop quite suddenly about three feet from the floor. When the dish contained anything like soup or stew the result was rather disastrous.

"I'm beginning to feel very inquisitive about these people," whispered Eustace to Edmund. "Do you think they're human at all? More like huge grasshoppers or giant frogs, I should say."

"It does look like it," said Edmund. "But don't put the idea of grasshoppers into Lucy's head. She's not too keen on insects; specially big ones."

The meal would have been pleasanter if it had not been so exceedingly messy, and also if the conversation had not consisted entirely of agreements. The invisible people agreed about everything. Indeed most of their remarks were the sort it would not be easy to disagree with: "What I always say is, when a chap's hungry, he likes some victuals," or "Getting dark now; always does at night," or even "Ah, you've come over the water. Powerful wet stuff, ain't it?" And Lucy could not help looking at the dark yawning entrance to the foot of the staircase—she could see it from where she sat—and wondering what she would find when she went up those stairs next morning. But it was a good meal otherwise, with mushroom soup and boiled chickens and hot boiled ham and gooseberries, red currants, curds, cream, milk, and mead. The others liked the mead but Eustace was sorry afterwards that he had drunk any.

When Lucy woke up next morning it was like waking up on the day of an examination or a day when you are going to the dentist. It was a lovely morning with bees buzzing in and out of her open window and the lawn outside looking very like somewhere in England. She got up and dressed and tried to talk and eat ordinarily at breakfast. Then, after being instructed by the Chief Voice about what she was to do upstairs, she bid good-bye to the others, said nothing, walked to the bottom of the stairs, and began going up them without once looking back.

It was quite light, that was one good thing. There was, indeed, a window straight ahead of her at the top of the first flight. As long as she was on that flight she could hear the *tick-tock-tick-tock* of a grandfather clock in the hall below. Then she came to the landing and had to turn to her left up the next flight; after that she couldn't hear the clock any more.

Now she had come to the top of the stairs. Lucy looked and saw a long, wide passage with a large window at the far end. Apparently the passage ran the whole length of the house. It was carved and panelled and carpeted and very many doors opened off it on each side. She stood still and couldn't hear the squeak of a mouse, or the buzzing of a fly, or the swaying of a curtain, or anything—except the beating of her own heart.

"The last doorway on the left," she said to herself. It did seem a bit hard that it should be the last. To reach it she would have to walk past room after room. And in any room there might be the magician—asleep, or

awake, or invisible, or even dead. But it wouldn't do to
think about that. She set out on her journey. The carpet was so thick that her feet made no noise.

"There's nothing whatever to be afraid of yet," Lucy
told herself. And certainly it was a quiet, sunlit passage; perhaps a bit too quiet. It would have been nicer
if there had not been strange signs painted in scarlet on
the doors—twisty, complicated things which obviously
had a meaning and it mightn't be a very nice meaning
either. It would have been nicer still if there weren't
those masks hanging on the wall. Not that they were
exactly ugly—or not so very ugly—but the empty eye-
holes did look queer, and if you let yourself you would
soon start imagining that the masks were doing things
as soon as your back was turned to them.

After about the sixth door she got her first real
fright. For one second she felt almost certain that a
wicked little bearded face had popped out of the wall
and made a grimace at her. She forced herself to stop
and look at it. And it was not a face at all. It was a
little mirror just the size and shape of her own face,
with hair on the top of it and a beard hanging down
from it, so that when you looked in the mirror your
own face fitted into the hair and beard and it looked as
if they belonged to you. "I just caught my own reflection with the tail of my eye as I went past," said Lucy
to herself. "That was all it was. It's quite harmless."
But she didn't like the look of her own face with that
hair and beard, and went on. (I don't know what the
Bearded Glass was for because I am not a magician.)

Before she reached the last door on the left Lucy
was beginning to wonder whether the corridor had
grown longer since she began her journey and whether
this was part of the magic of the house. But she got to
it at last. And the door was open.

It was a large room with three big windows and it
was lined from floor to ceiling with books; more books
than Lucy had ever seen before, tiny little books, fat
and dumpy books, and books bigger than any church
Bible you have ever seen, all bound in leather and

smelling old and learned and magical. But she knew from her instructions that she need not bother about any of these. For *the* Book, the Magic Book, was lying on a reading desk in the very middle of the room. She saw she would have to read it standing (and anyway there were no chairs) and also that she would have to stand with her back to the door while she read it. So at once she turned to shut the door.

It wouldn't shut.

Some people may disagree with Lucy about this, but I think she was quite right. She said she wouldn't have minded if she could have shut the door, but that it was unpleasant to have to stand in a place like that with an open doorway right behind your back. I should have felt just the same. But there was nothing else to be done.

One thing that worried her a good deal was the size of the Book. The Chief Voice had not been able to give her any idea whereabouts in the Book the spell for making things visible came. He even seemed rather surprised at her asking. He expected her to begin at the beginning and go on till she came to it; it obviously wouldn't have occurred to him that there was any other way of finding a place in a book. "But it might take me days and weeks!" said Lucy, looking at the huge volume, "and I feel already as if I'd been in this place for hours."

She went up to the desk and laid her hand on the book; her fingers tingled when she touched it as if it were full of electricity. She tried to open it but couldn't at first; this, however, was only because it was fastened by two leaden clasps, and when she had undone these it opened easily enough. And what a book it was!

It was written, not printed; written in a clear, even hand, with thick downstrokes and thin upstrokes, very large, easier than print, and so beautiful that Lucy stared at it for a whole minute and forgot about reading it. The paper was crisp and smooth and a nice smell came from it; and in the margins, and round the big coloured capital letters at the beginning of each spell, there were pictures.

There was no title page or title; the spells began straight away, and at first there was nothing very important in them. They were cures for warts (by washing your hands in moonlight in a silver basin) and toothache and cramp, and a spell for taking a swarm of bees. The picture of the man with toothache was so lifelike that it would have set your own teeth aching if you looked at it too long, and the golden bees which were dotted all round the fourth spell looked for a moment as if they were really flying.

Lucy could hardly tear herself away from that first page, but when she turned over, the next was just as interesting. "But I must go on," she told herself. And on she went for about thirty pages which, if she could have remembered them, would have taught her how to find buried treasure, how to remember things forgotten, how to forget things you wanted to forget, how to tell whether anyone was speaking the truth, how to call up (or prevent) wind, fog, snow, sleet or rain, how to produce enchanted sleeps and how to give a man an ass's head (as they did to poor Bottom). And the longer she read the more wonderful and more real the pictures became.

Then she came to a page which was such a blaze of pictures that one hardly noticed the writing. Hardly— but she *did* notice the first words. They were, *An infallible spell to make beautiful her that uttereth it beyond the lot of mortals.* Lucy peered at the pictures with her face close to the page, and though they had seemed crowded and muddlesome before, she found she could now see them quite clearly. The first was a picture of a girl standing at a reading-table reading in a huge book. And the girl was dressed exactly like Lucy. In the next picture Lucy (for the girl in the picture was Lucy herself) was standing up with her mouth open and a rather terrible expression on her face, chanting or reciting something. In the third picture the beauty beyond the lot of mortals had come to her. It was strange, considering how small the pictures had looked at first, that Lucy in the picture now seemed quite as big as the real Lucy; and they looked into each other's eyes and the real Lucy looked away after a few minutes because she was dazzled by the beauty of the other Lucy; though she could still see a sort of likeness to herself in that beautiful face. And now the pictures came crowding on her thick and fast. She saw herself throned on high at a great tournament in Calormen and all the kings of the world fought because of her beauty. After that it turned from tournaments to real wars, and all Narnia and Archenland, Telmar and Calormen, Galma and Terebinthia, were laid waste with the fury of the kings and dukes and great lords who fought for her favour. Then it changed and Lucy, still beautiful beyond the lot of mortals, was back in England. And Susan (who had always been the beauty of the family) came home from America. The Susan in the picture looked exactly like the real Susan only plainer and with a nasty expression. And Susan was jealous of the dazzling beauty of Lucy, but that didn't matter a bit because no one cared anything about Susan now.

"I *will* say the spell," said Lucy. "I don't care. I will." She said *I don't care* because she had a strong feeling that she mustn't.

But when she looked back at the opening words of the spell, there in the middle of the writing, where she felt quite sure there had been no picture before, she found the great face of a lion, of the Lion, Aslan himself, staring into hers. It was painted such a bright gold that it seemed to be coming towards her out of the page; and indeed she never was quite sure afterwards that it hadn't really moved a little. At any rate she knew the expression on his face quite well. He was growling and you could see most of his teeth. She became horribly afraid and turned over the page at once.

A little later she came to a spell which would let you know what your friends thought about you. Now Lucy had wanted very badly to try the other spell, the one that made you beautiful beyond the lot of mortals. So she felt that to make up for not having said it, she really would say this one. And all in a hurry, for fear her mind would change, she said the words (nothing will induce me to tell you what they were). Then she waited for something to happen.

As nothing happened she began looking at the pictures. And all at once she saw the very last thing she expected—a picture of a third-class carriage in a train, with two schoolgirls sitting in it. She knew them at once. They were Marjorie Preston and Anne Featherstone. Only now it was much more than a picture. It was alive. She could see the telegraph posts flicking past outside the window. She could see the two girls laughing and talking. Then gradually (like when the radio is "coming on") she could hear what they were saying.

"Shall I see anything of you this term?" said Anne, "or are you still going to be all taken up with Lucy Pevensie."

"Don't know what you mean by *taken up*," said Marjorie.

"Oh yes, you do," said Anne. "You were crazy about her last term."

"No, I wasn't," said Marjorie. "I've got more sense than that. Not a bad little kid in her way. But I was getting pretty tired of her before the end of term."

"Well, you jolly well won't have the chance any other term!" shouted Lucy. "Two-faced little beast." But the sound of her own voice at once reminded her that she was talking to a picture and that the real Marjorie was far away in another world.

"Well," said Lucy to herself, "I did think better of her than that. And I did all sorts of things for her last term, and I stuck to her when not many other girls would. And she knows it too. And to Anne Featherstone of all people! I wonder are all my friends the same? There are lots of other pictures. No. I won't look at any more. I won't, I won't"—and with a great effort she turned over the page; but not before a large, angry tear had splashed on it.

On the next page she came to a spell "for the refreshment of the spirit." The pictures were fewer here but very beautiful. And what Lucy found herself reading was more like a story than a spell. It went on for three pages and before she had read to the bottom of the page she had forgotten that she was reading at all. She was living in the story as if it were real, and all the pictures were real too. When she had got to the third page and come to the end, she said, "That is the loveliest story I've ever read or ever shall read in my whole life. Oh, I wish I could have gone on reading it for ten years. At least I'll read it over again."

But here part of the magic of the Book came into play. You couldn't turn back. The right-hand pages, the ones ahead, could be turned; the left-hand pages could not.

"Oh, what a shame!" said Lucy. "I did so want to read it again. Well, at least, I must remember it. Let's see . . . it was about . . . about . . . oh dear, it's all fading away again. And even this last page is going blank. This is a very queer book. How can I have forgotten? It was about a cup and a sword and a tree and a green hill, I know that much. But I can't remember and what *shall* I do?"

And she never could remember; and ever since that day what Lucy means by a good story is a story which reminds her of the forgotten story in the Magician's Book.

She turned on and found to her surprise a page with no pictures at all; but the first words were *A spell to make hidden things visible*. She read it through to make sure of all the hard words and then said it out loud. And she knew at once that it was working because as she spoke the colours came into the capital letters at the top of the page and the picture began appearing in the margins. It was like when you hold to the fire something written in Invisible Ink and the writing gradually shows up; only instead of the dingy colour of lemon juice (which is the easiest Invisible Ink) this was all gold and blue and scarlet. They were odd pictures and contained many figures that Lucy did not much like the look of. And then she thought, "I suppose I've made everything visible, and not only the Thumpers. There might be lots of other invisible things hanging about a place like this. I'm not sure that I want to see them all."

At that moment she heard soft, heavy footfalls coming along the corridor behind her; and of course she remembered what she had been told about the magician walking in his bare feet and making no more noise than a cat. It is always better to turn round than to have anything creeping up behind your back. Lucy did so.

Then her face lit up till, for a moment (but of course she didn't know it), she looked almost as beautiful as that other Lucy in the picture, and she ran forward with a little cry of delight and with her arms stretched out. For what stood in the doorway was Aslan himself, the Lion, the highest of all High Kings. And he was solid and real and warm and he let her kiss and bury herself in his shining mane. And from the low, earthquake-like sound that came from inside him, Lucy even dared to think that he was purring.

"Oh, Aslan," said she, "it was kind of you to come."

"I have been here all the time," he said, "but you have just made me visible."

"Aslan!" said Lucy almost a little reproachfully. "Don't make fun of me. As if anything *I* could do would make *you* visible!"

"It did," said Aslan. "Do you think I wouldn't obey my own rules?"

After a little pause he spoke again.

"Child," he said, "I think you have been eavesdropping."

"Eavesdropping?"

"You listened to what your two schoolfellows were saying about you."

"Oh that? I never thought that was eavesdropping, Aslan. Wasn't it magic?"

"Spying on people by magic is the same as spying on

them in any other way. And you have misjudged your friend. She is weak, but she loves you. She was afraid of the older girl and said what she does not mean."

"I don't think I'd ever be able to forget what I heard her say."

"No, you won't."

"Oh dear," said Lucy. "Have I spoiled everything? Do you mean we would have gone on being friends if it hadn't been for this—and been really great friends—all our lives perhaps—and now we never shall."

"Child," said Aslan, "did I not explain to you once before that no one is ever told what *would have happened?*"

"Yes, Aslan, you did," said Lucy. "I'm sorry. But please—"

"Speak on, dear heart."

"Shall I ever be able to read that story again; the one I couldn't remember? Will you tell it to me, Aslan? Oh do, do, do."

"Indeed, yes, I will tell it to you for years and years. But now, come. We must meet the master of the house."

❦ The Dufflepuds Made Happy ❦

C. S. Lewis

Lucy followed the great Lion out into the passage and at once she saw coming toward them an old man, barefoot, dressed in a red robe. His white hair was crowned with a chaplet of oak leaves, his beard fell to his girdle, and he supported himself with a curiously carved staff. When he saw Aslan he bowed low and said,

"Welcome, Sir, to the least of your houses."

"Do you grow weary, Coriakin, of ruling such foolish subjects as I have given you here?"

"No," said the Magician, "they are very stupid but there is no real harm in them. I begin to grow rather fond of the creatures. Sometimes, perhaps, I am a little impatient, waiting for the day when they can be governed by wisdom instead of this rough magic."

"All in good time, Coriakin," said Aslan.

"Yes, all in very good time, Sir," was the answer. "Do you intend to show yourself to them?"

"Nay," said the Lion, with a little half growl that meant (Lucy thought) the same as a laugh. "I should frighten them out of their senses. Many stars will grow old and come to take their rest in islands before your people are ripe for that. And to-day before sunset I must visit Trumpkin the Dwarf where he sits in the castle of Cair Paravel counting the days till his master Caspian comes home. I will tell him all your story, Lucy. Do not look so sad. We shall meet soon again."

"Please, Aslan," said Lucy, "what do you call *soon?*"

"I call all times soon," said Aslan; and instantly he was vanished away and Lucy was alone with the Magician.

"Gone!" said hê, "and you and I quite crestfallen. It's always like that, you can't keep him; it's not as if he were a *tame* lion. And how did you enjoy my book?"

"Parts of it very much indeed," said Lucy. "Did you know I was there all the time?"

"Well, of course I knew when I let the Duffers make themselves invisible that you would be coming along presently to take the spell off. I wasn't quite sure of the exact day. And I wasn't especially on the watch this morning. You see they had made me invisible too and being invisible always makes me so sleepy. Heigh-ho—there I'm yawning again. Are you hungry?"

"Well, perhaps I am a little," said Lucy. "I've no idea what the time is."

"Come," said the Magician. "All times may be soon to Aslan; but in my home all hungry times are one o'clock."

He led her a little way down the passage and opened a door. Passing in, Lucy found herself in a pleasant room full of sunlight and flowers. The table was bare when they entered, but it was of course a magic table, and at a word from the old man the tablecloth, silver, plates, glasses and food appeared.

"I hope that is what you would like," said he. "I have tried to give you food more like the food of your own land than perhaps you have had lately."

"It's lovely," said Lucy, and so it was; an omelette, piping hot, cold lamb and green peas, a strawberry ice, lemon squash to drink with the meal and a cup of chocolate to follow. But the Magician himself drank only wine and ate only bread. There was nothing alarming about him, and Lucy and he were soon chatting away like old friends.

"When will the spell work?" asked Lucy. "Will the Duffers be visible again at once?"

"Oh yes, they're visible now. But they're probably

all asleep still; they always take a rest in the middle of the day."

"And now that they're visible, are you going to let them off being ugly? Will you make them as they were before?"

"Well, that's rather a delicate question," said the Magician. "You see, it's only *they* who think they were so nice to look at before. They say they've been uglified, but that isn't what I called it. Many people might say the change was for the better."

"Are they awfully conceited?"

"They are. Or at least the Chief Duffer is, and he's taught all the rest to be. They always believe every word he says."

"We'd noticed that," said Lucy.

"Yes—we'd get on better without him, in a way. Of course I could turn him into something else, or even put a spell on him which would make them not believe a word he said. But I don't like to do that. It's better for them to admire him than to admire nobody."

"Don't they admire *you?*" asked Lucy.

"Oh, not *me,*" said the Magician. "They wouldn't admire *me.*"

"What was it you uglified them for—I mean, what they call *uglified?*"

"Well, they wouldn't do what they were told. Their work is to mind the garden and raise food—not for me, as they imagine, but for themselves. They wouldn't do it at all if I didn't make them. And of course for a garden you want water. There is a beautiful spring about half a mile away up the hill. And from that spring there flows a stream which comes right past the garden. All I asked them to do was to take their water from the stream instead of trudging up to the spring with their buckets two or three times a day and tiring themselves out besides spilling half of it on the way back. But they wouldn't see it. In the end they refused point blank."

"Are they as stupid as all that?" asked Lucy.

The Magician sighed. "You wouldn't believe the

troubles I've had with them. A few months ago they were all for washing up the plates and knives before dinner: they said it saved time afterwards. I've caught them planting boiled potatoes to save cooking them when they were dug up. One day the cat got into the dairy and twenty of them were at work moving all the milk out; no one thought of moving the cat. But I see you've finished. Let's go and look at the Duffers now they can be looked at."

They went into another room which was full of polished instruments hard to understand—such as Astrolabes, Orreries, Chronoscopes, Poesimeters, Choriambuses and Theodolinds—and here, when they had come to the window the Magician said, "There. There are your Duffers."

"I don't see anybody," said Lucy. "And what are those mushroom things?"

The things she pointed at were dotted all over the level grass. They were certainly very like mushrooms, but far too big—the stalks about three feet high and the umbrellas about the same length from edge to edge. When she looked carefully she noticed too that the stalks joined the umbrellas not in the middle but at one side which gave an unbalanced look to them. And there was something—a sort of little bundle—lying on the grass at the foot of each stalk. In fact the longer she gazed at them the less like mushrooms they appeared. The umbrella part was not really round as she had thought at first. It was longer than it was broad, and it widened at one end. There were a great many of them, fifty or more.

The clock struck three.

Instantly a most extraordinary thing happened. Each of the "mushrooms" suddenly turned upside-down. The little bundles which had lain at the bottom of the stalks were heads and bodies. The stalks themselves were legs. But not two legs to each body. Each body had a single thick leg right under it (not to one side like the leg of a one-legged man) and at the end of it, a single enormous foot—a broad-toed foot with the toes

curling up a little so that it looked rather like a small
canoe. She saw in a moment why they had looked like
mushrooms. They had been lying flat on their backs
each with its single leg straight up in the air and its
enormous foot spread out above it. She learned afterwards that this was their ordinary way of resting; for
the foot kept off both rain and sun and for a Monopod
to lie under its own foot is almost as good as being in a
tent.

"Oh, the funnies, the funnies," cried Lucy, bursting
into laughter. "Did *you* make them like that?"

"Yes, yes, I made the Duffers into Monopods," said
the Magician. He too was laughing till the tears ran
down his cheeks. "But watch," he added.

It was worth watching. Of course these little one-
footed men couldn't walk or run as we do. They got
about by jumping, like fleas or frogs. And what jumps
they made!—as if each big foot were a mass of springs.
And with what a bounce they came down; that was
what made the thumping noise which had so puzzled
Lucy yesterday. For now they were jumping in all
directions and calling out to one another, "Hey lads!
We're visible again."

"Visible we are," said one in a tasselled red cap who
was obviously the chief Monopod. "And what I say is,
when chaps are visible, why they can see one another."

"Ah, there it is, there it is, Chief," cried all the others. "There's the point. No one's got a clearer head
than you. You couldn't have made it plainer."

"She caught the old man napping, that little girl
did," said the Chief Monopod. "We've beaten him this
time."

"Just what we were going to say ourselves," chimed
the chorus. "You're going stronger than ever to-day,
Chief. Keep it up, keep it up."

"But do they dare to talk about you like that?" said
Lucy. "They seemed to be so afraid of you yesterday.
Don't they know you might be listening?"

"That's one of the funny things about the Duffers,"

said the Magician. "One minute they talk as if I ran everything and overheard everything and was extremely dangerous. The next moment they think they can take me in by tricks that a baby would see through—bless them!"

"Will they have to be turned back into their proper shapes?" asked Lucy. "Oh, I do hope it wouldn't be unkind to leave them as they are. Do they really mind very much? They seem pretty happy. I say—look at that jump. What were they like before?"

"Common little dwarfs," said he. "Nothing like so nice as the sort you have in Narnia."

"It *would* be a pity to change them back," said Lucy. "They're so funny: and they're rather nice. Do you think it would make any difference if I told them that?"

"I'm sure it would—if you could get it into their heads."

"Will you come with me and try?"

"No, no. You'll get on far better without me."

"Thanks awfully for the lunch," said Lucy and turned quickly away. She ran down the stairs which she had come up so nervously that morning and cannoned into Edmund at the bottom. All the others were there with him waiting, and Lucy's conscience smote her when she saw their anxious faces and realised how long she had forgotten them.

"It's all right," she shouted. "Everything's all right. The Magician's a brick—and I've seen *him*—Aslan."

After that she went from them like the wind and out into the garden. Here the earth was shaking with the jumps and the air ringing with the shouts of the Monopods. Both were redoubled when they caught sight of her.

"Here she comes, here she comes," they cried. "Three cheers for the little girl. Ah! She put it across the old gentleman properly, she did."

"And we're extremely regrettable," said the Chief Monopod, "that we can't give you the pleasure of seeing us as we were before we were uglified, for you wouldn't believe the difference, and that's the truth, for there's no denying we're mortal ugly now, so we won't deceive you."

"Eh, that we are, Chief, that we are," echoed the others, bouncing like so many toy balloons. "You've said it, you've said it."

"But I don't think you are at all," said Lucy, shouting to make herself heard. "I think you look very nice."

"Hear her, hear her," said the Monopods. "True for you, Missie. Very nice we look. You couldn't find a handsomer lot." They said this without any surprise and did not seem to notice that they had changed their minds.

"She's a-saying," remarked the Chief Monopod, "as how we looked very nice before we were all uglified."

"True for you, Chief, true for you," chanted the others. "That's what she says. We heard her ourselves."

"I did *not*," bawled Lucy. "I said you're very nice *now*."

"So she did, so she did," said the Chief Monopod, "said we were very nice then."

"Hear 'em both, hear 'em both," said the Monopods. "There's a pair for you. Always right. They couldn't have put it better."

"But we're saying just the opposite," said Lucy, stamping her foot with impatience.

"So you are, to be sure, so you are," said the Monopods. "Nothing like a opposite. Keep it up, both of you."

"You're enough to drive anyone mad," said Lucy, and gave it up. But the Monopods seemed perfectly contented, and she decided that on the whole the conversation had been a success.

And before everyone went to bed that evening something else happened which made them even more satisfied with their one-legged condition. Caspian and all the Narnians went back as soon as possible to the shore to give their news to Rhince and the others on board the *Dawn Treader,* who were by now in considerable anxiety. And, of course, the Monopods went with them, bouncing like footballs and agreeing with one another in loud voices till Eustace said, "I wish the Magician would make them inaudible instead of invisible." (He was soon sorry he had spoken because then he had to explain that an inaudible thing is something you can't hear, and though he took a lot of trouble he never felt sure that the Monopods had really understood, and what especially annoyed him was that they said in the end, "Eh, he can't put things the way our Chief does. But you'll learn, young man. Hark to *him*. He'll show you how to say things. There's a speaker for you!") When they reached the bay, Reepicheep had a brilliant idea. He had his little coracle lowered and paddled himself about in it till the Monopods were thoroughly interested. He then stood up in it and said, "Worthy and intelligent Monopods, you do not need boats. Each of you has a foot that will do instead. Just jump as lightly as you can on the water and see what happens."

The Chief Monopod hung back and warned the others that they'd find the water powerful wet, but one or two of the younger ones tried it almost at once; and then a few others followed their example, and at last the whole lot did the same. It worked perfectly. The huge single foot of a Monopod acted as a natural raft or boat, and when Reepicheep had taught them how to cut rude paddles for themselves, they all paddled about the bay and round the *Dawn Treader,* looking for all the world like a fleet of little canoes with a fat dwarf standing up in the extreme stern of each. And they had races, and bottles of wine were lowered down to them from the ship as prizes, and the sailors stood leaning over the ship's sides and laughed till their own sides ached.

The Duffers were also very pleased with their new name of Monopods, which seemed to them a magnificent name though they never got it right. "That's what we are," they bellowed, "Moneypuds, Pomonods, Poddymons. Just what it was on the tips of our tongue to call ourselves." But they soon got it mixed up with their old name of Duffers and finally settled down to calling themsleves the Dufflepuds; and that is what they will probably be called for centuries.

That evening all the Narnians dined upstairs with the Magician, and Lucy noticed how different the whole top floor looked now that she was no longer afraid of it. The mysterious signs on the doors were still mysterious but now looked as if they had kind and cheerful meanings and even the bearded mirror now seemed funny rather than frightening. At dinner everyone had by magic what everyone liked best to eat and drink. And after dinner the Magician did a very useful and beautiful piece of magic. He laid two blank sheets of parchment on the table and asked Drinian to give him an exact account of their voyage up to date: and as Drinian spoke, everything he described came out on the parchment in fine clear lines till at last each sheet was a splendid map of the Eastern Ocean, showing Galma, Terebinthia, the Seven Isles, the Lone Islands, Dragon Island, Burnt Island, Deathwater, and the land of the Duffers itself, all exactly the right sizes and in the right positions. They were the first maps ever made of those seas and better than any that have been made since without magic. For on these, though the towns and mountains looked at first just as they would on an ordinary map, yet when the Magician lent them a magnifying glass you saw that they were perfect little pictures of the real things, so that you could see the very castle and slave market and streets in Narrowhaven, all very clear though very distant, like things seen through the wrong end of a telescope. The only drawback was that the coastline of most of the islands was incomplete, for the map showed only what Drinian had seen with his own eyes. When they were finished the Magician kept one himself and presented the other to Caspian: it still hangs in his Chamber of Instruments at Cair Paravel. But the Magician could tell them nothing about seas or lands further east. He did, however, tell them that about seven years before a Narnian ship had put in at his waters and that she had on board the lords Revilian, Argoz, Mavramorn and Rhoop: so they judged that the golden man they had seen lying in Deathwater must be the Lord Restimar.

Next day the Magician magically mended the stern of the *Dawn Treader* where it had been damaged by the sea serpent and loaded her with useful gifts. There was a most friendly parting, and when she sailed, two hours after noon, all the Dufflepuds paddled out with her to the harbour mouth, and cheered until she was out of sound of their cheering.

MARK ALBERT VAN DOREN

(1894–1972)

Mark Van Doren, celebrated American poet, critic, novelist, and short-story writer, was born in Hope, Illinois. He studied at the University of Illinois and Columbia University, where he became professor of English. During World War I, he served in the infantry, and then, in 1924, he succeeded his brother Carl as literary editor of *The Nation*. He held this post until 1928. Although Van Doren wrote several novels and a number of brilliant critical works, he is best known for his poetry. His books of verse include *Spring Thunder* (1924) *7 P.M.* (1926), *Now the Sky* (1928), *Jonathan Gentry* (1931), *A Winter Diary* (1935), *The Seven Sleepers* (1944), *The Country Year* (1946), and *Spring Birth* (1953). In 1940 he was awarded the Pulitzer Prize for *Collected Poems: 1922–1938*.

Few think of Mark Van Doren as a writer of short stories, probably because he has published only one collection of short fiction (*Collected Stories*, 1962). "The Tall One," taken from that volume, clearly reveals that poetry is not the only genre in which Van Doren excels. As is true of most well-written stories, "The Tall One" can be read on more than one level. Some readers will see it as a poignant and moving domestic drama chronicling the hardships of a poor woodcutter and his family, with a bit of the supernatural thrown in for good measure. An entertaining tale well told, but little more. Others, however, may perceive the work as a sensitive and illuminating commentary on man's age-old problem of maintaining unquestioning faith in a divine being when faced with Job-like tribulations. This is a tale which emphasizes man's powerlessness in the grip of forces much greater than himself, but it is also a testimonial to man's dignity and courage. Van Doren's style is smooth and lucid—the reader will be hard pressed to find a blemish in this meticulously structured narrative. The discipline and economy of the poet are evident here.

❧ The Tall One ❧

Mark Albert Van Doren

The woodcutter's wife was not helping him today because their youngest child, the fourteenth she had borne him in a dozen years, was ailing from the raw spring weather. She was two miles away, in the little house by the third turning of the wood road he had trimmed till it was fit for chariots to pass over. No chariots ever came, but he liked to think that if they did they would have gentle going.

As he chopped and stacked the ash poles he would sell in early summer he paused now and then to glance along the wood road, as far as to the first turning there by the big beeches, and imagine he saw two white horses coming with her behind them. In his fancy he much admired the straight way she stood in the chariot, or cart, or whatever it was she drove. She was his wife whom he loved, and she was not here today, bending to pick up the lighter lengths and place them neatly in a pile.

He missed her because of the help she gave him and because she was good company in the woods. Sometimes he scolded her for wandering off to look at the small flowers that had opened since yesterday among the rocks and ferns, but he was not serious about this, and she knew it. Or he hoped she did. When she was not with him he was less sure that he treated her as well as she deserved. She was still straight and fair, in spite of her childbearing, and even if she never had new clothes to wear she wore the ones she had so that they

253

looked as if they belonged on her and no other woman. She deserved everything, and some day he would tell her so if he could find the words.

It was not of her alone, however, that he was thinking as he worked this afternoon. There were the children too—eleven of them, for the first three had died. And the oldest living ones were girls who couldn't help him in the woods. But that was not it. He was thinking of them all, and of their mother too, as of a dozen souls who depended utterly on him. On his body, that is. On his stout arms and legs, and on his lungs through which air came and went. Their very lives, he said, hung on the chance that he would never break one of his bones beyond repairing, or be felled by one of his own trees so that it crushed the soft life inside his ribs, or expose himself to wet winds that caused a fever in the chest, with pain and swelling till a man choked and died.

The thought of this was itself painful, so that he caught his breath. He remembered how his brood had appeared to him when he walked into the house day before yesterday, looking for some wedges he had gone to fetch from the oak shelf in the chimney corner. His wife, flushed with her cooking at the fireplace where new sticks of shagbark hickory were ablaze, had been surprised at his coming home so early, and had asked him what the matter was. But the little ones had not seen him, for they were asleep in a row on the warm floor, near the fire. Five of them, including Luke, the lame one, curled there with jam on their faces and their arms flung every-which-way as they slept. Their legs, too, except for Luke's, that wouldn't bend. Their mother went back with him to the woods, helping him carry the wedges; and still thinking, it seemed to him, whatever she had thought when she supposed something was the matter. This would be something—certainly it would—about his getting hurt. She knew, too, though she never spoke of it, how much they all depended on his strength, which must not fail. The little ones didn't know. They had gone on snoring without a worry in their heads. That was how they expressed their faith in him. Nothing could happen to their father.

And nothing ever had. The ax had never slipped and cut his foot—a deep cut, that wouldn't heal—and his shoulders were still safe in their sockets. But what if something did happen, in the way of matters over which no man has control?

Only *she* controlled them, he said. And he was not thinking of his wife.

She was someone he had never seen, but he prayed to her every day under his breath. He had got into the habit of doing it—quietly, that is—so his wife wouldn't hear him. He wasn't sure he could convince her that she existed. But she did, and he had even given her a name. She was The Tall One, and she stood over him, guarding him against accidents. Not only him, perhaps, for he could believe that she had many men in her charge. This was why she needed to be tall. How otherwise could she overlook so many choppers in so many distant woods? She was tall and serious, and wore a green robe which fell clear to the ground. He was sure of that, for he saw her in his dreams. She could control things. She could put out a hand and prevent axes from slipping. She made sure that trees fell where they should. But a man had to let her know that he knew she was there. Otherwise she would miss him in her rounds, or even arrange for something to go wrong and punish him. He prayed to her every day, under his breath, beseeching her not to stay away too long, and never to forget him. There had been moments when he tried to conceive a sacrifice that would please her. He would give her anything, but he had so little. Perhaps it was because he had never offered her a sacrifice that Luke's legs had withered, beginning two years ago when he came home from wading in the cold swamp. Perhaps Luke could have been saved, if anyone had known in time.

Because he was alone today he spoke her name aloud. It was the first time he had done so.

"Tall One," he stood up and said, a little startled by his own boldness, and by his voice that went so far among the ash trees, "is there anything I have left undone or spoken? Come near me if you will and let me see you, and say whether or not I do my duty by your goodness."

The prayer didn't sound right to him. It sounded like a priest's, and he was not a priest. But he had no better idea how to put his case. And he surely couldn't talk to her as if she were an ordinary person.

Then she was there. It happened so suddenly that he almost fell back on the blade of his ax, which was lying where he had dropped it when he decided to speak.

She was tall indeed, and the robe she wore was the same shade of green that he had dreamed. But her face was more beautiful. Stern, yet very beautiful.

She was standing between two ancient ashes whose bark seemed to reflect in its ridges the color of her robe, for the moss there took on a deeper hue, as if happy in the privilege of confessing its true cause.

"You called me," she said, looking down at him as calmly as if this were an everyday occurrence, this coming to him when he said her name. "Why was that?"

He frantically dropped to one knee in the mold he had been trampling.

"Stand up," she said. "I have no doubt of you." For the first time she smiled.

He stood up, embarrassed because he didn't know how to begin. But when she smiled again he could.

"Tall One, I am haunted by fears that my children may starve. And my good wife, who sometimes helps me here."

"I know," she said.

"If I should hurt myself—badly, so that I could never do this work again, but would have to sit useless in the corner while my young ones lay like a row of thin sticks on the floor, accusing me because I could not bring them food or warmth—and my wife, too, for what could she do then, knowing only how to care for what

I give her, and sometimes to help me in the woods?—it is with thoughts of them I am haunted. That is why I—called your name, hoping you would come, yet fearing you had only been a dream."

She moved a little, so that her robe rustled.

"You dream of me?"

"I do, I do," he said, "and every day I speak to you, under my breath."

"When you think you dream, I am with you also. But why just now did you say my name aloud?"

"Because—" and he hesitated— "because my fear was stronger than before. And because it came over me that a sacrifice was necessary."

She frowned. "Your fear was stronger, and your faith was weaker than on other days."

"No, no!" he said. "My faith is such that if a sacrifice is needed I will make it. I wanted to tell you I was ready. But I didn't know—"

"You didn't know what thing of yours I would take from you so that all the others could be safe. Or what child, so that the others—"

She stopped because he was staring at her dumbly.

"Or what wife."

He dropped to both knees and put out his two hands that were so hard and square from their long toil. But he said nothing, for his new fear made him as ignorant as a stone.

"Now," she said, "you are more afraid of me than you are of trunks and blades and sharp winds. You do not trust your own skill among the things and places that are dangerous. But neither do you trust me who am the owner of those things, those places. You have no faith that I will keep them friendly. Have I not always done so?"

He nodded, and tears started in his eyes.

"Yet now I am to be paid. Very well. Your wife is the full price."

He tried to go forward on his knees, to kiss the hem of her green robe, but both his legs felt as if they had gone to sleep.

"Stand up," she said.

She must have known he couldn't, for she smiled a little cruelly when he failed.

"Your wife, or else the child that is lame. Either one of them will buy safety forever, for the others at home, and of course for you."

"Luke!" It was the only word he could say, and he said it hoarsely in his great fear for the little one whom for two years he had carried tenderly on his shoulders. Not Luke. It must not be Luke.

That was why he said the name, hoarsely, as if he were sick. But she seemed to have a different understanding, for she retreated a step, as if the conversation were about to close.

"Very well, then, you say Luke."

"No, no!" And he had strength to stand. "I said it only so that you would know—"

"I know," she said. "You are willing."

"But I am not!" he shouted. Then he became ashamed. "I mean—I only said his name. I wanted to talk more about him."

Her figure faded rapidly among the trees. She was going and his heart grew faint again. He could scarcely hear the last words she spoke before she disappeared.

"Go home," she said, "and see what has happened to Luke."

He stood as white as a mushroom, staring at the place where she had been.

Luke!

Then he started running, his ax abandoned where it was and his brown jacket forgotten on the dead limb where he had hung it when the sun grew warm an hour ago.

He ran down the wood road he had trimmed to where it turned by the big beeches; to where it turned again, and he had fancied a chariot might be preparing to round the curve behind two white horses; and then to where it showed him his cottage chimney with blue smoke curling lazily out of its mouth.

There was Luke himself, running on thin legs to meet him.

Nobody else. And the boy's legs, though they were thin, worked perfectly. They pounded the turf like the happy legs of a little dog. And Luke was crying something loudly to his father.

"Forgive me, Tall One!" The woodcutter stopped where he was and raised his eyes, though there was no one except Luke to be seen. "My faith *was* little. Yet see how you have rewarded it! He is well again. I do not deserve it, but he is well again!"

Luke, however, did not stop running. He came closer and closer, and now his father saw that the little boy was not thinking of his legs. He was not running to show how well they were. It was as if they had never been withered from the waist down.

His face bore another message.

"Mother!" he cried. "She is—"

But the woodcutter did not hear at first. He was still bewildered by his own happiness.

"Your legs," he said. "You ran to meet me. Look at me, Luke."

"Mother!" cried Luke again, evading the woodcutter's arms thrust out to embrace him. "She is dead."

The woodcutter heard this.

And as he heard it he raised his eyes again. The branches of a white oak to which a few of last year's leaves were clinging were all he saw. But those leaves, lofty and colorless in the cool wind, had shaped themselves until they looked like a face that smiled. A cruel smile, only for him.

"Tall One!" he groaned, and let Luke lead him into the house.

His children stood in a ring about their mother, who lay on the one bed they owned, her bed and his bed. Her limbs were as straight as the ash lengths she had piled for him yesterday, and her face was as pale as a candle.

The children broke their ring so that he could enter it. He did so, looking down through their silence as one after another they lifted their faces to see why it was that he said nothing.

What he said at last even the oldest of them failed to comprehend.

"Tall One," he said, "you are powerful! When I prayed to you I was as ignorant as a rock around which trees have wrapped their roots. The rock is ignorant still, but I am not. I know that you are powerful. Should I never have prayed to you? But I was not free to be silent. And now I am not free to enjoy the safety I have bought. It will never give me pleasure; and all of these young ones will weep forever. Yet I cannot call you wrong. You gave me what I asked for, even though I was ignorant of its meaning. I do not blame you, Tall One. I still will pray to you, every day I will pray to you, and not under my breath. I will pray aloud, saying how great the strength is that wraps me, and hoping that hereafter all will be well at least with these. With Luke, for whom I thank you, and for all the others.

"Tall One, I will never doubt or disobey you while I live, or ask you for what I shouldn't have. And I will tell you of my grief for her. Every day I will tell you. Not as blaming you, but as remembering one without whom you must teach me how to live."

The children stared at him, thinking he was mad. For he didn't sound like their father. He sounded like a priest, and said strange things.

They did not hear the other voice, high in the smoke that had gathered among the rafters.

But he did, and raised his eyes.

He saw her dimly in the blue smoke, smiling at him without cruelty as she said:

"Look down and see what I am doing."

He looked down, and at the same moment the children clapped their hands.

His wife was opening her eyes, and her cheeks were as red as the embers of hickory that hissed in the fire.

"Where have you been?" she said. "All of you—

where have you been? Luke, dear, you mustn't try to do that!"

For Luke was climbing onto the bed to kiss her.

"Look at Luke!" the rest of them cried. "He's well!"

"Look at all of us," her husband said, though it was difficult in his joy to speak so she could hear. "We're safe."

"Safe!" She sat up suddenly and laughed. Another laugh sounded among the rafters, but when they looked up they knew it could be only an echo. Even the woodcutter saw nothing now. "You're always worrying about that," she said.

But then she cried as Luke ran out with his brothers to play in the dry lot this side of the swamp.

LLOYD ALEXANDER
(1924–   ).

Lloyd Alexander was born and brought up in Philadelphia. As a boy he loved to read fairy tales, folklore, legends, and, especially, the adventures of King Arthur and his knights of the round table. His interest in literature was so strong that while still a teenager he decided to become a writer, and subsequently spent long evening hours hunched over his writing desk. After a brief and uneventful stay at Westchester State College, he joined the army, hoping to find there a more exciting and adventurous life style—one which might provide the raw materials for later works of fiction. His assignments in military intelligence carried him first to England, and later to Wales. It was most certainly the rugged grandeur of the Welsh landscapes which inspired the settings of the *Chronicles of Prydain*. When the war ended, Alexander was stationed in Paris, where he met and married a French girl, Janine. Still enthusiastically pursuing his career as writer, he attended the University of Paris with the intention of learning more about his craft. A short time later the decision was made to return to the city of his youth. In Philadelphia, the aspiring young writer held a number of different jobs while attempting to get his works published. For the next seventeen years he experienced only moderate success with his adult fiction, but then he turned to children's literature with *The Time Cat* (1963), and his fortunes took a dramatic turn for the better. Since that publication, he has written a number of popular and award-winning fantasy works, but he is best known for the five volumes which comprise the "Prydain

Cycle": *The Book of Three* (1964), *The Black Cauldron* (1965), *The Castle of Llyr* (1966), *Taran Wanderer* (1967), and *The High King* (1969) which was the recipient of the 1969 Newberry Award. Mr. Alexander is currently writer in residence at Temple University, Philadelphia, Pennsylvania.

Tolkien has his Middle Earth, Lewis his Narnia, and Alexander his Prydain. Each is a classic example of the key ingredient of high fantasy—a magical other-world. "The Foundling" is only one of the many stories Alexander has set in that wondrous world of Prydain, where all things are possible. It is a brief, but rich, tale which is especially noteworthy for its mythic underpinnings. It should not take the reader long to discover the similarities between the three crones who find and rear Dallben, "greatest of enchanters of Prydain," and the three Fates of classical mythology. But Orddu, Orwen, and Orgoch are not the cold and impersonal figures of the myth. Rather, they are three garrulous old women with unforgettable and distinctive human personalities. The Alexander touch is also evident in the wry humor which permeates the narrative. The story is entertaining, but also instructive. It is a thoughtful commentary on the curious admixture of anguish, suffering, hope, and joy which characterizes every man's existence.

❦ The Foundling ❦

Lloyd Alexander

This is told of Dallben, greatest of enchanters in Prydain: how three black-robed hags found him, when he was still a baby, in a basket at the edge of the Marshes of Morva. "Oh, Orddu, see what's here!" cried the one named Orwen, peering into the wicker vessel floating amid the tall grasses. "Poor lost duckling! He'll catch his death of cold! Whatever shall we do with him?"

"A sweet morsel," croaked the one named Orgoch from the depths of her hood. "A tender lamb. I know what I should do."

"Please be silent, Orgoch," said the one named Orddu. "You've already had your breakfast." Orddu was a short, plump woman with a round, lumpy face and sharp black eyes. Jewels, pins, and brooches glittered in her tangle of weedy hair. "We can't leave him here to get all soggy. I suppose we shall have to take him home with us."

"Oh, yes!" exclaimed Orwen, dangling her string of milky white beads over the tiny figure in the basket. "Ah, the darling tadpole! Look at his pink cheeks and chubby little fingers! He's smiling at us, Orddu! He's waving! But what shall we call him? He mustn't go bare and nameless."

"If you ask me—" began Orgoch.

"No one did," replied Orddu. "You are quite right, Orwen. We must give him a name. Otherwise, how shall we know who he is?"

"We have so many names lying around the cottage,"

265

said Orwen. "Some of them never used. Give him a nice, fresh, unwrinkled one."

"There's a charming name I'd been saving for a special occasion," Orddu said, "but I can't remember what I did with it. No matter. His name—his name: Dallben."

"Lovely!" cried Orwen, clapping her hands. "Oh, Orddu, you have such good taste."

"Taste, indeed!" snorted Orgoch. "Dallben? Why call him Dallben?"

"Why not?" returned Orddu. "It will do splendidly. Very good quality, very durable. It should last him a lifetime."

"It will last him," Orgoch muttered, "as long as he needs it."

And so Dallben was named and nursed by these three, and given a home in their cottage near the Marshes of Morva. Under their care he grew sturdy, bright, and fair of face. He was kind and generous, and each day handsomer and happier.

The hags did not keep from him that he was a foundling. But when he was of an age to wonder about such matters, he asked where indeed he had come from, and what the rest of the world was like.

"My dear chicken," replied Orddu, "as to where you came from, we haven't the slightest notion. Nor, might I say, the least interest. You're here with us now, to our delight, and that's quite enough to know."

"As to the rest of the world," Orwen added, "don't bother your pretty, curly head about it. You can be sure it doesn't bother about you. Be glad you were found instead of drowned. Why, this very moment you might be part of a school of fish. And what a slippery, scaly sort of life that would be!"

"I like fish," muttered Orgoch, "especially eels."

"Do hush, dear Orgoch," said Orddu. "You're always thinking of your stomach."

Despite his curiosity, Dallben saw there was no use in questioning further. Cheerful and willing, he went about every task with eagerness and good grace. He drew pails of water from the well, kept the fire burning in the hearth, pumped the bellows, swept away the ashes, and dug the garden. No toil was too troublesome for him. When Orddu spun thread, he turned the spinning wheel. He helped Orwen measure the skeins into lengths and held them for Orgoch to snip with a pair of rusty shears.

One day, when the three brewed a potion of roots and herbs, Dallben was left alone to stir the huge, steaming kettle with a long iron spoon. He obeyed the hags' warning not to taste the liquid, but soon the potion began boiling so briskly that a few drops bubbled up and by accident splashed his fingers. With a cry of pain, Dallben let fall the spoon and popped his fingers into his mouth.

His outcry brought Orddu, Orwen, and Orgoch hurrying back to the cottage.

"Oh, the poor sparrow!" gasped Orwen, seeing the boy sucking at his blistered knuckles. "He's gone and burned himself. I'll fetch an ointment for the sweet fledgling, and some spider webs to bandage him. What did you do with all those spiders, Orgoch? They were here only yesterday."

"Too late for all that," growled Orgoch. "Worse damage is done."

"Yes, I'm afraid so," Orddu sighed. "There's no learning without pain. The dear gosling has had his pain; and now, I daresay, he has some learning to go along with it."

Dallben, meanwhile, had swallowed the drops of liquid scalding his fingers. He licked his lips at the taste, sweet and bitter at the same time. And in that instant he began to shake with fear and excitement. All that had been common and familiar in the cottage he saw as he had never seen before.

Now he understood that the leather bellows lying by the hearth commanded the four winds; the pail of water in the corner, the seas and oceans of the world. The earthen floor of the cottage held the roots of all plants and trees. The fire showed him the secrets of its flame, and how all things come to ashes. He gazed awe-struck at the enchantresses, for such they were.

"The threads you spin, and measure, and cut off," Dallben murmured, "these are no threads, but the lives of men. I know who you truly are."

"Oh, I doubt it," Orddu cheerfully answered. "Even we aren't always sure of that. Nevertheless, one taste of that magical brew and you know as much as we do. Almost as much, at any rate."

"Too much for his own good," muttered Orgoch.

"But what shall we do?" moaned Orwen. "He was such a sweet, innocent little robin. If only he hadn't swallowed the potion! Is there no way to make him unswallow it?"

"We could try," said Orgoch.

"No," declared Orddu. "What's done is done. You know that as well as I. Alas, the dear duckling will have to leave us. There's nothing else for it. So many people, knowing so much, under the same roof? All that knowledge crammed in, crowded, bumping and jostling back and forth? We'd not have room to breathe!"

"I say he should be kept," growled Orgoch.

"I don't think he'd like your way of keeping him," Orddu answered. She turned to Dallben. "No, my poor chicken, we must say farewell. You asked us once about the world? I'm afraid you'll have to see it for yourself."

"But, Orddu," protested Orwen, "we can't let him march off just like that. Surely we have some little trinket he'd enjoy? A going-away present, so he won't forget us?"

"I could give him something to remember us by," began Orgoch.

"No doubt," said Orddu. "But that's not what Orwen had in mind. Of course, we shall offer him a gift. Better yet, he shall choose one for himself."

As Dallben watched, the enchantress unlocked an iron-bound chest and rummaged inside, flinging out all sorts of oddments until there was a large heap on the floor.

"Here's something," Orddu at last exclaimed. "Just the thing for a bold young chicken. A sword!"

Dallben caught his breath in wonder as Orddu put the weapon in his hands. The hilt, studded with jewels, glittered so brightly that he was dazzled and nearly blinded. The blade flashed, and a thread of fire ran along its edges.

"Take this, my duckling," Orddu said, "and you shall be the greatest warrior in Prydain. Strength and power, dear gosling! When you command, all must obey even your slightest whim."

"It is a fine blade," Dallben replied, "and comes easily to my hand."

"It shall be yours," Orddu said. "At least, as long as you're able to keep it. Oh, yes," the enchantress went on, "I should mention it's already had a number of owners. Somehow, sooner or later, it wanders back to us. The difficulty, you see, isn't so much getting power as holding on to it. Because so many others want it, too. You'd be astonished, the lengths to which some will go. Be warned, the sword can be lost or stolen. Or bent out of shape—as, indeed, so can you, in a manner of speaking."

"And remember," put in Orwen, "you must never let it out of your sight, not for an instant."

Dallben hesitated a moment, then shook his head. "I think your gift is more burden than blessing."

"In that case," Orddu said, "perhaps this will suit you better."

As Dallben laid down the sword, the enchantress handed him a golden harp, so perfectly wrought that he no sooner held it than it seemed to play of itself.

"Take this, my sparrow," said Orddu, "and be the greatest bard in Prydain, known throughout the land for the beauty of your songs."

Dallben's heart leaped as the instrument thrilled in his arms. He touched the sweeping curve of the glowing harp and ran his fingers over the golden strings. "I have never heard such music," he murmured. "Who owns this will surely have no lack of fame."

"You'll have fame and admiration a-plenty," said Orddu, "as long as anyone remembers you."

"Alas, that's true," Orwen said with a sigh. "Memory can be so skimpy. It doesn't stretch very far; and, next thing you know, there's your fame gone all crumbly and mildewed."

Sadly, Dallben set down the harp. "Beautiful it is," he said, "but in the end, I fear, little help to me."

"There's nothing else we can offer at the moment," said Orddu, delving once more into the chest, "unless you'd care to have this book."

The enchantress held up a large, heavy tome and blew away the dust and cobwebs from its moldering leather binding. "It's a bulky thing for a young lamb to carry. Naturally, it would be rather weighty, for it holds everything that was ever known, is known, and will be known."

"It's full of wisdom, thick as oatmeal," added Orwen. "Quite scarce in the world—wisdom, not oatmeal —but that only makes it the more valuable."

"We have so many requests for other items," Orddu said. "Seven-league boots, cloaks of invisibility, and such great nonsense. For wisdom, practically none. Yet whoever owns this book shall have all that and more, if he likes. For the odd thing about wisdom is the more you use it the more it grows; and the more you share, the more you gain. You'd be amazed how few understand that. If they did, I suppose, they wouldn't need the book in the first place."

"Do you give this to me?" Dallben asked. "A treasure greater than all treasures?"

Orddu hesitated. "Give? Only in a manner of speaking. If you know us as well as you say you do, then you also know we don't exactly *give* anything. Put it this way: We shall *let* you take that heavy, dusty old book if that's what you truly want. Again, be warned: The greater the treasure, the greater the cost. Nothing is given for nothing; not in the Marshes of Morva—or anyplace else, for the matter of that."

"Even so," Dallben replied, "this book is my choice."

"Very well," said Orddu, putting the ancient volume in his hands. "Now you shall be on your way. We're sorry to see you go, though sorrow is something we don't usually feel. Fare well, dear chicken. We mean this in the polite sense, for whether you fare well or ill is entirely up to you."

So Dallben took his leave of the enchantresses and set off eagerly, curious to see what lay in store not only in the world but between the covers of the book. Once the cottage was well out of sight and the marshes far behind him, he curbed his impatience no longer, but sat down by the roadside, opened the heavy tome, and began to read.

As he scanned the first pages, his eyes widened and his heart quickened. For here was knowledge he had never dreamed of: the pathways of the stars, the rounds of the planets, the ebb and flow of time and tide. All secrets of the world and all its hidden lore unfolded to him.

Dallben's head spun, giddy with delight. The huge book seemed to weigh less than a feather, and he felt so light-hearted he could have skipped from one mountaintop to the next and never touched the ground. He laughed and sang at the top of his voice, bursting with gladness, pride, and strength in what he had learned.

"I chose well!" he cried, jumping to his feet. "But why should Orddu have warned me? Cost? What cost can there be? Knowledge is joy!"

He strode on, reading as he went. Each page lightened and sped his journey, and soon he came to a village where the dwellers danced and sang and made holiday. They offered him meat and drink and shelter for the coming night.

But Dallben thanked them for their hospitality and shook his head, saying he had meat and drink enough in the book he carried. By this time he had walked many miles, but his spirit was fresh and his legs un-weary.

He kept on his way, hardly able to contain his happiness as he read and resolving not to rest until he had come to the end of the book. But he had finished less than half when the pages, to his horror, began to grow dark and stained with blood and tears.

For now the book told him of other ways of the world; of cruelty, suffering, and death. He read of greed, hatred, and war; of men striving against one another with fire and sword; of the blossoming earth trampled underfoot, of harvests lost and lives cut short. And the book told that even in the same village he had passed, a day would come when no house would stand; when women would weep for their men, and children for their parents; and where they had offered him meat and drink, they would starve for lack of a crust of bread.

Each page he read pierced his heart. The book, which had seemed to weigh so little, now grew so heavy that his face faltered and he staggered under the burden. Tears blinded his eyes, and he stumbled to the ground.

All night he lay shattered by despair. At dawn he stirred and found it took all his efforts even to lift his head. Bones aching, throat parched, he crept on hands and knees to quench his thirst from a puddle of water. There, at the sight of his reflection, he drew back and cried out in anguish.

His fair, bright curls had gone frost-white and fell below his brittle shoulders. His cheeks, once full and flushed with youth, were now hollow and wrinkled, half hidden by a long, gray beard. His brow, smooth yesterday, was scarred and furrowed, his hands gnarled and knotted, his eyes pale as if their color had been wept away.

Dallben bowed his head. "Yes, Orddu," he whispered, "I should have heeded you. Nothing is given without cost. But is the cost of wisdom so high? I thought knowledge was joy. Instead, it is grief beyond bearing."

The book lay nearby. Its last pages were still unread and, for a moment, Dallben thought to tear them to shreds and scatter them to the wind. Then he said:

"I have begun it, and I will finish it, whatever else it may foretell."

Fearfully and reluctantly, he began to read once more. But now his heart lifted. These pages told not only of death, but of birth as well; how the earth turns in its own time and in its own way gives back what is given to it; how things lost may be found again; and how one day ends for another to begin. He learned that the lives of men are short and filled with pain, yet each one a priceless treasure, whether it be that of a prince or a pig-keeper. And, at the last, the book taught him that while nothing was certain, all was possible.

"At the end of knowledge, wisdom begins," Dallben murmured. "And at the end of wisdom there is not grief, but hope."

He climbed to his withered legs and hobbled along his way, clasping the heavy book. After a time a farmer drove by in a horse-drawn cart, and called out to him:

"Come, Grandfather, ride with me if you like. That book must be a terrible load for an old man like you."

"Thank you just the same," Dallben answered, "but I have strength enough now to go to the end of my road."

"And where might that be?"

"I do not know," Dallben said. "I go seeking it."

"Well, then," said the farmer, "may you be lucky enough to find it."

"Luck?" Dallben answered. He smiled and shook his head. "Not luck, but hope. Indeed, hope."

PETER S. BEAGLE

(1939–   )

Peter S. Beagle, a young and talented freelance writer, was born in New York City. He graduated from the University of Pittsburgh in 1959 and then went on to Stanford, but did not complete the graduate work begun there. Instead, he left for Europe, spending most of his two-year stay in Paris. After his sojourn on the Continent he returned to California to devote even more time and energy to writing. Since his return he has produced a steady stream of quality essays, reviews, short stories, and novels. He currently resides in Santa Cruz, California, with his wife and three children.

Beagle's diversity is nicely shown through his full-length works. For example, *I See By My Outfit* (1965) is a fascinating nonfiction account of a motor-scooter trip Beagle took across the United States, while *The Last Unicorn* (1968) is a brilliant novel of high fantasy. It is the latter work which has firmly established him as one of the most respected writers of fantasy literature on the contemporary American scene. Beagle's latest creation bears the intriguing title of *Lila The Werewolf* (1974). It is a novelette about an honest-to-goodness modern vampire named Lila. Those who appreciate Beagle's satire and distinctive brand of humor should like this out-of-the-ordinary piece of short fiction. Other works include *A Fine and Private Place* (1960) and *The California Feeling* (1969).

It is not difficult to understand why Beagle received the coveted O. Henry award for "Come Lady Death" (1960). It is a carefully structured story which features a smooth, highly polished prose style. More specifically, it has the "high style" displayed by only the most gifted of fantasy writers—notables such as Lord Dunsany, E. R. Eddison, and Evangeline Walton. It is this style which is primarily responsible for the arresting strangeness which permeates the tale. The setting and atmosphere are so carefully handled by Beagle that the reader quickly forgets that the action is taking place in an eighteenth-century London mansion. The final effect of the narrative is so convincing that the reader feels himself placed in a secondary magical world as distinct as Narnia or Prydain. After all, it is not a commonplace reality which allows for the appearance of Lady Death at a fairy-tale-like grand ball. Beagle has a flair for the dramatic; a trait which results in a suspenseful, fast-paced narrative. At the risk of being accused of a poor pun, it is safe to say that this story has a haunting beauty which remains with the reader long after the text has been shelved.

❧ Come Lady Death ❧

Peter S. Beagle

This all happened in England a long time ago, when
that George who spoke English with a heavy German
accent and hated his sons was King. At that time there
lived in London a lady who had nothing to do but give
parties. Her name was Flora, Lady Neville, and she
was a widow and very old. She lived in a great house
not far from Buckingham Palace, and she had so many
servants that she could not possibly remember all their
names; indeed, there were some she had never even
seen. She had more food than she could eat, more
gowns than she could ever wear; she had wine in her
cellars that no one would drink in her lifetime, and her
private vaults were filled with great works of art that
she did not know she owned. She spent the last years
of her life giving parties and balls to which the greatest
lords of England—and sometimes the King himself—
came, and she was known as the wisest and wittiest
woman in all London.

But in time her own parties began to bore her, and
though she invited the most famous people in the land
and hired the greatest jugglers and acrobats and
dancers and magicians to entertain them, still she
found her parties duller and duller. Listening to court
gossip, which she had always loved, made her yawn.
The most marvelous music, the most exciting feats of
magic put her to sleep. Watching a beautiful young
couple dance by her made her feel sad, and she hated
to feel sad.

And so, one summer afternoon she called her closest friends around her and said to them, "More and more I find that my parties entertain everyone but me. The secret of my long life is that nothing has ever been dull for me. For all my life, I have been interested in everything I saw and been anxious to see more. But I cannot stand to be bored, and I will not go to parties at which I expect to be bored, especially if they are my own. Therefore, to my next ball I shall invite the one guest I am sure no one, not even myself, could possibly find boring. My friends, the guest of honor at my next party shall be Death himself!"

A young poet thought that this was a wonderful idea, but the rest of her friends were terrified and drew back from her. They did not want to die, they pleaded with her. Death would come for them when he was ready; why should she invite him before the appointed hour, which would arrive soon enough? But Lady Neville said, "Precisely. If Death has planned to take any of us on the night of my party, he will come whether he is invited or not. But if none of us are to die, then I think it would be charming to have Death among us—perhaps even to perform some little trick if he is in a good humor. And think of being able to say that we had been to a party with Death! All of London will envy us, all of England."

The idea began to please her friends, but a young lord, very new to London, suggested timidly, "Death is so busy. Suppose he has work to do and cannot accept your invitation?"

"No one has ever refused an invitation of mine," said Lady Neville, "not even the King." And the young lord was not invited to her party.

She sat down then and there and wrote out the invitation. There was some dispute among her friends as to how they should address Death. "His Lordship Death" seemed to place him only on the level of a viscount or a baron. "His Grace Death" met with more acceptance, but Lady Neville said it sounded hypocritical.

And to refer to Death as "His Majesty" was to make him the equal of the King of England, which even Lady Neville would not dare to do. It was finally decided that all should speak of him as "His Eminence Death," which pleased nearly everyone.

Captain Compson, known both as England's most dashing cavalry officer and most elegant rake, remarked next, "That's all very well, but how is the invitation to reach Death? Does anyone here know where he lives?"

"Death undoubtedly lives in London," said Lady Neville, "like everyone else of any importance, though he probably goes to Deauville for the summer. Actually, Death must live fairly near my own house. This is much the best section of London, and you could hardly expect a person of Death's importance to live anywhere else. When I stop to think of it, it's really rather strange that we haven't met before now, on the street."

Most of her friends agreed with her, but the poet, whose name was David Lorimond, cried out, "No, my lady, you are wrong! Death lives among the poor. Death lives in the foulest, darkest alleys of this city, in some vile, rat-ridden hovel that smells of—" He stopped here, partly because Lady Neville had indicated her displeasure, and partly because he had never been inside such a hut or thought of wondering what it smelled like. "Death lives among the poor," he went on, "and comes to visit them every day, for he is their only friend."

Lady Neville answered him as coldly as she had spoken to the young lord. "He may be forced to deal with them, David, but I hardly think that he seeks them out as companions. I am certain that it is as difficult for him to think of the poor as individuals as it is for me. Death is, after all, a nobleman."

There was no real argument among the lords and ladies that Death lived in a neighborhood at least as good as their own, but none of them seemed to know the name of Death's street, and no one had ever seen Death's house.

"If there were a war," Captain Compson said, "Death would be easy to find. I have seen him, you know, even spoken to him, but he has never answered me."

"Quite proper," said Lady Neville. "Death must always speak first. You are not a very correct person, Captain." But she smiled at him, as all women did.

Then an idea came to her. "My hairdresser has a sick child, I understand," she said. "He was telling me about it yesterday, sounding most dull and hopeless. I will send for him and give him the invitation, and he in his turn can give it to Death when he comes to take the brat. A bit unconventional, I admit, but I see no other way."

"If he refuses?" asked a lord who had just been married.

"Why should he?" asked Lady Neville.

Again it was the poet who exclaimed amidst the general approval that this was a cruel and wicked thing to do. But he fell silent when Lady Neville innocently asked him, "Why, David?"

So the hairdresser was sent for, and when he stood before them, smiling nervously and twisting his hands to be in the same room with so many great lords, Lady Neville told him the errand that was required of him. And she was right, as she usually was, for he made no refusal. He merely took the invitation in his hand and asked to be excused.

He did not return for two days, but when he did he presented himself to Lady Neville without being sent for and handed her a small white envelope. Saying, "How very nice of you, thank you very much," she opened it and found therein a plain calling card with nothing on it except these words: *Death will be pleased to attend Lady Neville's ball.*

"Death gave you this?" she asked the hairdresser eagerly. "What was he like?" But the hairdresser stood still, looking past her, and said nothing, and she, not really waiting for an answer, called a dozen servants to her and told them to run and summon her friends. As she paced up and down the room waiting for them, she asked again, "What is Death like?" The hairdresser did not reply.

When her friends came they passed the little card excitedly from hand to hand, until it had gotten quite smudged and bent from their fingers. But they all admitted that, beyond its message, there was nothing particularly unusual about it. It was neither hot nor cold to the touch, and what little odor clung to it was rather pleasant. Everyone said that it was a very familiar smell, but no one could give it a name. The poet said that it reminded him of lilacs but not exactly.

It was Captain Compson, however, who pointed out the one thing that no one else had noticed. "Look at the handwriting itself," he said. "Have you ever seen anything more graceful? The letters seem as light as birds. I think we have wasted our time speaking of Death as His This and His That. A woman wrote this note."

Then there was an uproar and a great babble, and the card had to be handed around again so that everyone could exclaim, "Yes, by God!" over it. The voice of the poet rose out of the hubbub saying, "It is very natural, when you come to think of it. After all, the French say *la mort*. Lady Death. I should much prefer Death to be a woman."

"Death rides a great black horse," said Captain Compson firmly, "and wears armor of the same color. Death is very tall, taller than anyone. It was no woman I saw on the battlefield, striking right and left like any soldier. Perhaps the hairdresser wrote it himself, or the hairdresser's wife."

But the hairdresser refused to speak, though they gathered around him and begged him to say who had given him the note. At first they promised him all sorts of rewards, and later they threatened to do terrible things to him. "Did you write this card?" he was asked, and "Who wrote it, then? Was it a living woman? Was it really Death? Did Death say anything to you? How did you know it was Death? Is Death a woman? Are you trying to make fools of us all?"

Not a word from the hairdresser, not one word, and finally Lady Neville called her servants to have him whipped and thrown into the street. He did not look at her as they took him away, or utter a sound.

Silencing her friends with a wave of her hand, Lady Neville said, "The ball will take place two weeks from tonight. Let Death come as Death pleases, whether as man or woman or strange, sexless creature." She smiled calmly. "Death may well be a woman," she said. "I am less certain of Death's form than I was, but I am also less frightened of Death. I am too old to be afraid of anything that can use a quill pen to write me a letter. Go home now, and as you make your preparations for the ball see that you speak of it to your servants, that they may spread the news all over London. Let it be known that on this one night no one in the world will die, for Death will be dancing at Lady Neville's ball."

For the next two weeks Lady Neville's great house shook and groaned and creaked like an old tree in a gale as the servants hammered and scrubbed, polished and painted, making ready for the ball. Lady Neville had always been very proud of her house, but as the ball drew near she began to be afraid that it would not be nearly grand enough for Death, who was surely accustomed to visiting in the homes of richer, mightier people than herself. Fearing the scorn of Death, she worked night and day supervising her servants' preparations. Curtains and carpets had to be cleaned, goldwork and silverware polished until they gleamed by themselves in the dark. The grand staircase that rushed down into the ballroom like a waterfall was washed and rubbed so often that it was almost impossible to walk on it without slipping. As for the ballroom itself, it took thirty-two servants working at once to clean it properly, not counting those who were polishing the glass chandelier that was taller than a man and the fourteen smaller lamps. And when they were done she made them do it all over, not because she saw any dust or dirt anywhere, but because she was sure that Death would.

As for herself, she chose her finest gown and saw to its laundering personally. She called in another hairdresser and had him put up her hair in the style of an earlier time, wanting to show Death that she was a woman who enjoyed her age and did not find it necessary to ape the young and beautiful. All the day of the ball she sat before her mirror, not making herself up much beyond the normal touches of rouge and eye shadow and fine rice powder, but staring at the lean old face she had been born with, wondering how it would appear to Death. Her steward asked her to approve his wine selection, but she sent him away and stayed at her mirror until it was time to dress and go downstairs to meet her guests.

Everyone arrived early. When she looked out of a window, Lady Neville saw that the driveway of her home was choked with carriages and fine horses. "It all looks like a great funeral procession," she said. The footman cried the names of her guests to the echoing ballroom. "Captain Henry Compson, His Majesty's Household Cavalry! Mr. David Lorimond! Lord and Lady Torrance!!" (They were the youngest couple there, having been married only three months before.) "Sir Roger Harbison! The Contessa della Candini!" Lady Neville permitted them all to kiss her hand and made them welcome.

She had engaged the finest musicians she could find to play for the dancing, but though they began to play at her signal not one couple stepped out on the floor, nor did one young lord approach her to request the honor of the first dance, as was proper. They milled together, shining and murmuring, their eyes fixed on the ballroom door. Every time they heard a carriage clatter up the driveway they seemed to flinch a little and draw closer together; every time the footman announced the arrival of another guest, they all sighed softly and swayed a little on their feet with relief.

"Why did they come to my party if they were afraid?" Lady Neville muttered scornfully to herself. "I am not afraid of meeting Death. I ask only that Death may be impressed by the magnificence of my house and the flavor of my wines. I will die sooner than anyone here, but I am not afraid."

Certain that Death would not arrive until midnight, she moved among her guests, attempting to calm them, not with her words, which she knew they would not hear, but with the tone of her voice as if they were so many frightened horses. But little by little, she herself was infected by their nervousness: whenever she sat down she stood up again immediately, she tasted a dozen glasses of wine without finishing any of them, and she glanced constantly at her jeweled watch, at first wanting to hurry the midnight along and end the waiting, later scratching at the watch face with her forefinger, as if she would push away the night and drag the sun backward into the sky. When midnight came, she was standing with the rest of them, breathing through her mouth, shifting from foot to foot, listening for the sound of carriage wheels turning in gravel.

When the clock began to strike midnight, everyone, even Lady Neville and the brave Captain Compson, gave one startled little cry and then was silent again, listening to the tolling of the clock. The smaller clocks upstairs began to chime. Lady Neville's ears hurt. She caught sight of herself in the ballroom mirror, one gray face turned up toward the ceiling as if she were gasping for air, and she thought, "Death will be a woman, a hideous, filthy old crone as tall and strong as a man. And the most terrible thing of all will be that she will have my face." All the clocks stopped striking, and Lady Neville closed her eyes.

She opened them again only when she heard the whispering around her take on a different tone, one in which fear was fused with relief and a certain chagrin.

For no new carriage stood in the driveway. Death had not come.

The noise grew slowly louder; here and there people were beginning to laugh. Near her, Lady Neville heard young Lord Torrance say to his wife, "There, my darling, I told you there was nothing to be afraid of. It was all a joke."

"I am ruined," Lady Neville thought. The laughter was increasing; it pounded against her ears in strokes, like the chiming of the clocks. "I wanted to give a ball so grand that those who were not invited would be shamed in front of the whole city, and this is my reward. I am ruined, and I deserve it."

Turning to the poet Lorimond, she said, "Dance with me, David." She signaled to the musicians, who at once began to play. When Lorimond hesitated, she said, "Dance with me now. You will not have another chance. I shall never give a party again."

Lorimond bowed and led her out onto the dance floor. The guests parted for them, and the laughter died down for a moment, but Lady Neville knew that it would soon begin again. "Well, let them laugh," she thought. "I did not fear Death when they were all trembling. Why should I fear their laughter?" But she could feel a stinging at the thin lids of her eyes, and she closed them once more as she began to dance with Lorimond.

And then, quite suddenly, all the carriage horses outside the house whinnied loudly, just once, as the guests had cried out at midnight. There were a great many horses, and their one salute was so loud that everyone in the room became instantly silent. They heard the heavy steps of the footman as he went to open the door, and they shivered as if they felt the cool breeze that drifted into the house. Then they heard a light voice saying, "Am I late? Oh, I am so sorry. The horses were tired," and before the footman could re-enter to announce her, a lovely young girl in a white dress stepppd gracefully into the ballroom doorway and stood there smiling.

She could not have been more than nineteen. Her hair was yellow, and she wore it long. It fell thickly upon her bare shoulders that gleamed warmly through it, two limestone islands rising out of a dark golden sea. Her face was wide at the forehead and cheekbones, and narrow at the chin, and her skin was so clear that many of the ladies there—Lady Neville among them— touched their own faces wonderingly, and instantly drew their hands away as though their own skin had rasped their fingers. Her mouth was pale, where the mouths of other women were red and orange and even purple. Her eyebrows, thicker and straighter than was fashionable, met over dark, calm eyes that were set so deep in her young face and were so black, so uncompromisingly black, that the middle-aged wife of a middle-aged lord murmured, "Touch of the gypsy there, I think."

"Or something worse," suggested her husband's mistress.

"Be silent!" Lady Neville spoke louder than she had intended, and the girl turned to look at her. She smiled, and Lady Neville tried to smile back, but her mouth seemed very stiff. "Welcome," she said. "Welcome, my lady Death."

A sigh rustled among the lords and ladies as the girl took the old woman's hand and curtsied to her, sinking and rising in one motion, like a wave. "You are Lady Neville," she said. "Thank you so much for inviting me." Her accent was as faint and as almost familiar as her perfume.

"Please excuse me for being late," she said earnestly. "I had to come from a long way off, and my horses are so tired."

"The groom will rub them down," Lady Neville said, "and feed them if you wish."

"Oh, no," the girl answered quickly. "Tell him not to go near the horses, please. They are not really horses, and they are very fierce."

She accepted a glass of wine from a servant and drank it slowly, sighing softly and contentedly. "What good wine," she said. "And what a beautiful house you have."

"Thank you," said Lady Neville. Without turning, she could feel every woman in the room envying her, sensing it as she could always sense the approach of rain.

"I wish I lived here," Death said in her low, sweet voice. "I will, one day."

Then, seeing Lady Neville become as still as if she had turned to ice, she put her hand on the old woman's arm and said, "Oh, I'm sorry, I'm so sorry. I am so cruel, but I never mean to be. Please forgive me, Lady Neville. I am not used to company, and I do such stupid things. Please forgive me."

Her hand felt as light and warm on Lady Neville's arm as the hand of any other young girl, and her eyes were so appealing that Lady Neville replied, "You have said nothing wrong. While you are my guest, my house is yours."

"Thank you," said Death, and she smiled so radiantly that the musicians began to play quite by themselves, with no sign from Lady Neville. She would have stopped them, but Death said, "Oh, what lovely music! Let them play, please."

So the musicians played a gavotte, and Death, unabashed by eyes that stared at her in greedy terror, sang softly to herself without words, lifted her white gown slightly with both hands, and made hesitant little patting steps with her small feet. "I have not danced in so long," she said wistfully. "I'm quite sure I've forgotten how."

She was shy; she would not look up to embarrass the young lords, not one of whom stepped forward to dance with her. Lady Neville felt a flood of shame and sympathy, emotions she thought had withered in her years ago. "Is she to be humiliated at my own ball?" she thought angrily. "It is because she is Death; if she were the ugliest, foulest hag in all the world they would clamor to dance with her, because they are gentlemen and they know what is expected of them. But no gentleman will dance with Death, no matter how beautiful she is." She glanced sideways at David Lorimond. His face was flushed, and his hands were clasped so tightly as he stared at Death that his fingers were like glass, but when Lady Neville touched his arm he did not turn, and when she hissed, "David!", he pretended not to hear her.

Then Captain Compson, gray-haired and handsome in his uniform, stepped out of the crowd and bowed gracefully before Death. "If I may have the honor," he said.

"Captain Compson," said Death, smiling. She put her arm in his. "I was hoping you would ask me."

This brought a frown from the older women, who did not consider it a proper thing to say, but for that Death cared not a rap. Captain Compson led her to the center of the floor, and there they danced. Death was curiously graceless at first—she was too anxious to please her partner, and she seemed to have no notion of rhythm. The Captain himself moved with the mixture of dignity and humor that Lady Neville had never seen in another man, but when he looked at her over Death's shoulder, she saw something that no one else appeared to notice: that his face and eyes were immobile with fear, and that, though he offered Death his hand with easy gallantry, he flinched slightly when she took it. And yet he danced as well as Lady Neville had ever seen him.

"Ah, that's what comes of having a reputation to maintain," she thought. "Captain Compson too must do what is expected of him. I hope someone else will dance with her soon."

But no one did. Little by little, other couples overcame their fear and slipped hurriedly out on the floor when Death was looking the other way, but nobody sought to relieve Captain Compson of his beautiful partner. They danced every dance together. In time, some of the men present began to look at her with more appreciation than terror, but when she returned their glances and smiled at them, they clung to their partners as if a cold wind were threatening to blow them away.

One of the few who stared at her frankly and with pleasure was young Lord Torrance, who usually danced only with his wife. Another was the poet Lorimond. Dancing with Lady Neville, he remarked to her, "If she is Death, what do these frightened fools think they are? If she is ugliness, what must they be? I hate their fear. It is obscene."

Death and the Captain danced past them at that moment, and they heard him say to her, "But if that was truly you that I saw in the battle, how can you have changed so? How can you have become so lovely?"

Death's laughter was gay and soft. "I thought that among so many beautiful people it might be better to be beautiful. I was afraid of frightening everyone and spoiling the party."

"They all thought she would be ugly," said Lorimond to Lady Neville. "I—I knew she would be beautiful."

"Then why have you not danced with her?" Lady Neville asked him. "Are you also afraid?"

"No, oh, no," the poet answered quickly and passionately. "I will ask her to dance very soon. I only want to look at her a little longer."

The musicians played on and on. The dancing wore away the night as slowly as falling water wears down a cliff. It seemed to Lady Neville that no night had ever endured longer, and yet she was neither tired nor bored. She danced with every man there, except with Lord Torrance, who was dancing with his wife as if they had just met that night, and, of course, with Captain Compson. Once he lifted his hand and touched Death's golden hair very lightly. He was a striking man still, a fit partner for so beautiful a girl, but Lady Neville looked at his face each time she passed him and realized that he was older than anyone knew.

Death herself seemed younger than the youngest there. No woman at the ball danced better than she now, though it was hard for Lady Neville to remember at what point her awkwardness had given way to the liquid sweetness of her movements. She smiled and called to everyone who caught her eye—and she knew them all by name; she sang constantly, making up words to the dance tunes, nonsense words, sounds without meaning, and yet everyone strained to hear her soft voice without knowing why. And when, during a waltz, she caught up the trailing end of her gown to give her more freedom as she danced, she seemed to Lady Neville to move like a little sailing boat over a still evening sea.

Lady Neville heard Lady Torrance arguing angrily with the Contessa della Candini. "I don't care if she is Death, she's no older than I am, she can't be!"

"Nonsense," said the Contessa, who could not afford to be generous to any other woman. "She is twenty-eight, thirty, if she is an hour. And that dress, that bridal gown she wears—really!"

"Vile," said the woman who had come to the ball as Captain Compson's freely acknowledged mistress. "Tasteless. But one should know better than to expect taste from Death, I suppose." Lady Torrance looked as if she were going to cry.

"They are jealous of Death," Lady Neville said to herself. "How strange. I am not jealous of her, not in the least. And I do not fear her at all." She was very proud of herself.

Then, as unbiddenly as they had begun to play, the musicians stopped. They began to put away their instruments. In the sudden shrill silence, Death pulled away from Captain Compson and ran to look out of one of the tall windows, pushing the curtains apart with both hands. "Look!" she said, with her back turned to them. "Come and look. The night is almost gone."

The summer sky was still dark, and the eastern horizon was only a shade lighter than the rest of the sky, but the stars had vanished and the trees near the house were gradually becoming distinct. Death pressed her face against the window and said, so softly that the other guests could barely hear her, "I must go now."

"No," Lady Neville said, and was not immediately aware that she had spoken. "You must stay a while longer. The ball was in your honor. Please stay."

Death held out both hands to her, and Lady Neville came and took them in her own. "I've had a wonderful time," she said gently. "You cannot possibly imagine how it feels to be actually invited to such a ball as this, because you have given them and gone to them all your life. One is like another to you, but for me it is different. Do you understand me?" Lady Neville nodded silently. "I will remember this night forever," Death said.

"Stay," Captain Compson said. "Stay just a little longer." He put his hand on Death's shoulder, and she smiled and leaned her cheek against it. "Dear Captain Compson," she said. "My first real gallant. Aren't you tired of me yet?"

"Never," he said. "Please stay."

"Stay," said Lorimond, and he too seemed about to touch her. "Stay. I want to talk to you. I want to look at you. I will dance with you if you stay."

"How many followers I have," Death said in wonder. She stretched one hand toward Lorimond, but he drew back from her and then flushed in shame. "A soldier and a poet. How wonderful it is to be a woman. But why did you not speak to me earlier, both of you? Now it is too late. I must go."

"Please, stay," Lady Torrance whispered. She held on to her husband's hand for courage. "We think you are so beautiful, both of us do."

"Gracious Lady Torrance," the girl said kindly. She turned back to the window, touched it lightly, and it flew open. The cool dawn air rushed into the ballroom, fresh with rain but already smelling faintly of the London streets over which it had passed. They heard birdsong and the strange, harsh nickering of Death's horses.

"Do you want me to stay?" she asked. The question

was put, not to Lady Neville, nor to Captain Compson, nor to any of her admirers, but to the Contessa della Candini, who stood well back from them all, hugging her flowers to herself and humming a little song of irritation. She did not in the least want Death to stay, but she was afraid that all the other women would think her envious of Death's beauty, and so she said, "Yes. Of course I do."

"Ah," said Death. She was almost whispering. "And you," she said to another woman, "do you want me to stay? Do you want me to be one of your friends?"

"Yes," said the woman, "because you are beautiful and a true lady."

"And you," said Death to a man, "and you," to a woman, "and you," to another man, "do you want me to stay?" And they all answered, "Yes, Lady Death, we do."

"Do you want me, then?" she cried at last to all of them. "Do you want me to live among you and to be one of you, and not to be Death anymore? Do you want me to visit your houses and come to all your parties? Do you want me to ride horses like yours instead of mine, do you want me to wear the kind of dresses you wear, and say the things you would say? Would one of you marry me, and would the rest of you dance at my wedding and bring gifts to my children? Is that what you want?"

"Yes," said Lady Neville. "Stay here, stay with me, stay with us."

Death's voice, without becoming louder, had become clearer and older; too old a voice, thought Lady Neville, for such a young girl. "Be sure," said Death. "Be sure of what you want, be very sure. Do all of you want me to stay? For if one of you says to me, no, go away, then I must leave at once and never return. Be sure. Do you all want me?"

And everyone there cried with one voice, "Yes! Yes, you must stay with us. You are so beautiful that we cannot let you go."

"We are tired," said Captain Compson.

"We are blind," said Lorimond, adding, "especially to poetry."

"We are afraid," said Lord Torrance quietly, and his wife took his arm and said, "Both of us."

"We are dull and stupid," said Lady Neville, "and growing old uselessly. Stay with us, Lady Death."

And then Death smiled sweetly and radiantly and took a step forward, and it was as though she had come down among them from a great height. "Very well," she said. "I will stay with you. I will be Death no more. I will be a woman."

The room was full of a deep sigh, although no one was seen to open his mouth. No one moved, for the golden-haired girl was Death still, and her horses still whinnied for her outside. No one could look at her for long, although she was the most beautiful girl anyone there had ever seen.

"There is a price to pay," she said. "There is always a price. Some one of you must become Death in my place, for there must forever be Death in the world. Will anyone choose? Will anyone here become Death of his own free will? For only thus can I become a human girl."

No one spoke, no one spoke at all. But they backed slowly away from her, like waves slipping back down a beach to the sea when you try to catch them. The Contessa della Candini and her friends would have crept quietly out of the door, but Death smiled at them and they stood where they were. Captain Compson opened his mouth as though he were going to declare himself, but he said nothing. Lady Neville did not move.

"No one," said Death. She touched a flower with her finger, and it seemed to crouch and flex itself like a pleased cat. "No one at all," she said. "Then I must choose, and that is just, for that is the way that I became Death. I never wanted to be Death, and it makes me so happy that you want me to become one of yourselves. I have searched a long time for people who would want me. Now I have only to choose someone to replace me and it is done. I will choose very carefully."

"Oh, we were so foolish," Lady Neville said to herself. "We were so foolish." But she said nothing aloud; she merely clasped her hands and stared at the young girl, thinking vaguely that if she had had a daughter she would have been greatly pleased if she resembled the lady Death.

"The Contessa della Candini," said Death thoughtfully, and that woman gave a little squeak of terror because she could not draw her breath for a scream. But Death laughed and said, "No, that would be silly." She said nothing more, but for a long time after that the Contessa burned with humiliation at not having been chosen to be Death.

"Not Captain Compson," murmured Death, "because he is too kind to become Death, and because it would be too cruel to him. He wants to die so badly." The expression on the Captain's face did not change, but his hands began to tremble.

"Not Lorimond," the girl continued, "because he knows so little about life, and because I like him." The poet flushed, and turned white, and then turned pink again. He made as if to kneel clumsily on one knee, but instead he pulled himself erect and stood as much like Captain Compson as he could.

"Not the Torrances," said Death, "never Lord and Lady Torrance, for both of them care too much about another person to take any pride in being Death." But she hesitated over Lady Torrance for a while, staring at her out of her dark and curious eyes. "I was your age when I became Death," she said at last. "I wonder what it will be like to be your age again. I have been Death for so long." Lady Torrance shivered and did not speak.

And at last Death said quietly, "Lady Neville."

"I am here," Lady Neville answered.

"I think you are the only one," said Death. "I choose you, Lady Neville."

Again Lady Neville heard every guest sigh softly,

and although her back was to them all she knew that they were sighing in relief that neither themselves nor anyone dear to themselves had been chosen. Lady Torrance gave a little cry of protest, but Lady Neville knew that she would have cried out at whatever choice Death made. She heard herself say calmly, "I am honored. But was there no one more worthy than I?"

"Not one," said Death. "There is no one quite so weary of being human, no one who knows better how meaningless it is to be alive. And there is no one else here with the power to treat life"—and she smiled sweetly and cruelly—"the life of your hairdresser's child, for instance, as the meaningless thing it is. Death has a heart, but it is forever an empty heart, and I think, Lady Neville, that your heart is like a dry riverbed, like a seashell. You will be very content as Death, more so than I, for I was very young when I became Death."

She came toward Lady Neville, light and swaying, her deep eyes wide and full of the light of the red morning sun that was beginning to rise. The guests at the ball moved back from her, although she did not look at them, but Lady Neville clenched her hands tightly and watched Death come toward her with her little dancing steps. "We must kiss each other," Death said. "That is the way I became Death." She shook her head delightedly, so that her soft hair swirled about her shoulders. "Quickly, quickly," she said. "Oh, I cannot wait to be human again."

"You may not like it," Lady Neville said. She felt very calm, though she could hear her old heart pounding in her chest and feel it in the tips of her fingers. "You may not like it after a while," she said.

"Perhaps not." Death's smile was very close to her now. "I will not be as beautiful as I am, and perhaps people will not love me as much as they do now. But I will be human for a while, and at last I will die. I have done my penance."

"What penance?" the old woman asked the beautiful

girl. "What was it you did? Why did you become
Death?"

"I don't remember," said the lady Death. "And you
too will forget in time." She was smaller than Lady
Neville, and so much younger. In her white dress she
might have been the daughter that Lady Neville had
never had, who would have been with her always and
held her mother's head lightly in the crook of her arm
when she felt old and sad. Now she lifted her head to
kiss Lady Neville's cheek, and as she did so she whispered in her ear, "You will still be beautiful when I am
ugly. Be kind to me then."

Behind Lady Neville the handsome gentlemen and
ladies murmured and sighed, fluttering like moths in
their evening dress, in their elegant gowns. "I
promise," she said, and then she pursed her dry lips to
kiss the soft, sweet-smelling cheek of the young lady
Death.

URSULA KROEBER LE GUIN

(1929–   )

Ursula Le Guin is now generally recognized as one of the most accomplished writers of both science fiction and fantasy on the contemporary literary scene. Born in Berkeley, California, she received her B.A. from Radcliffe in 1951, and her M.A. from Columbia University in 1952. While studying in Paris on a Fulbright fellowship, she met and married Charles A. Le Guin, an historian. Her close friends describe her as a sensitive, quiet, and modest individual who shuns the limelight. Although Ursula Le Guin is best known as a writer, she has also established a fine reputation as a teacher through her work with the University of Washington's Science Fiction Writers' Workshop. The Le Guins now live in Portland, Oregon; they have three children.

Although Ms. Le Guin points out that she has written sf and fantasy works since the age of six, the success of her professional writing career was assured in 1964 with the publication of her first novel, *Rocannon's World*. This sf work was followed by a number of others in the same genre: *Planet of Exile* (1966), *City of Illusions* (1967), *The Left Hand of Darkness* (1969), *The Lathe of Heaven* (1971), and, most recently, *The Dispossessed* (1974). Illustrative of the high quality of her science fiction is the fact that in 1970 *The Left Hand of Darkness* received both the Nebula and Hugo Awards, the highest honors which can be bestowed upon a writer of sf. In the realm of fantasy literature, Le Guin has published the popular, and critically acclaimed, *Earthsea Trilogy*, which consists of *A Wizard of Earthsea* (1968), *The Tombs of Atuan* (1972), and *The Farthest Shore* (1972). Recently, she has published a collection of short stories (containing both sf and fantasy) entitled, *The Wind's Twelve Quarters,* and *Wild Angels,* a collection of poetry. She was the recipient of the Boston Globe–Hornbook award for excellence in juvenile fiction in 1968.

In her fantasy Le Guin carefully and convincingly creates a secondary magical world, complete with its own history, geography, customs, traditions, language, and people. Detailed maps, à la Tolkien, are included to help the reader gain his bearings and subsequently follow the action of the narrative. "The Rule of Names," is one of two short stories through which Le Guin first enters this magical realm of Earthsea, and it illustrates several of the emphases which later appear in the trilogy, notably the author's concern with the nature of magic and with the ancient belief that an individual's being is somehow contained in her/his name. Particularly effective in this story is her superb handling of foreshadowing. Through this device Le Guin allows the careful reader to solve the mystery of Mr. Underhill before it is divulged by the author herself. The story, while it shows an earlier, less mature Le Guin in both style and characterization, shows nonetheless an already fine talent. "The Rule of Names" succeeds on its own merits.

❧ The Rule of Names ❧

Ursula Kroeber Le Guin

Mr. Underhill came out from under his hill, smiling
and breathing hard. Each breath shot out of his nostrils
as a double puff of steam, snow-white in the morning
sunshine. Mr. Underhill looked up at the bright De-
cember sky and smiled wider than ever, showing
snow-white teeth. Then he went down to the village.

"Morning, Mr. Underhill," said the villagers as he
passed them in the narrow street between houses with
conical, overhanging roofs like the fat red caps of toad-
stools. "Morning, morning!" he replied to each. (It was
of course bad luck to wish anyone a *good* morning; a
simple statement of the time of day was quite enough,
in a place so permeated with Influences as Sattins Island, where a careless adjective might change the
weather for a week.) All of them spoke to him, some
with affection, some with affectionate disdain. He was
all the little island had in the way of a wizard, and so
deserved respect—but how could you respect a little fat
man of fifty who waddled along with his toes turned in,
breathing steam and smiling? He was no great shakes
as a workman either. His fireworks were fairly elaborate but his elixirs were weak. Warts he charmed off
frequently reappeared after three days; tomatoes he enchanted grew no bigger than canteloupes; and those
rare times when a strange ship stopped at Sattins Harbor, Mr. Underhill always stayed under his hill—for
fear, he explained, of the evil eye. He was, in other
words, a wizard the way walleyed Gan was a carpenter;

by default. The villagers made do with badly-hung
doors and inefficient spells, for this generation, and relieved their annoyance by treating Mr. Underhill quite
familiarly, as a mere fellow-villager. They even asked
him to dinner. Once he asked some of them to dinner,
and served a splendid repast, with silver, crystal,
damask, roast goose, sparkling Andrades '639, and
plum pudding with hard sauce; but he was so nervous
all through the meal that it took the joy out of it, and
besides, everybody was hungry again half an hour afterwards. He did not like anyone to visit his cave, not
even the anteroom, beyond which in fact nobody had
ever got. When he saw people approaching the hill he
always came trotting out to meet them. "Let's sit out
here under the pine trees!" he would say, smiling and
waving towards the fir grove, or if it was raining, "Let's
go have a drink at the inn, eh?" though everybody
knew he drank nothing stronger than well-water.

Some of the village children, teased by that locked
cave, poked and pried and made raids while Mr. Underhill was away; but the small door that led into the
inner chamber was spell-shut, and it seemed for once
to be an effective spell. Once a couple of boys, thinking
the wizard was over on the West Shore curing Mrs.
Ruuna's sick donkey, brought a crowbar and a hatchet
up there, but at the first whack of the hatchet on the
door there came a roar of wrath from inside, and a
cloud of purple steam. Mr. Underhill had got home
early. The boys fled. He did not come out, and the
boys came to no harm, though they said you couldn't
believe what a huge hooting howling hissing horrible
bellow that little fat man could make unless you'd
heard it.

His business in town this day was three dozen fresh
eggs and a pound of liver; also a stop at Seacaptain
Fogeno's cottage to renew the seeing-charm on the old
man's eyes (quite useless when applied to a case of detached retina, but Mr. Underhill kept trying), and
finally a chat with old Goody Guld, the concertina-
maker's widow. Mr. Underhill's friends were mostly

old people. He was timid with the strong young men of the village, and the girls were shy of him. "He makes me nervous, he smiles so much," they all said, pouting, twisting silky ringlets round a finger. "Nervous" was a newfangled word, and their mothers all replied grimly, "Nervous my foot, silliness is the word for it. Mr. Underhill is a very respectable wizard!"

After leaving Goody Guld, Mr. Underhill passed by the school, which was being held this day out on the common. Since no one on Sattins Island was literate, there were no books to learn to read from and no desks to carve initials on and no blackboards to erase, and in fact no schoolhouse. On rainy days the children met in the loft of the Communal Barn, and got hay in their pants; on sunny days the schoolteacher, Palani, took them anywhere she felt like. Today, surrounded by thirty interested children under twelve and forty uninterested sheep under five, she was teaching an important item on the curriculum: the Rules of Names. Mr. Underhill, smiling shyly, paused to listen and watch. Palani, a plump, pretty girl of twenty, made a charming picture there in the wintry sunlight, sheep and children around her, a leafless oak above her, and behind her the dunes and sea and clear, pale sky. She spoke earnestly, her face flushed pink by wind and words. "Now you know the Rules of Names already, children. There are two, and they're the same on every island in the world. What's one of them?"

"It ain't polite to ask anybody what his name is," shouted a fat, quick boy, interrupted by a little girl shrieking, "You can't never tell your own name to nobody my ma says!"

"Yes, Suba. Yes, Popi dear, don't screech. That's right. You never ask anybody his name. You never tell your own. Now think about that a minute and then tell me why we call our wizard Mr. Underhill." She smiled across the curly heads and the woolly backs at Mr. Underhill, who beamed, and nervously clutched his sack of eggs.

" 'Cause he lives under a hill!" said half the children.

"But is it his truename?"

"No!" said the fat boy, echoed by little Popi shrieking, "No!"

"How do you know it's not?"

" 'Cause he came here all alone and so there wasn't anybody knew his truename so they couldn't tell us, and *he* couldn't—"

"Very good, Suba. Popi, don't shout. That's right. Even a wizard can't tell his truename. When you children are through school and go through the Passage, you'll leave your childnames behind and keep only your truenames, which you must never ask for and never give away. Why is that the rule?"

The children were silent. The sheep bleated gently. Mr. Underhill answered the question: "Because the name is the thing," he said in his shy, soft, husky voice, "and the truename is the true thing. To speak the name is to control the thing. Am I right, Schoolmistress?"

She smiled and curtseyed, evidently a little embarrassed by his participation. And he trotted off towards his hill, clutching his eggs to his bosom. Somehow the minute spent watching Palani and the children had made him very hungry. He locked his inner door behind him with a hasty incantation, but there must have been a leak or two in the spell, for soon the bare anteroom of the cave was rich with the smell of frying eggs and sizzling liver.

The wind that day was light and fresh out of the west, and on it at noon a little boat came skimming the bright waves into Sattins Harbor. Even as it rounded the point, a sharp-eyed boy spotted it, and knowing, like every child on the island, every sail and spar of the forty boats of the fishing fleet, he ran down the street calling out, "A foreign boat, a foreign boat!" Very seldom was the lonely isle visited by a boat from some equally lonely isle of the East Reach, or an adventurous trader from the Archipelago. By the time the boat was at the pier, half the village was there to greet it, and fishermen were following it homewards, and cowherds and clam-diggers and herb-hunters were puffing up and down all the rocky hills, heading toward the harbor.

But Mr. Underhill's door stayed shut.

There was only one man aboard the boat. Old Seacaptain Fogeno, when they told him that, drew down a bristle of white brows over his unseeing eyes. "There's only one kind of man," he said, "that sails the Outer Reach alone. A wizard, or a warlock, or a Mage . . ."

So the villagers were breathless hoping to see for once in their own lives a Mage, one of the mighty White Magicians of the rich, towered, crowded inner islands of the Archipelago. They were disappointed, for the voyager was quite young, a handsome black-bearded fellow who hailed them cheerfully from his boat, and leaped ashore like any sailor glad to have made port. He introduced himself at once as a sea-peddlar. But when they told Seacaptain Fogeno that he carried an oaken walking-stick around with him, the old man nodded. "Two wizards in one town," he said. "Bad!" And his mouth snapped shut like an old carp's.

As the stranger could not give them his name, they gave him one right away: Blackbeard. And they gave him plenty of attention. He had a small mixed cargo of cloth and sandals and piswi feathers for trimming cloaks and cheap insense and levity stones and fine herbs and great glass beads from Venway—the usual peddlar's lot. Everyone on Sattins Island came to look, to chat with the voyager, and perhaps to buy something—"Just to remember him by!" cackled Goody Guld, who like all the women and girls of the village was smitten with Blackbeard's bold good looks. All the boys hung round him too, to hear him tell of his voyages to far, strange islands of the Reach or describe the great rich islands of the Archipelago, the Inner Lanes, the roadsteads white with ships, and the golden roofs of Havnor. The men willingly listened to his tales; but some of them wondered why a trader should sail alone, and kept their eyes thoughtfully upon his oaken staff.

But all this time Mr. Underhill stayed under his hill.

"This is the first island I've ever seen that had no wizard," said Blackbeard one evening to Goody Guld, who had invited him and her nephew and Palani in for a cup of rushwash tea. "What do you do when you get a toothache, or the cow goes dry?"

"Why, we've got Mr. Underhill!" said the old woman.

"For what that's worth," muttered her nephew Birt, and then blushed purple and spilled his tea. Birt was a fisherman, a large, brave, wordless young man. He loved the schoolmistress, but the nearest he had come to telling her of his love was to give baskets of fresh mackerel to her father's cook.

"Oh, you do have a wizard?" Blackbeard asked. "Is he invisible?"

"No, he's just very shy," said Palani. "You've only been here a week, you know, and we see so few strangers here. . . ." She also blushed a little, but did not spill her tea.

Blackbeard smiled at her. "He's a good Sattinsman, then, eh?"

"No," said Goody Guld, "no more than you are. Another cup, nevvy? Keep it in the cup this time. No, my dear, he came in a little bit of a boat, four years ago was it? just a day after the end of the shad run, I recall, for they was taking up the nets over in East Creek, and Pondi Cowherd broke his leg that very morning—five years ago it must be. No, four. No, five it is, 'twas the year the garlic didn't sprout. So he sails in on a bit of a sloop loaded full up with great chests and boxes and says to Seacaptain Fogeno, who wasn't blind then, though old enough goodness knows to be blind twice over, 'I hear tell,' he says, 'you've got no wizard nor warlock at all, might you be wanting one?' 'Indeed, if the magic's white!' says the Captain, and before you could say cuttlefish Mr. Underhill had settled down in the cave under the hill and was charming the mange off Goody Beltow's cat. Though the fur grew in grey, and 'twas an orange cat. Queer-looking thing it was after

that. It died last winter in the cold spell. Goody Beltow took on so at that cat's death, poor thing, worse
than when her man was drowned on the Long Banks,
the year of the long herring-runs, when nevvy Birt here
was but a babe in petticoats." Here Birt spilled his tea
again, and Blackbeard grinned, but Goody Guld
proceeded undismayed, and talked on till nightfall.

Next day Blackbeard was down at the pier, seeing
after the sprung board in his boat which he seemed to
take a long time fixing, and as usual drawing the taci-
turn Sattinsmen into talk. "Now which of these is your
wizard's craft?" he asked. "Or has he got one of those
the Mages fold up into a walnut shell when they're not
using it?"

"Nay," said a stolid fisherman. "She's oop in his
cave, under hill."

"He carried the boat he came in up to his cave?"

"Aye. Clear oop. I helped. Heavier as lead she was.
Full oop with great boxes, and they full oop with
books o' spells, he says. Heavier as lead she was." And
the stolid fisherman turned his back, sighing stolidly.
Goody Guld's nephew, mending a net nearby, looked
up from his work and asked with equal stolidity,
"Would ye like to meet Mr. Underhill, maybe?"

Blackbeard returned Birt's look. Clever black eyes
met candid blue ones for a long moment; then Blackbeard smiled and said, "Yes. Will you take me up to
the hill, Birt?"

"Aye, when I'm done with this," said the fisherman.
And when the net was mended, he and the Archipelagan set off up the village street towards the high green
hill above it. But as they crossed the common Blackbeard said, "Hold on a while, friend Birt. I have a tale
to tell you, before we meet your wizard."

"Tell away," says Birt, sitting down in the shade of a
live-oak.

"It's a story that started a hundred years ago, and
isn't finished yet—though it soon will be, very soon. . . .
In the very heart of the Archipelago, where the islands
crowd thick as flies on honey, there's a little isle called

Pendor. The sealords of Pendor were mighty men, in the old days of war before the League. Loot and ransom and tribute came pouring into Pendor, and they gathered a great treasure there, long ago. Then from somewhere away out in the West Reach, where dragons breed on the lava isles, came one day a very mighty dragon. Not one of those overgrown lizards most of you Outer Reach folk call dragons, but a big, black, winged, wise, cunning monster, full of strength and subtlety, and like all dragons loving gold and precious stones above all things. He killed the Sealord and his soldiers, and the people of Pendor fled in their ships by night. They all fled away and left the dragon coiled up in Pendor Towers. And there he stayed for a hundred years, dragging his scaly belly over the emeralds and sapphires and coins of gold, coming forth only once in a year or two when he must eat. He'd raid nearby islands for his food. You know what dragons eat?"

Birt nodded and said in a whisper, "Maidens."

"Right," said Blackbeard. "Well, that couldn't be endured forever, nor the thought of him sitting on all that treasure. So after the League grew strong, and the Archipelago wasn't so busy with wars and piracy, it was decided to attack Pendor, drive out the dragon, and get the gold and jewels for the treasury of the League. They're forever wanting money, the League is. So a huge fleet gathered from fifty islands, and seven Mages stood in the prows of the seven strongest ships, and they sailed towards Pendor. . . . They got there. They landed. Nothing stirred. The houses all stood empty, the dishes on the tables full of a hundred years' dust. The bones of the old Sealord and his men lay about in the castle courts and on the stairs. And the Tower rooms reeked of dragon. But there was no dragon. And no treasure, not a diamond the size of a poppyseed, not a single silver bead . . . Knowing that he couldn't stand up to seven Mages, the dragon had skipped out. They tracked him, and found he'd flown to a deserted island up north called Udrath; they followed his trail there, and what did they find? Bones again. His bones—the dragon's. But no treasure. A wizard, some unknown wizard from somewhere, must have met him single-handed, and defeated him—and then made off with the treasure, right under the League's nose!"

The fisherman listened, attentive and expressionless.

"Now that must have been a powerful wizard and a clever one, first to kill a dragon, and second to get off without leaving a trace. The lords and Mages of the Archipelago couldn't track him at all, neither where he'd come from nor where he'd made off to. They were about to give up. That was last spring; I'd been off on a three-year voyage up the North Reach, and got back about that time. And they asked me to help them find the unknown wizard. That was clever of them. Because I'm not only a wizard myself, as I think some of the oafs here have guessed, but I am also a descendant of the Lords of Pendor. That treasure is mine. It's mine, and knows that it's mine. Those fools of the League couldn't find it, because it's not theirs. It belongs to the House of Pendor, and the great emerald, the star of the hoard, Inalkil the Greenstone, knows its master. Behold!" Blackbeard raised his oaken staff and cried aloud, "Inalkil!" The tip of the staff began to glow green, a fiery green radiance, a dazzling haze the color of April grass, and at the same moment the staff tipped in the wizard's hand, leaning, slanting till it pointed straight at the side of the hill above them.

"It wasn't so bright a glow, far away in Havnor," Blackbeard murmured, "but the staff pointed true. Inalkil answered when I called. The jewel knows its master. And I know the thief, and I shall conquer him. He's a mighty wizard, who could overcome a dragon. But I am mightier. Do you want to know why, oaf? Because I know his name!"

As Blackbeard's tone got more arrogant, Birt had looked duller and duller, blanker and blanker; but at this he gave a twitch, shut his mouth, and stared at the Archipelagan. "How did you . . . learn it?" he asked very slowly.

Blackbeard grinned, and did not answer.

"Black magic?"

"How else?"

Birt looked pale, and said nothing.

"I am the Sealord of Pendor, oaf, and I will have the gold my fathers won, and the jewels my mothers wore, and the Greenstone! For they are mine. —Now, you can tell your village boobies the whole story after I have defeated this wizard and gone. Wait here. Or you can come and watch, if you're not afraid. You'll never get the chance again to see a great wizard in all his power." Blackbeard turned, and without a backward glance strode off up the hill towards the entrance to the cave.

Very slowly, Birt followed. A good distance from the cave he stopped, sat down under a hawthorn tree, and watched. The Archipelagan had stopped; a stiff dark figure alone on the green swell of the hill before the gaping cave-mouth, he stood perfectly still. All at once he swung his staff up over his head, and the emerald radiance shone about him as he shouted, "Thief, thief of the Hoard of Pendor, come forth!"

There was a crash, as of dropped crockery, from inside the cave, and a lot of dust came spewing out. Scared, Birt ducked. When he looked again he saw Blackbeard still standing motionless, and at the mouth of the cave, dusty and dishevelled, stood Mr. Underhill. He looked small and pitiful, with his toes turned in as usual, and his little bowlegs in black tights, and no staff—he never had had one, Birt suddenly thought. Mr. Underhill spoke. "Who are you?" he said in his husky little voice.

"I am the Sealord of Pendor, thief, come to claim my treasure!"

At that, Mr. Underhill slowly turned pink, as he always did when people were rude to him. But he then turned something else. He turned yellow. His hair bristled out, he gave a coughing roar—and was a yellow lion leaping down the hill at Blackbeard, white fangs gleaming.

But Blackbeard no longer stood there. A gigantic tiger, color of night and lightning, bounded to meet the lion. . . .

The lion was gone. Below the cave all of a sudden stood a high grove of trees, black in the winter sunshine. The tiger, checking himself in mid-leap just before he entered the shadow of the trees, caught fire in the air, became a tongue of flame lashing out at the dry black branches. . . .

But where the trees had stood a sudden cataract leaped from the hillside, an arch of silvery crashing water, thundering down upon the fire. But the fire was gone. . . .

For just a moment before the fisherman's staring eyes two hills rose—the green one he knew, and a new one, a bare, brown hillock ready to drink up the rushing waterfall. That passed so quickly it made Birt blink, and after blinking he blinked again, and moaned, for what he saw now was a great deal worse. Where the cataract had been there hovered a dragon. Black wings darkened all the hill, steel claws reached groping, and from the dark, scaly, gaping lips fire and steam shot out.

Beneath the monstrous creature stood Blackbeard laughing.

"Take any shape you please, little Mr. Underhill!" he taunted. "I can match you. But the game grows tiresome. I want to look upon my treasure, upon Inalkil. Now, big dragon, little wizard, take your true shape. I command you by the power of your true name—Yevaud!"

Birt could not move at all, not even to blink. He cowered, staring whether he would or not. He saw the black dragon hang there in the air above Blackbeard. He saw the fire lick like many tongues from the scaly mouth, the steam jet from the red nostrils. He saw Blackbeard's face grow white, white as chalk, and the beard-fringed lips trembling.

"Your name is Yevaud!"

"Yes," said a great, husky, hissing voice. "My true-name is Yevaud, and my true shape is this shape."

"But the dragon was killed—they found dragon-bones on Udrath Island—"

"That was another dragon," said the dragon, and then stooped like a hawk, talons outstretched. And Birt shut his eyes.

When he opened them the sky was clear, the hillside empty, except for a reddish-blackish trampled spot, and a few talon-marks in the grass.

Birt the fisherman got to his feet and ran. He ran across the common, scattering sheep to right and left, and straight down the village street to Palani's father's house. Palani was out in the garden weeding the nasturtiums. "Come with me!" Birt gasped. She stared. He grabbed her wrist and dragged her with him. She screeched a little, but did not resist. He ran with her straight to the pier, pushed her into his fishing-sloop the *Queenie,* untied the painter, took up the oars and set off rowing like a demon. The last that Sattins Island saw of him and Palani was the *Queenie*'s sail vanishing in the direction of the nearest island westward.

The villagers thought they would never stop talking about it, how Goody Guld's nephew Birt had lost his mind and sailed off with the schoolmistress on the very same day that the peddlar Blackbeard disappeared without a trace, leaving all his feathers and beads behind. But they did stop talking about it, three days later. They had other things to talk about, when Mr. Underhill finally came out of his cave.

Mr. Underhill had decided that since his truename was no longer a secret, he might as well drop his disguise. Walking was a lot harder than flying, and besides, it was a long, long time since he had had a real meal.

SYLVIA TOWNSEND WARNER

(1893–   )

Sylvia Townsend Warner, novelist, poet, and short-story writer, was born at Harrow-on-the-Hill, Middlesex, daughter of a schoolmaster. Educated privately, she displayed a love for both music and literature very early in life. Her interest in music rapidly developed into an expertise which brought her recognition as an expert on Renaissance music. Her writing career began with the publication of *The Espalier* (1925), a warm and witty book of poems. Since that initial volume she has published a number of collections of verse, including *Time Importuned* (1928), *Opus 7* (1931), and *Rainbow* (1932). Her novels, like her poems, are characterized by a whimsical wit and a polished style. Some of her best known works in this genre are *Lolly Willowes* (1926), *Mr. Fortune's Maggot* (1927), *The True Heart* (1929), *Summer Will Show* (1936), *The Corner That Held Them* (1948), and *The Flint Anchor* (1954), Recently, Ms. Warner has published some delightful short works of high fantasy in *The New Yorker*. Her collections of short fiction include *A Garland of Straw* (1943) and *Museum of Cheats* (1947). Ms. Warner has also written an excellent biography of T. H. White (1968).

"Beliard," one of Warner's most recent short stories of high fantasy, is extraordinarily rich in fairy lore. Here the reader will find elfin kings and queens, magic springs, werewolves, sundry enchantments, and much of the other paraphernalia of the fairy tale as well as of the Gothic fantasy. However, Warner's sprightly wit, subtle satire, and wry humor create a curious tone and

311

atmosphere which make the work distinctive. There are echoes here of Shakespeare's treatment of Oberon, Titania, and their fairy train, in *A Midsummer Night's Dream*. In both these works Puck appears, and in both, the fairyland and elfin aristocracy display the same idosyncrasies and vanities possessed by their human counterparts. Warner's prose style is energetic, but polished, and the narrative thread of her story is strong. It is entirely fitting that such a remarkable tale should exhibit such a strange and surprising ending.

❧ Beliard ❧

Sylvia Townsend Warner

There was a time when the spring called Barenton was the most renowned thing in the fairy kingdom of Brocéliande—more renowned than the court, than any of its queens, than Vivien who imprisoned Merlin in her spells; more renowned and better thought of. Its water was cold, even in the sweltering days of late summer. It had never been known to freeze over. Winter and summer, the spring jetted in a quiet twirl of silver from the sandy bottom of the pool, filled it always to the same level, and flowed away unseen through a bed of reeds. It was as though it had a life of its own, apart from the rest of the world. There was nothing striking about it, except itself. The peasant women who resorted to it sometimes found a lady there, bathing or sitting thoughtfully beside it. She was tall, stately as a queen, and always very pleasant, talking to them in the patois. It was as if she too had a life of her own, apart from the world of Faery; for she was visible to any mortal, familiar as a neighbor, and helpful in their mortal misfortunes. But as time went on and religion spread through the district, they came to mistrust her and be of two minds about her character; when they resorted to the spring they did so secretly, and if she happened to be there they crossed themselves and drew back. And so by degrees it became a sin to go to the spring, and also a waste of time, since one had only to go to the new church to find Our Lady of Brocéliande

313

and the stoup of holy water, with no sin about them and always available.

Dando the Cosmographer, the Court Archivist, who wrote the standard work on Elfindom, maintained that Barenton was coeval with the stones of Carnac, and that the Kingdom of Brocéliande was formed around it, probably about the time when the forest, overthrown by the Great Gale, had put up enough second growth to afford shelter to the vagrant tribe of Fairies, or Peris, driven out of Persia by the magicians Aaron and Moses. He held that the first settlement consisted of simple reed huts round about the spring, and that it was not till much later that the court was established in another part of the forest, over two miles away. Be this as it may (Dando's conclusions were questioned by some later scholars), the court of Brocéliande paid a respectful lip service to Barenton—such as the Dean and Chapter of Salisbury might pay to Stonehenge. It figured in sonnets (ladies as pure, and even colder). Its water was an ingredient in the famous Eau de Brocéliande, till it was superseded by a distillation of Hamamelis. A ceremonial picnic took place beside it every twenty-five years, and if a visitor happened to be of the party Queen Melior would tell the legend of the beautiful lady who bathed there at midnight on Mid-summer Eve—to which an ambassador from the Scottish Kingdom of Elfhame had replied by telling her of a kraken in Loch Ness. Apart from these polite acknowledgments, Barenton fell into disesteem. It was in an uncouth part of the forest, all midges and brambles, and had regrettable associations with poaching mortals, who soused their scabby children in it and threw in farthings for luck. True, it was a very long time since any poaching had gone on; only peasants desperate for firewood or acorns ventured so deep into the forest. But its reputation was dubious—not to speak of that bathing person, whoever she was. Dando had no doubt who she was: one of those indigenous fairies of Brittany, contemporary with the Nine Maidens of miraculous power mentioned by Pomponius Mela, whom common speech referred to as "the Old Lot." Dando, invisibly frequenting alehouses and the company of midwives, learned that the indigenous fairies were still remembered by mortals. It was from two old women scalding a pig that he heard about the fairy who pulled a drowning boy from the pool of Barenton and took such pity on him that she followed him into the mortal world to be his nurse.

It was from Dando grown very old and ramshackle, that Beliard heard the same story in his childhood, and he was immediately seized by a passionate longing to be nursed by a fairy. His nurse and nursemaids were fairies; his mother, Lady Pervenche, was a fairy of unblemished lineage; he was born into the most distinguished of Elfin courts; he had never seen anything but fairies—and he longed with childish violence to be nursed by a fairy. Now he was grown up, unassuming and short-sighted, but for all that a credit to his upbringing. He had an intermittent ambition to play the flageolet, and used to steal off to the pool of Barenton where he could practice undisturbed.

He was working at the open-pipe octave, where a hoot at the bottom and a squeak at the top are equally hard to avoid, when he heard approaching wings and saw Puck, the old whipper-in of the royal pack of werewolves, and four stout kennel lads carrying buckets alight by the pool.

"Sorry to disturb Your Lordship, I'm sure," said Puck righteously. "And if it had been tomorrow, we wouldn't have. But today's their last chance, poor creatures! Tomorrow, it'll be worms."

"Do you mean the pack is to be killed?"

"No. He wouldn't do that. It would be hurting their feelings. And he's all for feelings, is My Lord Melilot. But he thinks it's hard on the lads to be fetching water from here, so the drinking troughs are to be filled from the rainwater tank. You can't drink rainwater without getting worms, that's a known fact. But it's no part of my place to know better. Time will prove, that's all."

They flew off. The ripples slapped against the bank, slowed, died into silence.

It was the end of September. The reeds were changing color, and they whispered more harshly, as though admonishing him. He had meant, this time, to work at his flageolet seriously, to practice every day, to master the chromatic scale, soar into the upper octave, play gavottes and airs with graces instead of the melancholy little tunes within the compass of a fifth, which had been all he could manage before. But the reeds were turning color, it would soon be too cold to practice by the pool, and he had not done half as well as he had intended.

As he was a bachelor, he still shared his mother's apartment. This made indoor practicing difficult. When he had gone up the scale without a hoot or a squeak, she would interrupt him with a "Don't go on, dear. You'll strain your heart," or ask why he didn't play those nice little tunes he used to play. Lying—practice had made him nearly perfect at that—he would explain that he had promised to attend a cockfight or play a match with So-and-So, and leave. Picking his way down back stairs, skirting the tennis courts, he would walk demurely till it was safe to run, run like a hunted stag till he came to the pool, recover his breath, take the flageolet out of its velvet sleeve, and begin his preliminary exercises. *Do, re, mi, fa, sol, la, si, DO. Do, mi, la, DO, la, mi, do.* And so on, a degree higher; for by now he could practice agility most of the way up the scale. The silver twirl rose through the stilly water, the unchanging level of the pool flowed away through the reeds and sank beneath a small swamp. And Lady Pervenche would glide along the gallery which the younger members of the court called "the Hen's Parade," to visit her friend Lady Renoncule (they belonged to the epoch when it was fashionable to be called after field flowers), to declare that Renoncule's Persis grew prettier every day, to drink a cup of chocolate, and to conceal her sorrows: for as she hoped to make a match between Persis and Beliard it would not have done to admit how much it distressed her to see Beliard always passed over when there was a court appointment going.

"Have you heard about poor old Dando? I must admit I had almost forgotten he was still alive."

Dando the Cosmographer was dying. He had been brought down from his garret and laid in the State Death Bed, amid black curtains and under a black tester. His mind was decayed, but he was conscious and complained that the mattress was lumpy. His feet were rubbed, his beard combed, he was given strengthening soups, and for a time he rallied and talked in a wandering way about things long past and forgotten. Once, he called for a secretary, as he wished to have an annotation set down. But he was far away from the cares of this world, for when the Queen's Justice Clerk arrived with two witnesses and suggested he might like to make his will, he replied there wasn't enough to trouble about. A couple of days before his end, he was heard to chuckle and sigh and repeat snatches of ballads learned in his alehouse days. A coughing fit nearly finished him, but he got the better of it and began to clamor about a boy: he wanted to see the boy. He became so insistent that they eventually asked him which boy. The boy who wanted to be nursed by a fairy, he said. It was plain he had some mortal boy in mind, and this made it even more impossible to oblige him. "Beli-ard!" he shouted. It was like the angry bellow of a ram. Beliard was fetched to the bedside. Dando's glance wandered up him from a boy's height to a man's. "Did you get her?" he asked. Beliard shook his head. "None left, none left," said Dando, and an attendant, thinking he spoke of his empty bowl, came up with more soup.

The funeral was superb. Music, specially composed in the antique style, was performed, and several panegyrics were spoken. Of these, the most eloquent came from the Archivist of a Kingdom in Wales, so small and unimportant that it had not been notified; but he had somehow heard the news and travelled to Brocéliande to praise Dando, above all for his compelling hypothesis of the Great Gale.

By the time all this was over, it had grown too cold to practice by the pool of Barenton. Beliard put away his flageolet and settled down to the customary gaieties. It was an implacably hard winter. There were skating parties on the ornamental moat, with braziers set at intervals along it. Lady Pervenche's ankles did not allow her to skate, but as she was young at heart she sat in an ice sleigh and was pushed by Beliard. Persis, she thought, could not fail to observe how strong he was, and how kindhearted: such a husband is a treasure for centuries. Observing Beliard's kindheartedness, Melilot skated up to them to suggest he should have the pleasure of pushing the sleigh for a few rounds. Beliard, who was more out of breath than any scale passage could have left him, was ready to accept, but Lady Pervenche cried out, "No, thank you, no, thank you! You are really too kind. But you have *other* duties, you know." She had known Melilot to be a scheming interloper ever since his appointment to the Mastership of the Werewolves, a post she had designed for Beliard.

Melilot smiled, bowed, hoped for another time, and skated away.

At the assembly that evening, Beliard detached himself from watching the cardplayers to make some atonement. Melilot bore no malice. His wish to please everybody extended into a belief that everybody was pleasing. When Beliard asked how the pack were doing, he said how grateful they were for an issue of blankets. "Splendid fellows! You should have seen how they snatched at them." Blankets were not his only innovation. He had begun to add vegetables to their diet. After a spell of carrots they looked much glossier—or so it seemed to him. If Beliard could spare time to look in at a morning feed—

Beliard woke the next morning with the agreeable thought of having something to do. As he neared the kennels he heard hammerings: they were breaking the ice on the rainwater tank. He remembered Dando's statement that the pool of Barenton never froze. Dando had some scientific explanation of why this was so, which Beliard could not remember. He had not read the Cosmography very attentively. He decided that after doing the polite at the kennels he would walk on and see for himself.

The snow was speckled with dead birds. They were so weightless with starvation that they lay on its surface like decorations on a pudding. The sky was lead-colored; the dull dazzle of snow wrenched at his short-sighted eyes. A shinier patch of snow, trodden down into ice, and a few trampled wisps of hay showed where fodder had been put out for the deer.

The pool lay before him, black and alarming. He felt his heart jolt. An old woman was crouched beside it. The hood of her peasant's cloak had fallen aside; he could see her grizzled hair, and the cadaverous face she bent over the water. It was because she was so unexpected that he had been frightened. But his fright kept him motionless, staring at the blotch of darkness she made. After a while she scrambled to her feet and made off through the reeds and was gone. In his fright he had almost forgotten his reason for being there. He went forward to the pool, and saw that the water was unfrozen, the spring twirling up as usual. Thus looked down into, the pool did not seem dark and alarming at all; the sandy bottom gave it an appearance of being sunlit. And the old woman was nothing to be alarmed by. The frost was everywhere, a stranglehold on mortals, on cattle licking snow with parched tongues. She had known in her old woman's memory that the pool of Barenton never froze, and had come with her pitcher, defying regulations, chancing the poacher's death on the gallows, to fetch water.

All the same, she had given him a fright.

He returned to the palace to be told what he had missed: the Queen had been reading aloud from the Cosmography.

The expense of the funeral had not been in vain.

Dando was rediscovered as a classic. His accounts of other Kingdoms were most entertaining, his theories ingenious, his solemn language a delight. Books Three and Four, "Of Brocéliande," and "Of Customs," were indisputably Dando at his best. Who could have believed that the quiet old man, so retiring in his habits, so shabby in his apparel, was—here opinions diverged, some saying, "Such a man of the world," others, "Such a master of the occult." The readings continued. There was talk of an abridged Cosmography—with some of the scandals, some of the Druidical bits left out—for children. Only the Directors of Piety held aloof. Dando should certainly not be abridged for children: his sources were dubious, his opinions those of an atheist. Nowhere in Book Three was there a word about Afrits—malign spirits peculiar to the Brocéliande dynasty, whose malevolence could only be warded off by the intervention of the Directors of Piety.

During all this, Beliard said nothing of his familiarity with the pool of Barenton; he wanted to keep it for his flageolet. The snow was still lying, the kennel lads hammering, when he visited it again. He had half an idea the old crone might still be drawing water from it. She was not there. It was natural to suppose that she was dead. He had taken his flageolet with him, and with freezing fingers he played a little tune, just to hear what it sounded like in that icy, dying world.

A week before the Spring Ceremony, there was a sudden thaw. He went to the pool two days running, and each time she was there. He had not the courage to approach her. He did not know what to think. Dando would have known. But he was glad that Dando was spared from knowing. It would have grieved him to know that the benign, stately lady who bathed there, sat musing on the bank, talked like a neighbor to the peasant women, had shrunken into this pitiable crone.

The Spring Ceremony took place in a violent hailstorm. The day after, it was warm as summer and the Directors of Piety emerged like tortoises and basked in justification. The Afrits had struck—Melilot had been killed by the werewolves. He had gone into their enclosure to distribute some tidbits, and stumbled over a bone. In an instant they rushed on him, pulled him down, and tore him to pieces. The court went into mourning, the Directors of Piety imposed a general fast, the opening of the hunting season was postponed, the Cosmography was put on the Index, Puck was sacked. In the storm of controversy over the future of the werewolves, various positions were put forward: They were a traditional glory; they were quite out of date; no one wanted them; they were the envy of every other court. Melior seemed to incline to the traditionalists; then, for she prided herself on her spontaneity, passed the death sentence. They were hanged.

With history being made at such a rate, it was easy for Beliard to slink off to the pool. As an excuse to himself, and an insurance against the disappointment he would feel if the old woman were not there, he took his flageolet. Once, when he was practicing, she passed behind him and sat down in her usual place. He wanted to speak to her—some noncommittal remark about the beauty of the morning—but he was afraid to. For all he knew, he was invisible to her: her survival (he was convinced by now she was a survival) hung on so delicate a thread that the smallest shock might blow her away. And that would be a cruel deed: if she were so faithful to the pool, she must love it a great deal. He looked at her as little as possible: a direct glance might fall on her like a blow. In the light of spring, her age was more apparent, and her ugliness. It was not a solemn ugliness: it was grotesque, a clay likeness of a frog.

When she was not there he felt a dull bereavement, like a bruise.

It was ironical that at this time he should hear so many evocations of her at court. With the Cosmography on the Index, not to admire Dando was dowdy. Barenton again figured in sonnets, but now—for fashions change—as the water of youth where the poet's mistress

had been immersed, where immersion would be super-
fluous. Book Four, "Of Customs," governed taste.
Round dances ousted cotillions, monoliths were a passion. Melior was importuned to revive the custom of
bathing in Barenton, and the Court Architect designed
a light tent. Beliard did not feel his tenancy menaced.
He knew that the more a project is talked of the less
likely it is to take place. Meanwhile he had found a
new way to practice undisturbed, by hiding in the
laurels and serenading Persis. His heart was cold, his
feelings engaged elsewhere, and he probably played the
better for this. One night it occurred to him to leave
his hiding place and to play by the pool. Persis had
opened her casement and said something about nightingales—but he stole away and followed the path,
which was now so familiar and in its hoarfrost of
moonlight curiously strange and peopled by mysterious
shadows.

She was there—a darker blotch of darkness in the
moonlight than ever by day. The impersonality of
moonlight made him bold. He walked up to her,
stopped beside her. She was staring down at what he
took to be the reflection of the moon in the water. But
it was not the moon. It was her own reflected face she
was staring at: a smooth, calm, youthful face, with
faintly smiling lips.

He felt no astonishment, no awe. He felt at ease and
profoundly contented, as though he had come to the
end of a journey and was looking down into the valley
which was his birthplace. The dawn wind brushed the
reed bed, he heard her breathe a slow, contented sigh;
she got up, gave herself a little shake, and hobbled
away. The sun had risen, the dragonflies were hawking
over the pool, the midges swarming round him, before
he walked back through the awakened forest.

It was as though he had won some transcendental
bet—a bet against all odds. She was one of the Old Lot,
persistent as the little twirl of the spring, indigenously
young. Her disguise of old age was as trifling as a cob-
web. He was so sure he had seen her that he was sure

he would see her again, her true likeness, her self smiling at herself in the pool. How would it be by daylight? Did she, did he need the moon? By now copies of the forbidden Book Three and Book Four were passing from hand to hand, vanishing up cuffs or into bodices. He borrowed a copy of Book Three and read it attentively. There was no particular mention of moonlight. Moonlight came in later, with the Druids. And why should moonlight be needed? If she had bathed only by moonlight, Dando would have said so. He went early to bed that night, and fell asleep in a trance of trust.

A dream stabbed him awake. In the dream, the Court Architect exhibited a small straw hat, saying it was the Queen's bathing tent. He woke in a panic. If that bathing scheme came to anything, she might be driven away, affronted by the invasion of her solitude. He would never see her again.

It was late; he had overslept. The Hens were rushing up and down their Parade, calling for daisy chains. In the Morning Saloon, the program for the day was being read out. The Queen with her ladies, pastorally dressed, would be carried to Barenton in litters. The bathing tent would be set up near the pool. The litter bearers and tent peggers would wait at a distance. Her Majesty, assisted by her ladies, would disrobe and enter the pool at noon precisely, wearing a gossamer shift and protected by a Chinese parasol. The Queen would bathe in the pool for five minutes. Bath towels, warmed, would be in readiness. After she had reposed, there would be a light collation and the party would start back, reaching the palace at 3 P.M. The program had been decided on overnight, at the last moment, but it was hoped that all would go smoothly.

"You'll be eaten alive by midges!" he shouted. Melior turned and beckoned him toward her. "Are they awful?" she asked. "Swarms of them," said he. "And frogs? Are there many frogs? I'm terrified of frogs." If he had kept his wits about him, he could have made as many frogs as midges and the bathing party might have been cancelled. It was a fatal omission.

Melior was so amazed that anyone in court could consider her welfare before his own that she kept him in conversation for some while after; and when she had thanked and dismissed him, and ordered that every member of the party should be sprayed with oil of verbena and the Court Physician be in attendance, and made a mental note to find some post for her honest man, Beliard was so buttonholed, questioned, and congratulated that he despaired of getting away in time.

But he was in time—she was there. And moonlight was not essential; the pool reflected her daytime face, which was slightly more rounded and mature. She seemed to listen to him as he poured out the news of the bathing party; the invasion of her privacy, his inability to protect her. But how could he tell if she really were listening? That momentary pucker on her brow might just as well have been a tremor on the surface of the pool. It would only be for a few hours, he assured her. By the evening, all would be as it had been.

"Beliard, dear! What are you thinking of? You mustn't be here. The Queen will arrive at any moment."

He heard the violins strike up, a clatter of voices, his mother's skirts catching on the grass as she hurried to take her place with the rest. He cast himself down headlong to kiss the face in the water. It vanished under his lips. The ripples darted up the bank, his mouth was full of grit, he felt the water evading him, deserting him. The reeds heeled over in the vehement current as the pool of Barenton drained away.

When the pages unrolled the carpet from the bathing tent to the rim of the pool, they saw Beliard lying face down on the wet sand, his hand clutching the last trickle of water from the spring.

The carpet was rolled up, the tent dismantled, the litters filled higgledy-piggledy, no precedence observed. Melior sat behind closed curtains, her gloves half buttoned, her mind in bitter disarray. Only that morning had she found an honest, disinterested courtier. He was not dead: the Court Physician had revivied him and diagnosed his malady. But he could never be given a post of confidence. Brocéliande would not accept a Minister with epilepsy.